A Brief Note About *Midnight Lover*

I was seventeen when I began this story. While working in a factory in 1999, a friend asked me to write her a short story. Tracie gave me the names of the four main characters, with basic descriptions, and asked me to decide everything else – the only other stipulation she gave was that Holly, the character based on her, would be given a dog called Max.

The result was a short story called *Midnight Lover*. We were both pleased with the outcome, and with a smile, the story was labelled in my head as 'complete', and put away.

About a year or so later, a random thought passed through my head, a scene almost perfectly-created, and I took the story back out. *Midnight Lover, Part Two: The Demon Child* didn't take long to write, and I sent the finished addition to my friend. Tracie was pleasantly surprised to receive a bonus extra to her story. Again, I filed it as complete… however, there was now an excited little voice in my mind telling me it may not be totally finished.

Part Three: Reborn and *Part Four: To Rise Again* were written in similar ways – random ideas popping into my head over the years, demanding to be set down, and then leaving me with this feeling of 'not quite there yet'…

Sometimes, stories almost explode out of you, the compulsion to start writing so strong that trying to move past it is almost impossible. *Part Five: From Shadows To Eternal Darkness* was like this, something past the Muses who usually whisper gently in the ear – this was more a deafening roar of noise that was only silenced by putting pen to paper. I knew when I started this chapter that I was in it until the end this time.

It is, without a doubt, the longest piece of writing I have ever done – both in word count and in time. In 2008 I finally wrote 'The End' on a story that had been with me for nine years. I then entered a period of mourning – it felt as though I had said goodbye to some very close friends, friends that I had spent so much quality time with.

I sent the finished manuscript to Tracie, along with a daft little page from an imaginary newspaper that I sometimes did the front page for (and only ever the front page), as a sort of memorial to it.

I have edited it since then, trying to bring the styles that changed over years into a little better alignment, but around ninety-nine percent of it remains the same. I prefer it that way.

I hope you enjoy reading it even half as much as I enjoyed writing it.

Beth x

Celebrations Ring Out!

Celebrations rang out today as announcements came through about a completed story.

Midnight Lover (a story about vampires) started out as a short story in 1999, and was finally finished yesterday.

The author, 26 year old witch Beth Murray, told this reporter that she was "extremely pleased" that the story was finally completed, adding that she was looking forward to starting new projects.

A number of possible different endings were leaked to various members of the press since the announcement of the completion was made - yet Miss Murray refuses to confirm or deny any of the possible story lines. With a grin, she simply stated that "there is only one way for people to find out the ending of *Midnight Lover*, and that is to read it!"

Yet reading it will not be as easy as it first seems. So far, there is only a single copy of the novel in circulation, and it is due to be handed over to a friend of the author.

"Tracie Atkinson was the reason that this story came into being. It was her request today, for a short story to be written for her, back in 1999, that first gave birth to the first 4 characters. And the story just seemed to grow on its own."

Miss Atkinson, 30 from Boston, is as yet unaware that the story has been finished, and will not be informed until the manuscript is presented to her.

When asked if that is definitely the end, if there was no chance of more being added, Miss Murray was direct.

"The story has taken 9 years to complete and has been the most enjoyable story I have written. But there has to be some sense of closure, for me, if I am to be able to move on to other stories. When I typed 'The End' on the last page, it was meant."

Copies of Midnight Lover as of yet cannot be purchased, but we are assured that copies of the book will be available from the author 'on demand'.

Pumpkin Falls Causes Mischief

The Magickal Police have issued a statement today, requesting information about a number of 'pumpkin attacks' that have occurred all over the UK in the last few days.

In seemingly co-ordinated strikes, hundreds of 'mischievous' witches have been dropping pumpkins from the sky, causing damage to garden gnomes, bird-baths, and potted plants. They then fly their broomsticks away (greatly exceeding the speed-limits for residential areas), leaving very few clues for the Magickal Police to follow. All of the properties that have so far been targeted have one thing in common: they are all homes of people who refuse trick-or-treaters, many bearing notes on doors asking trick-or-treaters not to call.

The MP have made these attacks among their top priorities and have asked that anyone with any relevant information contact them immediately on *MAGICK524779*, (or *MAG27 on all digital crystal balls*).

see a related article on page 17

Beth Murray (signature)

Dedication:

Midnight Lover will always and forever be dedicated to
Tracie Atkinson, my amazing friend who inspired
not only the words on the following pages,
but has inspired me in so many ways.
She has helped me to push past the boundaries of my comfort zones,
giving me the courage to travel to places I had only dreamed of
visiting,
encouraging me to continue to grow as a person –
and, in a way that only the closest friends can,
telling me straight on those occasions when I act like an idiot.
So, Tracie, this is for you, with my love,
(and always with the unofficial title of *Sunnyside Up)*

And huge thanks also goes to my dad,
Allan Murray, who has proofread
everything I have ever published,
and who's editing skills I wouldn't be without.
Eternally grateful xx

Part One

The Midnight Lover

She stood at the door of the church, arms circling her chest to keep the cold away. No stars shone through the dark clouds and the moon was only a whisper in the sky. Despite the wind, she still felt warm; knowing that she would be seeing Michael again always seemed to keep the chill away.

Michael wasn't around very much. He worked elsewhere and he'd be gone for a few nights, then she would find a note posted through the door and sometimes even on her bed, asking her to meet him – it had scared her the first time, but had also excited her. She had decided that being in her twenties stopped her from being too concerned, whether that was for good or for ill. And it was only ever a few hours at night that she saw him. Always, like clockwork, on the final stroke of midnight, he would appear to hold her again.

As the bells of the church began to chime, Holly stared across the graveyard, past the stones and the gate, into the street where she knew that her dark-haired lover would soon appear.

Michael was so different to his brother, Ryan, who was meeting Jesse on the other side of the village. Neither Holly nor Jesse could see any resemblance. Michael had dark hair while Ryan had mousy-brown. Michael had green eyes, Ryan blue. The only thing that made them alike was their skin-tone, both pale, as if they had never spent a single day in the sun.

As she heard the last chime of the church bells, she saw a shape moving towards the gate. Holly stayed where she was, waiting for Michael to come to her. He walked slowly, sedately, his face almost glowing in the contrast of darkness. She could see his red lips from where she stood and saw something dark pooled at one corner of his mouth. The moment that Holly saw it Michael seemed to realise it was there and wiped his mouth and chin with the back of his hand.

It felt like an eternity, but finally he reached her and she walked into his outstretched arms, feeling his cold skin under his clothes. They kissed gently, softly, before he moved his head to hold her closer to him.

"I missed you."

Michael's voice was rough and as sexy as ever, and Holly felt her heart beating faster as it did each and every time he spoke.

"I wish you didn't have to go away all the time." Her head rested easily on his shoulder and she could feel his breath on the back of her neck.

"Need to, unfortunately."

Holly sighed and Michael pulled out of the embrace. He took her hand, kissed it, and then led her out of the churchyard. She was shaking but she didn't know if it was the cold or if it was because Michael was back with her. Or a combination of the two.

He noticed her shivering and removed his black suede jacket, placing it around her shoulders. If it had been anyone else she would have objected but she knew that Michael didn't feel the cold as much as she did. She looked at him and saw that, as usual, Michael wore black jeans and a plain black T. shirt. It no longer surprised her that Michael could wear short sleeved tops in the middle of winter. Like his absences, it was just another thing about her boyfriend that she was beginning to get used to.

Under a streetlamp, Michael stopped and his hand pulled free of hers and moved to Holly's hair. He took the bobble from it and watched it fall past the middle of her back, the light catching on it. His fingers ran through the blonde strands, not letting it fall over her eyes. "You're so beautiful."

Instead of feeling happy, those words made Holly feel sad and lonely. The expression of complete loss that filled his eyes would not allow her to feel anything else. She felt his cold hand on her cheek and she lifted her own hand to wipe away the tears that were forming in Michael's eyes.

Before she could say anything, question his sadness, he took her hand from his face and began to walk again, holding her hand tightly as if afraid to let go.

They walked in silence, Holly concentrating solely on Michael's presence and not where her feet were taking her.

When they stopped, Holly turned and looked at him, confused that they had gone straight to her house.

"I have to go." Michael said, still holding her hand tightly. "I just had to see you tonight. Let you know I was around again."

"Will I see you tomorrow night?"

He smiled gently. "Of course." His lips touched her softly on her cheek.

Holly suddenly turned her head and kissed him full on the lips. For a second he responded and the kiss turned passionate, then Michael moved backwards a step. "I'll see you tomorrow."

He walked away, leaving Holly standing on her doorstep with his jacket still on her shoulders. She closed her eyes and let herself into her home, unsure about how to feel about Michael's strange behaviour.

"What took you so long, Michael?"

Ryan stood under the cover of the church, exactly where Holly had stood only twenty minutes earlier.

Ryan was cocky. That was the first thing that Michael had noticed about him at their first meeting. Just a cocky kid, but with a hell of a lot of potential. It was abundantly clear that he thought he knew everything, the way he stood, the way he walked, and especially the way he talked. But, with time, Michael knew that it would change.

"I walked Holly home."

Ryan smiled. "Ah, yes. The lovely Holly."

Ryan had a lot of character flaws, but it was the smugness that always made Michael mad, especially when the topic was Holly.

"How'd things go with Jesse?" Michael wasn't really bothered, he just wanted to steer the conversation away from his girl.

"Good. As always."

"Make sure you don't forget yourself." Michael stared at Ryan, ensuring the boy knew that this was serious. "If you hurt Jesse then Holly'll get hurt." *And,* Michael thought, *If Holly gets hurt, you'll die in a way you never thought was possible.*

"Gotcha. Don't hurt Holly." Ryan looked at his companion closely. "You really got a thing for her, huh."

The smile faded from his face when he saw Michael nod. He shrugged. "Didn't think people like us could."

Ryan started walking away, Michael watching him as he steered around headstones. *People like us? That's a joke.*

He followed, not rushing. He had all the time in the world.

The sunlight shone through Holly's window and she awoke to find Jesse standing by the bed, the light bouncing off the frames around Jesse's eyes. Holly groaned and closed her eyes briefly before sitting up, leaning against the headboard.

"So? What happened with the gorgeous Michael last night, Hol? You look knackered."

Holly laughed at Jesse's raised eyebrows. "Nothing. Like usual."

Jesse sat on the edge of the bed. "He still pulling away?"

She nodded. "I don't get it. Every time I try and take things a bit further he backs off."

Jesse smiled, tilting her head forward so that her glasses slipped down to the tip of her nose. She looked at Holly over the rims. "Tell Auntie Jesse."

Holly laughed. "I'm okay."

It was her turn to look at Jesse, appraising her room-mates and friend's appearance, watching as she straightened the glasses. "Bit of a nasty bite. Mosquito?" She saw Jesse put a hand to her neck to try and cover the love-bite. "See things are going fine between you and Ryan."

"Sure." Jesse looked at her friend seriously. "Alright if I have the place to myself tonight?"

Holly smiled slyly. "Pushing things further along yourself, are you?"

Jesse blushed slightly. "D' you mind?"

She shook her head. "Course not. I want to talk to Michael tonight anyway. It might be easier if we're somewhere neutral."

Jesse hugged her friend fiercely before jumping off the bed. "Cheers mate." She started to bound out of the room, then turned back. "You know, you should be grateful for one thing. At least you know he's not just after you for your body."

As Jesse left Holly shouted after her. "I wouldn't it mind if he was!" She heard her friend laugh and smiled herself before slumping back down on the mattress. *Just be careful, Jesse.* A secret prayer, one that not even Holly heard completely.

The dozens of candles burned brightly, illuminating the softly-furnished living-room, music playing quietly on the stereo. Jesse had opened the bottle of white wine and placed it next to the two glasses on the small coffee table. Everything looked perfect, including herself, she had the house to herself, everything was set. She looked at the clock and saw the minute hand move. Seven o'clock on the dot. The knock on the door came as no surprise; much like Michael, Ryan was always on time.

Jesse walked to the door and let Ryan in, smiling as he

stepped inside. He closed the door behind him and she walked into the living-room and picked up the bottle of wine, her back to her boyfriend.

His hands curled around her waist, caressing her stomach. She felt his lips on her neck, kissing her gently, sending shivers down her back. Ryan whirled her around to face him, making her lose her grip on the bottle, neither of them noticing when it landed on the edge of the table and broke. They kissed intensely, and she felt his teeth on her lips. The kiss became more passionate and she could taste blood. Ryan broke off and moved his mouth onto her neck again. The taste of blood was still on her tongue when Jesse felt the pressure on her neck, knowing that he was giving her another love bite. She took hold of the hands that had encircled her waist again. She lifted them up and began to kiss them seductively. She almost crushed them between her own when pain raced through her body. She felt warmth run down her neck and onto her chest, and she pushed Ryan away with her body. Her back still to him, she lifted her hand up and felt the place that the pain was centred.

When the tips of her fingers came away sticky and red she turned to Ryan for an explanation, eyes widening. He stood before her, mouth covered in her blood, breathing quickly. His eyes had changed: the colour was the same but the amusement that had always been there had been replaced with a primal hunger. He stepped towards her, Jesse stepping back to compensate and cutting her feet on the broken glass of the bottle.

The look of fright on her face stopped Ryan from moving any further towards her and, instead of continuing, he turned briskly and walked from the room.

Jesse felt light-headed, her head swimming. Before the front door swung shut, and before she fainted, bleeding from her lips, her neck and her feet, she heard Ryan's voice.

"Michael's gunna kill me."

"I'll see you tomorrow."

Holly saw Michael looking around them from the corners of his eyes. He'd been distracted for the last fifteen minutes, the way he had abruptly told her that he should walk her home, cutting their night short after only an hour, and before she could even attempt to talk to him. During the walk he'd continually looked over her shoulders as if sure that someone was following them.

"Okay."

He kissed her forehead and simply walked away.

Angry, disappointed, she opened the door and hoped that Jesse and Ryan had finished whatever had been started, or at least taken it to a more private room. Holly smelled wine as soon as she closed the door and peeked her head around the living-room door, hoping that she could skirt through without being seen to the stairs at the far end of the room.

She had expected to see her friend and Michael's brother making out on the sofa. What she saw instead was Jesse, pale and collapsed on the floor with blood on her neck, near a broken bottle in a pool of spilled wine.

Holly ran to her side and saw that she was still breathing. "Thank God."

Gathering all the strength she had, Holly picked Jesse up by the armpits and put her down, almost dropping her, onto the sofa. The first place she looked was Jesse's neck. Deep looking marks sat in the skin that had already started to turn purple around blood that had already dried, yet they didn't look too serious - nothing that she thought would kill her, anyway. Looking again at the broken wine bottle on the floor, she looked at Jesse's feet. A few cuts, again nothing serious, and no sign of any glass embedded there. And, finally, Holly looked at Jesse's mouth. At first, Holly thought that her friend had been hit, but when she looked closer she saw small tears in Jesse's gums, like she'd been pricked with needles.

"Jesse?"

No response.

"Jesse!"

Holly was surprised into a laugh when her unconscious friend snorted once and began to snore. Hoping that she wasn't making a mistake by not taking her straight A&E, Holly decided to let her friend sleep.

Holly sat at Jesse's side and eventually fell asleep herself, dreaming of a river of blood.

"How could you be so stupid?!"

Ryan backed away from Michael, almost tripping over his feet. He had never seen Michael angry before and, now that he had, he decided he never wanted to see it again.

When Ryan began to mumble something Michael interrupted. "It was a rhetorical question, asshole. Keep your fucking mouth shut. I need to think."

Michael walked away and started pacing in front of a large headstone, closing his hands into fists then opening them: closing, opening, closing, opening.

"For Christ's sake, will you stop doing that?!" Ryan whispered, but Michael heard.

"For *Christ's* sake?" He laughed cruelly. "How appropriate. We're standing next to a church. Maybe Christ *will* help." He looked at Ryan. "I sure hope he does, 'cos I can't think of any way to sort out this fucking mess you caused." Michael sat down on a headstone and sighed heavily. Calmly, he said, "If I lose her I'll kill you." He looked at Ryan, who was shocked to see tears in Michael's eyes.

"I'll kill you."

"It was Ryan."

Holly's hand came away from her mouth. "But what happened?"

She sipped the vodka that she had just poured and went over to sit next to her friend, passing her the other glass.

"Jesse?" She turned Jesse's head to face her. "What happened?"

Jesse held her vodka with shaking hands and drank half of it in one go, enjoying the way it burned her all the way down to her stomach and leaving a warm trail down her throat. "We were making out and he started to give me a love-bite. Then he bit me!" She sighed.

Jesse turned and looked out of the window at the sunshine. "But it wasn't just that. He changed."

Holly looked at the mark on Jesse's neck. "What do you mean?"

Jesse shook her head slowly. "I'm not sure, just that he changed. His whole body stance, like a predator on the hunt. His eyes were so intense. And," she paused, emptying the glass. "His teeth were sharper, longer."

She looked at Holly, not liking what she saw there. "I'm not mad and I'm not making this up, Holly. His teeth..."

Holly stood and walked to the window. Outside, people walked, minding their own business, while inside her house everything had been turned on its head. "I'll speak to Michael tonight, tell him what's happened."

"Just be careful, Holly. I don't trust Ryan anymore. I mean, thinking about it, I don't know anything about him, not really! And you don't know anything about Michael, either."

Holly's expression tightened a little. "I'll be fine," she said as she left the room.

Jesse looked at the wall across from where she sat, staring at the decorative crucifix that hung there, knowing that she was probably being stupid but not caring.

"He told me."

Holly was shocked. "How can you be so calm about this? Your brother attacked my best friend and you're acting like it's the most natural thing in the world!"

Angrily, she turned to walk away but Michael caught her arm and turned her back to him. "I'm mad as hell about what he did! But when I get angry I cannot hold my temper and I will not allow myself to hurt you." He realised that he was squeezing her arm and let go. "I'm going to meet with him now. We'll sort out everything."

"'Sort everything out'?!"

Michael tried to kiss her but she turned her face away. He sighed and slouched off, leaving her alone in the churchyard.

Holly turned and watched him go, for once feeling warmer without him there.

Confused and disturbed, she started back home, trying to distract herself from her turmoil by looking at the way that things changed in the dark. When she arrived home she found it empty.

He watched the woman and Ryan, knowing that he too was being watched. With women like this one Ryan always did the talking. He was confident, cute and cocky and that, Michael had come to believe, was exactly what the girls liked. As long as they could pay. He himself found approaching prostitutes an awkward experience, but he was from a different time.

She obviously liked Ryan straight away, her body language gave that away. He was telling her the old routine, that he had to get his money but would be straight back. She watched him go with clear disappointment.

Ryan walked over to where Michael hid in the shadows. "So? What d'ya think?"

Michael looked back at the woman. She was big, easily twenty-five stone. She wore a short skirt, a couple of inches higher and it wouldn't cover anything. Her low-cut top covered her protruding stomach, but not much else. Make-up was plastered all over her face. Compared to the other girls working the street, he doubted that she got much business, but she looked like an easy target. "Not bad."

"Same deal as usual?"

Michael looked at the man that was meant for him, what Ryan had referred to as the 'same deal' for the last decade. "Sure. Why break tradition?"

Ryan took some money from his trouser pocket then emerged from the shadows, walking back towards the prostitute while Michael focussed his attention on his own prey. He was still aware of her watching him but he managed to concentrate on the pimp who had started talking to a couple of other girls. Michael gave Ryan time to take the prostitute away before walking forwards, keeping his eyes focussed entirely on the man. He reached the corner and stopped, letting his prey see him, not making any attempt to speak.

Finally the man became aware that Michael was watching him. "Something occurring, mate?"

It came out sounding like *occurrrrring* and Michael had to stop himself from smiling at the Norfolk accent. It just didn't sound right for a pimp.

"Can I talk to you? I need to ask you something." He looked back at the woman then back at him. "Without the workers."

The pimp nodded at the woman and she left then turned back to Michael, obviously weary. "So what can I do for ya?"

Jesse watched Michael talking to the man, an arm slung around his shoulder, leading him slowly away into a space between two buildings. She moved from where she had crouched, grimacing at the aches that had accumulated, and walked towards the place they had disappeared. She could hear her own feet loud on the pavement and hoped that Michael couldn't.

Jesse spotted them, the man slouching on the ground looking nervous, Michael leaning over him. He had his back to her, knowing that they were talking but able to hear the words.

Abruptly, the man with the moustache stood up quickly and moved away from Michael. For a reason that Jesse couldn't see the moustache-man's anger turned to fear and he backed away, hitting his back on the wall behind him. He slid to the floor, returning to his original position. His eyes were fixed on Michael's face, the fear turning to complete terror.

Jesse only watched as Michael crouched beside him and placed a restraining hand on the man's neck. Her own hand covered the bite that Ryan had given her without realising she was doing it. Frowning, she watched as Michael moved his head forward, covering the man's mouth and turning his face to one side, unable to see what he was doing.

She gasped when Michael turned towards her, his mouth coated in blood, and Jesse fled the street.

Michael disposed of the body then walked the short distance to the hotel and straight into the room in which Ryan had led the prostitute.

The woman that Ryan had fed on was sprawled on the bed. He had covered her body with the once-white sheet and Michael gazed at the raised shape, knowing that the woman would never hover around the street corner again.

"How badly this time?"

Ryan, unlike Michael, liked to play around before he fed. After threatening them with worse if they screamed, he would use his nails and his teeth to scar his victim; a few cuts here, a few bites there: scaring them until they lost all their fight, scaring them as he scarred them, mentally exhausting them until they almost begged to be taken.

Smiling widely, Ryan whipped the sheet off, exposing the naked corpse.

Michael, usually not easily shocked by Ryan's sick games, had to turn away. But it was too late: the image had burned itself into Michael's brain. The woman had been completely mutilated. Instead of a single bite on the woman's throat, it had been slashed all the way across. Dried blood went down her neck and covered her breasts where both nipples had been ripped off, with bites covering the surrounding flesh. Her huge stomach had been slit open and her intestines hung out, spread over the mattress. Her legs were the worst. A chunk of her left calf had been torn off, and nail marks stretched around both thighs down to the ankles.

He looked at Ryan. "You're a cruel bastard."

Ryan shrugged, but he at least dropped the grin. "So, did Jesse see everything?"

Michael nodded. "I'm still not sure that this is a good idea, though. There must have been an easier way."

Ryan shrugged again and uttered a simple statement. "It's slightly dramatic, but I still think it's the only way for you to keep Holly."

"Holly! You home?"

Jesse closed the front door with a slam and walked into the living-room, a little unsteady on her feet. It had taken her almost an hour and forty minutes to walk from the town back to the outskirts of the village. And counting the time it had taken her to buy the two bottles of vodka (and drinking half of one sat on a wall near the shop) she'd been gone hours. She sat down heavily on the sofa and with shaking hands lifted the remains of the open bottle to her lips, drinking deeply.

Footsteps on the stairs caught her attention and she looked up, watching Holly closing her nightgown as she descended the stairs.

"Holly. Oh, thank God. We need to talk about...." She drifted off as she saw Michael appearing at the top of the stairs, putting his jacket on.

"About what?" Holly said serenely as she reached the bottom step.

"Doesn't matter." Jesse took another swig of vodka, covering her bite with her free hand, seeing Michael walk down the stairs.

"I'd better be going." Michael kissed Holly, catching Jesse's eye for a second, then left, leaving Holly staring at the place he had disappeared, smiling contently.

The moment the front door clicked closed, Jesse jumped up and grabbed Holly by the shoulders. "Please." She said, looking into Holly's eyes. "Please, for God's sake, please tell me you didn't sleep with him!" She searched Holly's eyes and realised that it was no good hoping.

Jesse pushed Holly away viciously. "Oh, how could you be so fucking stupid?!"

"Jesse?" The happiness on her face disappeared in an instant. "How can you-"

"I saw him kill someone, Holly. I saw him kill a man and drink his blood."

"What? Don't be so stupid, Jesse! Of course he didn't-"

"He did! I watched him do it! And he saw me, he knew I was watching, he-"

Holly, tears flowing from her eyes, looked at her friend with disgust. "Shut up! Just because your boyfriend gets off on sick shit like that, don't try and poison me towards Michael."

"Holly-" Jesse wanted to say that she was telling the truth, but Holly cut her off before she could get any words out.

"Spend the night here, Jesse. But first thing tomorrow, pack your things and you get the hell out of my house! I will not let you destroy my relationship just because yours has gone to shit."

Holly strode up the stairs and Jesse jumped when she heard the bedroom door slam. She sank to the floor and gazed up at the top of the stairs, dazed and wondering what had just happened.

"He's beautiful, Michael."

Holly picked up the golden-retriever puppy and held him close to her. She looked at the blue collar around his neck and whispered the name printed on it. "Max."

Michael watched her cuddling the dog and felt pleased that he had made her so happy, especially after the pain he'd caused her by manipulating Jesse the way he had. He thought about last night, about sleeping with her, touching her and loving her. He'd never thought that he could feel like this again. He had been wondering if he'd done the right thing. Now, seeing Holly with the puppy he was sure that he had.

* * *

For three weeks Jesse observed Holly. She saw her friend walking the dog, always with Michael, and always at night. Michael was around all the time when it was dark, disappearing only for an odd hour every few nights. She no longer followed him to his feeds; instead she was determined that the thing - even though Jesse knew what he was, she still couldn't even think the word vampire - would cause no harm to her friend. Jesse watched the house constantly, sleeping only when she had to, hardly eating.

Finally, Jesse built up the courage to try and speak to her friend, and approached the house. She knocked on the door, the winter sun strong on the back of her neck and immediately heard the dog start to bark. She heard nothing else.

Using the key she still had, Jesse let herself into the house. She walked in and closed the door behind her, shutting the sunlight off once again from the curtain-shielded house.

As soon as the rays of the sun were banished from the hall, Jesse saw Holly's golden-retriever. It emerged from the shadows of the living room, a growl coming from deep in its throat. It paced slowly forward, its eyes locked on Jesse. Then, without warning, it pounced.

She felt teeth in her calf, pain that sank in the flesh even further than the rows of teeth, followed by a sudden liquid warmth on her ankle. Jesse held back the scream that threatened to erupt from her lungs and grabbed the dog by its neck, trying to stop it doing any more damage.

"Max."

The dog relinquished its hold on Jesse and backed off immediately, never once taking its eyes from Jesse's. It moved to the foot of the stairs and when Jesse looked up she saw Holly halfway up.

She couldn't stop staring at her friend, at the differences that she hadn't noticed in her night-time stalking. Her skin had paled and to Jesse it made her look even more beautiful. Her eyes seemed more aware, filled with brightness, making Holly look more alive than she ever had before.

"Good guard dog, Holly. Bet he doesn't attack Michael like that."

Holly walked slowly down the rest of the stairs, her black satin skirt shifting near her ankles as she moved, and stood next to Max. "Probably because he knows Michael would never hurt me."

"And I would?" Jesse saw that Holly's eyes were no longer focussed, and she seemed almost asleep on her feet. Max resumed his growling.

"You'd better go, Jesse." Holly sat down and placed a loving arm around Max's neck. "I really don't think that Max likes you very much."

Scared of leaving Holly alone in her bizarre state but scared of what Max would do if she didn't, Jesse turned and walked out of the door. Talking to Holly hadn't worked so it was time she had a talk to Michael.

"Michael."

He turned his back on Holly's door to see Jesse standing in front of him. Her hair was held back in a greasy ponytail, her clothes were creased and dirty. She looked a mess, but also so much stronger than the last time he had seen her.

"You're right," he said, responding to what he read in her eyes. "We've got to talk." He gave one last look at Holly's door and stepped away from it.

Together they walked, a cloudy sky above them hiding the stars, Jesse keeping him at a distance she considered safe, and keeping a tight grip on the crucifix in her pocket. Michael led the way and Jesse found herself in the churchyard where Michael and Holly used to meet. He stood inside the doorway of the huge building and Jesse stood opposite, not allowing herself to be caged in.

"So. Let's talk." His expression had changed; he'd become more sure of himself.

"Tell me what you are." She refused her eyes permission to fall from his - he would not stare her out!

"You know what I am." Amusement; his voice and his face showed only simple amusement.

"Are you afraid to say it?"

"I'm a vampire." So matter-of-factly.

"Are you going to change Holly into one of you?"

Losing some of this authority, Michael stepped back a little, the amusement leaving him instantaneously. "No." A whisper that seemed to catch in his throat. "I love her too much to do that." He sighed deeply, and shook his head. "And even if I had ever planned to, there's something else now."

He looked at her and Jesse simply stared back.

"Holly's pregnant."

Things grew even darker around Jesse, becoming hazy and unreal, as her eyes rolled upwards and she collapsed on to the ground.

The smell of mould and damp crept into her nostrils, and even before she completely came to, she knew that she was no longer in the churchyard. Jesse remembered why she had been there and sat up in a hurry. Her head hit something hard and she slumped backwards onto her elbows. Black spots danced in front of her eyes and she closed them again to stop from fainting once more, her stomach rolling. Once the sick feeling had passed she opened her eyes again.

Jesse saw, amidst all the shadows, two figures moving. A match was lit and the flame was transferred onto a candle, which Michael held. He passed it to Ryan, who avoided Jesse's eyes.

"Are you okay?" Michael walked carefully over to her and handed her a glass of water, his other hand raised palm towards her, a gesture of placation. After a few moments hesitation Jesse accepted the glass from him without speaking.

Jesse looked out of the corner of her eye and realised that she sat on the lower level of a bunk-bed in a small room. Dust covered everything and she saw that wherever the bedroom was, it had obviously not been used for quite a while.

"Ryan. Do you mind?" Michael kept his eyes on the young woman while Ryan lit a few more candles before leaving the room. Seconds later they both heard a distant front door open and close.

Jesse looked at Michael, rolling the glass between her hands, all her fear gone. "Did you really say that Holly was pregnant?"

He nodded, keeping quiet as he sat on a small cushioned chair opposite her.

"How is that possible?" She put a hand to her forehead, trying to still the headache that had just appeared. "I'm not exactly a fan of films like that, but the one's I've seen..."

"All rubbish." His voice was depressed and his hands twirled and twisted with each other - they looked like they were having some insane fight. "It's rare, really, incredibly rare. But I have heard of it happening. But..." He stared at his hands, unable to meet Jesse's eyes. "I've never heard of either mother or child surviving, in any form."

"What?" All of her uncomfortable feelings were consumed by anger. "What do you mean neither mother or child survive?"

She stood, making sure that she didn't hit her head again, and dropped the glass on the wooden floor. Her feet crunched on the broken glass as she moved towards Michael. "You bastard! You've killed her!"

Michael looked up too late, to see her approaching him, anger plastered all over her face. "We don't know that!"

Jesse no longer heard him, her mind completely blanked his voice out, as she twisted the crucifix in her pocket, accidentally cutting her fingers on a jagged edge. The only things that she could concentrate on were Michael's face and the weight of the silver crucifix. As she walked, her fingers turned the item, causing more cuts on her skin without feeling them.

Without warning, even to herself, the crucifix that had been in her pocket found its way out and, using Jesse's strength, plunged itself deep into Michael's chest. The moment Jesse realised what she had done she removed her hand from the silver item and stood back, breathing hard.

Michael's face paled and he slumped lower in his seat, his hands trying to catch the dark blood that poured from his chest. He looked up at Jesse, eyes pleading. Bubbles of blood forming on his lips and he gargled. "Try to… protect.. her…"

All she could do was watch, mesmerised despite the disgust at herself. He didn't burst into flames or disappear in a puff of smoke. For a few seconds nothing happened, just the continued flow of blood as he slipped off the chair. The blood stopped flowing and he grew older; wrinkles formed on his brow and around his eyes, his hair grew grey and then white before falling out completely, the skin on his bald head turning mottled, diseased. His face collapsed in on itself and then became little more than a crater. His body thinned and shrunk, folding into a pile at the base of the chair. Jesse kicked at the clothes to find that nothing filled them.

Holly jumped as Max began to howl violently as if he was in pain. She ran into the living-room to find Max looking up at the ceiling.

"Max?" She walked slowly towards him, then stopped abruptly when he turned to face her. Holly stifled a scream. Max's eyes were bloodshot and blood dripped from his jaws. There didn't seem to be any injury that she could see, and she didn't care once it began pouring from his mouth. All she could do was watch as grey hair began to appear on his fur, and she finally started to back away. She tripped on her own feet and went sprawling awkwardly onto her back. As a shot of pain raced through her spine, she heard a low growl, and lifted her head up slightly.

Holly saw Max inching slyly towards her, blood-soaked muzzle wrinkled, and she raised her legs up to her belly in response. At her movement, he came at a run, and Holly kicked her legs up and away from her, squinting her eyes closed as her feet connected with her beloved pet.

She heard a thud accompanied with a squelching sound and, when she found the courage to look up, she saw Max's twitching body impaled momentarily on a picture hook before the dog's weight tore the hook from the wall.

A sharp pain in her stomach took her attention from the animal. It stopped as soon as it had started and a thought, without knowing exactly what it meant, flew into her head. *It's over!*

An hour after killing Michael, and one hour after Max's death, Jesse again let herself into Holly's home.

An incredible stench, similar to rotting red meat, filled her nostrils as soon as she walked in, but Jesse ignored it. Keeping an eye out for Max, she walked up the stairs and into Holly's room, where she found her friend packing clothes into a bag, tears pouring from her eyes.

"Holly?"

Holly turned around to see her friend standing in the doorway, and she ran into her arms, allowing Jesse to stroke her blonde hair, clutching her tightly. "I killed him." The words came out amidst sobs and Jesse gently pushed her away so she could look into her eyes.

"No, *I* killed him, Holly. Michael will never come near you again."

Jesse tried to take Holly back into an embrace but it was Holly's turn to push Jesse away, holding onto the woman's arms and looking as if she'd just been slapped.

"What do you mean, he'll never bother me again?"

Jesse couldn't find any words to answer, her mouth opening

and closing with no sound. She backed away from Holly when she saw the violence in her friend's eyes, Holly closing the distance.

"What have you done?" Holly's voice growing shrill, more anguished. "Jesse, what the fuck have you done?" They were out of the bedroom, Jesse walking backwards to keep out of Holly's reach.

"What have you *DONE*?!"

Too late, Holly saw what was about to happen. The anger flew out of her voice to be replaced with panic, her arms reaching out to try and prevent it. "JESSE!"

The scream echoed around the house as Jesse slipped backwards down the stairs, the scream falling short as Holly heard the sharp and loud snap of bones breaking.

Holly ran down the stairs to where Jesse's tangled body lay. With trembling hands, she reached out but couldn't bring herself to touch her friend as she looked at the glazed eyes behind the broken glasses. Not knowing what else to do, Holly raced back upstairs. Less than ten minutes later, with two bags of clothes and a couple of personal belongings, she ran from the house.

* * *

Seven Months Later

Sweat poured from her face, her chest heaved and she tried to slow her breathing. The midwife and nurse spoke to her encouragingly as she gave the final push.

Her body trembled as the midwife held the baby that she'd produced, placing it onto Holly's chest. She looked down at the child, wonderingly. The baby girl did look like her father: a shock of dark hair, beautiful and alert green eyes.

"Maybe Jesse was wrong." The words came out as a whisper of exhausted hope and the nurse looked at her nervously.

Holly stroked the baby's cheek, feeling completely happy for the first time in months. She smiled and her daughter nuzzled against her, her lips pulling back to expose tiny sharp teeth.

The scream of horror rang through the room, bouncing off the tiles, until the injection of pethidine ran through Holly's veins, turning the scream into a whimper of despair and heartbreak.

Part Two

The Demon Child

She walked into the bedroom, the unusual silence filling her mind. Laura was nowhere in the house, Michelle knew that in her heart and in her stomach, had known it from the second she had stepped foot through the front door. Her daughter was gone.

The room was no different to the normal organised chaos that Michelle was accustomed to seeing, though she did notice that a few personal belongings were missing. On the table where the necklace she had given Laura for her twelfth birthday usually sat when it wasn't being worn, was an envelope. Shaking, Michelle picked up the letter and saw that it had her own name printed on it; Laura had never called Michelle 'mum', she had always known the truth about the adoption.

Michelle's stomach jumped uneasily at the sight of her adopted daughter's handwriting laid out upon the multiple pages, and began to read.

Michelle. I'm so sorry I had to do things like this, but if I'd told you what's been going on you'd send me to a shrink! I know that what I'm going to tell you is strange but it's all true. I swear that it's all true.

Do you remember when I was little, I told you about the man and the woman that would visit me at night? They knew my mother and my father. They told me about what happened to them.

I'll do my best to set you and Paul straight. God, this could be a very long letter.

The first time I saw Ryan, that I can remember anyway, I think I was about six. He sat on my window sill and told me that he had been watching me ever since I had been born. He brushed the hair from my face and told me that he could see both Holly and Michael in my eyes. That was the first time I ever heard my parents' names.

I remember hearing you on the stairs and Ryan told me he'd come back. Can you remember? I ran out to you and told you a friend of my parents came to visit me. You'd blamed it on a dream. You smiled, kissed my forehead and told me that you were sure that my parents were always watching over me.

You misunderstood, but I understand why.

When I was a little older, he visited with a lady. It was a full moon, and they looked beautifully-pale.

Ryan, his brown hair swept back from his forehead, had the most gorgeous blue eyes I had ever seen. Even now, I don't believe that I have ever seen eyes like that. One minute, they were filled with such passion, such happiness. The next they looked so sad. His lips always fascinated me. They were ruby red, made even darker by the paleness, the whiteness, of his skin.

The lady, Jesse, was extraordinary. Her brown eyes always held the same expressions as Ryan. She stayed completely quiet the first time I met her, never speaking and not once taking her eyes from me.

I won't go into detail of every time I met with Ryan and Jesse, you'd be reading for the next five years if I did. So I'll leave it at this: they visited me often and left me feeling like I had a real connection with my parents.

Last year, I got a letter from Ryan, asking me to sneak out to meet them the next night. I was a little nervous, especially at the words 'I have to show you what you are.' At the time I thought he meant 'I have to show you who you are'. I know now that I was wrong, but all I knew then was that I was curious.

So, I did as he'd asked. I checked that you and Paul were asleep and crept out of the house. It was dark, it was cold, and I was scared, even though our street is always quiet. You never let me out alone at night, the whole experience was terrifying. But it was also wonderful. I felt more real. Everything had changed. The streets seemed to move with my footsteps. I could hear people speaking but could see no one. I could feel the night. I know how weird that sounds, but it's the only way I can describe it.

I saw Ryan and Jesse standing at the corner at the end of the street and walked quickly towards them. They had their backs to me, but I knew it was them. When they turned to face me, I stopped dead, my heart beating fast, and just looked at them. There was something about my friends that I suddenly didn't trust, a feeling that made my stomach turn. It went almost as quickly as it appeared, but it left me confused.

Instead of walking towards them, I waited until they reached me. Ryan immediately hugged me, and it felt wrong, somehow awkward. He seemed to sense this as well and pulled away from me.

"There's no easy way to do this, Laura." He glanced at Jesse who looked away instantly. "Come on."

We walked for about five minutes and I straggled behind a little, not understanding my feeling – I wanted to come home. Ryan stopped in front of a terraced-house. A 'sold' sign stood in the garden amongst the overgrown plants and weeds, faded and battered. The windows were bordered up and I could see black material behind the wooden boards.

Jesse unlocked the door and swung it open for me. It was pitch black in the doorway and I refused to move until a light had been switched on.

Ryan wandered off somewhere in the house and Jesse closed the door and turned to face me. "I've got something for you."

I watched as she pulled something out of her trouser pocket. Her eyes held that familiar sadness, which always seemed to deepen when she looked at me. The photograph was folded up, and old. She walked away from me and I followed her into the small living room.

We sat in silence for a few moments then she handed me the photo. I opened it up and saw the woman, blonde, beautiful. Her eyes were smiling, and she was laughing at whoever had taken the picture. I could see the similarity between her and myself. I looked at Jesse and she nodded.

"That's Holly, your mother."

I stared at the picture for a long time. My eyes were still focussed on my mother when I asked, "What happened? Why did she give me away?"

"I think she couldn't cope with what you were. Your father had died, maybe she just couldn't cope with you on her own. She had no family, no one to help." I saw a tear creep down her face.

"What do you mean she couldn't cope with what I was? What happened?"

Jesse sighed and wiped her face with the back of her hand. "She left you at the hospital, and disappeared." Tears were flowing freely from her eyes. "They found her a week later. Found her body."

I'd never known my mother, had never known Holly. But as she said those words, as she told me that my mother was dead, I felt sick, like someone had punched me in the stomach. I'd always had the hope of maybe meeting her one day.

Before I could really react to the news properly, Ryan appeared in the doorway. Jesse nodded and Ryan left again. She stood and held a hand out to me, which I took straight away. We walked upstairs and into one of the bedrooms. Ryan stood next to a bed and I saw a woman there. She had make-up plastered all over her face; it made her look ugly.

We walked over to Ryan, and Jesse let go of my hand. I felt Ryan put a hand on my shoulder and we watched as Jesse sat on the edge of the bed.

The woman looked up at Jesse and smiled. She really could have been pretty if it hadn't been for the make-up. Her eyes reached Ryan, still smiling, then she saw me and her smile faltered. She looked at Jesse and Ryan again, obviously seeking an explanation. Ryan flashed his good-natured smile but it was only when Jesse smiled at her that she seemed to relax.

Jesse moved closer to her and brushed the hair from the woman's neck. For a moment, I wanted to be where Jesse was, to be doing what she was doing, and I looked up at Ryan, but he only pointed at the bed. After a few moments I looked.

I saw the blood.

It didn't look like ketchup or any of the fake stuff like in the films. I never, not for one second, believed it to be anything other than what it was. It was blood, over her neck. Jesse was drinking it. And the woman didn't even struggle. A feeling, a wanting, hit me. I saw the blood flow over the woman's chest and I wanted it, wanted to taste it. I think I actually took a step forward, eyes fixed only on that red line. Then I felt Ryan's arm, that had been draped over my shoulder the whole time, fall away. And the hunger seemed to fall with it. I no longer wanted that blood, I didn't even want to be anywhere near Ryan and Jesse.

I looked at Ryan. Then I ran, as fast as I could. Not once did I look back but my pace slowed as I neared home. I began to walk, my heart still beating fast, blood pumping through my veins. My legs ached and I had a stitch in my side, but I felt safer. I walked slowly, enjoying the silence of the night.

I heard no footsteps behind me and almost screamed, when a hand touched my shoulder. I turned and saw Jesse. Her eyes were filled with that sadness again and I saw tears threatening to spill. She showed nothing of what I had just seen.

We began to walk towards the park. Not talking, but I felt that Jesse was thinking hard, trying to ready herself for whatever it *was that she had to tell me.*

I sat on the swings and, after a moment's pause, Jesse sat on the one next to me. She was still silent and I took time to marvel at the peacefulness that was around me. The night, it seemed, changed the whole world.

"Your mother and I were good friends."

Her voice shocked me out of my thoughts and I looked at her. Her hands twisted in her lap and she looked into the playing fields.

"What happened?" My voice came out weak and strained.

I won't tell you everything she had said, it would be a waste of time, but I'll sum it up for you. My mother, Holly, fell in love with my father, Jesse was seeing Ryan; everything was normal. My mother and father slept together and she fell pregnant. By that point, Jesse knew what Ryan and my father were. It still seems insane to me, so I can imagine what you'll think when you read this. They were vampires. Jesse killed my father and she and my mum had an argument. Jesse fell down the stairs and nearly died. Ryan saved her by turning her into one too. Then they tracked my mother down.

I'd been crying by the time that Jesse had finished talking. I'd taken the photograph from my pocket and stared at it. My mother. Half of me thought Jesse was crazy but half of me believed her.

I asked her why they'd done this, why they couldn't just let me be a normal kid.

Jesse had turned to me, almost angrily. "You're all I've got of her. If we let you be, in time you'll die."

My heart dropped into my stomach at that. I was a kid! I'd never thought about death before.

"If I let that happen to you, I'll lose whatever was left of Holly. I won't let that happen." She'd turned to me then, hands resting firmly on my shoulders, eyes burning deeply into mine. "You have to be with me always."

It was all so strange and, for a second I felt like someone dangerous was watching me, waiting to see how I'd react. Then that feeling left. I'd walked away from her then, telling her that I needed time to think, that I didn't want to see either of them for a couple of weeks. And, thankfully, they did as I asked.

I know you'll remember this next bit, Michelle. You were so worried about me, about the books I was reading. Remember? I found every book I could about vampires, but there was no truth in any of them, except one. Sunlight would kill Ryan and Jesse, but not me. I wore the crucifix you had given me and neither of them shied away from it. They'd never lived in coffins, nor did they change into bats or wolves. Their faces did not change when they wanted to feed: they remained as beautiful as ever. No, the only truth in those books seemed to be about sunlight, for them at least.

When Ryan visited me, we talked about them and I must have asked him a hundred questions. I asked him how old he was, but he just shook his head and refused to answer. I asked why the sunlight didn't kill me or even hurt me, and again he just shook his head. He said that he didn't know anything more than I did, that my father had mentioned that the rare cases of vampire pregnancies had resulted in both baby and mother dying, so he didn't know what to expect.

When Ryan had left, I was more confused than ever. Go with them and see what would happen, or stay with you and Paul? My head whirled around, going down one path and then the other. I was scared but I was also curious. If I stayed, I'd always be curious. If I went I would lose the only parents I'd ever known. I'd have Ryan and Jesse, but I'd lose you. And I wasn't sure if I really trusted them anymore.

I didn't sleep well that night, and when I finally did, I dreamed I was on a boat. The boat was tied somewhere, but I couldn't see land. I looked at the water, and it wasn't water but blood. My thoughts were torn in two. Half of me wanted to grab the rope and pull on it until I made the boat reach land. The other part of me wanted to jump in, to bathe myself in the blood. And before I knew what was happening my two thoughts became one and I dove out of the boat.

I woke up with a coppery taste in the back of my throat, and I knew that taste. It was blood. And I wanted more of it. The depth of the feeling scared me but I couldn't deny that it was there. My throat was thirsty for it, my body longed for it. It seemed I'd made my decision.

During the day I felt distracted. I didn't want to be there and I longed for the sun to set and for the night to begin. It took over my thoughts, this new hunger. I started hating school, started to shy away from my friends. The one thing that stopped me from joining Ryan and Jesse was the thought of you, Michelle, and Paul. How *could I leave you?*

Two nights ago, Ryan came to see me again. He told me that he and Jesse were leaving, that I had to make my decision. Stay, or go with them? Suppress what I was, or embrace it?

So, I guess I've made my choice. I can't help what I am. I can only do what feels most natural to me now. I have to go.

I love you, Michelle. And I love Paul. You treated me like I was your own. But now I have to find out exactly what I am, and who I am. And you can't help me with that.

I'll miss you more than you will ever know. That's the only thing I am sure of now.

I'll love you always.

x-Laura-x

Michelle ran from Laura's room, still holding the letter. She rang Paul at work and told him to come home. When he asked if it was Laura she just told him to get home.

The phone was slammed back on its cradle. It was five-nineteen. An hour and five minutes before the sun would disappear from the sky.

They sat at the kitchen table, two cups of coffee in front of them, both untouched and cold. Paul read the last of the letter and placed it on the table. He looked carefully at his wife. "You can't really believe this?"

Michelle looked from the window where she had watched the sun begin its descent. Carefully she shook her head.

Paul stood. Hands in pocket, he stood at the kitchen sink and looked outside, where his daughter was somewhere. "I don't know what this is really about, but she'll be home soon."

Night descended. Laura walked out of the house with Jesse at her side. Ryan locked the door and they walked together down the road. It was cold but Laura had declined Jesse's offer of a jacket. As it bit at her skin it reminded Laura that all of this was real, not some weird delusion. It made her feel alive.

They did not have to walk long before they found someone.

His clothes were dirty, his hair unwashed, his breath stinking of cheap whiskey and he couldn't walk straight. Laura didn't want to, not to *him*, but Jesse reassured her.

The man stumbled and Laura rushed to his aid, asking him if he was okay. The man smiled gratefully, and with his slurred speech thanked her. Laura gently and subtly steered him away from the street lamps and into a small alley behind a pub.

She told him to sit and he did, falling rather than sitting. Ryan and Jesse joined them within minutes.

Ryan walked up to the man and didn't bother with his usual niceties. His teeth locked onto the man's neck, puncturing the skin, letting the blood flow. He pulled away before he became too hungry and stood back.

The man, a drunk who had been on the streets since his wife had thrown him there two years before, looked at Ryan, his eyes filled with shock. He saw movement and looked at the young girl as she moved towards him.

Laura looked at the man, pretending not to register the fright in his eyes. She looked at his throat and at the blood that flowed from the holes that Ryan had created. The hunger that had only been a dull throb for the past weeks, now filled every part of her. Her mouth locked onto his throat and she began to drink.

The taste filled her throat then slowly reached her stomach. Instead of abating, the hunger increased and the sound of his heart beat filling her body thrilled her. This was the meaning for everything, her whole life had been leading up to this point.

When she had finished, she wiped her mouth with the palm of her hand and looked at Ryan and Jesse. They looked proud, yet somehow puzzled.

Smiling, she stood and they walked away.

"You've tried all of her friends?"

Paul nodded, noticing that Michelle had hardly taken her eyes from the window since the sun had set. "Nobody's seen her today. Not that they're admitting to their parents, anyway."

He stared at the darkness, where Laura was hiding somewhere, and sighed. "We need to ring the police, Michelle."

He heard his wife's gasp and turned. What he saw shocked him.

As Laura walked through the door, Michelle heard herself make a mewling sound in the back of her throat. *Oh my God. She's beautiful!* Instead of happiness, that thought made her feel cold and she suppressed a shiver that wanted to take control. Her little girl had always been pretty, but she had known that when Laura got older she would be considered by most to be plain. But now that had changed. Her hair, which had always been dark, now looked jet black. And her eyes! They sparkled and, even from a distance, Michelle could see her daughter's green eyes. *Oh, dear God. She's so beautiful!* The despair she felt started the tears she had been holding back ever since she had found Laura gone.

Without saying a word, Laura walked to Paul and kissed him on the cheek then walked to Michelle and kissed her.

Then Laura left. Michelle and Paul walked to the door to see their daughter walking away with two others. Without knowing that the other was doing the same, they touched their cheeks, wondering why the cold where she had touched them was lingering, too stunned to do anything else.

They walked in silence, feeling the crisp October night. There was something wrong, the two elder of the three felt it. In much as the same way headaches indicated an electrical storm on its way for some, their bodies tingled.

Ryan and Jesse were knocked to the ground before they even sensed anyone close to them. It hadn't hurt but they were too stunned by the force they had been hit with to do anything.

Someone, one of *them*, was restraining Laura, trying to stop her struggles. Something was whispered in the girl's ear, neither Ryan nor Jesse able to hear what, but Laura stopped struggling and relaxed in an instant, a smile appearing on her young face.

The vampire lifted the hood that shadowed her face. When she spoke, she spoke to both Ryan and Jesse, with passion and venom in her voice and eyes. "You will never touch my daughter again."

Ryan looked at Jesse and she looked straight back at him. When they looked back at Laura, they saw Holly walking away with her daughter in to the night.

Part Three

Reborn

She had watched Holly since before the youngster had given birth, knowing instinctively that there was something special about the rare pregnancy. When the woman had fled the hospital she had followed, realising that the others she had seen close by would watch the child.

The vampire, a loner, was ancient. She'd wandered for the last few centuries, trying to find just one thing that could end the unbearable boredom. And in Holly she had seen it. She'd sensed a change in Holly's physical state, one that, in all her years, she had never witnessed in any other: the woman had, after all, successfully carried a vampire child, and the child's blood had begun mixing with her own, starting to change her. It intrigued Ania, for in all her years she had never witnessed such an alteration. She didn't know if the change would actually complete or if it would stop before.

So she watched. But always from a distance.

Holly had run, despite her own body telling her to return to her daughter. But her sanity was in jeopardy and she simply couldn't. Her heart knew what, rationally, she knew couldn't be real, and so she had to run from it. In the darkness, she could feel the vibrations all through her body as her feet hit the pavement. When she had reached a fair distance away from the hospital she slowed her pace and walked through the night.

It was cold for a June night but she felt no need to find shelter; the cold kept her in reality. She walked on the unfamiliar pavements, watching for anybody nearby that would seem threatening. Her heart had slowed its pace and she walked with it, staying parallel to the river, her pace never changing. The moon shone clearly over the water, illuminating it with a beauty that Holly had never noticed before. The dark held a fascination for her, one that she had missed previously, in the life before vampires were a part of it. As she moved, she wondered how it felt, how Michael had felt, never seeing daylight, always hiding in the shadows. The thoughts, instead of scaring her, made her even more curious.

As she walked, she fantasised about what it could have been like.

Ania walked behind Holly, keeping her distance, watching. She knew the danger that was approaching and was intrigued. She wanted to know how the woman would cope. If things looked too bad, she would intervene - she didn't want the woman to die or to even be harmed, she just had to know how things would develop. In the darkness she could see Holly drawing closer to the man, and stayed with her.

Her stomach began to jump maddeningly as she saw the figure rise from the shadows. She saw a glint of light, and felt sweat form on her brow as she realised that the man held a knife. Holly wanted to take her eyes from him and keep walking naturally, but her eyes refused to leave the metal reflecting the moon. She felt awkward, her legs seemed unsteady and moving in an unfamiliar fashion.

The man stepped forward and blocked her path. He swayed slightly from side to side, his mean eyes bloodshot in the darkness. He raised the knife towards her, creeping slightly forward as Holly stepped backwards. His arm darted out and grabbed Holly's wrist, the sudden movement and the pain of his grip making her cry out.

Instead of being scared Holly suddenly felt invigorated. She could feel the blood pumping through her temple and she looked at the man, not reacting. When he raised the knife and tried to catch her cheek she simply backed away slightly. The man's hand slipped and she calmly watched as his hand dropped down onto the blade.

He cried out with surprise when the woman's wrist broke away from his hand and grabbed his own. Instead of running like they always did, she caught his other hand and squeezed hard, making him drop the knife. She lifted his hand up and watched silently as the blood dripped onto the ground.

Without thinking, Holly lifted his hand to her lips and allowed the blood to drop onto her tongue. The taste, small as it was, burned her throat as it worked its way along. Her eyes closed momentarily before opening again to look directly at the man who had tried to attack her. She stepped closer, almost taking him into an embrace. Her gaze swept slowly over his neck, and she moved her head closer, not noticing the smell of cheap alcohol that surrounded him.

Before she could stop herself, her teeth sank into the soft flesh and that taste enveloped her whole body. She drank deeply, holding onto his body with her formerly-unknown strength to prevent him from falling to the ground.

He passed out and she let him slip from her grasp. Holly

looked at his crumpled body, no sense of comprehension in her mind. She realised what she had done, vaguely realising what had happened, what she'd become. She turned around sharply at the approaching footsteps.

The woman walked slowly, obviously enjoying herself, never taking her eyes from Holly's. Her dark hair threaded with silver hung over the black velvet coat she wore. Beneath the long coat, Holly saw the black trousers and a black top, but her eyes never ventured far from the woman's face. Her eyes held an expression that Holly recognised from both Michael and Ryan, the same long-lived hunger.

Holly felt a sliver of fear reach into her heart and she looked down again at the body, fallen at her own feet. A part of her felt revulsion, but her body wasn't capable of that emotion - it craved for more of what it had just tasted.

A hand, cold and pale, gently touched her shoulder, light as a feather and Holly felt only comfort in it. Here was someone who could help her. Someone who could explain everything she needed to know. Slowly she looked up.

The woman's blue-grey eyes stared into her own, and Holly could see age in them that wasn't evident anywhere else in the woman's face. Her lips, full and voluptuous, were dark red, almost frighteningly so when compared to the whiteness of her skin. And she wasn't just pale as Michael and Ryan had been, but completely white as if her skin was made out of marble.

"I'm Ania."

Her voice was silvery, musical, sweet. But somehow it was too sweet, like an apple that hasn't quite ripened yet. It made Holly's head ache, even while she wished that the woman in front of her would continue to speak.

"I'm Holly." She glanced back down at the man at her feet and sickness rolled over her. Her stomach cramped and before she could stop herself, she leant away and vomited, gagging even harder when she saw the mess that she had brought up - nothing but blood.

That cold hand stroked her back and Holly was unable to suppress a shiver. Slowly, she stood up straight, wiping her mouth with the back of her hand. Her body was shaking, and the cold began to attack her.

In a fluid motion that Holly nearly missed, the woman who

had introduced herself as Ania whipped off her velvet coat and draped it around Holly's shoulders. The warmth stopped her from shivering, but she still felt totally ill.

"You haven't turned completely yet, that's why your body's reacting. It just needs time to adjust to the change in nourishment."

Holly looked at her, then looked back at the man on the ground. That sickness rolled over her once more but Ania turned her away before it could take hold.

"You need to come with me now. Looking at that man is not helping you."

Not totally sure that she wanted to go anywhere with her, Holly nevertheless allowed herself to be led away.

The night seemed darker than before, more menacing, the beauty of it now gone. The water that they walked alongside looked deadly, the moon reflected there more like a deformed skull, smiling and insane. The lights from the streetlamps were rusty, the colour of bloody daggers left to corrode, and the air was filled with a smell. It burned its way through her nose and into her throat so that she could almost taste it. And it tasted like the man's blood. It tasted like death.

"What did you mean," she said as they walked slowly through the streets. "That I haven't completely turned?"

For a long time, Ania said nothing. Holly was just about to repeat her question when the woman opened her mouth and began to talk, still walking, her hand still on Holly's arm.

"Before I answer, Holly, I must tell you a little of myself."

Holly nodded, although it seemed that no reaction was needed. Ania didn't look at her or even in her direction, she just continued to move.

"I have lost count of the years I have spent in the darkness, and I don't know the date or even the year that I was turned. I was already ancient when the Black Plague destroyed so many people's lives, I was old when the greatest minds believed that comets were harbingers of doom. And I had been turned long before Jesus Christ was strung upon his crucifix and left to die. I began my life, before darkness, when two moons ruled the nights instead of only one."

Holly stopped at that, unable to comprehend it in any real way, but when she realised that Ania wasn't going to stop, she caught up.

Ania simply nodded once Holly was back at her side. "I have

wandered around this world, simply filling the centuries with anything." Here she stopped and turned to face the young woman who was not a vampire, yet was not, strictly speaking, human any more. "In all my years, never have I come across anyone like you. For all I know you may well be the first to go through this type of change. And your daughter may also be the first born vampire."

Despite how she had fled from her child, how she had abandoned her, Holly felt a great surge of anger at that. "How do you know of my child?"

Ania smiled, neither warm nor cold, and simply looked at her for a moment. "You saw me for what I was, Holly. The moment your eyes saw me you knew that I was a vampire. You were able to see *me*. Did you expect that *I* had not seen *you*?"

"You've been following me? For how long?"

Ania waved this question away. "This is unimportant. You do not have to fear for your daughter. There were others following you, although they did not sense me. They will watch your child." At the startled look on Holly's face she quickly added, "And protect her, I am sure."

"You can't know that."

"All the same, I *do* know it." She looked carefully at her companion. "You are of no use to her at the moment, Holly. How can you raise a child, when you presently cannot look after yourself?"

"But that's-"

Ania held a hand up, and Holly stopped immediately. "I can help you get through this. If you trust me to."

Resignedly, Holly nodded.

"Let me teach you. And when you are ready, when you have gone through your change, when you have completely turned, I will help you claim back your child."

"How can I trust you?"

Ania laughed, a sound so genuine and startlingly beautiful that Holly couldn't help smiling in response. Her eyes fixed on Holly and another shiver coursed through her body.

"Who else are you going to trust, Holly? Who else can help you?"

And Holly realised that there was no one.

The house that Ania led her to three nights later was small, a two bedroom cottage set back from a main road. There was a small garden surrounded by a fence that was barely standing. Weeds had almost overrun the whole area, and the place had a disused feel to it. The curtains were drawn but the windows were open. Holly looked at this before speaking.

"Is it a good idea to leave your windows open? Anyone could get in."

Ania smiled, an action that lit up her pale face. "Oh, I don't need to worry about that. Apparently this place is haunted. I don't even have any trouble with kids throwing stones. I'm left completely alone."

She removed a key from her black trousers and unlocked the door.

Judging from the outside Holly had expected the inside to be just as unkempt. But she was pleasantly surprised. It was very neat, very warm, and very cosy. It was cluttered but this just added to its charm. It felt homely. In fact, it felt like home.

Ania saw the surprise on Holly's face and was comforted by it. It was good to know that, despite her advanced age, she was still able to shock people.

When they had settled, Ania on a small armchair in one corner of the room and Holly curled up on the sofa in another, her shoes kicked off and with a hot cup of tea, Holly realised that she was really tired. It came on all of a sudden, one minute she was wide awake and enjoying the comfortable room and the next she was yawning. It wasn't really surprising. She'd gone through a lot in the last few days.

"Wow," she said, covering her mouth as another gigantic yawn took over, straining her jaw. "I don't usually get tired so quickly."

Ania nodded towards the window. "The sun is on its way up. It is just your body's way of telling you to hide away before it rises."

Holly looked at her sleepily. "Where should I go?" The idea of coffins sprung to mind, and the thought horrified her. She wasn't dead and there was no way in hell she was putting a foot inside a wooden box.

Ania seemed to understand what she was thinking. "When I said 'hide away', I didn't mean in a coffin. That's just fiction."

She watched as Holly yawned once again. "But we can talk about that after you've slept. Just lay down where you are and close your eyes. Sleep finds you no matter where you are."

Carefully, Holly sat her cup down on the floor and lifted her legs up on the sofa, resting her head on the arm of the furniture, sure that she would not be able to fall asleep. She'd never been able to sleep during the day and didn't expect that to change in a hurry.

Less than a minute later she was gently snoring. Ania stood and first closed all of the windows, making sure that the curtains were covering the windows properly. She had no idea how long Holly's transformation would take, and she didn't want the young girl to find out the hard way that sunlight could hurt. She picked up the soft throw that lay on top of the sofa and gently placed it over Holly's sleeping body. With a cold hand - it had been a long time since her hands had been warm - she brushed a stray lock of blonde hair from the girl's face.

On her way back to her own room, Ania looked back at the strange sleeping form. She hadn't realised until then just how lonely she had been. It felt good to have a companion again.

Holly woke as the last hint of sunlight drifted from the day. The darkness was not yet fully formed and she had no trouble seeing everything around her. The home of her teacher, *her* new home, was filling with shadows, all of them welcome.

She stayed where she was, covered by the white throw, simply staring at the ceiling and watching as the colours gently changed before her eyes.

It all seemed like a dream to her now: running away from her child, attacking the drunk, meeting Ania. But, no - not all of it seemed like a dream after all. What was still very fresh in her mind, still totally vivid, was drinking the man's blood - that, more than anything was real, and she was not able to deny it, no matter how much she wanted to. Even as she thought about it her mouth cramped for that taste, wanting the real thing to fill it, to flow over her taste buds. To quench her.

For a second, she could actually taste it, that bitter coppery taste, and the smell filled her nostrils. She could feel her own blood pumping through her system, and looked down at her wrist, knowing that blood was in easy reach, even if it was her own. Sweat broke out on her brow and she raised her wrist to her face, letting her lips trace the path of the veins underneath the skin, morbidly wondering what it would feel like to piece her own skin with her teeth.

Even as her mouth opened to find out, her mind came back from wherever it had been, and she allowed her wrist to drop back onto the sofa. She was totally shocked at herself; she was breathing heavily, as if she had just run a race. Although her ears picked up no sound she became aware of a presence behind her.

"Don't be too concerned about that, Holly." Ania walked into view and sat in her chair, taking her place from last night. "That's just your body reacting to what it needs." She tried to smile, but it wasn't successful. "You'll go through worse than that before it's complete."

Sarcastically, Holly looked at her and scoffed. "That's supposed to be comforting?!"

Ania didn't look offended, didn't look much of anything. "No. It's not. But I'm not going to lie to you; believe me, you'll only hate me after you go through it if I do."

Holly raised herself onto her elbows. "But you don't know, though, do you?"

Ania's brow creased, confused.

"Well, you said that no one's been changed like this, didn't you? How do you know that it will be the same? It could be easier for me, couldn't it?" Holly had been scared by what Ania had said and was now hanging onto any idea that could offer a small comfort.

Ania, who had been resting back comfortably in her chair, leant forwards and looked at Holly seriously. "You're right. It could be easier. I *don't* know how this will happen for you. But you have got to prepare yourself for the fact that it may be the same. Or it might even be worse."

For a brief second Holly forgot to breathe. Then she laughed at the expression of uncertainty she saw on the woman's face. "I've given birth, Ania, remember? What's more painful than that?" She began to laugh but soon stopped when Ania didn't join in.

Ania spoke only one word, but it was enough to destroy all of Holly's false hope. "Plenty."

And it was only hours later that Holly found out that her new companion had been right; there was *plenty* that hurt more.

It started as nothing more than a dull throb in her bones, as if something had a hold of every part of her skeleton and was applying pressure - not a lot, just enough for her to notice. Minutes after noticing it for the first time those throbs became a little more intense. But Holly, believing it to be nothing more than shock to everything that had happened, ignored it, neglecting to mention it to Ania.

They had left the house, the space of the fields next door just too inviting to be ignored. They had walked for almost half an hour through field after field, enjoying the changes that the night brought to the world and its scenery, when Holly collapsed onto the ground clutching her stomach and trying her hardest not to scream.

Heat ripped through her body, wave after wave after wave of liquid fire, burning everything else from her mind. The pain was like nothing she had ever experienced before and it made giving birth seem like a stubbed toe in comparison. Tears of terror sped from her eyes, yet she refused to scream, biting down on her lip.

Ania knelt beside her, trying to hold the thrashing figure without success, despite all of her extraordinary strength. "Holly? Holly, is it the fire? Has the fire taken you over?"

She howled through gritted teeth as another wave took her over, but she managed to nod.

Ania stood up, then bent back down. Gathering all the strength she could muster, she picked the woman up in her arms and began to sprint towards her house. It took her only three minutes, her hair flying back behind her and Holly howling at the moonlit sky like a wounded animal. As gently as she could, she put Holly onto her bed and stood back, watching.

"It shouldn't be happening so quickly, Holly. You should have had a warning. Your bones should have changed first."

She spoke through clenched teeth. "They did. I felt them. Oh-my-god this huuuurrrts."

Ania swept a hand through her hair. It shouldn't be happening this damned quick! That's why it was hurting her so much - the process was taking half the time it should. She sat on the bed and stroked Holly's head, feeling at a complete loss. "I have to go out for a little while, Holly. I swear to you, I won't be long."

Holly gave no indication that she had heard, and her howls were becoming softer. Ania sighed. The girl was sinking into the pain, which was the best thing. Soon she would sleep and let her body adjust the way it had to.

Quietly, Ania left, wrapping her cloak around her; becoming just another shadow in the dark.

Holly was sinking into the pain, that much was true, and while the pain didn't lessen it didn't hurt quite so much. In a way, she understood that she was simply distancing herself from it all, just allowing her body to do what it had to do despite her protests. Her mind was beginning to relax, letting peace come over her again, when she saw something.

Holly's eyes seemed to have changed too, her vision seemingly improved. She knew it was the middle of the night but she had no problem seeing everything. Everything, including the something dark that was scuttling on the ceiling; and not a small thing either. It was easily the size of a young adult, but it moved like a spider. It scrambled quickly from the corner of the room, rustling and scratching against the plaster.

It was directly over Holly when it stopped moving. Holly was laying on her back and could clearly see the thing that was above her. It had something that looked like a leather cape wrapped around its body which at least explained the rustling. It clung to the ceiling, although even with her newly-improved eyesight, Holly couldn't see how.

Then the thing above her turned over so that its back was against the ceiling and it was looking down at the blonde girl below her, still hanging securely above her.

Its face was disturbingly old, as old as the ages, and seemed only very slightly feminine. Its eyes were dead yet still they saw Holly. It smiled, old black gums moving back to reveal elongated teeth, all of them the same length and dangerously sharp. They were yellow and ancient, stained with God-alone knew what, and Holly knew instinctively how they'd feel ripping into her.

The being on the ceiling slowly spread her arms, lifting out the thing that Holly had mistaken as a cape. But as the woman reached out she saw that it wasn't a cape but leathery wings. She could even see the bones that ran inside the skin, holding it taunt. Small claws extended out and the talons were covered in dark stains. She wasn't able to delude herself that they were anything but the residue of blood.

Holly tried to get out of bed, to move so that she was no longer directly underneath that creature. But she seemed to have no control of her body, none of her muscles seemed connected to her anymore and she couldn't move, couldn't even twitch her finger. She became aware of the sweat running down her face and couldn't raise a hand to wipe it away. She was paralysed.

The thing above her seemed to understand that Holly was now trapped, and its grin widened.

Holly saw this and tried to scream out for Ania, forgetting that her companion had gone out, but not even her voice would obey her any more. Holly had gone past being scared and straight to terrified. Here she was, not only paralysed, but now it looked like she was to become easy prey for a thing that she couldn't even explain.

She heard a high pitched mewling and the woman dropped. It happened so quickly that Holly didn't even see it. One minute the woman clung to the ceiling somehow and the next she was perched on Holly's chest, cutting off the air to her lungs. Pain ripped through her body but she could do nothing to try and ease it.

A smell came to her as the woman's face moved closer, like rotten meat that had been left spoiling in the sun. But underneath she could smell something else as well, like old clothes found after decades in a damp attic. It was the smell of death.

The woman opened her wings again and the claws on the ends came closer to Holly's throat, slowly, *deliberately slowly*, until they were wrapped around her neck. Even as the woman was choking the life out of Holly, her face moved closer and closer until their noses were almost touching. Holly, whose mind had become suddenly sharpened saw a disturbing thing in the woman's eyes: equal measures of insanity and happiness; hate and love. Murder and compassion.

When she thought that she could take no more, surely no more, the creature's mouth clamped down onto hers. She was being simultaneously strangled to death and given the kiss of life by the same disturbing creature. She could feel stale air being forced into her, could taste the acidic hint to it, and tried to fight against it, already knowing that it was pointless. So that she wouldn't have to be looking into the things face when the end came, Holly focused hard and was able to at least close her eyes. Then she gave in to her fate.

Ania dropped the man to the floor, hoping that he wasn't going to slip away before Holly had a chance to feed. The sooner she became adjusted to blood, the better she would be.

She walked upstairs to check on Holly and stopped on the threshold. Holly had gone pale, her breathing forced, her body rigid. She looked dead, laying there, the creature perched on her chest. So it was happening. The Hag had come to claim Holly for her own.

Knowing that nothing could be done, Ania went back outside and sat on the ground and waited for the damned being to leave and for it all to end.

Two hours later, Holly opened her eyes. Outside the darkness was whole, something she could almost touch. The room was now empty, no sign of the creature that had come to kill her, the creature that had *succeeded* in killing her. She had no idea how that could be; she was after all breathing, could feel the air in her lungs, could feel her heart beating hard in her chest, could see everything in detail. Yet she didn't doubt it - she had been killed.

Slowly, a part of her sceptical that she would be able to move at all, Holly sat up. There was no pain in her chest where the creature had been sat and no evidence that the thing had been there at all, but she trusted her own memories completely. That thing had been there, had killed her.

She walked out of the room and downstairs. She glanced at the man lying unconscious on the kitchen floor without much interest. She had no reason for thinking that Ania was outside, yet she was sure. And, as she opened the door, she saw her companion sitting elegantly on the ground, back to her. She seemed not to hear Holly as she approached and turned slowly when Holly touched her shoulder, a sad smile on her face.

"It is done." Ania said softly.

Holly nodded and sat next to her, reaching a hand out and gently caressed Ania's face.

Ania allowed this for a moment before gently removing Holly's hand with her own. Instead of dropping her hand, Ania held Holly's. "You see now?"

And Holly did. Ania's skin was still pale compared to

Holly's, but the degree had lessened slightly. Holly looked carefully at her hand when Ania let go, turning it over and seeing, really *seeing*, how pale her skin now was. She had never been tanned, but now she was positively pallid.

The moon shone down on the two vampires, one as old as time and the other newly reborn, with total indifference, lighting their skin with its own light.

"Who was she? The creature that killed me, who was she?"

Ania smiled wide enough to expose her sharp teeth. "The Hag. It is she who kills our mortal sides and then gives us a new existence."

They both spun round as they heard an almost silent groan from inside the house.

"Go inside, Holly. Feed now, then we'll talk."

A fire ignited in Holly and her blue eyes darkened. She didn't need to be told twice. As she stood, she looked at Ania. "Aren't you coming in?"

"No. I've had my fill for tonight."

Without another word Holly walked back into the house. The man was still lying on the floor, but he was beginning to stir. As she looked at him she could almost see the blood beneath his skin, and her whole body ached for it. She ran her tongue over her teeth and was glad when she found them a little sharper than they had previously been.

Slowly she knelt beside him and gently caressed his forehead, looking at him. He was quite handsome and she was glad that he was going to be her proper first. It seemed right. She bent over him and kissed him once on the lips, her way of thanking him, then sank her teeth into his throat.

He writhed once and then was still again, the strength leaving him as quickly as it had arrived, and he never regained consciousness.

Holly thought that she was going to explode. The sensation was extraordinary. The blood was hot as it passed down her throat and every part of her felt invigorated. The room seemed to brighten, to take on a heightened sense of *realness*, and Holly was amazed. She could feel the blood slowing its rush into her mouth and knew that his heart no longer forced it around his body. She had had enough. Until the next time, at least. And she was already looking forward to it.

Amazed by how easy it all felt to her, she wiped her mouth and licked the tiny dots of blood from her fingers, and walked back outside. The night was brighter, the world clearer. She had never felt so alive, and the thought made her laugh. How strange to finally feel really alive only when she was dead.

Ania, who had herself experienced everything that Holly was feeling, laughed with her. "There's one last thing we have to do." She nodded inside. "To stop a trail always dispose of the body. It's safer."

Holly nodded, and as they set about the task they finally began to talk.

"The Hag was the first," Ania said as she lifted the corpse and easily carried it outside. "Nobody knows how old she is, or how it all happened. All we know is that it is she who completes the turning. Without her intervention, we would have the thirst but our bodies wouldn't be able to digest the blood."

"So it would be like what happened the first time I fed? Being sick?"

"That's exactly right, I've seen it happen on many occasions." She dropped the body gently onto the ground. "Can you grab me that spade from over there?" Ania asked, pointing towards the far end of her garden.

"Sure." Holly went and retrieved it. "So, what's it all about? Why does she do it the way she does?"

Ania began to dig the dirt. "She steals our life by extracting all of the air, which is why she sits on the chest. And she strangles to make sure that we die. Then she breathes her own air into us, filling our empty lungs with her own life."

"Yeah, but that wouldn't *do* anything, surely? Scientifically I mean, how could that transform us?"

Ania smiled. "I don't know, Holly. There's a magic in it, I know that much. Other than that..?" She shrugged. "I find it best not to think about the 'hows' too much. What's the point when the answers cannot be found?" Quickly she bent down and dragged the body into the hole she had dug.

It was deep enough for their requirements. When Ania grabbed the shovel Holly took it from her. "Let me do it. I've gotta get used to it."

Ania handed the shovel over and watched as Holly slowly filled the hole back up. "So, is it always that quick?"

"No. I think that because you carried a vampire child; it must have speeded it up." Ania looked at Holly, who obviously wasn't satisfied with that answer. "Look, there isn't a specific time for her to arrive. It seems to take longer in the younger vampires, probably because their bodies haven't matured yet. It just depends how quickly the initial infection spreads."

"Infection?" Holly looked alarmed at this.

"Yeah, it's the best way to describe it. It's a blood disease, passed on by infected blood being passed into the blood of another, and I believe your child's blood infected your own."

"Oh." She looked down at the patch of newly shovelled ground, feeling a sadness but no real remorse. "This is hard for me to take in."

"It gets easier, believe me."

Holly looked at her companion, her *friend*, and smiled. "Yeah, I guess it does."

* * *

Ania gathered Holly's feeds for almost a whole year, letting Holly discover the best method of killing for herself, but never actually watching or advising. A vampire's feeds were a private and intimate thing, the *ultimate* intimacy, between victim and hunter, and she wouldn't dream of intruding on that.

On the anniversary of Holly's visit from The Hag, Ania walked into the living room with something in a rectangular and thin box and silently passed it to her.

"What's this?" Holly looked at Ania.

She simply shrugged. "Only one way to find out."

Holly opened it and separating the tissue paper to bring out some black material. She separated the cloths and found herself holding a set of clothes: A pair of black trousers, a black top, and a black cloak, almost identical to Ania's. Holly lifted them up to see them better. "They're beautiful, Ania, thank you." She smiled mischievously. "What is it, have I finally gotten my uniform?"

Ania grinned back. "No. You don't get that for two hundred years." She grew a little more serious. "It's easier to blend into the night when you're wearing black, and it's easier to hunt when people don't really see you. And the cloak, for me is what I grew up wearing. But I've found in recent years, that when people see you, if you look a little eccentric, they don't remember your face all that well; they only remember what it is that made you look different."

The word 'hunt' had sent a shiver through Holly's spine, but it was totally pleasurable. "I'm going on the hunt?"

She nodded. "You're ready. Long overdue actually; I just wanted to make sure. I didn't know how things could change, if your change would be permanent. I didn't want to risk putting you in a situation that you weren't prepared for."

Holly smiled, holding the clothes to her face, and feeling the softness on her newly pale skin.

"Change and we'll go."

Less than ten minutes later they stepped out onto the streets, two dark figures walking towards the town centre. "It's easier to pull someone away from a crowd." Ania whispered. "They're less likely to be missed immediately."

Holly nodded. Excitement filled her at the prospect of her first hunt. Her first hunt! No more relying on Ania to supply the food, no more waiting patiently in the house for Ania to bring her someone to feed on.

The crowds of people passed by them. Ania pointed out a few people that were possibilities. Holly nodded, and pinned her sights on a man about her own age. He and his friends were obviously drunk by the way that they swayed and the raucous way they laughed. The one she had picked out was handsome and, although she didn't admit it, he looked more than a little like Michael.

She glanced at Ania, who nodded, and Holly broke away from her mentor, heart hammering loudly in her chest. She made her way to him, glad that he had fallen behind his friends to unsteadily bend down and attempt to tie his shoelace. When he stood, she gently put a hand on his arm.

He turned and looked at her. The lust that crept into his eyes when he saw the beautiful woman that stood in front of him was obvious, and he smiled widely at her. He didn't give his friends another thought, simply allowed her to take his hand and followed where Holly led him.

They walked slowly past bars and clubs, both ignoring the noise that came from inside and the people that they passed. Neither of them spoke, they just walked, neither aware that many other eyes followed their progress.

They stopped behind a club, and Holly pushed him back against the wall, the bass of the current song being played from inside vibrating through the brickwork. He grabbed her and pulled her closer so that their bodies crushed against each other. He kissed her passionately and she allowed him to for a few minutes, enjoying the feeling that it gave it, responding with equal passion; it had been a long time since she had been kissed that way, and she allowed herself to be swept along. The excitement of the kiss made her senses peak, and she finally became aware of the people watching them.

She chose to ignore them, deciding that all they were seeing were a couple of adults enjoying themselves. She kissed his cheeks, his chin, his neck. She felt the blood beneath his skin pounding and gently forced her mouth to close, sinking her teeth into his flesh.

The sound he made was halfway between a gasp of pain and a moan of pleasure, and it increased the sensuality of the moment. Yet before she could take more than a few mouthfuls of his blood, she was grabbed roughly by the nape of the neck and yanked away from him. She felt the man's skin tear beneath her teeth, and heard him yelp like a wounded animal.

Hands held her away from him and she turned to face her attackers, meaning to use them to satisfy the thirst she felt. A group of eight, men and women, were stood around her, and she saw them immediately for what they were. Vampires. More of her kind, each of them looking at her with hatred.

"This is our area." One of them rasped, and Holly turned her attention to him.

"I'm sorry," she said, almost whispering, feeling her fear like a physical object in the pit of her stomach. "I didn't know-"

"Well you do now." Another said, this one a woman, moving closer to her. "This area is ours, and we don't tolerate the new in our area." She smiled viciously. "Not enough to go around, and it makes it more likely that we'll all get discovered."

The hand on her neck dropped away, and Holly started to back away, observing carefully as they matched her step for step, moving closer as she moved away.

Even afterwards, she wasn't sure what happened; it all went so quickly. But she heard a low growl and then her would-be attackers were being thrown away from her, landing in untidy piles heaped on the ground behind the club.

Ania stood in the midst of it all, but Holly found no comfort in the intervention. She had never looked more beautiful, nor more terrifying. Her hair was swept back from her face and her blue-grey eyes flamed with savage fury. She lunged, like a large cat, towards the vampires, who tried to pick themselves up to get away. She caught the ones stupid enough to try and escape and used her nails on their throats. Soon, the cracked concrete was coated with blood, rich and red, yet Ania didn't stop her frenzied attack until all of them lay motionless on the ground.

It didn't make much sense to Holly, but Ania spoke to the fallen and broken bodies. "I have existed longer than all of you combined. *I* am not new, and this is *not* your territory! Think of doing that again, and I'll kill you."

Her eyes had almost regained their usual serenity when they landed on Holly, but Holly couldn't get the image of Ania's attack from her mind. With a steady hand, Ania pointed to the boy Holly had been feeding on before she was interrupted. "Finish, Holly, then we'll go. They will remain unseen, but we still need to leave soon."

Although Holly no longer felt much like feeding, she obediently walked over to the man. His eyes were wide, but glazed and distant, and Holly knew that he had seen much of what had happened. Yet he didn't fight when Holly put her lips back onto that spot where the blood still flowed. As soon as her tongue tasted the coppery liquid her thirst returned and she forgot everything else.

Instead of disposing of the body, Ania led her away as soon as she was done. Holly walked slowly, wary of her companion. She thought back over what Ania had said. "What did you mean when you said you'd kill them? I thought that you had."

Ania looked at her, knowing that the woman was now a little scared of her, and saddened because of it. "There is only one way to kill a vampire, Holly, and that is sunlight. You can hurt another, empty their veins upon the ground, even make them go through the physical sides of it – destruction, decomposition - but we always come back. Unless sunlight gets you, that is."

Holly's mind whirled, but with only one thought: Michael. Jesse said she had killed him. But how had she done it? Was it sunlight, or was it some other way? Her feet refused to take another step. "My daughter's father. My friend said she'd killed him. But if it wasn't sunlight, does that mean he may still be alive?"

Ania stopped also and looked at the girl. Hope shone from Holly's eyes, and Ania desperately wanted to say something, wanted to let Holly know what she knew, that Michael had wandered in his own hell, but had found Holly again - Holly just didn't know it. And the two of them had reached an agreement that Holly was only to know when she had learnt what she needed to learn. It was agonising for him, but he knew that his lover had to concentrate on being what she was for now. And when she was ready, the three of them would come together to retrieve the lost child.

But for now, all Ania could do was nod. "Yes, if it wasn't sunlight, he could be alive."

Tears fell from Holly's eyes. She had given him up as lost, and now there was a chance she still might be with him again.

They walked on again, Holly lost in her own thoughts, seeing in her mind the moment when she would be reunited with her lover.

He watched them, glad that Holly was okay. Ania had protected her well. But he couldn't help but feel more than slightly resentful. It should be *him* looking out for her. It should be *him* walking with her, answering her questions. But he understood. He had found her again, and he wasn't going to leave her, whether she knew it or not. She was okay, and that was enough for now.

He turned away from them and walked back into the town again, hunting for himself now.

Holly stole glances at Ania as they neared their home. Ania was aware of this, but gave no sign. She knew that Holly had things to say and questions that she needed to ask, but also knew not to prompt her - she'd ask what she needed to ask when she was ready.

As they got closer to the house Holly had gathered her nerves together. "You scared me tonight."

Ania continued to walk on in silence for a while, not commenting. Finally she said, "I know I did, Holly. But I won't apologise for doing so."

Holly was shocked at this. She hadn't consciously thought about an apology, but she realised that she had been expecting one nonetheless. "Why?" She sounded peevish even to herself, and felt ashamed of it. Who was she to judge this creature, this ancient being?

Again, Ania kept her silence. It was only when they were settled in the house for the rest of the night that she turned to her new companion. In the cosy light of the living room, with a single lamp chasing the shadows into the corners, she faced Holly.

"When you saw Michael for the first time, Holly, what did you think of him?" She realised that she had slipped up, that she had mentioned Holly's former lover by name despite the youngster never having told her, but luckily Holly didn't pick up on it.

"He was so beautiful." She smiled to herself, lost in her memories. "I was walking through the streets in the evening - I had been having trouble sleeping - and he was suddenly there in front of me. God, he was so beautiful! I know that's not something you usually say about a man, but he was. Mostly, it was his eyes that I noticed. Stunning, intense, but there was always a sadness in them, as if no matter what he was doing, there was something keeping him from being truly happy."

"Beautiful." Yes, he was definitely that, she had seen his beauty for herself. "But nothing else of his nature, his *true nature*, shone through? You never got a glimpse of what he truly was?"

She shook her head, her blonde hair waving around her face. "No, nothing."

Ania nodded. "We get better at hiding what we are." She looked deeply at Holly, hoping that she would be able to get her meaning across. "What we are, Holly, are true selves, isn't beautiful. We feel compassion, we feel love, we feel hate; we remain the people we were before. But, always, underneath, there is the thirst burning through us and, ultimately, *that* is what we are. We're death. We kill, we feed, we move on. We touch people's lives and they always see us the way you saw Michael - as something beautiful to be loved, admired. But that it not what we *are*."

Holly's eyes had widened. She'd never thought of it like that, hadn't really thought about that side of it too much at all.

Ania sighed. "I'm not going to try and frighten you, Holly. Like I said, we do feel things; and we usually feel them more passionately because of what we are, but you need to understand there is that other side to us. You glimpsed it in me tonight. And it was only a glimpse; I barely allowed the surface to be scratched. You are right to be afraid, but not of me. Be afraid of my nature - *our* nature - but not of me. I will never hurt you like I hurt those others tonight.

"But you need to understand that other side of us, especially in yourself. You've been a vampire for a year now, and you're a killer. And, as much as you may hate it, it'll make you stronger." *And you'll need to be stronger for the years ahead,* she thought. *You have so much to claim back for yourself and you need to be ready.*

It was alright for Ania to tell her not to be afraid, but Holly was. The idea that she was now a killer and must kill for the next God-knew how many years *terrified* her. But she could already feel it in herself. She had been scared when Ania had attacked those other vampires. But, thinking back, hadn't there been a part of her eager to join in? Even now, she was anxious to get back out, to get back into the hunt.

Nevertheless, she stretched and yawned. "The sun must be on its way up. I'm going to go to bed." She stood and walked over to Ania, kissing her on the lips. "I'll see you when the night descends, Ania." She strode quickly up to her room.

Ania knew that the sun would be another hour at least before its killer rays shone upon the earth and also knew the real reason for Holly's departure. Rather than what they had spoken of, her mind was on her lover. And probably would be for a long time yet. And, speaking of which...

She walked briskly to the front door and opened it, stepping out into the night. He was stood under one of the trees that bordered her garden, looking at her as she walked towards him. "You can come inside now. She's gone to bed."

Michael walked back to the house with beside Ania. As always when he was so close to Holly, all he wanted to do was to go to her and to take her in his arms. But, despite himself, he agreed with Ania. Holly needed to concentrate on what she was, on becoming the strongest she could be. And then, when she was tough enough to take back her child - *their* child - then he could be with her again.

He sat on the chair that was still slightly warm from Holly's body, and could smell her, her perfect natural perfume. He took a few moments to relish it, knowing that that was the closest he was going to get to her for some time, before looking at Ania.

"How do you think she did tonight?"

Holly lay in her bed, thinking of Michael. She must have drifted off without knowing it, because she heard his voice. She couldn't make out the words, but she could hear his voice, calm and in total control. How she wished that he was there, just to be able to hold him once would be worth everything she had to give.

Her dream changed dramatically. She was with the man she had killed, her first hunt. The vampires came to kill her, to drive her out of their area. They clawed at her, bit her, kicked her. The pain was immense, and she looked around for Ania. Ania would be there, would come to save her. Ania would destroy those that threatened her.

But nobody came. She attempted to fight back, but she wasn't strong enough. She was overpowered and forced to the floor. She tried to crawl away, but managed only a few feet before a foot planted itself in her back, forcing her to fall flat on her face. Pain bit into her as her face was smashed onto the concrete. She was turned over, and looked up at those that were taking such delight in her pain. She could hear them laughing, a chorus of insane delight.

Their laughter was what she needed to hear. Her thirst, which hadn't been satisfied, burnt within her and she used it as a tool. They were trying to stop her from feeding! They were trying to stop her nature from coming forwards. In her head, she heard Ania's voice.

Be afraid of my nature - of our *nature. You're a killer. And, as much as you may hate it, it'll make you stronger.*

She found that strength now and forced herself up, ignoring the hands that tried to push her back down, as a wolf would ignore something as insignificant as a fly. Her hair flew around her face, although she could feel no breeze. The vampires that had hurt her, had *taunted* her with their laughter, backed away from her.

They could now see her true self, could feel the killer that was in her, and she laughed viciously at them. She let the killer in her take over and moved quickly among them, throwing them against the walls, pounding into them, all the time laughing her own harsh laugh.

When they all lay still upon the ground, she looked up, her racing, breathing hard and fast. Ania was stood next to her, smiling her own killer smile. Holly looked down at herself. Their blood covered her hands, her face, and she loved it. *This* was what she was. *This* was her nature. And she regretted nothing.

She awoke knowing that it was too early for her to rise. The sun was still in the sky, she could feel the heat of it in the room even though there was no other evidence of it other than soft reflected light spilling in from the edges of the curtains.

She laid back down, her heart hammering in her chest. She was shocked at herself, even though she knew that she hadn't really attacked those others, it had only been a dream. But she could feel the strength still in her, thrumming through her veins. Ania had been right. She was a killer. She had found her nature.

Ania saw the change in Holly when she saw her that night. There was no physical change in her, yet it was still easy for her to see. It was there in her eyes. It was the look of an animal anxious for the kill. Ania was glad. Despite the inevitable remorse and future denials that would come, for her to have begun finding it could only be a good thing. She began to believe that Holly could be ready far sooner than she'd anticipated.

"It's happened." It wasn't a question, yet Holly answered it anyway.

"Yes." She smiled, and Ania saw the killer look leave her eyes. But it had been there, and would be again.

"Ready?"

The killer was back instantly at the thought of the hunt. "Yes," she simply repeated.

They walked into the night together for the second time, not just two vampires but two assassins, and only one was aware that a third followed closely behind.

Michael saw Ania turn to look at him and was shocked. She had never acknowledged him while with Holly, in case Holly caught the glance. For her to look at him now was significant, but he didn't know what it meant. He followed as they walked to the centre of town as he had the night before. He watched with interest as Holly broke away from Ania after only a couple of minutes. He watched her walk out of sight, a longing for her so deep that it drove even the thirst from him - temporarily, at least. When he was sure that she was preoccupied, her walked over to Ania.

"I don't think you have to wait too long for her, Michael."

Confused, he was only able to look at his lover's guide.

"Satisfy your thirst, then go to the house. Wait for us there."

His heart hammered in his chest. Was it possible, so soon, yet after so long? Was she really telling him that tonight he could be back in Holly's arms?

She simply nodded at him before turning her back on him and leaving to satisfy the pangs of her own thirst.

Holly saw the man she had chosen walk over to an empty doorway. He stood and looked back out. After a few seconds he saw her and smiled. She walked slowly to him, enjoying the rush that had started to fill her. She kept her eyes on his, not letting them drift to his neck as they wanted to.

She reached him and the thirst had hold of her. She no longer cared about keeping up the pretence. Passionately, she pushed him backwards, and before his back even had time to hit the locked door her teeth had latched on to his exposed neck. The blood spouted into her mouth and she gulped it down greedily, giving in to what she was.

The man was dead quickly, drained of most of his blood before he even had a chance to ask himself what was going on. She let him slump to the ground and wiped the blood from her chin and mouth, licking her fingers.

She remembered what Ania had always told her, and picked the man up. He was very light, and Holly had to wonder if he had been so before. She walked with him in the shadows, making sure that she stayed out of people's sight. She found a large bin behind a shop and opened it, still holding the man in her arms. Before she threw him in on top of a stack of cardboard boxes, she searched through his pockets and smiled softly when she found a lighter. She lit the cardboard that was beneath him, watching as the flames took hold. She left, leaving the bin to its fate.

With his blood flowing through her body, Holly felt great. She wandered the streets looking for Ania, but in no real rush. The night was young and it enchanted her, a similarity between it and the night she had fled, leaving her daughter behind. A hand fell on her shoulder and she saw Ania standing beside her. The vampire also looked radiant and they looked at each other and laughed, the laughter of the well-fed. Those people on the streets near them heard the laughter and moved on quickly.

Ania began to feel anxious as they walked back to the house. She knew that Michael would be there, and she was happy for them both, but still she was worried. What if she wasn't doing the right thing? What if Holly wasn't ready for this? She still had a lot to learn and a lot of strength she still needed to find.

"What's wrong, Ania?" Holly was looking at her friend, notably concerned. She was picking up the unease from Ania, and it bothered her that Ania *could* be uneasy about anything.

"Nothing. I'm fine." Her answer brisk and slightly barbed.

No, you're not. Holly thought, but she said nothing else. Ania would tell her if she wanted her to know and wouldn't if she didn't: it was really that simple.

Maybe it was because of Ania's obvious tension, but as they got nearer to the house Holly also began to feel nervous. Butterflies danced excitedly in her stomach and she felt breathless, as if the air was filling with a more viscous substance.

She looked at Ania as she saw that the lights had been switched on in the living room. She knew that they had been switched off before they'd left. She was shocked to see that Ania wasn't surprised, and became more anxious as Ania nodded at her to go in.

Her whole body was shaking, and the killer part of her now felt nowhere near – had seen those lights and took its leave; she simply felt weak. Cautiously, hand trembling badly, she opened the front door and walked in.

At first, she was sure that she was dreaming. He was stood by her chair in the living room, a mirage of beauty, looking directly at her. His dark hair was slightly longer than she remembered, but it was his eyes that caught and held her. His green eyes, looking totally happy for the first time, despite the tears that were slipping from them.

She couldn't move at first, could only stand there and look at him, taking in every part of him. She had been right, her memory had not tricked her; he was utterly beautiful.

When he smiled and whispered her name, her paralysis broke and she raced to him. His arms wrapped themselves around her waist, tightly, securely, and he kissed her lips, their tears merging together.

"Michael," she whispered, hardly able to believe that he was here with her once more, after these years, she was finally back where she belonged. "What took you so long to come back to me?"

They were just words, but Michael answered her, touching her to make sure that she was actually there, and not a figment of his memory-induced imagination. "That's a long story." He looked at Ania, who smiled at him gently. "But we've got time, Holly." Michael looked back into his lover's eyes. "We've got so much time now."

Part Four

To Rise Again

The streets looked familiar yet he didn't know where he was - didn't even know *who* he was. The only thing that he *did* know was that the night was a comfort, and that he hid himself away as soon as the darkness began to lighten, usually in barns and abandoned houses. He always made sure that, no matter where he was, there was no chance of the sun reaching him.

On the third night after waking up on the dirty floor of a tumbled down house he became aware of something burning in him, setting not only his body on fire but his soul as well. He craved something, but had no idea what it was. He wandered the almost-deserted streets that he vaguely recollected, feeling agitated and weak. His body was in desperate need of something, and he could remember the taste of it - a coppery, red taste - but not what it was.

His feet hurt, his whole body ached and he was tired. No, not just tired. He was exhausted. He felt old, ancient, and he realised that he didn't even know what he looked like. He didn't know what colour his hair was or what colour his eyes were. He couldn't even guess his age.

So, that burning in himself temporarily pushed aside, he began to search for something else. It didn't take him too long to find a shop window that was reasonably clean, and he looked at his reflection in disbelief.

His clothes were creased and faded, but that didn't surprise him - he'd been laying on a dirty floor for God-knew how long and been sleeping rough for a few days. No, it was his face that took up all of his attention. He was old, at least ninety, which at least explained the aches in his body, and his hair was grey and wispy, his eyes a dull blue.

Feeling more unnerved now that he knew exactly how he looked, he moved on, aimlessly moving in his shuffling walk. There was something out there that he needed, if only he knew what it was and how to get it.

He slept the day away, curled up in the hay in a farmer's barn, hearing the voices of men working directly below him through his dreams. The sun went down and he awoke. He'd had a dream that could be termed a nightmare – it certainly left him feeling anxious.

It had been totally clear and he could remember every detail. He'd been lying on his back, staring at the night sky, watching as stars twinkled above him. He'd felt cold, a wind blowing hard against his tough skin, but he hadn't been concerned with that. He was watching the stars as they appeared, forming patterns in the sky. Pain had shot through his body, centred through his chest, and blood had erupted from his chest, showering him with small red raindrops. Strangely he hadn't been scared, only slightly concerned at this. He began to close his eyes, waiting for death to take him. As the world grew dimmer he'd stretched his hand out, reaching for someone that wasn't there, calling her name out to the world he was leaving.

That name still hung on his lips and he spoke it aloud, marvelling at the feelings that surged through him - hope, sadness, and love.

"Holly."

Something tried to get through then, some half-formed memory. He had time to glimpse a beautiful blonde-haired girl, smiling and laughing as she cradled a golden-retriever puppy. So happy, and for the second that he'd seen her, he'd felt happy.

When he tried to concentrate on the memory it faded, leaving him more confused than ever. Who was that girl? Who was Holly? Why did the thought of her leave him sad and happy at the same time?

Knowing that it was useless to try and force the memory to return, he straightened himself up as much as he could, brushing the dry, prickly hay from his hair and clothes and carefully stepped down the ladder until his feet were firmly on the ground.

That fever was back in him, stronger than ever. He questioned himself again, seeing if he could trick his mind into supplying an answer as to what it was he needed. But it was no use, his mind refused to cooperate. Annoyed, he walked steadily from the barn, hearing a humming that was close by.

The woman was walking in the darkness, obviously enjoying the night. She was young, barely out of her teenage years, dark hair tucked behind her ears. She seemed to have no purpose for being outside, but he knew that sometimes the night just had to be answered.

She turned suddenly and saw him watching her. Her face wrinkled up as she saw him and he could understand that so well - he'd seen his face and knew how he looked. Still looking at him cautiously, she stumbled and fell, cutting her hand on a piece of farming equipment.

That burning increased at the sight of the red liquid - he was being consumed by it, his whole being was a walking inferno. Finally he knew. Finally he knew what it was that his body craved.

With speed that he had no idea he possessed, he went to her and wrapped strong hands around her throat, never taking his eyes from her bleeding hand. She gasped once and then fell silent.

He became aware of the teeth inside his mouth, became aware of their sharpness. Without hesitation, he bent her head away from him so that he had complete access to the soft flesh of her neck, using his teeth to break the skin, but barely tasting the saltiness of her skin - there was only one taste that he had any interest in now.

It was ecstasy! His mouth cramped with pleasure as that hot red liquid coursed its way down his throat, coating it. He was totally gripped by it now, and the blood wasn't coming out quick enough for him. He pushed his teeth together then pulled, spitting out the lump of flesh that he had just relieved the girl of. The blood came out in a gush, and he bathed his face in it, knowing that he was smearing it over his face, not caring. It was here! Finally, he had what he needed.

When the blood stopped pumping from the wound, he just let the body fall to the ground, leaving it where it was. He walked from the farm, wiping the blood from his face, a face that had a few less wrinkles than a few moments ago.

He fed three more times that night, attacking his prey with speed that he was fast becoming accustomed to. He left the bodies where they were, hidden slightly out of view but not concealed properly. He had no more thoughts of the girl with blonde hair, his mind consumed by that red fire that was dampened slightly each time he killed.

He passed by windows as he walked, but didn't even glance at them; he had seen what he looked like and had no urge to remind himself further. But if he had looked he would have been surprised. Although a lot of age still remained in his features, a lot more had simply disappeared. His face bore fewer wrinkles, and his white hair was now peppered with black strands. His blue eyes, previously dull and uninteresting, were now sparkling with the fire that he felt within him. He hadn't noticed that the aches of the night before were gone, either, or that he walked quicker and steadier.

He walked for miles, no longer searching for anything - he had had his fill on blood for one night, and now just enjoyed the powers of the darkness. The wind was cool on his face, blowing his hair back, and the stars glittered and sparkled in the dark sky.

As the night started to lift, he began to feel tired and knew that it was time to rest. He looked around him and began to panic. He'd left the town that he had been walking through without registering it properly, and everywhere he looked now there were fields, small bushes and lone-standing trees, not a single house in sight. Not one thing to shelter him from the rays of the sun.

His pulse quickened, and sweat began to escape from his pores. The dark wasn't as dark as it should be, and he knew that it wouldn't be too long before the sun began its ascent. He had to find somewhere to hide - and soon.

Not knowing where to go, he turned in a complete circle, looking for the slightest indication that a house was nearby. There was nothing. He thought about going back the way he had come, but he couldn't remember even leaving the town, let alone how far back it was. He thought his best bet was to go forwards and hope for the best.

He began to jog, then to run, and finally to sprint. With each minute that passed, his anxiousness increased. Each minute that passed meant that the sun was a minute closer to him. He glimpsed a dull light in the distance, and nearly stopped, fearing that he was too late. But as he ran, he saw that it was too dim to be the sun. It was a candle, burning steadily in a house window.

Relief flooded through him, but he didn't slow down. He wasn't going to relax until he was safely hidden. He didn't care if he had to kill every occupant of the house in order to gain entry - what was another kill to him now?

He easily vaulted over the gate that blocked his entry and was raising his fist to hammer on the door when it swung open, startling him.

A man stood in the doorway, a strange look on his face. He looked amused and irritated at the same time. He didn't speak, just regarded the killer with interest. After a moment, yet still before the killer could speak, the man opened the door wider and gestured for him to enter.

He walked in without another thought, grateful when the

door closed behind him.

"We didn't think that you were going to make it."

The man with white hair that was no longer purely white looked at the other man closely. He had short blonde hair, piercing grey eyes, pale skin, and looked to be about thirty. He wore brown trousers and a white shirt open at the collar.

"What do you mean, you didn't think I was going to make it? How did you know to expect me?" When the man in front of him didn't answer, he asked a different question. "Who are you?"

The man smiled and it lit up his whole face. "Finally, a sensible question. I'm Kian." He held his hand out and the other man shook it, noticing the length of Kian's fingernails. They looked like they could do some damage.

"I'm Michael." He froze, shocked at himself. Was that his name? If not, why did he say it? He searched into himself and found that it felt right, anyway, so he said it again, confirming to himself that that was who he was. "Yes, I'm Michael."

Kian laughed, a sound that was slightly creepy. "Yeah, it's always a little confusing when we come back." Without expanding on his comment he walked out of the hall, and into a small living room, where he extinguished the candle and closed the thick black curtains.

He turned and looked at the new-comer, sizing him up and taking in every detail. "Come. You need your rest, young Michael."

Michael stood where he was for a few moments, looking at Kian curiously. Young? Had he really called him *young*? He thought that Kian was being sarcastic. After all, he was easily three times older than the man who stood before him. But, looking deep into Kian's gorgeous grey eyes, he decided that, somehow, the man was being serious.

"What are you?" The question popped out of his mouth before he even knew that he was going to speak. Before Kian had a chance to answer, Michael asked another question, this one far more important. "What am *I*?"

Kian smiled, exposing teeth that were as sharp as Michael's, and simply shook his head. "These questions can wait." He saw that Michael was going to interrupt and held a hand up to still him. "They will be answered, those and more, but for now you need to regain your strength. And the sunlight hours are no time for the dead to walk or talk."

Michael frowned, but Kian had already started to walk up a flight of stairs and he had no real choice but to follow.

The stairs were carpeted in a dark maroon and the walls were decorated in strange jagged symbols, but with each step that Michael climbed he could feel his strength diminishing and everything except a good day's sleep became unimportant. When they reached the landing, Kian led him into a small bedroom. Without another word passing between them, Kian gently kissed Michael on the cheek before leaving, closing the door behind him.

It was pitch black but Michael found that he had no trouble seeing around him. The room was about twelve feet squared, with only a double bed and a chair as furniture. There was nothing else, except a window. It was draped in thick black velvet curtains, which Michael pulled aside. He was not shocked to see the black paint that had covered the glass. He dropped the curtain back, glad to see that it concealed the window perfectly.

Sleepiness stole over him once again and he yawned, feeling tears rise in his eyes. He walked to the bed and noticed a change of clothes that had been left there. He held them up, looking at the black shirt and black trousers with no real surprise. He knew that when he it was time for him to awaken at the dawning of the night and put this new ensemble on they would fit him perfectly.

He placed them onto the chair, and stripped out of his own dishevelled clothes, feeling better when not a stitch of cloth touched his skin. He pulled the cover aside and got into the bed, loving the way the cool sheets felt on his naked flesh. He laid his head upon the pillow, utter contentment at the feeling of laying in an actual bed, and closed his eyes.

Before the sun touched the horizon, Michael was asleep.

The night had descended once more when Michael opened his eyes. He knew that the sun had vanished, knew it in his body, and was keen to see the night again. The thirst was back in him and it needed to be quenched.

He became aware of someone watching him, and looked at the figure that was seated on the chair. She had long red hair which curled around her shoulders and green eyes shone out from pale skin. She smiled at him, exposing the sharp tips of her teeth, yet didn't speak.

He continued to look at her, feeling unsure of himself, nervous. After minutes of silence, she stood and approached the head of the bed. She held the clothes that had been lain out for him that morning, casually draped over one arm, and held her free hand to Michael.

He looked at it, noticing the small dark tattoo that had been inscribed onto her wrist, before placing his own hand in hers. She helped him to stand and he remembered, too late, that he wore nothing under the cover.

As the quilt dropped from his body the woman made no attempt to disguise the way she was looking at him. Her eyes moved hungrily down his body, taking in every curve of his muscles, every shape of him. He could see the desire in her eyes and looking at her he could feel the same desire mirrored in himself.

Instead of giving him the space he needed to get dressed, she stepped closer to him, pressing her clothed body against his naked one. He slipped his arms around her waist, feeling the cotton of her shirt move underneath his fingers. It whispered against her skin, and he could feel himself responding to that whisper.

She moved her head towards him, so close that he could taste her breath on his tongue and their lips met, gently and tentatively. Michael pulled away slightly, so that he could see into her green eyes. He saw the passion there, a flame dancing in her eyes.

He moved in to kiss her again and this time there was nothing shy about it. The dam of their excitement was knocked aside and they let the waters flood them. Michael relieved the woman of her clothes and when they fell onto the bed, there was nothing to separate their flesh.

They moved together, and burned together, two creatures of the night, bound completely to each other for the time that they had. It was an experience that Michael would never forget - more so for the knowledge that was revealed after. For that time of utter sweetness, was to be entombed in a cavern of darkness, but it was because of that darkness that made the memory so much sweeter, like a single grain of sugar lost in a mountain of salt.

But for those that live in darkness, the light can sometimes be a trick of the mind.

He dressed while she watched from where she lay, nothing covering her naked form. She lovingly watched as his muscles flexed and relaxed, taking the time to enjoy the feelings that he aroused in her. It had been a long time since she had dared look at another the way she was looking at Michael. Kian would never allow it. This knowledge saddened her, but she was resigned to it. Kian allowed her to have her little encounters, but she was his, for now and all eternity. She had promised herself to him, and if he even suspected that Michael meant anything more than a little fun there would be an eternity to suffer.

Finally dressed, Michael turned to face her, a smile on his face that lit up his blue eyes. "I don't even know your name." He perched on the bed next to her.

She raised herself up on to her elbows and kissed him gently on the lips before replying. "I am Caroline." Then she uttered the words that she dreaded saying, wishing with all that she had that they weren't true. "I am Kian's, and Kian's I will remain until time has ended."

Michael looked at her in disbelief. Kian's? She was with Kian? God, what had he just done? Kian had given him a place to shelter from the day and he had repaid him by sleeping with his lover.

She saw the apprehension on his face. "Worry not, Michael. He knows what I came to you for and has no qualms with it. He knows as well as I do that eternity is too long a time to be faithful to just one."

Sensing that the incredible moment that they had spent together was truly finished, Caroline also began to dress, keeping her eyes on what her hands were doing and not seeking his gaze as she so wanted to do.

Michael could only stare at the woman. "I don't know what is happening!" he suddenly yelled. "Tell me what is going on!"

Caroline only shook her head. "It is not my job to guide you, Michael, or to help you discover who you are. It is Kian's job to tell you who and what you are."

She finished dressing and left the room, looking back at him when she was over the threshold. "Kian will be waiting for you in the lounge. It's best not to keep him waiting for too long."

And with that she left, leaving Michael sitting on the bed,

wondering what kind of a place he had stumbled into.

Kian was sitting in a straight-backed chair, a fire roaring in the fireplace in front of him. He wore clothes identical to Michael's, and at first didn't acknowledge Michael when he entered, he just continued to stare into the flames. Michael sat on the black leather sofa that was across from Kian and took advantage of the man's silence, allowing his eyes to take in the details of the room. It was painted scarlet with black and white paintings dotted the walls. Each of them showed extremes of weather; lightning storms, tornados, huge tidal waves crashing down onto rocky landscapes.

"I hope Caroline made you feel welcome."

Michael jumped when Kian spoke, momentarily taken by surprise. He turned to look at him and was unnerved by the humour in the man's grey eyes. He nodded, not wanting to go into details of the private moment he and the girl had shared.

Kian nodded in response, then turned back to the flames. "We're just like fire, you know, Michael. We burn for as long as we are fed, always hungry, never sated for long. We can die out, only to rise again when circumstances allow."

To Michael this seemed like a speech used dozens, maybe hundreds, of times before, yet he listened to each word, hoping that Kian would begin to make a bit of sense and stop talking so metaphorically.

"Yet unlike the fires, we have only one weakness." Kian looked at Michael, the humour totally gone from his face. "You know what that is, even if you don't understand why. You were hiding from it when you found us."

"The sunlight." Michael whispered, barely loud enough for it to reach his own ears, yet Kian nodded as if he'd heard.

"Yes, the sun." He stood and walked to the fireplace, feeding another cut of wood onto the flames. When the fire had taken hold of it he again looked at his guest. "Have you had any memories since you awoke? Any, even half-glimpsed?"

Michael nodded, thinking about the girl he had seen, the blonde whose name was almost-certainly Holly. "Yes, but nothing that I can make sense of."

"The streets that you wandered before coming here, they are familiar to you?"

Again, Michael nodded, feeling goosebumps break out over his body despite the warmth of the fire. How could he know that?

"And me? Do I seem familiar to you?"

Michael shook his head. "No. I don't know you."

"Ah." Kian was smiling, bit it was strange, infused with both sadness and passion. "Look closely, Michael. There is nothing about me that you remember, nothing, not even a feeling?"

Michael shook his head again, but suddenly he wasn't sure. Something was nagging at him, something in the back of his mind, something making him doubt himself.

Kian nodded once more, as if expecting this. He walked out of the room and Michael heard locks being turned. Intrigued, he joined Kian by the front door.

"We're going out." Kian looked at Michael, looking at the grey still in the man's hair. "You need to feed, and then there are things that you need to see."

Not sure that he trusted him Michael nevertheless left the house by Kian's side, with a feeling that they had walked this way once before.

He felt stronger, more sure of himself, and knew that others could also feel it. He could tell by the way that groups steered away from him when they noticed him watching them. They had nothing to fear; his belly was full with the blood of two people and the thirst had slackened.

Kian smiled when Michael joined him again, looking again at the hair on his companion's head. He nodded slightly, seeing what it was that he had needed to see, and they walked through the streets of the night, observing their prey with no desire to hunt.

That feeling of recognition increased with every step and the whole thing was driving Michael insane. It was just so frustrating to know that he remembered something, but not knowing how or why or when he had been here before. Even some of the faces looked familiar, although he was sure - well, pretty sure - that he had never seen them before.

He swept a hand through his hair, and stopped moving. There was something different. He passed his hand through his hair again, opening himself to the sensation. It was impossible, but his hair felt thicker, healthier, *younger*. He studied the hand that he had used to move his hair and his heart began to beat quicker in his chest. The lines on his hand were gone, simply erased. The skin looked youthful and supple, the hands of someone who had grafted hard in his life, but was still relatively young.

Kian had also stopped, and was looking at Michael, watching him as he searched himself.

Michael looked up, his eyes wide and frightened. "What's happening to me? Kian, what the hell is going on?" He looked back down at his hands then back at his companion. "Tell me what I am!"

Kian sighed, looked around him and seeing no one around them he took Michael by the hand and began to guide him on. After a few quiet moments he began to talk.

"Michael, I could tell you what you are. I could tell you how I know you. But I don't have all of the answers that you need, I don't know all of your existence, or your thoughts, or your feelings. There are some things that you need to discover about yourself. That's where I'm taking you - to somewhere that should make your memories accessible."

Michael watched Kian, ignoring all else, still walking to their destination. There was something about this man that he just didn't trust. "So, tell me what you can."

Kian sighed, in annoyance. "You don't remember me at all, but it is because of me that you are here." He looked at Michael, searching his eyes for something that he didn't see - recollection or understanding. "Do you know what you are, Michael? You don't need to know the name for it, but look inside yourself and answer me. Do you know what you are?"

They walked in silence for a moment, Michael searching himself intently. Did he know what he was? No. Did he know the *nature* of what he was? Yes, he knew the answer to that, had known since he had first quenched that red thirst. He was a creature of the darkness, of the night. He was a stalker, he was a slayer, an executioner. He was a hunter. He was a -

"I'm a killer." He looked at Kian, not to see if he had given the right answer, but to confirm it. To look into the eyes of another killer and see himself there.

Kian nodded. "Yes. You're a killer. The name of what you are is unimportant, just a word to cause fear in people's hearts and souls. But the *essence* of what we are is vital. To know that is to know all you really need to."

Michael thought that perhaps Kian was understating the issue, but he let it go. With any luck, *he* would be able to find out what was really needed.

They walked quickly, passing people without their knowledge. Maybe they felt a cold breeze pass by, maybe they sensed a deeper darkness near them, but most simply felt nothing. And those who did feel something shrugged it off as nothing.

The town gave way to fields, and Michael felt a sense of recollection nagging at him as he passed old buildings, but it was just a feeling. He could still remember nothing of his life.

Kian sensed his impatience, and his annoyance changed into anger. There was a time when the boy beside him - and compared to himself, Michael *was* just a boy - had hung on his every word, eager to learn. But he forced himself to remember that that was a long time ago, and things had changed so much. Including the boy who walked beside him.

After an hour of walking, with hardly any words passing between them, Kian finally stopped. Michael looked around him and felt his heart jump into his throat, although he had no idea why the ruins in front of him could make him react so intensely.

The building was standing, but only just. Windows had been smashed, doors removed from their frames, and walls were crumbled and damaged. The land in front of the house which had once been a garden, was now just a jungle of weeds and rubble from what remained of the house.

He looked up to a window to the left of the house, a fraction of a memory stirring in him. He saw a girl looking out of the window, young, youthful and beautiful. Then the memory faded and he was left looking at only shadows. Moving slowly, Michael walked to the place where the front door had once stood, and hesitated. This place had an air of sadness surrounding it. Should he go in? Wasn't it best for memories of grief to be left unremembered?

"Good or bad, I need to know." he whispered to himself and took a tentative step over the threshold, a shiver working its way through his body.

He walked a few steps in, then looked back to see that Kian had stayed a safe distance from the house. "Aren't you coming?" The idea of being here, alone, filled him with unease. He didn't want to remember what he had to remember on his own.

Kian shook his head. "No. This place is for you, Michael. I have no rights here." He looked up at the dark sky. "If you linger too long and you can't make it back to the shelter before the day dawns, there is still a cellar and it is still standing. You can hide there if you need to."

He nodded, as if confirming it to himself, then turned and began to stroll away, not looking back.

Michael waited until Kian was out of sight then turned back to face the empty hallway in front of him. He didn't want to be here, not on his own. He didn't want to confront his memories alone. But he knew that he had no choice - he *was* alone, and he had to know who he was. Kian was wrong; knowing *what* he was came nowhere near to being enough.

Taking a deep breath, he walked further into the house.

The wallpaper was peeling from the walls, mould growing over most of it. The carpet was wet underneath him and he could feel it sucking at him, trying to grab his shoes from his feet. It smelt dank and rotten, and the air was thick with moisture. He walked slowly from empty room to empty room, looking and searching for anything that would trip his mind up, tricking it into spilling some of its secrets; but there was nothing. It wasn't a house anymore, it was just a collection of stones that had been left empty and uncared for far too long.

He walked slowly up what remained of the steep stairs, ignoring the banister after seeing that it was beginning to fall away from the wall. The steps themselves weren't much better, bowing alarmingly under his weight. He moved along the landing, seeing the same as he had downstairs - a lot of mouldy walls and nothing else. He went into the room where he had 'seen' the girl and found it as he had expected - only an empty space that had once been a home for someone.

He had hoped that this room would cause his mind to react and was disappointed when nothing happened. He felt tired in a way that made his heart ache. The house was a shell that was vacant of anything, and whatever Kian had hoped for just wasn't going to happen. Michael accepted that he was never going to know about his past, and thought that maybe it was for the best. He could feel the sadness underneath the nothingness of his memories, and things like that probably were best left forgotten.

He dragged his feet, thinking about going back to the refuge with no answers, and his heart skipped a beat. The idea of telling Kian that the whole thing had been a waste of time wasn't something he really wanted to consider - there was something in the man's eyes that made Michael distrust and fear him immensely. The man was dangerous. Michael knew that, *sensed* that, even if he didn't know the reasons behind it.

So, he trekked back downstairs and found the door to the cellar. It smelled identical to the rest of the building, but he thought that he could rest there comfortably enough to be able to think, and it was safe in case he fell asleep before the sun rose.

He laid down upon the cold wet ground, put his arms under his head and closed his eyes. His disappointment still overwhelming him, Michael fell asleep, and dreamed dreams that were not dreams. In his sleep his mind unlocked the door and the tidal wave of his memories crashed through.

* * *

Michael stood and watched as she walked away, angry at himself, but more angry at her. She was letting her father split them up, and that was just wrong. He'd suggested that they run away, but she was having none of it. She was happy to just move on, probably end up an old maid. Well, if that was the way she wanted it, it was fine with him.

He stormed away from the house, keeping close to the trees so that no one would spot him. It didn't occur to him that, since he was so upset, his discretion meant that he did *care that she didn't get into any trouble.*

He walked along the road, nothing more than a mud-trap, and tried to keep his thoughts away from Tracie. But that was no good. The more he tried not to think about her, the more his mind went back to her.

They had been together for two months, and he knew that he loved her, probably even more than she loved him. And it had been good, as well. The only time that they argued was when the conversation moved on to her parents.

Michael had an idea that her mum was okay about it all. It was just her father. He didn't want anyone taking his little girl away from him. Not that Michael had any intention of doing that, but it wasn't how he saw it.

The night had grown darker around him and a chill had seeped into the air. The road was deserted - no one strayed at night. There had been too many reports of devils in the area, the type that stole your blood and kept your soul. Not that he believed any of it; they were just stories and stupid superstitions that entertained and scared the local children. But all the same, he began to check over his shoulder regularly.

He bit in a scream when a cold hand touched his shoulder. He turned to see the thing that had scared him, expecting to see a grotesque figure, one of the devils that he didn't believe in. Instead, he saw a man with white skin and grey eyes that seemed to pierce deep into his soul. The blonde hair was cut short but still framed his pale face.

"I'm sorry," the man said, taking his hand from Michael's shoulder. "I didn't mean to startle you."

Michael studied the man's eyes and saw the amusement in them. He was quite sure that the man had intended to startle him. But he was too relieved to find that it was a man and not a soul-stealing monster that the man's attention wasn't too worrying.

"Can I help you with something?" Michael peered around to see if maybe the man had gotten his cart stuck in the road or something. But there was no sign of a cart, or anything else for that matter.

"Well, I had hoped that I could accompany you back to the village, if that was where your feet were leading you." The man smiled, which totally disarmed Michael. It was the smile of someone who knew that he was being stupid, but was going to continue anyway. "I don't know if you have heard, but there are stories of devils on the air, and I am nervous wandering around the night on my own."

Michael laughed gently. "I'm sure that what you have heard are just stories, but I will walk with you. It will be nice to have some company on such a long walk."

The man nodded, and Michael felt a twinge of unease. It was nothing that he could put his finger on, but it left him feeling odd.

He shook it off, and the two men began to walk along the

road together. Suddenly the man stopped and turned to face the boy he now walked with. "I'm so rude." he said, extending out his hand. "I haven't even introduced myself. My name is Kian."

Michael shook the offered hand. "I'm Michael. It's a pleasure to meet you, sir."

They began to walk again and Kian began to talk. "So, is it work or a maiden that has left your face so long, young sir?"

Michael looked at the man and laughed. "It is a maiden, but unfortunately she is no longer my maiden. It seems her loyalty to her father's wishes has overridden anything she felt for me." He was shocked to discover how easy it was to talk to this stranger, especially about a subject as painful as this.

Kian was nodding, as if he understood exactly. "In my experience, young Michael, girls have a way of coming around, given time and space enough to think about their choices and options. Maybe, if you leave her alone, she will realise where her heart lies. And, who has the power to ignore their heart?"

Michael glanced at the man, wondering if he was right. Maybe she would come around. If he understood this man, all he had to do was wait. "Thank you, sir. That is something I shall have to think on."

They walked in silence, Michael pondering what the man had said. It was possible, then, that Tracie was not completely lost to him. And despite his earlier conviction that he didn't care, he felt his heart lift.

His thinking stopped when Kian turned suddenly to face him, stepping in front of him.

"If you could have one wish, young Michael, what would it be?"

Michael felt his jaw drop slightly. What a strange question to ask. "If I could have..? What do you mean, if I could have one wish?"

Kian was watching Michael with a strange intensity. "Indulge my curiosity, young sir, as my curiosity often controls my voice. If you could have one wish granted, any wish at all, what would you wish for?"

Michael's mouth had suddenly gone very dry. There was something wrong here. The air had turned heavy and the darkness was almost tangible; he could almost feel it pressing against him. He realised the situation he was in - on a road that was deserted, with a man he didn't know, miles from anywhere. Miles from help should he need it.

"I don't know. I've never thought about things like that." He said with a nervous laugh, hoping that Kian would drop the subject, but it seemed that his answer wasn't good enough.

"Well, think about it now!" Kian sounded irritated, almost angry. "Think hard, young sir, for sometimes wishes really are granted." When Michael didn't respond, Kian continued. "Would you destroy your enemies? Have power, riches? Or would you, perhaps, wish for an eternity to spend with your maiden? An eternity with her by your side? To watch all of those fall apart with age, while you and your lover stayed young?"

Michael's eyes widened. Forever with Tracie? Forever with her next to him while her father had no choice but to age? Eternity with his love? "And who could grant me such a wish, if I were to make it?"

Kian smiled but Michael did not see the hardness that edged it. "Someone who is close to you, young sir."

Michael chose to ignore the glint in the man's eyes. He was lost in the fantasy of him and Tracie together with no one to oppose them. "And you could grant me and my love eternity?" He looked at Kian sceptically, yet eagerly.

"I could grant you, Michael. If your lady were to accept the gift, it is best that you be the one to bestow it on her."

Michael smiled. Of course she'd accept it - who wouldn't?! "How would it be possible? No one can grant eternity." But how his young heart hoped that he was wrong. The vision that he had in his mind was unshakeable.

"I shall ask you again, my friend. If you could have one wish, what would you ask for?" Kian's tainted blood pounded through his temples, through his entire body. Through his soul. It was always better if they came willingly. They just had to be offered the right incentives.

Michael smiled, still lost in his dream. "For eternity."

Kian smiled his hard smile again, only this time Michael saw the edge, like a knife. And he wanted to take it back. Something was wrong. Very wrong. He suddenly began to think about deals with devils.

Slowly, Kian moved closer to Michael, until he was face to face with the boy. "Granted."

Michael tried to move away, but a strong hand shot out with uncanny speed and grabbed his shoulder. Kian pulled Michael towards him, forcing him closer. His other hand grabbed the side of the boy's head and forced it backwards, exposing the soft skin of his neck.

Michael shouted out when the man's sharp teeth sank into his throat, and his whole body clenched. He could feel the blood being sucked from his body, but he was unable to move. Black stars began to dance in front of his eyes and the strength ran out of his body. He began to sag, but Kian held him steady.

Michael's eyes closed, his thoughts becoming vague and unimportant. His worries for Tracie were gone, but so was everything else. A voice spoke through the cloud that had descended upon him, but the words were incoherent.

And then a warm feeling was coming over him. He could think clearly once more, could see, could hear. Could taste. And what he tasted was tangy, yet tasty. It was copper that he could taste, and there was only one other thing that he knew of that tasted that way.

He began to struggle as he realised what was happening, smearing Kian's blood over his face. The blood was coming from a gash in Kian's hand and that same hand was being pushed against his face, and there was no way to escape it.

It only went on for minutes, and Michael soon knew that he didn't want it to stop. That taste was penetrating his whole being; he liked it and his body ached for more.

Finally, Kian let go of Michael's head and the boy collapsed onto the cold ground. Something was happening to him, and he began to shake. His eyesight, good to start with, became clearer still, and he could see through the darkness, could see every detail of the night, every marvellous wonder of the dark.

Kian stood over him and smiled. "Eternity is yours, young Michael. And you are now mine."

Michael closed his eyes and smiled.

Tracie sat at her vanity table brushing her long brown hair, trying to ignore the tears that refused to stop leaking from her eyes. He blamed her, she knew that he did, but what could she do? Her father had said that if he ever found out that she had seen him again, she would be sent away. And as much as the idea of not being able to be with Michael hurt her, not being able to see him at all would kill her.

She wiped at her eyes, trying to control her emotions. She turned suddenly, heart beating loudly in her chest, as something small hit her window. Quickly, she crossed the room and looked out onto the ground below.

Michael stood there and, as he saw her, he dropped the handful of small pebbles back onto the ground. Worried that her father would see him, but still pleased that he was there, she motioned to him that she was going to go down.

Quickly, she wrapped her gown around her and walked out of her room. As she passed her parents' bedroom she could hear the reassuring snores of her father and the pressure around her heart eased. As quickly as she could, she rushed down the stairs and outside.

Michael was hiding behind a clump of bushes and she ran over to him. There was something strange about him, an excitement in his eyes, and she felt herself reacting to it. She threw herself into his arms, loving it when they wrapped around her. Swiftly, they hurried into the shelter of the trees.

She tripped over a tree root and fell onto the ground. Because of the way she was holding onto him, he too fell, almost landing on top of her. They started to laugh and he put his lips onto hers to stop the sound.

He kissed her passionately and she responded, letting her passion take a hold over her, letting all of her cares fall away. They reacted to each other's bodies, allowing all previous restraints to be broken. He began to kiss her neck, and something in the way he kissed her set an alarm off in her head. She pulled away from him, looking at the expression on his face. At the sight of the hunger in his eyes she moved away, looking at him warily. He had changed, and she began to feel scared.

"What's happened to you, Michael?"

Michael grinned, and his teeth seemed more prominent. "I've been granted a wish."

There was something in the way he was looking at her, something in his eyes that had nothing to do with his lust for her. It *was a dark look, especially when his eyes happened on her throat.*

"What wish?"

He could sense the blood rushing around her body, but more so in her neck. He could hear it, and the more he fought to ignore it the less he was able to. He tore his gaze from her flesh and forced himself to look into her eyes.

"A wish for us, Tracie. A wish that means that I can spend forever with you, with no one to stop us."

He moved towards her again but she held a hand up, stopping him from reaching her. "What have you done, Michael? In the name of all that is, tell me what it is that you have done?"

Michael smiled at her, not sensing - or disregarding - her fear. "The tales of creatures roaming here are true. I met one tonight." He saw the look on her face, the widening of her eyes, and shook his head, laughter on his lips. "But not everything is true, Tracie. He's given me a gift - an eternity with you, if you accept what I have to give you."

Tracie was shaking her head, tears trickling down her face.

Slowly, she stretched out a hand and touched his face, feeling how cool his skin was beneath her warm hand. She moved her hand down his cheek and down to his neck, pulling the collar of his shirt aside so that she could see his throat. The wounds were clear, even in the darkness, and the blood was still drying and hardening.

She gasped and pulled her hand away, feeling stained. She held her other hand to her mouth, looking at Michael in a way that startled him. She was scared. No - more than that: she was terrified of him. He reached out to her, and she scrambled away from him. Looking at her, he pulled his hand back, holding them both up, palms facing her, letting her know that he didn't mean to harm her.

"Haven't you been listening to what people are saying, Michael?! Haven't you heard what happens to those who accept this 'gift' that has been given to you?"

He looked at her blankly, and she sobbed.

"You'll kill, Michael. You'll kill people." She paused and looked at him. "Is that why you came to me? Am I to be your first victim?" She was looking at him warily, backing away as she was talking, slowly getting to her feet.

He felt as though she'd slapped him. "I'd never harm you, Tracie! I love you!"

Tracie was shaking her head. "I can't believe that, Michael. The damned can't love." Slowly, she still backed away. "I love you, but I can't be near you. I just can't!"

Quickly, she began to run towards the edge of the trees.

"No!" He shouted, and began to move towards her. He saw the look on her face as she looked back at him, and it forced him onwards. He had to stop her, had to make her listen, had to make her see that it was because he loved her that he had done what he had done. He grabbed her by the arm and pulled her back forcefully, not meaning for what happened next. She fell roughly to the ground, hitting her shoulder against a tree, scraping the skin. Blood began to flow, and Michael looked at it, transfixed.

Before he knew what he was doing, before he could even try and stop himself, he lunged at his lover, shoving her against the ground and sunk his teeth into her throat.

She screamed out and, using her body as a lever, she pushed against him, but Michael held on. Knowing that she had no other choice, she grabbed hold of his head by his thick hair, hair that she had lovingly touched in the past, and pulled him off of her. The pain as he ripped a chunk of her flesh away was almost unbearable, but she did bear it. When he leapt towards her again, she kicked out at him, knocking him backwards. Then she was on her feet, moving quicker than she'd ever thought she would be able to, hurrying to the sanctuary of her home.

The door closed behind her and she leant against it, knowing deep within herself that she was safe from him. After a few moments, she walked to the bathroom and found what she could to clean and cover the injury. With that done, she walked back to her bedroom, closed and locked the door behind her, and found one of her scarves. She wrapped it around her throat, sat down on her bed, and began to cry.

Michael walked amongst the trees, trying to shake the memories from his mind. How she had looked at him. The way her blood had tasted in his mouth. The way he had felt when he had attacked her. And he could hear his own voice saying, over and over again, I'd never harm you, Tracie! I love you!

As he walked, he felt a pounding begin in his body. At first, he dismissed it as his blood as it pulsed around his body, but within minutes it had increased, and there was no way he could dismiss it.

He sank to the ground, his whole body burning. Yet it wasn't painful, more aggravating than anything else. Not knowing what else to do, he cried out the name he had learnt only hours ago.

"Kian. Help me, please!"

Only silence answered him and he lay down upon the forest floor, staring up at the night sky, his arms wrapped around himself. He closed his eyes, hoping that the sensation would subside a little.

He heard faint footsteps moving towards him and opened his eyes. Kian stood over him, looking down at him with a mixture of compassion and humour. It was a combination that Michael found disturbing.

"What have you done to me?"

Kian smiled at the man who was going through the change, shocked and intrigued that it had begun so quickly. He had only known a few that had adjusted so easily. "Only what you asked of me, Michael."

Slowly, he crouched onto the ground beside him. "I can stop it now, if you want. Still there is time for the process to be reversed. But to do that, you will have to die, young sir. So, I give you the choice: Let the fire take you and live for eternity or ask me to take the fire from you and die."

Michael whimpered as a burst of pain - real pain - swallowed him. He had a choice to make, and it took a moment for him to decide. Any life was better than none. "I ask for what you have given me. I ask for eternity."

Kian stood and smiled. "Then come with me, young Michael. And I will help you do what needs to be done. I will prepare you to welcome Her."

Michael shivered at those words for a reason he could not explain, but allowed Kian to help him up. With the man who had set all of these things in motion almost carrying him, they walked.

The change took an age to Michael, although he had no idea of the actual time. He lay in a bed in Kian's home, a place where the light never entered, and let the burning take him over. It could have been hours, but he was sure that it was longer than that - a couple of days, maybe even as long as a week.

He had no relief from the pain that blazed through him, but

found that he could distance himself from it, sending himself away from it for a short time. Kian visited him often, talking to him and explaining the things that Michael would have to know in order to survive.

One night, with the pain having subsided for a short time, Michael opened his eyes to see something moving on the ceiling of his room. It was draped in black, and darted across the ceiling with a clicking noise that grated on Michael's every nerve.

It loomed above him, and he could hear a low mewling noise, like a cat in heat, or perhaps a spider looking at a trapped fly. He knew that something was about to happen, could feel it just as he could feel the burning through his body. He could feel it in the air that had grown thick and oppressive.

Suddenly, it allowed him to see its face, and Michael felt his soul shrinking away. But the thing smiled, as if it knew exactly what was going on in Michael's mind.

It descended upon him and, thanks to Kian, he at least knew what to expect.

The night had never smelled sweeter or clearer, nor felt fresher. The dark was darker, yet also clearer, and everything looked more real than he remembered it.

He stood in the dark, looking out over everything that surrounded him, taking it all in, embracing it. Kian joined him and stood next to Michael in silence, letting him feel the things that he needed to feel.

After a while he turned to his newest companion. "Go now, young friend. Go and feed and then do what it is that you need to do. The night belongs to you now."

Michael smiled. Yes, the night. And the night was calling him, just as the need grew stronger in him. To feed, to have that taste in his mouth. Yes.

He began to walk away, not even looking back when Kian called out to him again. "Watch the night, Michael! Return here before the sun appears on the horizon! And if this home is beyond your reach, find shelter!"

Kian could only watch as Michael walked briskly for his hunt, the arrogance of youth in his stride.

He felt revived, steady and strong. The woman's blood now flowed in him, and it gave him a sense of well-being. People were hiding in their homes and it was only by chance that he had come across the woman, old and unafraid. He had gone to her, had given her peace from the many ailments that consumed her.

And now, he trekked across fields to fulfil the other burning that was in him. He travelled to see his beloved.

The house was dark but he had no doubt that she was there, hiding like the rest of the people in the area. Too many had heard tales of creatures in the night, but none understood. None knew how it felt to be this free, with only the limitations of the sun.

He stood in front of the house, looking up towards Tracie's window. He could see the light from a candle flickering, and it comforted him. If a candle burned, then maybe her love for him still burned. Maybe she waited for him.

He gathered a collection of small stones and began to throw them. After the third, he saw movement in her room, and his heart gladdened. She appeared at the window and looked downward. He saw her hand snake up to the scarf she wore around her neck, and his heart sank.

She left his sight, and Michael was lifting his hand to throw some more of the pebbles when he heard the sound of locks being turned. He turned to the door and saw his lover standing inside.

"Why do you come here, Michael?" Her voice was tinged with fear, but it didn't haunt her eyes as it had on their last meeting.

"For you, my love. Always for you." He looked at her, then at the scarf that hid her wounds. Shame and anguish clear in his words, he spoke. "I am sorry for hurting you. I had no control."

She laughed mockingly, but the sadness he saw in her eyes were real. "And now you do?" She looked at the way he hung his head, and nodded. "You have control because the sickness in you has been fed tonight. Is that not so?"

He forced himself to meet her eyes. "Yes. That is so."

The tension between them had grown, and Tracie was sad to find it so. There had been a time, when her love had still been himself and not a devil in disguise, when she would have laughed at the idea of being uncomfortable with him. But now he was dead, for how could one live by surviving on death?

"Forgive me for not taking your word, sir." she said, curtly, *gently unwrapping the scarf from her throat. "But I have reason to doubt."*

Michael saw the marks on her neck and cringed. The wounds had not healed and he could see that blood still wept from them. The skin surrounding the holes had become red and infected, and he knew that the infection would probably spread.

"Let me help you, Tracie." he said, looking into her eyes once more. "Let me give you the gift given to me. Let me take care of you."

Tracie looked at him in disbelief, feeling tears track down her cheeks. "No, Michael. Not now, not ever. I would rather die than live forever damned." She saw the shock on his face, and a part of her still longed for him, for him to make it all better. But she refused to pay for happiness with her soul.

"I want you to leave, Michael. And if you ever loved me, you will go. And not return."

Michael could feel his own tears passing from his eyes, but still managed to look at her without being fazed. "I loved you then. I love you now. I will always love you, Tracie. I shall do as you have asked."

Before Tracie realised that he had even moved Michael was standing next to her. She gasped and tried to move away, but he grabbed her shoulders and held her firm. He looked at the marks on her neck, then looked at her. Gently, he kissed her on the forehead and then on the lips, before backing away from her.

"I never meant to hurt you, my love. Forgive me."

He turned and ran into the night, leaving Tracie with the cold touch of his kiss still on her lips. After a few moments, she went back inside, leaving the dark to those who were ruled by it.

* * *

Michael threw himself into learning everything that Kian had to teach. Others like themselves arrived at the house, only to leave days later. None stayed for long and no one made any impression on the boy who now had nothing, and an eternity to wallow in it. He lived for the night and for the lessons that Kian gave him. He ignored all else, distracting himself so that thoughts of Tracie were kept away.

For three weeks, he managed to keep her out of his head, to keep his thoughts only on what he was becoming; finding out the nature of what he was.

But then Michael began to grow distracted. The things that Kian said had to be repeated in order for Michael to grasp them. It was raining, the sound of thunder filling the world, lightning attacking the sky, making the very air tingle.

"Enough of this, Michael!" Kian said, closing the book from which he had been reading. "Go and do what it is you have to do in order for your mind to function again."

Michael dragged his eyes away from the flames in the fireplace. "Pardon?"

Kian sighed. "I know you have been troubled lately. And I also know that you do not know what ails you. So go! Go out into the dark and walk. Wherever your feet take you is where you need to be."

Michael looked back into the flames and then rose from the chair. "Thank you, Kian."

As Michael left, Kian sighed again. Sometimes he thought that there was just no hope for that boy.

The rain attacked his body, yet he hardly felt it. His mind was filled with Tracie, and he knew immediately where his feet were taking him. Things had to be said to her, he had to tell her that there was nothing to fear. He had to persuade her.

As he neared the house, the air grew more oppressive, more deadly. His feet slowed, as if he were treading water. He was finding it hard to breathe, the air catching in his throat.

He stood in the spot he had occupied so many times before and looked up at the window. All was dark but he knew that he had to see her, and her being asleep wasn't going to stop that. He walked straight to the front door, and tried the handle. It turned easily in his hand and he let the door swing open in front of him. Slowly, he stepped over the threshold.

The house had an air of illness, of sickness, of death approaching, and it froze him. He suddenly knew why he had been called to this place. Hoping that he was wrong he silently sprinted up the stairs, finding the way to Tracie's bedroom straight away. He opened the door slowly and peered in.

At first, nothing seemed amiss, until he spotted the figure

lying underneath a bundle of blankets. He moved slowly towards the bed, thinking that maybe he had it wrong, and this was not his lover's room after all.

The woman lying on the bed looked old, haggard, and faded. Her hair was listless and worn and her face was sickly-yellow. The marks on her neck were clear, though, and he knew that it was Tracie who lay in front of him, Tracie who was ill. Who was dying.

He sat on the edge of the bed and held his face in his hands, letting the tears flow.

She stirred beside him and looked at him as he wept. She reached an aging hand out to him and gently touched his arm. He turned to her, saw her smile.

"You came to say goodbye, my love?"

Michael shook his head. "No. There need be no goodbye. Let me help you. Let me heal you. Let me take you somewhere where illness doesn't exist."

Gently, she shook her head, ignoring the pain that flowed through her. "No, Michael. It is not natural. And I would rather die a natural death than live an unnatural life."

He shook his head. "You don't mean that. You can't mean that." He looked into her eyes and saw only death looking back at him.

"I can and I do." She smiled sweetly and for a second Michael saw the real Tracie there, hidden beneath the mask of death. "I know you love me, Michael. You would not weep for me if you didn't. But I cannot accept what you have to give. I'm sorry."

Anger welled up in him and he jumped away from the bed and glared down at her. "I could give you my gift whether you wish to accept it or not! You don't have the strength to fight me!" But even as he said it, he realised that it wasn't true. He loved her too much to go against her wishes.

And Tracie saw it too. "You couldn't do that, Michael. You want to, I see that, but you couldn't. Not when you love me as much as you do."

He collapsed by the bed and held her hand to his face, so that she could feel his tears.

"If you love me, then say goodbye and walk away." She felt him shake his head. "Yes. If you love me, you will leave here, Michael. Leave here with the knowledge that I die how I lived.

Under the grace of all there is."

He looked up at her, his eyes red and sore, and managed a feeble smile. "Then I leave, my love." He leant towards her and kissed her slowly. Their last kiss.

Before he could begin to cry again, Michael walked from her room, leaving her alone as she had asked.

Slowly, Tracie closed her eyes, still feeling his lips on hers, his love answering to her own. Now she could die. Now she could be at peace.

Michael's hair was wet, his clothes sodden, but it didn't matter to him. His heart was breaking into a million pieces, and nothing mattered to him. How was he to survive? What was the point of eternity with no one to share it with?

Kian was waiting for him in his usual place when Michael returned.

"When will you leave, Michael?" he asked from his chair. Yet he looked only at the rain outside the window.

"Tomorrow night. I cannot stay here. Too many things will haunt me." He looked into the fireplace. "They'll haunt me anyway." he added softly to himself.

Kian nodded. It was as he'd expected. "Nothing can persuade you to stay?"

Michael shook his head. "No. With my love dying, nothing else matters to me now. It is best that I leave."

Already, Kian had decided on what steps must be taken, but to say so to his companion would be most unwise. "You are welcome here anytime, young Michael. When you need this sanctuary, it'll be waiting for you."

"Thank you, Kian. For everything." He walked upstairs to his room, not hearing when Kian left the house five minutes later.

She was screaming. He heard it even before he woke. His lover was screaming.

He bolted up in his bed, sweat breaking out on his cold skin. Where was she? He looked around his room, but found nothing there. Quickly, he dressed, and ventured out into the hall. He followed her screams and found Kian guarding another room.

He smiled at Michael as the boy approached. "Now you have

no reason to leave, my friend."

"What have you done?!" He screamed and pushed Kian away from the door. He scrambled for the key that was in the door and turned it. Quickly, he opened the door.

She lay on a bed, her hands and feet bound with twine. He could see her skin, no sign of illness remaining, was now milky-white. White, except for the splashes of red near her mouth, red with blood. Kian's blood. He rushed to her, her screams loud in his ears and tried to hold her. She saw who was there and began to struggle more.

"You said you wouldn't! Michael, you told me you wouldn't!"

He held her still and looked at her closely, making sure that she could see his face clearly. "As much as it pained me, my love, I was bound by your wishes. I promise you, I had nothing to do with this."

She looked at him, her struggles stopping. "Do you swear to me, Michael? As my lover and my love, do you swear?"

He could feel his anger building up, but not at her. At himself; and at Kian. His mentor. "I swear it to you, my love, I swear."

Tears fell from her eyes. She stilled as Michael freed her from her bonds, letting his swift hands work her free. She sat up as soon as she was able to, looking at her hands, at the way they seemed to shine in the darkness.

"So pale, Michael. My skin, just like yours." She began to sob and sank into his embrace when he offered her comfort.

Slowly, he stroked her hair, feeling her pain, her sorrow as strongly as he would have felt his own. Her tears were seeping through the material of his black shirt and he could feel their warmth on his chest. Their warmth. Gently, he pushed her away from him and looked deep into her eyes. Her skin had paled, yet the change was not complete, couldn't be, not so soon. There might still be time.

She was searching his eyes, looking into his soul, and knew. Knew what he was thinking without a sound passing between them. Knew that he was going to save her in the only way that was left.

Fresh tears, of love and of salvation, fell from her eyes, mirroring his own. "Yes, my darling." she whispered. "Yes, my love, my lover. Save me."

Michael took her in his arms, ignoring the figure that lingered in the doorway, watching. He kissed her slowly, their tears mingling together, a union that was unique and uniquely powerful because of it.

He gathered her into his arms and lifted, carrying her out of the room, passing Kian without a single glance.

Into the night he took her, to perform the final act of his love.

Back into her own home he took her, lying her on her own bed, her last resting place. He stood and looked at her lying there, as she looked back at him, a smile on her lips, engulfed in beauty.

They kissed once more and Michael watched as her eyes closed, and she waited. Tears spilled from his eyes even as he pierced the skin of her neck, feeling no joy as her blood poured into his mouth. He drank the blood from her body, taking her into himself and only stopped when the flow of life stopped, her heart beating no longer.

Michael stood and looked down at her again. Her skin was pale still, but had lost that glow, had taken on the pallor of death. With traces of blood still on his lips, he kissed her own, still curled in a restful smile, a parting kiss, then left the room, leaving the scent of death behind.

Slowly, he walked into the night, walking out of the village, and away from all he had ever known.

* * *

He awoke on the floor of the cellar, gasping and crying out, the memory of the taste of Tracie's blood lingering on his lips.

Kian. Kian had forced his hand, had forced him to kill his love, had put them both through hell, and for what? For a moment he wondered, but could think of no reason. Forcefully, Michael wiped the tears from his face, and walked out into the night. There was a purpose in his stride, and he trekked back to the false sanctuary.

Kian was sitting in the room that he frequented, with Caroline sat at his side. Michael slammed the door shut behind him, making Caroline jump. Kian, however, sat expressionless in his chair. With one look at Michael's face, the woman who bore Kian's mark tattooed on her wrist left the room, leaving the two male vampires alone.

Without a word passing his lips, Michael walked to Kian's side and looked down on him. When the man turned to face him, Michael saw a strange smile on his face.

"So, your memories have returned?"

"Enough of them have." Michael said, trying to keep the indescribable anger that he felt out of his voice. "If I ever see you again, Kian, I will kill you. I will make you suffer the way that you made Tracie suffer."

And for the last time, Michael left the house of Kian. He did not see the sorrow hidden behind Kian's mask of indifference, and wouldn't have cared if he had.

Michael wandered through the nights alone, seeking nothing, only surviving. He dismissed everything, caring about nothing. Months passed, and Michael started to become more curious. He wondered how it would feel to walk into the sunlight, wondered what it would be like to have the sun fall onto his face. Would it hurt? Would the pain be unbearable? Would he even care? He started to take chances, leaving it until the last minute before seeking shelter from the only thing that could kill him.

It was purely chance that he wandered into that street. He didn't know the area, didn't know any of his own kind, although he had seen them stalking their own prey. And he didn't care to know them. They were as unimportant as everything else in the world.

He turned a corner and saw two of his own, just walking along the road, one an obvious novice and the other who obviously knew what she was doing. The older of the two had dark hair streaked with grey. The other had beautiful blonde hair that reached down past her back.

There was something in the way that she moved, the set of her back that brought goosebumps to his arms. There was something about this girl that he knew, that he wanted. That he loved.

His heart seemed to jump out of his body, and he quickly moved into an alleyway, sinking to the ground. A flood of memories were breaking through again and he had no way to stop them.

He saw everything: Meeting her, holding her, touching her. Making love to her. And he saw her smile, heard her laugh, could smell her. He could see others with her, and recognised them. His companion, whom he had changed and trained, and her friend. He could remember everything. *Everything.* He relived his death, feeling the crucifix being stabbed into his chest. Could feel the pain all over again. But, more than that, he heard his own voice saying 'Holly's pregnant'.

Holly? Yes, that's her name. Holly. God, how he loved her. He remembered now. How could he have forgotten? It had taken him centuries to find someone he loved as much as Tracie, and he had just forgotten.

As quickly as he could manage it, Michael got to his feet and ran back out into the street. He saw the couple walking away and ran through the crowds of people, trying to catch up. He was soon out of breath, so when he shouted Holly's name, there was no chance of her hearing it.

But the other one did. She turned and looked at him, really *seeing* him, seeming to mark him in her memory before turning away again.

Michael stopped and stood where he was. And what of the child? What of *his* child? There was so much he didn't know, so much he had to find out. He searched the streets, a hunter once more. For hours he sought for the woman who had carried his child, but found no trace of her.

He was about to give up, to seek out a place for the day, when a strong hand touched his shoulder and turned him around.

The woman he had seen, the woman who had seen *him*, stood before him, with murder in her eyes. "Why do you look for her?"

Michael looked at her, losing himself in the blue-grey eyes. "She's my love. And she bore my child."

The woman looked at him curiously, all anger and aggression leaving her face. "What do you want from her?"

Michael smiled, yet feeling angry. "I want *her*." He looked at her, daring her to mock him.

Instead, she smiled softly at him. "She is yet to learn all she needs in order to survive. If you come into her world now, she will be unfocussed, unable to train as she needs to. Can you wait for her?"

Michael felt his heart swell and break at the same time. To know that she was there, *could* that be enough? "I can wait." he said simply.

She smiled and nodded. "Good."

* * *

He looked at his lover, who lay safe in his arms for the first time in over two years, and kissed her firmly on the mouth. Ania stood in the kitchen, looking out into the darkness that was becoming tinged with light.

"It is time for us to say good-day."

Slowly, Ania walked into the living room, to see them stand up together. She was glad to see how happy Holly looked, but she was still concerned. She just hoped that this good news wouldn't impede Holly in doing what she needed to do, that Michael hadn't come back into her life too soon.

She watched as Holly led Michael upstairs, and decided it may be more prudent to remain in the living room, to give them some extra privacy.

Stretched out elegantly on the sofa, she lay awake for hours, thinking, staring at the ceiling above her, wondering if the three of them would actually be able to find the child.

And about what it would mean if they did.

Part Five

From Shadows To Eternal Darkness

The mid-November rain fell heavily upon the ground and all those who walked in the streets were soon drenched, their clothes becoming stuck to their skin. The darkness was dense, and the light from the street-lamps was dulled as the raindrops fell past them.

A woman walked slowly away from the few people who were unlucky enough to have been caught in the downpour. The hood on her black cloak did little to stop the rain from saturating her dark hair. The darkness was so intense that even her pale skin looked darker, but no one strayed into her path. There was an air of danger around her that made her unapproachable.

A couple, reunited three years previously, watched her as they, too, walked through the rain, their hearts growing heavier as the lone woman walked away from them. They both had different insights into their friend's behaviour, yet neither had broached the subject yet. Talking about it would make it more real and they weren't ready for that: a little bit of ignorance wasn't total bliss, but it did make things a little easier to cope with.

Holly felt the last of her hunger departing as Ania walked into the distance, and she wondered if Ania was going to have another disturbed day of sleep. Although it had scared her each time it happened, she was hoping it would happen again. At least that way she might have a chance at finding out what was going on in her teacher's mind.

She'd heard her talking in her sleep for the last week. Not that she'd heard anything significant, mainly three names, Katherine and Maria and Elizabeth, and something that sounded like a place. But the fear and anger with which the words were spoken was enough for her to be scared. She'd even thought about asking Ania about it, just dropping it into the conversation. But every time she was about to broach the subject, an image popped into her head - how Ania had looked when she had attacked the group of vampires that had tried to hurt her. And the memory of it, the pure fury that had been on Ania's face and in her eyes when she had looked at them, was enough to stop her from saying anything.

So now she watched Ania with a sadness that was second to only one other thing in her heart.

Michael also watched Ania, and wondered how long it would be. He knew exactly how Ania was feeling, had felt it himself in his years of wandering - although he knew that it would be more intense for Ania. He just hoped that, when Ania did decide to leave, she would still fulfil her promise to Holly.

Although he was just as anxious to be united with his child, he knew that Holly was beginning to find it unbearable. She was using her time to prepare, and using it well, but soon it would cease to be enough. She wanted her daughter back in her life.

He put a protective arm around his lover and they began to walk back to the house.

Ania was aware of their eyes on her, could feel their concern, but it didn't help the feelings that were in her heart. She raised her face up to the sky so that the rain fell directly upon it, and felt herself being refreshed. The feeling, she knew, wouldn't last for long but it was enough to stop her from going crazy.

It felt so fitting, that a creature such as herself should roam in the rain, with only darkness for company. There was a solitude that she felt completely at home with, and, really, wasn't that the problem? Wasn't that a part of what Holly and Michael were picking up from her? That need to be alone?

The rain began to lighten and she knew that the stars would shine down on her again before the night was over. And that was good. She needed to consult herself, needed to consult her true feelings and that was always better done with the stars to offer her a bit of perspective.

But it would be awhile. Better to go and wait the time away with a little bit of company. That was the only problem with solitude - sometimes it got a little lonely.

They were sitting on the stoop of the house, arms around each other, and she couldn't help but smile. So many people thought of them as evil; Ania wondered if they would be able to keep that opinion if they could see the love shared between the two vampires in front of her.

"Did you have a good hunt, Ania?"

Michael looked at the woman, the ageless being, with suspicion. Not of her motives or of her thoughts towards them, but there was something that she was hiding. He had an idea that it was from her past, and he knew from experience that the past had a way of hurting centuries on, but there was something that crept into her eyes on occasion. Some *thing* that lurked just below the surface, and it was that that he didn't trust.

"Thank you, Michael. Yes. It was very satisfying." She caught a glimpse of what was happening in his mind, and had to suppress a grim smile.

"Are you coming in now, Ania?" Holly looked at her friend and mentor, not wanting to receive either possible answer.

Ania looked at the way that they were sat together, then up at the November night sky. It was almost clear, the stars beginning to appear. "No, not yet. The night still calls."

They both nodded, then went into the house, Holly giving Ania a smile before the door closed.

Ania sighed with relief. She knew that the night was also calling them, but for a different reason. Hopefully their need would be satisfied before she returned home. Confident that the pair were safely inside (although why she would be worried about their safety, she had no idea), she began to run.

She gathered speed quickly, the hood of her cape falling down, allowing her hair to escape and fly behind her. She ran over the wet, muddy fields with no hesitations, her grace never faltering once, jumping over roots and rocks without so much as glancing at them. Her blood pounded through her body and she was consumed with the light-heartedness and exhilaration that she felt. Her mind was, for once, free from memories, free from the guilt that haunted her, only the sound of her feet hitting the ground mattered. But she knew that it wouldn't last for long - it never did. When she stopped running those memories would just catch right up with her. She couldn't shake them: they were quicker than her, and had more stamina. They could run forever.

When she had run for fifteen minutes, she stopped, looking around at fields that were identical to the ones miles behind her, near her home.

The sky was now mostly cloudless, and the stars shone down on her indifferently. She loosened the cord at the neck of her cloak, and laid it upon the ground, not worrying that she was getting it dirty. Then she lowered herself upon it, placed her hands beneath her head, and just looked upwards.

She loved and loathed the stars in equal measure. They watched over everything that happened in the universe with total indifference and coldness, letting everything below them know that nothing that happened to any one person ever really mattered. Letting people know that nothing was important. Yet they also reminded Ania that she had so much left to do, so much left to conquer and defeat. So much left to experience.

The patterns were known to her, yet they had changed so many times in her life-time, changed so many times since she first learnt them as a child in her true home that, through one war or another, no longer existed. She wondered if she would still be around to see them change again. This, as always led her to think about how the end would happen for her. Would she just blink out of existence? Would she grow tired of it all one day and decide to see the sun rise? Or would the world end with her still wandering through it, searching for her forgiveness, her redemption?

She began to grow restless, the stars having provided the answer that, really, she had known all along. She knew what was to be done.

She picked up her cloak, holding it so that the dirt wouldn't transfer onto her, and began to walk home, the stars still twinkling above her. The walk took longer than the run had, but it gave her time to reflect on a few more things. Also it gave Holly and Michael time to finish their other business.

Ania hoped, as she neared her home, that she had tired herself out enough so that her sleep would be peaceful.

Holly was fighting it, but didn't know if she was going to win. She glanced over at her lover as he lay beside her and gently brushed away a lock of his black hair from over his closed eyes. He slept soundly, breathing slowly, and she ached with love for him.

She felt her eyes growing heavy, her body telling her that now the sun was up it was time for her to sleep, but she refused to give in. Ania had come home almost three hours ago and had gone almost straight to bed. So far, the youngest of the vampires had heard nothing being said, but she was determined to listen anyway, just in case.

If she could hear Ania speaking again in her sleep, then maybe she would be able to figure out what was going on in her head, and could help Ania, stop her from feeling as disconnected as she obviously was.

Also, Holly wanted to know if the dreams that she had been having herself had anything to do with Ania's. She knew how crazy it was, but some of her dreams lately had been completely confusing, and she believed that she was somehow picking them up from her friend.

Holly yawned, feeling tears being squeezed out from closed eyes, and her resolve began to weaken. She opened her eyes wide once more in a last-ditch effort to keep awake, but they slowly drooped closed. Soon, she was asleep, her body relaxing almost instantaneously.

Almost as soon as she fell asleep, Holly was woken by sounds coming from Ania's room. Her body urged to her go back to sleep, but her mind was completely awake. Quietly, she got out of bed and walked to the door of Ania's room. Slowly, she pushed it open so she could see inside.

On the bed, in a heap of covers and sheets, Ania slept; but not soundly. She thrashed wildly and low groans came from her partially open mouth.

Holly jumped when Ania spoke, and her words chilled every part of Holly's soul.

"No. Please, no. Don't. No! No, please! Not that! Please! Just let me die!"

Holly began to weep at the softness of those words without being aware, and hurried over to Ania's side. She reached an arm out and gently began to shake her.

Ania's eyes flew open, and she shrank away from Holly's touch, almost falling out of the bed. Her mind still saw the things from her past and, still half-consumed by her dream, she saw them standing in front of her. The man and the creature that had turned her, both as insane as the other, madness dancing in their eyes.

"Ania, it's okay. It's me. It's Holly."

The dream was beginning to fade, and Ania was relieved to see that it was true. The creatures that had taunted and tortured her were not here, were dead and long gone, and the only person here was her worried-looking friend.

Ania tried to laugh, without success. It came out sounding almost-hysterical. She looked down at the sheets that were twisted around her, then smiling, looked back at Holly. "Looks like I had another bad dream."

Holly thought that that was the understatement of the century, but thought better of saying it. Here was the opportunity that she had been waiting for, the chance to finally start asking the questions. She opened her mouth to speak.

"Are you sure you're alright?"

Ania sighed tiredly. "I'm fine. Go back to bed."

Holly nodded, and turned to go, hating herself that she was letting the opportunity go by. Yet she felt relieved as well. She stopped at the door and, without turning back around, asked the only question she felt safe asking. "You sure everything's okay?"

Ania, who knew that things hadn't been okay for her since the night of Elizabeth's death, answered with the only answer she could give. "Fine."

Holly walked back to bed and crawled beneath the covers. Michael stirred and placed a protective arm around her. Feeling safe, she closed her eyes and let sleep take her, and soon she dreamed, dreams of a midnight garden where flowers were the colour of the night and filled with the scent of blood.

Ania, however, could not sleep. She knew that she should, she knew that she would need all the rest she could get, but she couldn't. The memories of her dream were still too fresh.

She laid back with her head resting on her arms and stared at the ceiling.

They were downstairs and ready to start their night's hunt when Ania walked into the kitchen. Both Holly and Michael looked at Ania in shock.

She wore a pair of dark faded jeans and a white shirt that made her skin look a little less pale. She still didn't look normal - no change of clothes or amount of makeup could do that - but she did look a little less strange. Her hair was tied behind her head, and she was carrying a bag.

Holly's heart had jumped up into her throat, where a lump had formed. She looked at Michael, and he hated to see the hope in her eyes.

"We're going, aren't we?" She asked, looking at Ania with expectancy.

Ania sat at the table, and looked down at the wooden surface, taking a few moments to organize what is was that she had to say, before looking back up. "I'm going. You and Michael are to stay here."

Holly looked as though she had just been slapped. Michael, however, didn't look at all surprised.

"You leave tonight." It wasn't a question.

"Yes."

Holly was looking at her two companions as if they were both insane. "What do you mean, we're to stay here? How can you expect me to do nothing while you search for my daughter?"

Holly had begun to rise from her chair, anger and danger flashing in her eyes. Michael put a hand on her arm, and when she turned her gaze on him, he saw the threat there. After a second though, her eyes softened and she sat back down.

"I'm sorry, Holly. But it's going to take a lot of time. And you still have a lot to prepare yourself for. I need to go alone."

Tears streaked down Holly's pale skin, but she didn't argue. "How long?"

"As long as it takes. I can't say for sure."

Holly looked up again, that killer spark dancing in her eyes again. But she didn't speak. Instead, she got up slowly and left the room.

Ania knew that she could probably do what she needed to do reasonably quickly. But this would give her the chance she needed to be alone. And that would then make it easier to be around Holly and Michael for a bit longer when she finally returned.

Ania looked at Michael. "You'll take my place. Teach her all that she needs to learn, and help her all that you can. Protect her. Make her embrace what she is."

Michael nodded. "I understand how you're feeling, Ania. Come back to her as soon as you can. She needs you to teach her."

Ania nodded. "If I can come back sooner I will. But, Michael..." She paused while she searched for the way to express her fears. "You need to protect her. There's something not quite right, somehow."

She saw that he didn't understand what she was talking about. And that was to be expected, really, wasn't it? Especially when *she* didn't even know what she was talking about.

"It's just a feeling that I've got, but I learnt a long time ago to trust my instincts. There's something wrong; I can smell in the air, and she needs to be protected and kept safe from it." She looked at him intensely, hoping that he would understand how important it was. "No matter what it takes."

He nodded, and Ania nodded back. Satisfied, she stood. "Tell Holly I said goodbye. And also tell her that I keep my promises."

Michael nodded and watched as Ania picked up her bag and walked out of the front door. He watched from the window as she walked away from the house.

She knew that he was watching, and she knew that Holly was also watching from the bedroom window upstairs. But she wouldn't turn around. If she did that, she would be too tempted to go back inside, too tempted to stay, no matter how loud the night was calling for her. And that would lead to something too disastrous to think about.

So she walked. She followed the road for a long time, the wind pushing her along, but too many people were walking in the night. It wasn't like when she had first been turned, not anymore. Then, people had avoided the night, seeking the shelter of their homes as soon as the sun had begun to set, protecting themselves from all the horrors that the night seemed to bring. Now, people had become more closed-minded. They didn't believe that the night harboured any dangers - not that they couldn't handle, anyway.

So the nights when she had been able to wander alone, totally isolated, were gone. It was easier to find prey, that much was true, but there was no real solitude, not anymore. So when the feelings of claustrophobia began to creep in on her again she turned her back on the road and began to stride quickly across the open fields, losing herself in the emptiness.

She walked for hours, crossing the land with ease, when a scream filled her head. Her keen ears pinpointed the sound, and she turned towards it, her hair flying backwards. She could hear the terror and fear that made up the sound. It was followed by a gunshot. She smiled and began to run towards it. There was blood being spilled somewhere close, and she intended to get her share.

Tony and Jack had gone out that night with their intention fixed clearly in their minds. It wasn't about stealing - although if they saw something that would fetch a decent price without being conspicuous, they'd take it; after all, they weren't stupid. It was the thrill of it all, the excitement, that they craved.

They'd circled the area in the car that they had stolen, looking for somewhere that met all of their criteria. The place had to be isolated, so that no nosy neighbours called the cops; but it also had to be on a decent road, just in case the cops showed up, so that they could get away easily. But above all, it had to feel right. If they even sensed that there could be trouble, they'd forget it. They trusted their instincts, and then let everything fall where it fell.

It was Tony who always led, and that was only right - he was the eldest. It was Tony who had stolen their father's shotgun. It was Tony who had stolen the car. And it was Tony who had chosen the farmhouse.

It had only taken one hit before the door buckled and opened and then they'd moved quickly. The light had been on upstairs, they'd seen it from outside, so that was where they went.

But the one thing that they didn't expect, the one thing that had never happened before, had happened. The man, the aging bloke who now sat cowering in the corner with his arm around his missus, had seen the car pull up outside the house.

Unaware that they had already been spotted, they'd walked up the stairs and to the only room that had a light on. The door was open and the pinkish light from a lamp had spilled out onto the landing. And they'd just walked in.

That, Jack thought, as he cradled his injured arm, black and grey dots dancing across his vision, had been their mistake. They'd gotten cocky from all the other jobs, and they'd walked straight into the room. And the woman had leapt out from behind the door, brandishing the knife.

So, now here he was, hardly able to stand, his stomach churning so much that he thought he might throw up any second, with a hole in his arm. And he knew it was serious. He was pressing down as hard as he could, but the blood was still gushing out from between the small gaps in his fingers.

And what was his big brother doing? The bloke who had promised their parents that he would look after the 'baby' of the family? The bloke that had ordered the oldish couple to strip, had bound them, and had then cut the woman using her own knife before shooting at the wall above their heads? Why, he was *laughing*! Laughing and enjoying the hell out of it all, while his little brother was steadily bleeding to death.

Jack heard a sound from out on the landing, a low animal growl. His mind fixed on a word, although he had no idea what it meant: Guttural. And it felt right to him. That was what the sound was, guttural. But he dismissed it. If they'd had a dog, it would have started barking when they'd first gotten into the house. So, he ignored it, and went back to concentrating on not passing out.

It had only taken Ania a few minutes to reach the house, her senses guiding her towards the blood. There was a pale light on in one of the upstairs rooms and she guessed that that was where all the excitement was. She rounded the corner of the house, and immediately saw the state of the door.

The smell of blood was stronger as she walked into the house and began to climb the stairs, and her body cried out for it - she hadn't fed yet, and the killer side of her began to awaken. She trailed her hand softly over the banister as she ascended, her feet making no noise as moved.

She walked along the landing, nearing the room. She glanced inside, and was pleasantly surprised when she could see into the room without having to get too close. There were mirrors built into the wall, covering wardrobe doors, and she could see everything.

She could see the couple that were cringing in a corner, both completely naked. Their wrists were bound together with what looked to be garden twine. The woman had a cut in the dip between her two large breasts, and blood had trickled down to her equally-large stomach. But she knew that that was not the blood she could smell. No, the blood that she could smell belonged to the boy, no older than twenty, that was swaying on his feet. His skin was pale, with a touch of grey, and he was obviously struggling to stay conscious.

But her attention fell almost immediately to the man who stood with a sick smile on his face. He was older than the other boy, but only by a couple of years, and he held a shotgun.

And it was the smile that she focused on.

She felt her hunger being pushed aside as her true-self, her *animal* self, began to edge forwards, and she gave in to it. In situations like this, she had learnt that the animal part of her was a lot better at acting swiftly and without thought.

There was nothing she hated more than people who killed and tortured for no reason. She was a killer, she had no illusions about what she was. But the deaths of her victims were only a means to her own survival, a natural life-cycle. She didn't kill for the sake of it. And she definitely didn't torture anyone. Not anymore.

Her thoughts were becoming dulled and her senses sharpened. And she welcomed it.

There it was again! There was that sound again! There was no way that Jack could ignore it now. It was closer and louder and a lot more dangerous than before. He was beginning to faint, he knew he was - the spots in front of his eyes had tripled, and they were moving a lot faster. It was almost as if he was becoming sea sick.

He heard that growl again, that low, harsh throaty sound, and in a flash of understanding he knew that it was neither animal nor human, but something in between the two.

From the corner of his eye, he saw a dark shape lunging through the air, knocking his brother onto the floor in front of him. Almost immediately, he felt himself being lifted from the ground and had time to glance a marble-white face, ugly yet intensely beautiful, as the creature moved its mouth closer to his neck. Pain ripped through his throat and he felt warmth rushing down the side of his neck. Then he knew no more.

Tony came to and the first thing that he was aware of, other than the pounding in his head, was how sick he felt. His stomach was churning and every time he moved his head the sickness increased.

Moving slowly, stopping every time he felt too close to throwing up, he got to his knees and raised his head. He saw the couple, still in the corner, but there was something different about them. They still looked scared, he could almost smell it on them. In fact, as he looked closer, they looked more scared than they had been when he was pointing a gun at them. But that wasn't what was different. They were still bound, although he couldn't see the bindings because-

Because there was a sheet over them both, covering most of their bodies. He started to get angry, despite how ill he was feeling.

Who the hell had covered them up?! He thought that it was Jack, *had* to have been, but that wasn't right. The kid would follow him to hell if he was told to. No, it had to be someone else.

He looked carefully at the couple in front of him. Yeah, they were scared, alright; their eyes were huge in their pale faces, and they were staring at something. But not at him. They were staring at something *behind* him.

Pain flooded his already hurt head as the person behind him grabbed him by the hair. He screamed loudly as he was dragged backwards, small clumps of his hair being ripped out by the roots. The last thing he saw as he was pulled out of the room was the discarded mound of blood soaked clothes. Despite the pain, he was able to recognise the clothes as his brother's. And, by the looks of things, his *late*-brother's.

He marvelled at the strength of the guy that was pulling him along the landing. It had to be a guy, he had no doubt about that. No woman could have that much strength, especially combined with the speed that they were moving. But his thoughts stopped abruptly when his already-pounding head had to endure the pain of him being pulled down the stairs.

The wind hit him as soon as he was taken outside, where he was flung to the ground. He lay where he was for the time being, concentrating solely on not vomiting. Slowly, he looked up.

In the darkness before him stood a woman, and despit everything, he had to suppress a grin. The bloke who had pulled hir down the stairs must have run into the shadows, or maybe back int the house, leaving this woman - a *woman!* - to look after herself.

Wavering on unsteady legs, he stood. Using every ounce of determination that he had, he forced himself to stop his drunken swaying. He regarded her for a minute, smiling his arrogant smile.

His smile fell when the woman, who had been standing about twenty feet away from him, was suddenly in front of him, so clos that he could see the hard whiteness of her skin.

She smiled, and her gums lifted enough for him to see the bloodstained teeth, the incredibly *sharp* bloodstained teend underneath. But still he wasn't scared. There was nothing that woman could do that could hurt him. Maybe if the bloke who h dragged him downstairs turned up again then he might have so trouble. But not now.

stupid little minds, let them shout, let them scream. She would let them do all of that, but they would have to direct it at her back - she refused to let them see the reaction on her face.

Footsteps crunched over the loose stones of the road, and she could tell from the uneven movement that it was Maria walking towards her.

"Your parents are freaks, Ania." Maria whispered, aiming her comments to the head hidden by the long thick black hair. "Your parents are freaks. And you're a freak just like them."

Ania felt something burning inside of her, something that was totally unknown to her (although she would get used to it, would relish it, and would use it as her most valuable weapon in the centuries and millennia to come). It boiled and seethed amongst her blood, forcing her to breathe harder to control it. The anger that she had denied herself from feeling through all of the years of mockery and cruelty, of always being shunned, of always being alone, was finally making its presence known, the adrenaline it produced rising swiftly in her body. And she liked it.

"We'll make your life a misery, Ania," Maria continued, not realising the real danger she was putting herself in. Not realising that she had begun to push the girl too far. "We'll make you wish that they had dragged you dead from the womb."

Ania turned quickly, her long black hair that was bound with a white ribbon whipping back behind her, and she looked at Maria, who stepped backwards, fear and uncertainty rising in her eyes. Ania regarded her for a minute, a hard smile appearing on her lips, the anger and menace clear in her blue-grey eyes, and she stepped slowly towards Maria.

For every step Ania took, Maria compensated by taken a step backwards. Ania stopped and just stared at the girl in front of her, the girl whose vanity had possessed her to make her nothing but a breathing doll.

Still smiling that dangerous smile, Ania began to whisper. "I hope you remember those words that have just passed your lips, Maria. Because they're going to have real meaning to you soon."

Maria's forehead creased in puzzlement, but what Ania said was remembered. And remembered too well.

The adrenaline began to leave her now and Ania felt the old feelings of insecurity begin to edge in once more, pushing the anger out of her. She saw over Maria's shoulder that Katherine, who had missed everything said, was beginning to walk over and knew that it was time for her to take her leave.

She turned her back on the two girls, one who still looked amused and the other who looked bewildered, and began to make her way out of the town and to her own home.

Ania sat quietly as her parents took their dishes to the sink. She said nothing, and nothing was said to her. It was the same way most evenings. Her mother, as usual, gave Ania a look of aversion as she and her husband walked towards the cellar door, and her father glanced at her only once, and it was devoid of any emotion.

She waited until she heard the door close before gathering her own things and taking them to the sink. She would wash them later, long after her parents had finished their rituals in the cellar and retired to bed. In the mean time she had a little while to wait before she could escape.

Once she heard movements below cease, meaning that they were well into their ceremony, Ania walked out of the house, closing the door quietly as she left.

She knew what her mother thought, knew that she believed Ania to be a disappointment to the family. After all, her mother wasn't shy about telling her that. In fact, she used it at every available chance, dropping it into almost every rare conversation. The fact that Ania wasn't a mystic like the rest of her family had been for generations, in her mother's eyes, meant that Ania was a disgrace. Her father, who had at least two generations of mystics in his own family, obviously felt the same. Although to give him a bit of credit, he didn't mention it half as much as Ania's mother did.

It was a cold night, but Ania didn't mind. The half-formed moons hung high in the night sky, and Ania felt her breath stolen as she looked up upon their beautiful faces while stars sparkled everywhere.

She loved the night, which is why she was so keen to disobey her parents on the only order they had ever given her. They had told her that she was not allowed out after the last of the sun's rays had disappeared from the sky, although they had never told her why. But she loved the night, it offered her a little hope in her life, and she'd be damned if she let them take away the only bit of comfort she had *ever felt.*

Plus, she had another little secret, and it was only in the night that she could explore it. Her parents thought that she wasn't a mystic, the people of the village weren't sure, but as she walked through the dark, her white dress stirring the long grass as she walked towards the woods, she could let her secret out, could admit it to the silent, deserted night-time world without fear of reprisals and accusations. Could admit what she was. She was a mystic, a witch, a magickal. She could see the future and decipher it, and travel to places she had never seen in the flesh, could travel without her body.

That she could do these things didn't scare her, nor did the idea that she was still learning the extent of her powers. What did scare her was the idea of people finding out. She didn't want to be rejected further by the people of the village. Nor did she want her parents knowing when all her life she had been rejected by them as well. If she told them, they would welcome her with open arms, and Ania knew that somehow the sudden acceptance would be worse than the constant rejection. Because they would be welcoming her powers and not her.

But as she walked into the woods, travelling amongst the trees, where the limited moonlight wasn't able to infiltrate, she felt all of these things just melt away: they ceased to matter, ceased to have any importance. She was living in her own world, the world in which she really belonged. As she moved further and further towards her special place she started to become the person she was always meant to be: there was no fear in her heart, no need to be accepted - the night had always made her feel welcome and had never turned her away. She felt herself becoming stronger, her sense of peace and contentment filling her to almost bursting point. There was nothing in the night that could take any of it away from her.

And there it was, in front of her, the place where her powers seemed to increase three-fold. The pool lay in a clearing and the moons were able to shine through the break in the trees, filling the pool with their light. She walked to its edge, stopping with the tips of her toes touching the water.

Knowing that she was alone, that no one ever came out here, especially in the dark, she felt no sense of shame or embarrassment. Slowly, she unbuttoned her white dress, letting the silky material fall onto the ground, then slipped out of her underwear. Her hands unwound the white ribbon that bound her hair and the black strands fell onto her soft shoulders.

The water was cold and it stole her breath away as she waded into the depths of the pool. She went deeper so that it covered her shoulders and she felt her heart speeding up. Holding her breath, she ducked quickly underneath the water, feeling her hair being lifted. After a few moments, she lifted her head up so that it was out of the water and she felt almost warm. She knew that that was impossible given the temperature of the water, but it was true all the same.

The moons were reflected on the surface of the water, and light drifted downwards. Ania looked at it in amazement - it was like bathing in pure light. She turned her attention upwards and gazed at the moons properly, seeing faces in the light. As she looked upon them, wishing for nothing but the peace she now felt, she asked the moons about her future and felt her eyes growing heavy almost immediately, but she didn't feel tired. She knew that there was something that she was to be shown, something that she had to see.

She closed her eyes, and let that eye inside her mind open wide to let the images in.

If anyone had happened upon her, the beautiful young woman lying naked in cold water, her eyes closed, they may have thought her to be dead. Would anyone have helped, even been worried? It was doubtful. There was no one who knew her, knew of her and her family, that would have been willing to interfere.

She remained that way for almost an hour, seeing the image that had been sent to her. It added to her comfort, and she opened her eyes with a smile on her face. What she had seen wasn't in any great detail, but for Ania, it was enough. Darkness was her life, her destiny and that had been the vision of her future: pure darkness, an endless night. And to her, that sounded perfect.

It was a month after her confrontation with Maria and Katherine, and Ania walked around the market without fear of any more trouble. Maria had more pressing matters on her mind.

Just as Ania's mother had predicted, Maria had lost her son. He had been born early, very small and weak, and had become ill. He had survived for almost two days, but the illnesses that had *worked their way into him had eventually taken him over.*

The thing that seemed the most strange, though, was that she had hardly seen Maria and Katherine together. The usually inseparable pair had been seen together only once, and that was less than pleasant. Katherine had approached Maria, but Maria had looked at her with such hatred that Katherine had left again in a hurry.

Ania stood at a stall, looking at some purple material that would be perfect for a new dress, when a soft and dejected voice spoke just behind her.

"Hello, Ania."

Slowly she turned around. Ania was not used to people talking to her, and she couldn't remember the last time that someone had approached *her for no apparent reason. She was more shocked when she saw who it was.*

Maria was a mess. Her dark blonde hair hung lankly to her shoulders, her skin was pale and covered in terrible spots, and dark circles surrounded her eyes. Her clothes were loose on her body, and she just looked terrible. She looked nothing like the girl who had tormented her only a month earlier.

"Hello, Maria." She looked down, as was the custom. "I am sorry for you loss, Maria. May the Gods protect you at this time. I offer my sympathy to you." She looked up, and met the woman's eyes.

A sad smile played on Maria's lips and she looked at Ania with understanding. "Thank you, Ania."

The silence was awkward, and Ania knew that there was something that Maria wanted to say. She was tempted to break the silence herself, to prompt Maria to say whatever it was, just to end the unusual exchange sooner. But she knew, despite her limited experience with people, that some things couldn't be rushed.

Maria's face was flushed, but she forced herself to look at Ania anyway, her fingers gently touching the cloth that Ania was holding. "I'm sorry for the way I've treated you, Ania. There was no need to hurt you like that. Please accept my apology."

Ania was stunned, and for a moment was unable to speak. Finally she found the words. "I accept you apology, and with thanks."

Maria nodded and turned away. Before she went, she looked

back. "That colour would look lovely on you, Ania."

Ania stood completely still, unable to move, or to even comprehend what had just happened. She watched the young woman walk away, her head lowered and feet shuffling on the ground. Ania was taken aback, but once Maria was out of sight, she felt more comfortable. She looked again at the material she had been admiring and realised that Maria was right - it would suit her very well.

Once she had purchased the material that she had chosen, and after gathering the few things that her parents needed, Ania began to walk back home. It was a long walk, over countryside that had begun to turn more colourful with the onset of winter. It was beginning to get dark, and she added more haste to her movements - it was fine to sneak out in the dark without her parents' knowledge but to arrive home after the sun had set would only lead to confrontation, and she didn't want that.

She approached The Wall, the broken down bricks that bordered the small town - even though her home was still acknowledged as being in the town, technically it wasn't, laying just outside.

As she was climbing over it, holding the skirt of her dress up so that it wouldn't become dirty, a scream flooded the air and she froze, one leg in the town proper and one leg on the land that had no real name. The hairs all over her body were stood on end, and her heart was beating heavily in her chest.

She knew where those screams had come from, had even seen glimpses of the house once, but had no intention of investigating. No one knew the person who lived there, and only rumours confirmed that it was a man - only friends-of-friends had ever been known to catch glimpses of him, no one willing to admit that they had been anywhere near.

She waited for a few moments, counting to a hundred before swinging her other leg onto 'her' side of The Wall. The evening had grown still and the silence unnerved her. She had been taught to read the signs of nature when she was younger, and knew that the eeriness that she could feel meant that an evil had been committed.

She knew that her parents would also have heard the scream, so she started to run, returning home quicker than she had planned, *the rays of the sun still illuminating the ground below.*

Her father sat at the table while her mother stood at the stove, cooking their supper. Ania greeted her parents and wasn't shocked or upset to receive only a single nod from her father as a response. Her arms felt lighter once she had unloaded her packages onto the small table by the door. Carefully, she lifted her own packages, including the fabric that she had decided to buy, and carried them up to her room.

It was simple, with nothing but a bed in the centre and a small desk and chair by the window, but it was filled with the warmth of the setting sun. As night fell it would grow cold, but there was a small fireplace that was ready to be lit when it turned too chilly.

She put the packages on her bed and unwrapped the material, a beautiful shade of dark purple. She held it against her body, closing her eyes so that she could picture how it would look on her, and twirled around slowly. As she began to lower it, to drape it across the length of her bed, she felt something prick her finger.

She looked down at her hand, and saw a small bead of blood forming on the pad of her middle finger. Curious about what could possibly have caused it, she looked down at the material. Reflecting the fading light, she saw something sharp and metal. She looked closer and saw a pin. She saw that the material looked a little strange, a little thicker on the other side, so she turned the material over.

The pin she had pricked herself on attached a small piece of white paper, barely three inches across. She freed it from the material, placing the pin on her desk before unfolding the paper.

There, in writing that was elegant, yet strangely childlike, her own name stared at her.

> *Ania.*
> *I wish to speak to you.*
> *Please meet me at The*
> *Wall, two hours after the*
> *night falls. I will understand*
> *if you decide not to.*
> *With Deep Regards.*
> *Maria.*

Ania read the small message about a dozen times before the reality of it was able to sink in to her mind. Maria wanted to meet her? Maria wanted to speak to her? The whole idea was so strange, the fact that someone would actually want to spend time with her, it just couldn't be real.

Yet she held the note in her hand, held it with a finger that was still seeping blood from the pinprick. It was this that forced her mind to accept it - the red spot on her finger.

Her heart felt heavy yet light at the same time. The idea of a trap crossed her mind - that maybe Maria and Katherine would be waiting together, meaning to hurt her somehow - but she refused to think of it. She would go, and she would wait in the shadows. She would see who arrived, and then she would decide what to do.

The gloomy part of her thoughts left her with that decision having been made, and she looked at the material once more. She hid the note underneath it, knowing that her mother and father never ventured into her room any more than necessary, but wanting to make sure that if they did they wouldn't happen upon it. She walked down the stairs to join her parents for supper feeling happier than she could ever have imagined.

Supper seemed to drag on for longer than normal and Ania knew that it was because she was anxious to take her leave. With the usual silence filling the house, her parents speaking little and of things that Ania was unfamiliar with, she felt a knot forming in her stomach and worries began to form in her mind. Would her parents venture into the cellar tonight, leaving her to roam on her own? She knew the answer, and it was a silly thing to worry about - her parents went into the cellar every evening, and always for a long time - but her mind had fixed on one thing that could go wrong, and refused to let it go.

When the meal was finally finished (and, although it amazed Ania when she realised it, sooner than normal) and the dishes were tidied away ready to be cleaned, her fears washed away. With no words at all to their child, her parents left the room.

She heard the customary squeak of the cellar door as it opened and closed. She rushed immediately to her room, and stripped her gown off. As quickly as she could, she donned another ensemble, complete with cloak and hood, and went into the night.

With the dark as her only consort, hidden inside clothes bearing the same colour as the night - a colour that she was, as yet, unaccustomed to wearing - she stole off into the dark, feeling free.

She approached The Wall by a different path, keeping the promise that she had made herself to judge the situation before deciding on what action to take. So, it took longer than it should have for the main path to come into sight. And when it did, her heart leapt upwards. All of her fears, it seemed, were completely unfounded.

Maria sat on the stones of The Wall, gazing off into the distance, looking as she had earlier that day: unkempt, uncared for, humbled, and lonely. Lonely was not a word that Ania had ever thought of in connection with the self-centred and vicious Maria. But circumstances had a way of changing things.

And it was because of this word that all-but loomed in Ania's mind and heart that took her to stand in front of the girl who had suffered such a terrible tragedy.

Maria looked both shocked and pleased to see the girl in front of her, and Ania felt another touch of panic. Not for any other reason except that she had never spent any real time with another person, child or adult, and had no idea of how to begin. So she said the thing that still filled her with a touch of wonder.

"I received your note."

Maria shocked both of them when, out of happiness that things had gone the way she'd hoped, jumped off of The Wall, and threw her arms around the girl that she had always ridiculed.

Ania, with closed eyes, felt her heart not only jump, but fly, higher than she had ever known it to. And it is this moment that she would always think of, every day in the years of her torture, lying on the cold hard ground of a maniac's home, while her body screamed out in pain. It is this moment that she would remember, feeling sick with humiliation, hatred growing and burning inside of her, a fire that was insatiable. It was this moment that paved the way for her future.

It was three weeks since their first meeting, and Ania had felt her happiness soar to new heights. It didn't matter what her friend had asked of her, she was just glad to have a friend. And Maria understood that, although Ania couldn't help personally, her parents *may be willing to.*

Ania wished more than anything that she could help Maria speak to her son, but since she had no experience with things like that, Ania knew that it could be dangerous to even attempt it. No, it would be better if her parents were the ones to contact the dead boy. She would ask them; not tonight - they might get suspicious about what she did while they were in the cellar - but tomorrow, when she returned from the market. Yes, tomorrow would be fine.

The night was uncommonly warm, giving the fact that End of Year was close and Ania prolonged her walk, strolling to take full advantage of the darkness. Her black cloak moved delicately around her ankles and she allowed the hood to drop, exposing her hair to the breeze. Surely there had never been a night like this one.

She felt nothing wrong as she approached her home, maybe the combination of her happiness and the pleasant night dulling her typically-keen senses, and she opened the door quietly.

She allowed the latch to drop silently into its catch and walked into the kitchen, removing her cloak.

Her hands felt cold, numb, and the cloak drifted to the floor as she came to a halt. Seated at the supper table were her parents, their characteristically inanimate faces now filled with fury. Ania could make no sound and her mind was wiped empty at their expressions, the only thing she was capable of thinking was a short sentence: The unthinkable has happened.

Her mother rose slowly from her seat and approached Ania with deadly-silent ease. With no hesitation and no warning she moved her arm backwards and struck out.

Ania was knocked backwards, her cheek stinging from the force of her mother's open palm. Her eyes brimmed with tears, but when they fell it was not from pain, physical or emotional, but with her own anger.

"Faithless child!" Her mother proclaimed, but with a peculiar dull tone to her voice. "That you should disobey the one rule we have ever given you!" She turned to her husband, who had not moved a single muscle.

"What did we do that we have such an insolent child?" She turned back to her descendant without giving him a chance to reply. "The disgrace on both our families, we have learnt to live with, a child with none of the gifts that our ancestors bestowed on us cannot

be cast aside purely for their lack of talents."

At this, Ania's blood began to boil, and yet her mother was not finished, so she bit her tongue.

"But a child who cannot obey a rule which would keep her safe, to live the life she has been given, is unthinkable. Not only are you a stain on our family, but ungrateful with it!"

She began to move away, but Ania, her temper at its peak, grabbed her mother's arm, the first time she had ever done anything against her parents. In her mind she recalled every time that her 'lack of gifts' had been mentioned with scorn, every time she had been made to feel unimportant and unworthy of her heritage. With a strength that she had never shown before, she whirled her mother around to face her once more, the eldest woman's eyes wide in amazement.

"Do not speak to me in that way, Mother. I will not endure it a moment longer."

Both of her parents looked at her as if they had never seen her before - and really, they never had.

"I have lived with your disapproval all of my life and will not live this way anymore. The gifts that you think are missing from me are here, right in front of you. And your own cannot be as powerful as you believe if you have not seen them." Ania didn't want to give her parents any chance to react to this bit of news, so she continued, dropping her mother's arm.

"The night is the one constant pleasure in my life and I'll not allow any to steal that from me. I have called on the night as often as I can, and will not stop now, above all when the reason for this rule is unknown."

She dropped her eyes, the anger ebbing away, leaving her feeling bleak and more alone than she ever had before. When she turned her gaze once more to her parents she spoke more softly. "My reasons for having left the safety of this house was to offer counsel to Maria Lhunder, she whose child died as you predicted. She wished for me to contact her son, but I am unable."

Her mother opened her mouth to speak, but it was Ania's father who spoke, lifting himself from his chair in order to stand next to his wife.

"That girl," he said, speaking as softly as his daughter had, no anger in his voice now, only a tiredness that seemed ageless.

"She is not to be trusted."

He raised a hand when both of the women of his home began to interrupt. "Allow me this."

He looked at Ania, and her heart nearly broke. There were tears in his eyes, and something else, something that she had never seen there before – a tentative love. Tears began to form in her own eyes and she nodded at him to continue.

"It is clear that you believe her to be a friend, Ania, but she is not. The reasons we have for you to stay away from the night and for staying away from Maria Lhunder are one and the same. She will lead you to darkness, but it is a darkness from which there can be no salvation. It is endless and timeless.

"You wish to help her with the death of her son, but if you do, you lead us to suffer the same fate as she has. If you continue your meetings with her, as she has lost a son we should lose a daughter. And no matter what you would believe of us, there is not a worse fate for us to have to endure."

Ania looked at her parents, the only family she had ever known, with new eyes, and yet she fought against what her father was saying, but not out loud.

"We cannot lose you, child. And so I ask of you, if not for your own safety, then for the survival of those who stand before you. Have no more contact with that girl, and if the darkness calls to you, fight against it."

Having never heard her father speak so to her before, Ania felt compelled to agree. But she secretly swore to herself that she would have to take her own counsel on the matter.

It was unimaginable to her, but the brief flash of lightning within her normally-docile home seemed to make the air clearer, easier to breathe. The three family members, who had not spent a night together since Ania had begun to leave her childhood, seated themselves around the supper table and talked. They talked until the sky began to lighten with the sun, and Ania slept soundly, with complete ease, when they finally retired to their rooms.

When she awoke, the day long past its midpoint, she remembered all that had been said that night, and decided to honour her parents. She would keep away from Maria. As for the night, she would decide on that when it next beckoned her.

As the night of End of Year came, Ania felt conflicted once more. In her heart, she knew that she should keep the promise she had made to her family, but her pride - and also the rebellious streak in her nature - made her want to go against them.

Maria had passed the note to her secretly, knowing instinctively that there had to be a reason for Ania not contacting her, and Ania had kept it hidden until she was safely closed off in her room. Once there she sat at her desk and carefully unfolded the note.

> Ania.
> I understand if you cannot meet me anymore
> (I sense that my request may have caused
> conflict within your home), but I
> wish to see you one last time, one more
> meeting of our friendship. Please meet me
> tonight, as the night reaches its peak. Go to
> The Wall, where we usually meet, and turn
> east. Follow the path of The Wall for two miles.
> Because of what lies farther in that direction,
> no one dares ventures that far, and we shall
> not be seen. Please, I beg of you.
> Your friend,
> Maria.

Ania felt her will torn in two. Things had changed for her recently and she had to make a choice. Did she go against her parents one last time and meet Maria, a girl who had, until of late, shown her nothing but vicious ridicule? Or did she obey her parents, who had always looked upon her as a disappointment, and lose someone she now called a friend.

She looked out of her window, as the streaks of light began to loosen their hold on the world to give way to the darker shades of night and she felt her decision made. The night was calling for her, and she wasn't strong enough to resist. It was a call that she had to answer.

And really, she thought to herself, a girl who was in most respects a woman, having lived her twenty turns of the seasons in almost-complete solitude. As long as my parents do not discover me disobeying, there can be no real harm. They are not always right.

So, for the last time, Ania began to wait out the day.

The rain was pouring down upon her, the hood of her cloak barely keeping her head dry, and she trudged her way towards The Wall. The sound of the rain attacking all that was in its path was all around her, almost deafening. She could hear nothing else above its noise.

The ground was wet and slippery but Ania had a natural grace in her movements, and sidestepped all of the slight obstacles that she found in her way. After what seemed like an eternity of walking, she reached the stones and turned obediently towards the east. Though the rain was still falling fast she was still able to see a great deal ahead of her, but the dark seemed darker in that direction.

She smiled to herself, doubting her own senses, reassuring herself that it was only because of what she knew to be in that direction, that her mind was playing its tricks on her. Had she heeded her own feelings, she may well have changed the direction of her destiny. But she moved towards that darker darkness, holding her head as high as the rain would allow.

Yet still, as she neared the two mile distance that Maria had given her, her heart began to understand what her mind refused that there was something amiss, something very wrong, and her steps began to falter. There was no sign of Maria, and the whole world was quiet; even the rain, although it fell at the same pace, seemed somehow muted.

Ania began to think about turning back, of just retracing her steps until she was safely home. Just as she was beginning to do just that, she heard her name being called.

She turned again to see Maria and her heart fell. There was something wrong - the appearance of her 'friend' was the last piece of proof that she needed.

As she looked at Maria, her father's words resounded in her mind. It is clear that you believe her to be a friend, Ania, but she is not. She will lead you to darkness.

Maria stood before her, her hair tidy and her clothes immaculate despite the weather. Her eyes were wide and full of contempt and her lips curled into a smile that would have looked fitting on an ill-tempered animal, one that is ready to bite.

trying to prove Maria's ignorance. It was clear from the woman's eyes what the response would be, so Ania kept quiet.

"Well, my 'friend', I'd better show you where your punishment will be coming from." Maria reached her hand out and grabbed Ania's face, her perfectly-kept nails digging into the soft flesh of Ania's cheeks, and made Ania look to the left of the clearing.

In the dark that was too-dark, Ania could see the tumbled-down house. The size was difficult to judge because of the trees that almost hid it, but Ania had the feeling that it was vast. And not one part of it looked inviting. Close to the front, she could see a closed door, dark and old, rot having eaten away most of the frame.

Maria laughed strangely, and in the darkness that emitted from that mostly-concealed building, Ania was sure that she heard something equally as insane quietly answer.

Maria let go and looked at the blood on her fingers. She held them close to Ania's face so that Ania could smell the fragrance of her own blood.

"Blood for blood, Ania."

In a twirl of sophisticated clothes drenched by the rain, Maria and Katherine left, leaving Ania alone.

Once they had passed out of sight, Ania began to experiment with her bindings, trying to tease them, trying to find some give in the shackles that held her. It took her a moment to notice that the door to the house, that had stood closed when she had first looked upon it, now stood open, revealing a dense blackness inside.

Sweat began to seep through her skin. Something had opened that door. Something had either gone in or come out. And Ania felt sure that it had been the latter. And that something had just moved, she'd heard it. Something close by, something moving almost silently.

Ania gasped as a flick of white rushed past her, leaving a lingering smell of decayed flesh in its wake. Her calmness had passed and she knew that she had to - had to - get out of her chains. There was something, some thing, *out here with her, and she had no illusions that it was anything other than the disaster that her parents had feared. Whatever this thing was, whatever this place was, it was to lead to darkness. A darkness that would never hold any comfort for her.*

The white thing was in front of her, gagging her with its

odour of putrid flesh, and she had time to glance at a marble-white complexion and eyes that danced with death and madness, before it struck, and pain like a million wasps set upon her neck.

She screamed a silent scream and then drowned in the night.

When Holly awoke, a scream held in check so as not to wake her lover, the images were still clear in her mind.

She had been bound to a tree, a chain wrapped tightly around her waist and her wrists held above her head. She and the tree had stood as one in the centre of a clearing, where only darkness entered. A feeling of despair had overcome her at the sight of an open door, and then terror engulfed her at the sound of movement around her.

It was then that she had woken, trembling, with tears lightly coursing down her cheeks. She knew instinctively that she was seeing what Ania was dreaming, and that it was not a dream but a memory.

Needing comfort, she turned and reached out for Michael, and her fear doubled instead of subsiding. Apart from herself, the bed was empty.

Still shaking slightly, she stood and walked downstairs. In the kitchen Michael sat at the table, looking out of the window, into the darkness of the night. At her approach he turned to look at her, and she saw something that she was not accustomed to seeing in his eyes - uncertainty.

"Michael?" She sat next to him, reaching for his hand. "Michael, what is it? What's wrong?"

Michael smiled, forcing the anxiety out of his eyes. "Probably nothing, Holly." He raised her hand and kissed it, meeting her eyes to try and put her at ease - and trying to put himself at ease.

The truth was, he didn't *know* what was wrong. But there was something, a feeling at the base of his spine, telling him that there was *something* wrong, something that wasn't quite right. He'd woken feeling cold, as if an ice-cold hand had touched him, and he knew that there was danger around. A danger that Ania had warned him of, a danger that Holly must be protected from.

As they dressed ready for their night of feeding, Michael tried to keep his mind clear of his worries, knowing that Holly would pick up on them without trying, but it was difficult. And when they ventured out into the night, that cold-feeling in his spine increased, as if someone was pressing a heavy weight against him.

When they separated, each pursuing their own victims, Michael stood for a few moments watching Holly, trying to understand the danger that he felt. Hidden in the shadows of an alley-way, he'd watched Holly approach a man, young and handsome, and he closed his mind to the bustle of the streets. He blocked out the noise, the talking, the movement, focussing completely on Holly. Although he was not sure, he felt that Holly was safe, that the threat that he was being consumed by wasn't against her.

Once Holly disappeared from sight, taking the young man whose life-span had become dramatically changed away from the crowds, Michael walked back into the streets, passing people without looking at them. He had to feed, the need was there, as always, but it wasn't insatiable yet - and he felt that it was safer to wait.

The feeling, whatever it was, was beginning to frustrate him, making his senses dull, allowing nothing but itself to be noticed. He walked along the pavements, leaving the crowd behind, finding himself in a maze of residential streets, and he allowed his feet to take him where they would, giving in to the instincts that had led him through most of his life, both natural and unnatural.

As he twisted and turned through the endless streets, the sensation began to subside and was soon replaced by the growing appetite. It was dangerous to choose a victim in a place like this, dangerous because he would be more noticeable talking to someone - people were sure to remember him approaching someone, but with the feeling of danger now having passed, he was left solely with the need he had known of for a long time.

Yet as he looked around, the pavements glistening in the rain, bouncing off the light from the street-lamps, he realised that he had no choice but to return to the town; there was not another soul around.

He began to walk back the way he had come, waiting for that sense of caution to overtake him again, but it didn't return.

Ania opened her eyes, feeling drained. Whenever her memories consumed her that way, she always felt the same - tired, restless, uneasy, and afraid. Afraid of what, she didn't know - it was most likely that it was all residue from the memories of how she'd felt before being turned. As she sat on the cold crypt floor, her back resting against the damp walls, the world around her dark, trying hard to block out the images that she had relived, her body began to burn with the somehow pleasant hunger.

She sensed that it was time to leave this house of the dead and find that one thing that could make her feel alive. Still feeling weak (although the prospect of blood had awoken her sufficiently), she got to her feet and waited for a bout of dizziness to pass. When her head had stopped spinning she walked to the mausoleum door. As she reached towards it a cold hand pressed itself against her back; this indication of something not quite right was pushed aside and ignored. It was true that she had never felt this bad before, but her hunger was becoming insatiable, clawing and clamouring to be fed. If she had looked passed it, looked for the hidden meaning, the pain that was to follow may have been averted, but her hunger had dulled every one of her senses; she swung the door open wide.

She shrieked as the midday sun burnt into the skin on the left side of her body, and she backed into the shadows of the crypt, looking at the rays of sunlight as they fell halfway into the entrance. Her face and neck burned, pain biting into her, attacking her. Knowing what was to be done, knowing that there was only thing she could do, she quickly stretched her arm back into the sunlight, fighting against the pain, and grabbed hold of the door. She pulled it back, closing the sun off, plunging the mausoleum back into blessed darkness once more.

Making sure that the door was secure, and distantly hoping that no one had seen the crypt open or heard her screams, she sank to the floor, howling silently, tears of agony coursing down her face. Her whole body was shaking, and the more she moved the more she became aware of the pain.

Her right hand trembled as she reached it up to touch her face. First it touched the right-hand side, feeling the cold-smoothness, touching the wetness of her tears. Then, mind hardened at what she expected to feel, she moved her hand to the part of her face that had been exposed to the day. Her fingers rasped against the burnt skin, as if they were touching sand-paper rather than skin. Pain, which had begun to be more bearable, reared up once more. Ania bit down on her bottom lip, but she ignored the blood that started to fill her mouth.

Dropping her hand, she saw something dark on her white fingers. It looked like soot, or burnt paper, but she knew that it was her skin, skin that had flaked off of her face as she had touched it.

She moved slightly, so that her back was resting against the damp, cold walls of the crypt and simply sat there, feeling the pain abating, looking at nothing but the wall in front of her, concentrating all of her will on making the pain fade to nothing.

Once this was accomplished, the pain hidden so far back in her mind that she could ignore it, she raised her two hands so that they were in front of her face. One was marble-white, smooth and unblemished by age or time; the other was a blackened mess, skin rough and burnt. She looked at the contrast between the two for what seemed an age, moving them this way and that, letting her brain take it all in.

She had never slept through the night before - not even in the early years of her unnatural life had she ever not woken to the night's call. As she pondered this, the pain now a distant memory, something else began to awaken again. It had been more than thirty hours since she had last fed, probably more like thirty-five, and her hunger was growing rapidly within her, demanding loudly to be heard. But there was nothing to feed on, not for hours yet, when the sun had set.

Ania began to breathe heavily, the walls of the mausoleum seeming to draw closer together, the amount of space being squeezed so that she felt as though the walls would soon close together, squashing her. It was an illusion, just a bout of claustrophobia, she *knew* that, but the knowledge did nothing to ease her mind; in fact it actually seemed to make it worse.

So she sat, her body shaking from a thirst that could not be quenched, from pain that was still there, and from her fears that had re-awoken from her memories. Tears streaked down her face once more and for the first time in millennia she allowed the sorrow that she felt for herself engulf her.

She stepped out into the night, feeling the cold wind soothe her damaged skin. She had guessed at the time, opening the door slowly this time, feeling the relief at seeing the darkness-filled night.

She closed the crypt door, making sure that it could not be

opened by anyone other than another of her kind, and simply stood, allowing the night to fill her. But she couldn't wait for long - the hunger had increased all day, filling her so that it was all she could think of.

She had changed out of her jeans and white shirt. The damage to her face, neck and hands would prevent her from getting too close to a victim unless she used her immense speed, and she simply did not have the strength for that yet. So she had once again donned her clothes of the night, the hood of her cloak sufficiently hiding her face.

She turned on the spot, her keen ears picking up sounds of cars driving on a main road over three miles away, of people laughing in an equal distance.

There! The sound of her victims, not far, either. She could hear the soft moans of the two youngsters as they enjoyed each other's bodies, less than a hundred yards away, hidden from her view by the wall they lay behind.

Smiling, Ania began to edge closer, taking her time. There was no need to rush - let them finish their last moment's peace before she would send them into peace-eternal. With the hunger trying to force her quicker, she sat on a headstone a stone's throw away from the wall and waited. When she heard their sighs of contentment, she began edging closer, her grace and light-footedness making sure that she made no sounds.

They were unaware of her presence as she peered over the wall, too preoccupied by the comfort that they felt from the nakedness of the person next to them. Before they even had a chance to recognise that something was wrong, Ania used her speed for an instant, breaking the necks of both of them, being precise enough to ensure that their bodies still lived while ensuring that they were left unaware of anything. It was a procedure that had taken her centuries to perfect, but which came in handy for attacking multiple victims.

Without any more delay, Ania gave way to the animal part of her, allowing it to attack the bodies with ferocity, the blood pumping forcefully into her mouth. She drank deeply, draining each of them completely.

When Ania came back to herself, the animal retreating safely inside of her having been sated for another night, she covered the remains of her victims with their own blanket and walked away.

On she walked, her feet moving her without her interference, that sense of oneness with the world around her - the only world that mattered, far away from the noise of people, from the bustle of the moronic streets and the idiotic worries of her prey - was growing in her and when she stopped walking, she was more than slightly disappointed to find that she had reached a refuge.

The building, in the middle of the woods, was modern. Large glass windows ran the length of the front of the building, and a large sign hung on the glass door. The *Night Cafe* looked like a normal cafe; the floors were clean, as were the tables and counters. Food and drinks were displayed behind the counter and small dark menus sat on all the small round tables.

About a dozen people were sat in the cafe, drinks in hands, some talking in small groups, others sitting alone. Ania was glad to see that there were still three spare tables.

As she walked in, leaving the early hours of darkness outside, the bright artificial light having been dampened down a little by pink bulbs to emit a pleasant rosy glow, Ania couldn't help but smile. If anyone happened to wander in here by accident, they would probably be none the wiser, would probably be served with coffee or a snack without any problems. They would certainly be free of attack - no vampire who valued their own existence would ever draw attention to a refuge.

She settled herself at a table and as she sat there she became aware of the eyes on her. She picked up a menu, ignoring them all as they turned to stare, knowing that they saw the paleness of her skin, green in comparison to their own. She knew what they would be thinking, knew that they would continue to stare, either openly or by forcing small peeks. And she was reminded of something that that occurred to her every so often: Even amongst her own, she was an outcast.

Normally this would amuse her, and she would be tempted to do something to enhance the strangeness in herself, but tonight was different. She needed to be alone. The sense of oneness with Nature had affected her more deeply than she had first thought, and being around others would drive her close to insanity.

She looked at the menu without seeing anything written upon and simply waited to see who would approach her first.

With luck, her own and every other vampire in the cafe, a

waitress approached her first.

"I need a room to stay." She said, locking her eyes with that of the blonde-haired waitress, wanting to make sure that the order was clear.

"I..I'm..I mean, I'm not sure if we have any." The waitress stuttered, trying to pull her gaze away from the dark-haired being.

From the corner of her eye, Ania saw another approaching the table. He was dark-haired and at first looked younger than the waitress until the difference in tone of skin was noticed; his was definitely paler than the waitresses.

He touched the woman on her shoulder and she finally managed to rip her eyes from Ania's. She looked gratefully at him and walked away, a little unsteadily, not looking back.

"We have room." He said, simply, looking at Ania with obvious curiosity; and obvious anxiousness. "I'm to assume you would like to go straight away?"

Ania smiled at him and saw him relax instantly - she seemed to have that affect sometimes. "You assume correctly."

With a pleasant nod of his head and a subtle wave of his hand he indicated that she was to follow him. She stood and heard the instant hush of all within the cafe. Her shoes clicked noisily as she followed the cafe owner across the linoleum, all eyes moved eagerly with her, and her relief peaked when she saw the doorway behind the counter being opened.

Almost as soon as she was through into the white corridor and the cafe owner closed the door behind them both, the noise within the cafe suddenly exploded, as everyone began to talk about the ancient being that had just been within their midst. The owner made an apologetic smile to Ania, and she smiled in return.

"I'm sure that you're used to such a reaction." He said in a gentle voice that, perhaps a few centuries ago had a Scottish accent - now only a hint of it remained.

"Yes. It is something I have had time to become accustomed to." Although she had said it with humour, even Ania was able to notice the tiredness that had tainted the words.

"I am Iain," said the owner, his dark eyes looking deep into the woman in front of him. "If there is anything I can do to further accommodate you, madam..."

Ania smiled. "I think the room will be enough, Iain. And

thank you." Although she was doing her best to fight it, she could feel her temper rising. There was no reason other for her tiredness, but that did nothing to change what was happening. It was almost as if her soul was burning.

Iain seemed to realise a little of how she was feeling for he nodded and began to walk onwards, leading the way down a small corridor which branched off in two directions. While Ania followed, he walked down the left branch of the corridor and stood in front of a very old-fashioned door.

Made from heavy wood with large bolts holding the iron belts in place along the wood, the door would have looked perfect in a castle, where as in the white almost-sterile looking walkway it simply looked odd.

Iain pulled a thin string out from inside his shirt and lifted it over his head. Secured to the string was a very heavy key, dark with age. He held it tightly and unlocked the door.

Ania was convinced that when the door opened, the hall in front of them would be made from stone, torches lit and burning brightly to lead their way along the damp and cold corridor. She laughed and felt all of the irrational anger leaving her, and for a moment Iain joined her.

The corridor was the same as the one on her side of the door, except for the colour - pale cream walls, clean, and fresh looking. Pale pink globes hung from the cream ceiling and small delicate paintings hung on the walls.

As Iain locked the door behind them and again led the way, Ania looked at the pictures without interest - they were just pictures to cover the walls, nothing of any interest. Doors were dotted in between the pictures, modern doors with modern locks, some open and others closed, and Ania smiled again. There seemed to be absolutely no consistency to the time period in which the safe-house decided to exist.

Iain stopped outside an open door and waited for Ania to stop beside him. He reached his arm inside and flicked on a light-switch and the same rosy glow that filled the rest of the sanctuary filled the small room.

Ania walked in and Iain followed, taking a key out of the door and handing it to her.

Iain looked at her with open curiosity for a second before

speaking. "There's no time-limit for you to stay. There is a buzzer that sounds every day at sunrise, and another at night-fall, so that there are no surprises if you sleep too well. There are no windows anywhere in this part of the building, so no sunlight can sneak in."

He paused, and Ania was sure that his curiosity was going to get the better of him. Instead, he smiled again. "When you do wish to leave, there is a black button behind the door. Just push it and go to the end of the corridor and I'll be there to unlock the door." Still smiling, he said, "I'll leave you now to get as comfortable as you can. It's nothing fancy, I'm afraid."

Ania looked at Iain without looking around the room. "It's perfect. Thank you."

Iain looked at her for a moment longer before leaving, and Ania closed the door, locking it immediately. Then she felt safe enough to relax a little, so she glanced around the room, laughing out loud. 'Nothing fancy', Iain had said.

There was a double bed pushed against the far wall, covered in a very soft-looking quilt, a small twenty-four hour digital clock mounted above; a rocking chair made from wicker stood in the corner on the right, while on the left a small door led into her own private bathroom, and a thick blue carpet covered the whole floor. Wood stood ready to light in a small fireplace next to the rocking chair, and a fire-guard stood before it.

Still laughing gently, Ania walked to the bed and sat down, almost sinking into the soft mattress.

He had watched through the window, mouth dropped open in surprise. It had been millennia since anything had been able to surprise him, but the appearance of this woman had managed it. And to think if he had arrived just two or three seconds earlier they would have been face to face.

Of course he had thought about her, her and the rest, but especially her; but never had he believed that he would stumble upon her again. After she had set the fire he had lost track of her, not knowing if she had survived or not, not knowing if it was revenge that had caused her to resort to arson or whether it was suicide. Or maybe even both.

Knowing that it would be foolish to follow the woman into the safe-house, he had turned his back on it and walked back into the night to find another place to wait out the sun.

The vampire, whose own skin was an exact shade to the woman he had just seen, only hoped that he would be able to find Ania again. After all this time.

Ania watched the flames, her eyelids dropping slowly, listening to the crackle as the fire steadily consumed the wood. Even when her eyes closed completely the sound and aroma of burning wood followed her, chasing her slowly into her dreams.

She stood watching the flames reach higher into the air, straining to reach the heavens. The building had gone up so quickly, and she felt her feeling of revenge turn to enjoyment as she heard the building in which she had been imprisoned for so long began to fall. The fire that she had started was doing its duty - it was chasing the dense blackness away, its light and heat eradicating the evil blackness that had covered this area for so long, cleansing it from the evil that she and the others had been induced to.

As the building collapsed completely she was at the scene of the second fire she had started in as many nights. But here, her revenge did not turn to enjoyment. She felt sickened at what she had done.

She looked at the house, the inferno that she had caused devastating the structure. But she could see something at one of the top windows. Elizabeth stood there, blood covering her face, mouth screaming silently. Yet she could hear screaming; even from where she stood, she could hear the screaming - the screaming of a mute child.

Ania started towards the house, meaning to put it right, to *somehow* make it better, but the house collapsed, that face falling into the firestorm. And even at her distance, Ania saw, too clearly, the terror in those young eyes before the flames obliterated everything.

Ania awoke, tears streaming down her face, and found herself staring into yet another fire. Despite the difference in size and location, it still took her a minute to realize that this fire was safe, this fire was not a killer: this fire wasn't strictly-speaking, a fire at all - most of the flames had extinguished themselves, leaving only a few embers smouldering and a few wisps of smoke trawling lazily up the chimney.

Breathing heavily, unconsciously wiping away the unnoticed tears from her face, Ania turned and looked at the clock above the bed. Its rosy number blinked silently into the room: 4:47pm, turning to 4:48pm while she watched.

Even though it was probably already getting dark - November was almost over and this time of year belonged to those of her own kind - Ania knew better than to risk it; clocks could be wrong. Better to wait until her body told her that it was time to leave.

Holly woke up and looked at the clock beside the bed. It took a few moments for her eyes to adjust enough to see where the hands were pointing. About a quarter-to-five. Not time to rise yet.

She looked to her left and saw Michael lying beside her, sleeping soundly. She looked at his features: beautiful, pale, and ancient, yet still young, eternally-young. She smoothed a lock of black hair away from his forehead, hair that would never change, would never turn grey, marvelling that he was there at all. For almost two years, she had thought him dead, destroyed, and yet there he was, his chest gently rising and falling as he breathed, sleeping peacefully.

Still looking at her love, she began to think of Ania. She knew Ania was the reason she had awoken. She thought deeply, trying to recreate the details of the dream she had had, but she couldn't remember it clearly. All she could remember was fire, wild and uncontrollable, fighting a thick unnatural darkness.

Unable to let it go, Holly stared at the ceiling to wait away the remainder of the day, until night was on them again. And she had the strongest feeling that Ania was doing the exact same thing.

Once again into the night Ania walked. The wind blew bitterly cold, a harbinger of true winter. The hood of her cloak blocked everything out except the noise of the wind. Clouds filled the sky, veiling the stars and the waning moons, and Ania could smell a coming storm in the air, crisp and electric.

The forest was unnaturally quiet as she walked beneath the shade of the trees, but Ania didn't notice. She did, however, sense that something was not quite right. There was something playing at the base of her spine and she felt as if she had been split, that there was some kind of duality happening within. She half expected to turn around and see herself walking behind.

Smiling at the thought, wondering how after all her years of wandering, all of her existence, she was still as fanciful as she had been as a maiden. Yet, even as she doubted her own senses, that feeling didn't abate - in fact, it seemed to grow. There *was* something behind her, something reaching out, its pale hand stretching towards her. Panic began to fill her ancient soul and she realised that she actually felt scared. She could almost feel it...

She whirled around a second before the hand reached her and felt as though the world was collapsing around her.

The wind blew harder and she fell backwards, too off-guard to stop the descent. As she fell, her eyes locked onto his; gorgeous green eyes, eyes of a cat hidden in a marble-white face, a mirror of her own complexion; handsome as she was beautiful, both in the deadliest of ways.

Lightning couldn't have moved as quickly as he did as he swept her into his arms before she could crash into the hard winter ground.

She couldn't breathe, had lost all of the air from her lungs, and she continued to look into his eyes even as she drowned. Her lips moved silently, but he heard as she whispered his name as she had once whispered her own so long ago.

Holly stopped walking, not noticing when her prey moved out of her sight. A voice she knew echoed in her head, Ania's voice, quiet, almost inaudible. It repeated a single name: Blaiden.

She stood where she was, unable to move. Luckily, she was hidden down a small alleyway, cloaked in shadows and away from anyone. As she paused, she could even catch a glimpse of the man Ania was thinking about.

His green eyes almost glowed beneath jet-black hair that flowed slightly past his ears. But it was his skin, as pale as Ania's own skin. He looked like a beautiful marble statue that had been brought to life.

Slowly, the name faded from Holly's mind and the image that had been so clear also diminished, and she became aware once more of her surroundings. Instead of trying to salvage her hunt she fled from the alleyway in search of Michael, not realising that she had barely missed becoming prey herself.

Iain was beginning to prepare a meal for a small group of human's that had wandered into the *Night Cafe,* smiling as he did, trying to ignore the look of hunger on the rest of his 'customer's' faces. He wasn't worried about the humans' safety: They were probably safer than any other human tonight.

He was pondering on the paradox of prey being safe in the company of their hunters when the door slammed open.

A creature walked into the room, carrying the ancient being who had stayed in a room only that day, and he was walking straight towards the door behind the counter, indicating to Iain to open it.

Iain never hesitated. Leaving the waitress to take care of the only order that had needed to be prepared for almost three weeks, Iain opened the door and led the two vampires, one walking tall, the other being carried, through the corridor, through the old door and to the room that she had stayed in that day.

With only a brief word of thanks from the male vampire, Iain left the room. Once the door was closed and he had heard the lock click, Iain swept a hand through his hair. He had thought that the female he had met last night was the oldest, but it looked as though she had a twin.

III

He heard the heavy door being unlocked and slammed the lids of his eyes closed quickly, but not before the light streamed in, temporarily blinding him. All he could see was the light imprinted on the darkness behind his eyes, but he could hear. The sounds of those around him, dozens of them, screaming in pain and anger, came through clear. He could hear their feet scuffling in the dirt of the garden as they scurried around trying to find somewhere to hide from the agony of the light.

He heard a thump, something heavy being unceremoniously thrown upon the stony ground. A low moan accompanied this, and he knew from experience that another one had been brought in.

He heard footsteps, slow and unhurried, moving back towards the door, which was closed loudly and the lock secured once more. As always, he waited a moment before opening his eyes. It took only a second for his eyes to readjust to the darkness that had been the centre of his life for so long.

The body lay a few steps away from him and he moved towards it, feeling the others beginning to reappear from their hiding places. It was only when he was standing beside it that he could see that it was a woman.

Yet no other features were discernible at first. Blood covered her; her visible skin was ripped and shredded, especially around her neck and chest. Blood tainted the long dark hair which hung in sticky clumps over her face. Her black dress and cloak were also stained with dirt and blood.

Knowing that the others would stay away, not wanting to bother themselves by caring for another, preferring their loneliness in the crowd, he picked her up. Carrying her like a child he walked towards the dark pool.

When she was laying beside the cool still waters, he returned to his 'bed'; the mound of blankets which had become his mattress and covers. From the box where his few personal items were he removed a pale blue handkerchief, one of the few things that he had been able to keep clean.

He returned to the unconscious figure and knelt beside her. Using the water from the pool, he began to gently wipe the blood from the woman's neck, cleaning the wounds as best he could.

She moaned uneasily throughout; the wounds were deep and jagged and he knew how painful it was. He'd been where she was now, so he knew the agony she suffered, and had suffered at the will of the creature.

As he cleaned her face, now able to see the beauty that possessed her, she opened her eyes.

Smiling as reassuringly as he could, he looked into those pale blue-grey eyes. "Don't worry." He whispered. "You're safe now."

Comfort filled those eyes as she looked at him.

"My name's Blaiden, and I'll keep you safe."

Slowly, her eyes began to close again, losing herself in life's one true defence, sleep. But as he watched, her delicate mouth opened slightly and he leant closer to her as she whispered her own name.

Blaiden looked at Ania, sleep stealing her away, and he smiled gently down upon her as he continued to clean her wounds.

Blaiden looked down at her as she slept beside him, sharing his bed. He heard the others as they moved around the garden in their usual rambling way, no purpose, just moving, but he didn't take his eyes from Ania.

For the past two days, she had slept almost continuously, waking occasionally to drink the water that he gathered for her from the pool, before closing her eyes once more. And other than initially telling him her name, she hadn't spoken a word, hadn't uttered a syllable - and yet her voice was clear to him in his mind.

He had known her before, not by name but by the reputation of her family. He had passed her on the streets when she had been only a child, had seen the fear and terrible loathing that had been induced whenever her family was around; the way that people had moved to the other side of the street just so that the family's gaze wouldn't fall upon them.

That same fear had been pushed onto him, yet he had also felt a kinship with them. More than once, before he had been brought to this devil's paradise, he had thought about approaching them. But he had never been brave enough to do so. What could he have said if he had found the courage? Could he have confessed his secret to them? That he was the same? Did he think, even now, that people would have accepted him, even though they had never accepted Ania's family?

Behind her closed eyelids Blaiden could see Ania's eyes moving rapidly, her forehead creased anxiously, her lips parting slightly to emit a faint sob, a quiet whimper.

He began to brush a strand of hair away from her face, and stopped with his hand above her. The strand wasn't like the black strands that covered her head. It was silvery-white. After a second, he allowed his hand to continue its descent and he smoothed it away.

As he touched the skin of her cheek, gently caressing it, Blaiden heard a whisper inside his mind, soft and unobtrusive. He closed his eyes for a second and the silver light of the moons filled his mind, the colour of her voice.

Searching his conscience and deciding that he was doing the right thing, Blaiden gently placed the palm of his hand flat upon her cheek, and closed his eyes.

At first it was a jumble of images and voices, his mind had opened too far. He concentrated hard, feeling pressure building behind his own eyes. Suddenly the images separated, blown gently apart like smoke; the voices faded and he could hear a single dialogue, faint yet terrifying in its gentleness.

'She will lead you to darkness, but it is a darkness from which there can be no salvation. It is endless and timeless'

With those words came a vision of a moonlit pool fading into darkness, a pure and untainted blackness.

With an effort, Blaiden backed away from the images, allowing Ania's thoughts to drift out of his mind and he opened his eyes. He kept his hand on her cheek for a moment while he looked at her.

She was so beautiful. Slowly, he leant forward and kissed her forehead, before removing his hand. He lay down beside her and, watching her breathing soundly, fell asleep.

When he awoke, the darkness of the garden gave no indication of the time. But since he wasn't even sure how many years he had spent here and as there was no routine to be followed, the time really had no meaning.

He stretched and yawned, his arms moving outwards. Suddenly he stopped, touching thin air. Anxiously he looked beside him. Ania wasn't there, and the side of the bed that she had occupied for however long she had been in the Dark Garden was cold to his touch.

He jumped up, trying to look everywhere at once. There would be no point asking any of the others if they had seen her - nothing short of food held any interest to them - and there was only one way that any got out of the Dark Garden. He slumped down upon the blankets that made his bed, despair filling him in a way that he hadn't believed was possible.

He looked up, amazed, as a cup of water was moved into his line of sight, a pale slender hand brushing his cheek. "I thought I'd begin to repay the kindness you've shown me, Blaiden."

There were no tears in his eyes but Blaiden felt as though there should have been as he slowly lifted his head to see Ania standing before him. She smiled down at him, her eyes glistening, passion and life sparkling from within her. Despite the damage to her skin and clothes, despite her hair hanging lank and unwashed, she was beautiful.

Without taking his eyes from her, unable to believe that she was actually standing there in front of him, alive and conscious, Blaiden watched as she gracefully sat down beside him, her own eyes not leaving his for a second. After a moment, he took the cup of water that Ania was still holding out to him, and just held it in his hand.

The silence between them wasn't awkward or uncomfortable as it should have been, but relaxed and secure. They simply sat together, looking at each other and feeling contentment with the company of another.

Finally Blaiden said what was circling through his mind. "I can't believe you're okay. I was worried that you weren't strong enough."

For a second, Blaiden saw a wall form behind her eyes, an unconscious act of protection. But then she softened, a smile engulfing her face. "You didn't see a lot when we connected, did you?"

Blaiden blushed, yet didn't drop his eyes. "No. I just wanted to see if you were okay."

She nodded. "I know. But if you had delved deeper you would have seen that I'm strong enough to deal with most things."

She took a sip out of her own cup, even now not looking away from him. "I think I'm stronger than even I know." She glanced around them, looking deep into the Garden. "From what I saw just now, I think I'm going to have to be."

At this, Blaiden did look away. He didn't want to ruin this feeling that was overwhelming him by talking about the reality of the situation that they were in. He wanted to live in the fantasy for just a little longer.

Ania sensed this for she changed the subject completely. "You know that you brought me back, don't you."

Smiling in a way that made him glow, Blaiden looked at her again. "Well, I guess that nothing can bring people out of a sleep like someone peering into their minds."

Ania laughed, but it didn't touch her eyes. "I need to say this and then we'll talk of happy things, Blaiden. You need to explain everything to me. I need to know what I'm going to be facing."

He nodded, the fantasy now chased away. "I shall, but not yet. Despair can wait for a short time."

The silence which followed was no longer secure, and when they talked of happier things the conversation was stilted and wooden, happiness not having played a large part in either of their lives.

The door opened hours later, the darkness of the garden never having changed, and five full brown sacks were flung inside. An explosion of noise filled the Garden, usually so deathly quiet, as the dozens of people rushed to where the sacks had fallen.

Blaiden and Ania were pushed and pulled as the group swarmed, everybody fighting each other to get a claim on some of the food, yet they were among the first to get there. Blaiden, who brandished a heavy wooden stick, managed to secure a large portion of stale bread and a joint of cooked meat, which by the texture and the smell was only hours away from spoiling. He gave the food to Ania while he kept the others away, occasionally swinging the stick in the air in front of them just in case somebody didn't realise what it was for.

When they got back to the relative safety of Blaiden's part of the Garden, they sat and watched the other inhabitants that were still fighting. As Ania watched, a thin, skeletal man tried to escape with an entire sack full of food. But its weight was too much for his meagre frame to cope with. He collapsed onto the ground, where the sack was pulled from him. He was left with nothing while five others pulled and pulled at the bag to try and get its entire contents.

The bag ripped and food flew off in every direction. A large portion of bread, stale and slightly mouldy, landed close to Ania's feet. Quickly she stood and whipped it up.

A small group of men, looking mad and strong, approached with menace in their eyes. Blaiden, sensing the possible threat to the one who he had sworn to himself to protect, rose quickly.

Without speaking, Ania turned and pushed Blaiden back down to the ground, handing him the loaf of bread before turning back to the approaching would-be-attackers.

They stopped in a semi-circle around her, and Ania quickly identified the leader as the one who was standing directly opposite her. Moving slowly Ania walked closer to him, a smile playing softly on her lips, her eyes sparkling with seduction. The man, who stood about six-foot-five, a rough beard covering the lower part of his face, and roughly the build of a small building, smiled back, and, laughing, motioned for his friends to back away.

Blaiden watched all of this, jealousy eating into his heart. Despite the setting, and despite the situation they were in, he too found the way she moved very seductive, and seeing it directed at someone else felt as though someone was cutting into his heart, a piece at a time.

Ania stopped in front of the man and stood gazing up at him. The man looked back at her, a different sort of hunger now in his eyes as he looked over her entire figure, seeing what lay beneath the clothes she wore. Slowly, she reached her arms up until they were around his neck, her left hand gently stroking his long, dirty hair, while her right crossed over his chest and gently stroked down his right arm.

Before the man could even conceive that something was wrong, Ania suddenly gripped his wrist, and, using the force of her own body, spun him around. Her right hand held his wrist in a vice-like grip and she thrust her hand upwards, jamming his arm up between his shoulder-blades.

He let out a howl of pain and the commotion around the Garden stopped. Everyone turned to watch as the small woman who had recently had a slim chance of surviving had physically outdone and defeated a man who was the same size as a bear.

Ania cared nothing for the people watching - with the exception of Blaiden - but she relished the feel of the man shaking with shock and pain, his cries now whimpers, as she held her grip fast. Whispering in his ear so that no one else could hear, Ania spoke.

"I'm going to let go of you, and you will walk away. You will not dare this again with anyone else in this dark place. You will leave everyone, including myself, in peace. And if you ever feel the need for vengeance remember this feeling: how it feels to have a woman besting you in front of everyone. Because if you ever try this again, I will not be so charitable."

She was smiling again, this the man could tell by the sound of her voice, and that scared him. She was actually enjoying this.

"Is that agreeable to you?"

The man nodded his head and Ania knew that she had to let him go now, or he would act out against her out of a need to recover some of his pride. Gently, she lowered the hand that still held him, letting the pressure off of his arm slowly.

Finally she let go, and he moved away from her quickly, turning to look at her, so that he could see where she was. There were tears in his eyes, but only a fierce serenity in hers, and that decided him. Not looking at anyone, he moved off into the depths of the Dark Garden.

Ania felt a small sense of shame trying to make her regret what she had just done, but that feeling of power was filling her, and she found it a very pleasurable feeling. Adrenaline still coursing through her veins, a hot pounding sensation, Ania walked back to Blaiden.

He looked at her uncertainly, the same way that everyone was looking at her, and he gave her the loaf of bread which had started the trouble when she asked for it.

Slowly, Ania approached the ancient looking man who had first tried to take the sack, who was still lying on the floor, watching her anxiously as she walked nearer. Gently, she helped him to his feet, and placed the bread into his shaking hands. A frown appeared on his face as he struggled to cope with this strange act of kindness, then managed a small, almost toothless smile before he began to *attack the bread with the few teeth he had left.*

Ania walked back to her place next to Blaiden and people began to lose their interest in her and drifted away, squabbling quietly over the few remaining scraps of food.

They sat in silence for a short time, picking at the spoiling food that they had managed to get. Blaiden stared at her openly, and after a few moments, Ania raised her eyes to meet his gaze. Without warning, his face broke into a smile, so warm and genuine that Ania's heart began to ache with wanting.

"You weren't joking when you said you were strong enough to deal with most things, were you?"

They smiled together, and briefly in the Dark Garden, it didn't seem quite so dark to either of them.

"It's time now, isn't it?" He turned to face her as she drank the water that he'd brought.

Ania looked into the depths of her cup, and felt a longing for the magical pool of her past, longing to step into its cooling depths, to feel the peace it brought.

"Yes, Blaiden. I think it's time for you to tell me everything."

Blaiden looked at her, feeling himself falling in the intensity of her eyes, losing all sense of emptiness.

"Tell me of yourself first, Ania. Tell me how you ended up in this place of devils."

He saw that wall build up in her eyes again, yet she began to talk, and as she spoke Blaiden lost all sense of himself. He knew then that he was hers.

She told him of her relationship with her parents, of the prophecy that she had seen for herself, and the prophecy told to her by her parents. She told him of her 'friendship' with Maria, and how Maria had deceived her.

As she spoke of Maria, the wall in her eyes was replaced by hatred, fierce and total, and Blaiden caught a glimpse of the strength that Ania hadn't even tapped into yet. Looking into her eyes as she talked, he felt scared of her, yet he was also pleased by what he saw: that strength would get her through this nightmare, he felt sure of it.

After she had told her tale, Blaiden looked at the bitter smile that formed on her lips. "Now, my friend," she said after a slight pause. "It's your turn to spin a tale."

Smiling, Blaiden now began to speak.

"My father died when I was a young boy; I had seen six End-of-Years. He caught a chest cold and died, after a long, painful fight.

"My mother remarried three years after. Both my brother and my sister had also married, and lived in their own homes. For almost eight years the three of us lived together. Not perfectly happy, but almost.

"The last End of Year that I saw in the world outside was perfect. We all ate too much, and I was allowed to have my first sample of the Wheat-ale that my step-father always had." Blaiden laughed at this, the memory filling him with happiness. "I can still remember what it tasted like, sour and bitter, but compelling.

"We all danced, we all sang; we celebrated the dying of the Sun and welcomed it back at the same time. My brother and sister joined us, along with their families (by then, my sister had two children, and my brother had five). We celebrated until the sun rose once more, then slept until it started its descent again."

"That does sound perfect." Ania said dreamily. Compared to how she had spent all of her End of Years: her parents in the basement performing their rituals, lost in their own world and Ania lost in her own world outside in the darkness. In fact, it sounded more than perfect.

Smiling, Blaiden nodded. "It really was. I thought that everything was going to be okay."

Ania frowned at this, her forehead creasing up. "You mean, about what you can do?"

Blaiden's smile faltered slightly but didn't disappear altogether. "Yeah." He ran a hand through his hair, distractedly. "It had been a while since I'd heard anyone's thoughts or seen anyone's memories. I'd actually managed to convince myself that it was all in my head; my imagination and nothing more." He laughed, quietly and without much humour.

Ania nodded, able to understand the need to be normal; she'd never been able to be normal, but she understood wanting to be normal. "So, what changed?"

A dark shadow passed over Blaiden's eyes, darker than their surroundings, and only a bare reflection of the pain and horror within him. "Kaytan - my step-father - and my mother argued really badly, two days after End-of-Year. He had been drinking more than *normal of his Wheat-ale and became too handy with his fists."*

Even now, after all the time he had spent in the Devil's Lair, he could still see the way that Kaytan had approached his mother, who was backed into a corner, blood dripping from a nose that looked broken and a lip that had already puffed up to twice its normal size. He could see the fury that filled the eyes of his step-father, and the utter terror that filled every part of his mother. He could hear the long, drawn-out raspy breath of the man who had taken the place of his father and the short sharp gasps that came from the woman who had borne him. Blaiden could remember how it felt to walk down the stairs, feeling disconnected from everything, as if he was walking in a dream; walking towards the man who was now towering over her. He could remember the feel of the length of wood that he held in his hands; the weight of it as he raised it above his shoulder. But most of all, he could remember the sound it made as it sliced through the air, the sound it made as it connected to Kaytan's lowered head, just above the nape of the neck.

Blaiden looked at Ania, fighting against the memories. "He beat my mother really badly - she had trouble getting to bed that night, even with my help. I had to stop him. I had just seen my eighteenth End of Year, I was taller that Kaytan, but I was still scared. Anyway, I hit him with a piece of wood, on the back of the head -" he touched his own head to show her where. "- and I left him lying on the floor, bleeding, while I helped my mother to her room."

Ania moved closer to him and placed a sympathetic hand on his arm, smiling sadly at him.

Blaiden smiled back at her, actually relieved to be telling his sad history to someone, and not just to someone - to Ania. *Although he didn't know it, he had been a resident of the Devil's Lair for almost three years, and yet other than a few brief exchanges, he had not spoken to anyone. And now, he had found someone to whom he could talk to and listen to, someone he could connect with.*

"What happened?" Ania asked sadly. Although she was keen to know the rest of his story, there was no real feeling of suspense - he was sat next to her in this dark place, so it obviously didn't end well.

"I made sure that my mother was safe in bed, then went back downstairs. I still held the cut of wood, and for a moment I just stood

looking at him. Then I checked his breathing, just to be safe."

That wasn't exactly true, but he felt that he didn't need to explain; that maybe Ania was already aware of it. He had checked to see if Kaytan was breathing, but he had only felt disappointed to find that Kaytan was still living: it complicated matters.

What drove him to do what he did next was the image of pain and humiliation that had filled his mother's eyes when she had looked at him.

He dropped the length of wood (which was splattered with his step-father's blood) and went outside to the woodshed. It was dark and bitterly cold and Blaiden could see his breath as it left his mouth; and yet he still felt warm, the adrenalin pumping through his body, hot anger flooding him. He grabbed what he needed and rushed back inside, not comfortable leaving his mother alone in the same house with Kaytan.

A blaze burnt brightly and strongly in the fire-place and its dancing flames cast equally-dancing shadows upon the form that still lay motionless on the floor. Blaiden's hands rolled the ball of twine restlessly to each other. Despite the anger and fear, Blaiden knew that if he went on with this there would be no turning back - he'd be bound by his decision.

While he stood there, contemplating the harming of his step-father, a sound drifted down through the wooden floorboards to reach Blaiden's ears. It was more distressing than screams of pain or screams of anger - he could act on those, could try and help. But the tormented sobs that he heard caused an ache within him that forced him to a decision. He had to act - really, he had no choice, unless he wanted to become accustomed to his mother's tears.

Now, his mind made up, he was able to proceed quickly and surely.

Blaiden looked at Ania. "I bound his arms and legs and dragged him out of the house. I dragged him through the woods." He gulped, trying to rid himself of the lump in his throat. "I pulled him along the ground, and I just kept walking: I didn't have a destination in mind, I just walked.

"Eventually, I stopped. I was tired, every part of me ached, especially my arms and upper back."

"Did Kaytan wake up when you stopped?"

He laughed dryly. "Not once. He didn't stir on the way, nor

when I stopped dragging him. I suspected then that he was dying because of the cold - I hadn't put a wrap around him or anything.

"A part of me did think that he was going to wake suddenly and attack me. I must have heard too many stories, I suppose."

"So, what did you do?" They now sat very close together and Ania was able to see the disgust in his eyes as he remembered.

"I used his bonds, loosening them slightly, just enough to be able to rearrange them. I sat him up against a tree and wrapped a part of the rope around his neck then continued to wrap it tightly around the tree as well, so there was no way he'd be able to get out without strangling himself first.

"I kept wondering though, even as my hands moved, if I was doing the right thing. I'd grown up with the man for eight years - but remembering what he had done to my mother, there was nothing else I could do. Even now, I'm sure of it."

Blaiden lapsed into another brooding silence, asking himself again, if he was sure of it. He shook his head slightly, clearing the useless question from his mind - it was the past and he was unable to alter things.

"What happened after you bound him?" Ania asked after waiting a few moments for Blaiden to continue.

"I began to walk back the way we'd come. Even in the dark I was able to follow the path we'd cut through the frost. I'd travelled a distance before I heard a loud crunch, like someone had stood on something large but incredibly brittle.

"I don't know what came over me after what I'd decided to do, but I ran as quickly as I could back to my step-father, sure that he was in trouble, wanting to help him." That dark cloud passed over Blaiden's eyes again but he forced himself to carry on. "When I reached the tree that I'd tied Kaytan to, I saw his body slumped on the ground by the tree, and at first I thought that he'd somehow managed to loosen the ropes enough to get free . But-"

"But, he hadn't." Ania interrupted, not asking, just completing the sentence. She felt suddenly queasy: she had a strong suspicion where this was leading.

He shook his head. "No, he hadn't. I could see the blood, wet and dark, on the tree, could see it changing the colour of the frost around him." Blaiden's skin paled as he remembered. "The blood was escaping out of his neck, just seeping out without any force, like

that all the windows were also locked (for his peace of mind).

After checking the last one in his and Holly's bedroom, he stood and gazed at the blonde-haired beauty asleep on the bed. He ran his hands through his thick black hair, leaving it sticking up. If anyone had seen him they would have laughed, but Michael was far from laughing.

He was scared: he was finally able to admit it to himself if not to his lover. It had been years since he had felt this unsure of a situation and he was beginning to doubt his own ability to deal with it. If it was just a case of protecting Holly he could do that without a second thought. But there was nothing concrete to protect her *from* - just the irritating, nagging feeling of something very, very wrong.

He yawned deeply, the call of a good day's sleep ringing loudly through his entire body. He was well fed and now he needed to be well rested. He began to undress but, after only removing his black T-shirt, doubt began to encroach on him. Quickly, he raced around the house, re-checking that all the doors and windows were still locked. He was on the landing, and stopped with his hand on the bedroom door. In his mind, he retraced his steps, trying to make sure that he had checked each door and window. Still anxious, thinking that he must have missed *one* of them, Michael returned back downstairs.

He went to the front door and found it was, indeed, locked. Then moving clockwise, he passed each window and the back door, jiggling each handle to ensure that they wouldn't move. He then did the same upstairs.

When he was finished, he again paused by the bedroom door. Doubt had started to push in again and again he turned to go back downstairs, but stopped on the landing.

His eyes had grown heavy and he knew that he had to sleep. Yet here he was, acting completely insane, by checking things that he already knew he had checked.

He raked his right hand through his hair again and, fighting against the compulsion to check (again!), walked back into his bedroom. Michael finished undressing and, naked, slipped in between the sheets, next to Holly.

Feeling his presence, Holly's arm sleepily wrapped around his waist, and Michael, feeling her chilled skin against his own, took her hand in his. And eyes closed, he fell asleep, still holding her as if his very existence depended upon it.

He'd been walking around the town since the daylight had started to drift from the sky, giving his unconscious mind the chance to map the area well so that even if things didn't go exactly to plan he would be less likely to end up caught in a dead-end. And, despite his ultimate goal, he was not willing to sacrifice his own life.

Tonight, the town centre was more crowded than normal. It was the third of December and the Christmas lights were scheduled to be switched on at midnight. It meant that he would be able to hide well amongst the crowds until it was time to act; and also that there wouldn't be too many people wandering around - they would all stay gathered for the lights.

Anthony Gibbons began to feel a chill in his spine that had nothing to do with the mild December night. It seemed to reach deeper than any cold wind could, seeming to touch through to his soul. He could feel them nearby and lifted the hood of his coat, so that his face became shrouded in its shadow, and peered out into the crowded night.

Out of the corner of his eyes, he caught a glimpse of two black shapes moving rapidly in the distance, and he felt the adrenalin begin to build up in his system. He had to put this all into action soon, before they had a chance to feed, before they could gain any more strength.

It was now or never.

One gloved hand delved into his jeans pocket and brought out a small, thin mobile phone. There was only one phone number stored on the silver phone's memory and that number was on speed dial. He pressed the button and lifted the phone to his ear. It rang only once before being answered.

In a soft voice, empty of any emotion, Anthony spoke only two words before ending the connection. "Stand by."

Moving deliberately unhurriedly, knowing that if he allowed the desire to act overcome his restraint then all would be lost, fifty-seven year old Anthony began to edge out of the ever-increasing crowds.

It took a while to work his way out from the midst of everyone, and when he had regained his freedom he was barely in time to catch sight of dark clothes disappearing around a corner. Yet still he didn't let himself move any quicker than a stroll. Panic did enter his heart as he rounded the corner to find that there was no one there in dark clothes, only a few stragglers heading past him. But it quickly subsided as he saw the female going down another street on his left and the male heading away on a street to his right.

He ignored the girl, and watched the man walking away, but purely out of the corner of his eyes, while pretending to look in a shop window. There was no reason for this, but instinct told him not to look directly at him, because if he turned -

Just as he thought this, the stranger in dark clothes *did* turn, scanning the streets with an anxious look on his face that looked out of place.

Anthony could feel sweat begin to break out on his skin, but as much as he wanted to he refused to turn and look at the dark-haired monster he had been tracking. His feet were itching, he wanted to flee, to get as far away as he could. But he held his ground, more out of terror of being spotted, and soon the man turned and continued on his way.

Anthony breathed a sigh of relief, then began to walk again, going down the almost-deserted street that the woman had travelled down. He got out his mobile phone again and once more rang the number.

"She's just gone down Broadwater Street."

"Copy that." Came the reply before the phone went dead.

Still ambling slowly, pretending to care about the items that were displayed in the shop windows that he passed, Anthony continued to follow the blonde with the pale skin. When she changed direction, the middle-aged man who looked good for his age stopped and stared continuously at some tacky watches in a jewellery store window, and dialled the number again.

"Laurey Pass."

"Yeah, I'm there." The young man on the other end of the phone said. "I see her now."

Anthony sighed, feeling both excited and anxious. "Take care, Mickey."

"Always."

Anthony hung the phone up and simply stood on the dark street with his eyes closed, the dark-orange light from the street-lamps reflecting on the windows. He could hear noise from streets away as people chatted excitedly about the switching-on of the Christmas lights. But the sound was distant, unreal. The only real thing was the noise of his heartbeat in the darkness, the sound of his blood rushing through his body.

That, and the danger that his son was currently in.

Yet despite his worry, Anthony continued to wait. He waited for a full two minutes before taking a shaky deep breath and gathering all the strength he had. When he was sure that the timing was right, he put the phone back into his pocket and took out the other item that was there, holding it so that it stayed hidden up the sleeve of his coat.

Now he dropped all pretence and walked quickly down the street, allowing his feet to guide him to the alley that Mickey had promised to try and lead her to.

As he rounded the corner of the alley, panic bit into his heart. She was walking closer to his son.

He moved quickly into the mouth of the dead-end, cutting off her only means of escape if she tried to flee. Using his fingers, he gently edged the knife out from the sleeve of his coat not caring if the blade happened to cut him or not.

As he watched on, unnoticed by either his son or the creature that was stalking towards the boy, Anthony felt himself being unwillingly drawn towards her. The way she moved, her hips swaying as she walked towards Mickey -

As she walked towards his son, the hunter moving in on her prey.

Quickly, all thoughts driven from him except one, he took a step forward, now holding the knife out in front of him and spoke in a quiet yet strong voice. "Keep away from my son."

Uneasy surprise was on her face as she turned to look at him, her blonde hair whipped backwards.

Over her shoulder Anthony could see the relief in Mickey's eyes, and watched proudly as his son took the small yet sharp wooden stake out of his pocket.

Both now smiling at each other, they held their individual weapons in their hands pointing them towards the startled-looking monster before them.

Anthony glanced over his shoulder for a split second as a cheer of approval rose from the ceremony in the other street.

"The lights have been lit," he said, looking back at the blonde. "Looks like the party's about to begin."

Walking away seemed to be the hardest thing he'd ever done. Every nerve in his body was fired up and he could feel the electricity coursing through his veins. Holly walked away in the opposite direction to the one he was travelling in, and it was killing him. All he wanted to do was go back and protect her, yet still his feet moved him onwards. The panic began to build in him, growing and growing, and suddenly it was too much, the compulsion just couldn't be denied any longer.

He stopped and looked backwards, looking at Holly's back as she continued to walk away. Michael scanned the small group of people that were on the street that he'd just left. There was a group of four people walking unhurriedly towards the centre of the town where the lights would shortly be switched on and a man who stood looking absently into a shop window.

There seemed to be nothing wrong despite the needle of unease that played in his spine. Reluctantly, knowing that it would be pointless to linger, Michael turned and walked away.

Although the first pangs of his hunger were beginning to appear, and although his keen eyes were searching for a suitable victim, Michael's only thoughts were with the woman he loved.

The further Michael walked the more intense his fear became and the stronger the compulsion to go back became. Step by step, by step; his fear grew with each movement of his feet. His thirst was forgotten and his eyes searched for nothing any more. His body began to shake and that needle grew to a spear of ice lodged in his spine.

His mind travelled back to the moment he had scanned the small group of people in the street. He saw the two men and two women as they walked, chattering happily, as they walked past the man studying the shop window.

The man studying the shop window...

As he thought back, he stopped walking, allowing every ounce of himself to go back to that moment. There was something wrong, something wrong with the man's face.

And in his head, he saw it. The man was sweating. It was so clear, those beads of sweat breaking out on his flushed skin and glittering in the lamplight.

His voice whispered into the darkness. "Who the hell sweats on a cold December night?"

That spear of ice in his spine turned to a spear of fire in an instant and Michael began to run, moving in a flash of black clothing, preying to the Gods that he had once believed in that he wasn't too late.

In the darkness of the safe-house Blaiden once more laid down next to Ania. He had fed quickly, not wanting to leave her for any longer than necessary. She wasn't safe in her present condition and he wasn't going to leave her unprotected.

The memories she was reliving had become jumbled. She had raved a few moments ago about a woman called Holly, and Blaiden knew that that was the name of the girl Ania was trying to help. And she was scared for the girl, that much was certain. Something bad was happening hundreds of miles away, and Ania had been forced to see it.

Blaiden received a flash of memory as he wrapped his arms around her, and the moment he saw it Ania spoke four words that sent a thread of fear through his spine.

"They smell of death."

For two days Ania and Blaiden spent in an almost-contented existence. True, they only ate the almost-spoiling food that their unseen host allowed them; true, they lived in a garden of darkness, where no light was able to enter. But they did *have each other. They had no privacy, and no other real comforts, but they had bound themselves to each other until their time together ended. Witnessed by no others, they were married, their souls bound to find each other while they walked upon the earth, in this life and all others.*

They lay in each others arms, their warm naked bodies touching, wrapped in a blanket. Ania's head rested on Blaiden's chest and she felt herself moving on a wave as it rose and fell with each breath, and under that, his heart beating strongly, beating just for her.

They lay in each others arms, neither talking, just being.

Suddenly, Ania sat up, the blanket dropping from her, revealing her young body, its soft flesh still ravaged by the wounds that had been inflicted upon her. Every part of her had become alert - something was on its way and whatever it was meant something bad.

"Ania? What is it? What's wrong?" Blaiden also sat up and touched her creamy, silky shoulder and the terror that had begun to fill her infected him as well. Through Ania, he could also feel a presence moving closer.

She looked back at him, fear clear in her blue-grey eyes, and he mirrored her expression. Blaiden nodded and together they both grabbed for their clothes. Whatever it was that was coming for them they had no intention of meeting it naked.

They dressed in clothes that were dirty and shredded, but felt better when they were clothed. Together they stood side by side, and waited; motionless and speechless they stood together, while the others in the dark garden continued to simply amble in their normal couldn't-care manner, completely unaware of the danger that was approaching them all.

But all movement stopped briefly with the sound of the heavy door being unlocked. The silence lasted for only a second before the rush of people stampeded away in search of hiding.

All but Ania and Blaiden. As expected, the door was swung open quickly, and light flooded the interior of the Dark Garden. Eyes closed against the painful light, both Ania and Blaiden could hear the sound of dozens of people entering the garden. Although they were unable to see the new arrivals, they could tell through the sound that these came voluntarily, and that they would not be staying.

Ania opened her eyes slightly, enough to see through the blinding-brightness, that they were all men, big, heavy and strong, and that they all seemed to be searching.

It suddenly went dark again and Ania soon realised that the door hadn't been shut but two of the heavy-set men were standing before her and her lover, cutting off the light from their faces.

As they were both grabbed, the thought of fighting crossed her mind, but she quickly dismissed it. These men were muscle-personified and she hadn't had a decent meal for so long - there was no way that she could get away. This was confirmed as the man picked her up and draped her over his shoulder like a rug. She was barely in time to close her eyes before the light hit her face again.

Ania heard Blaiden grunt behind her and knew that the same thing was happening to him too. Then her ears picked up the sounds of weak cries happening all over the garden. It seemed that there were more than the two of them being removed from this place.

But Ania doubted that it was to help her escape.

While being transported out of the Garden she kept her eyes closed, but could still see the light through her eyelids. She was carried for what seemed an age, with her eyes firmly closed to prevent the spasmodic attack of sunlight from infiltrating.

Eventually the man carrying her stopped and she was roughly lifted from his shoulders and dropped upon the ground. The earth that her hands touched was softer than that in the garden she had been taken from, and she felt sure that she could still feel the sun on her skin. But it was hard to tell with her eyes still closed.

The others were dumped on the ground in the same fashion as she was, and they all heard the sixteen men retreat from them. As in her previous place of imprisonment, a heavy door was slammed shut, but not just one lock was used. Still in her self-imposed darkness, Ania counted four.

Not daring to speak or move, Ania experimented in opening her eyes slightly, allowing a small amount of sunlight to seek its way through. After having spent so long living in a continuous state of darkness it hurt like hell but gradually it eased. Slowly, Ania continued opening her eyes a little at a time, stopping so that she could become accustomed to the increase in light, and then repeating the whole thing.

When she was finally able to look around, Ania was amazed by what she saw. Although light came through hundreds of sky-lights, the two acre-squared garden was still a dark garden. It took a while, but Ania pulled her gaze away from the bizarre scenery and focussed on the other people who had also been brought to the new garden.

There were fifteen other people sat upon the ground and all of them were working hard to open their eyes in exactly the same way as she had. But only one of them concerned her.

She moved to Blaiden quickly, who had only managed to open his eyes a quarter of the way. "It's okay, Blaiden." she said, crouching beside him and putting a hand on his shoulder. "I'm here, we're fine."

He turned his unopened eyes to her and his beautiful smile transformed his face, removing the worry and the uncertainty, and filling it with wonder. "I can't see you properly yet, but I think I can see enough to know you're lying."

Smiling herself, Ania sat down, removing her hand from his shoulder and taking hold of his hand. "Well 'fine' maybe going too far, but we're still alive and together."

Blaiden's smile slipped a notch and when he spoke a small quiver had worked its way into his voice. "It's time for me to tell the rest of my story now, is it not, Ania?"

Although she was feeling unsure and afraid, Ania couldn't help but continue to smile.

"Yes, my love. Now it is story time once more."

Smiling again, Blaiden turned his face towards the sound of her sweet voice. "It'll pass the time, at least." he said, followed by a surprisingly-genuine burst of laughter. "Although," he added, "I can think of better ways to spend whatever time we have."

He adjusted himself a little, trying to ease the ache in his back following his unceremonious drop to the ground.

"When I last talked of my life before this place, I told you of how Kaytan had been killed, of how I realised that the place in which I had found myself was too dark. Of running through the trees."

Ania nodded, then remembered that Blaiden was not able to see. "You began to talk of something chasing you." She was aware of the others nearby also listening in.

Any look of humour was washed quickly from his face as he began to weave the web of his story again, still experimenting opening his eyes.

"I was running as quickly as I could manage. With the depth of the darkness I had to work hard to avoid the trees, and I nearly fell over the protruding roots and rocks a couple of times. It felt as though I was running for an age, but I don't think it was longer than two or three minutes.

"But, no matter how long I was running, for the entire time I could hear something running behind me.

"I was out of breath within seconds and every one of my muscles seemed to be on fire, but the thing that pursued me made no sounds, except the occasional snapping of frost-ridden twigs on the ground.

"The thing that was behind me obviously grew tired of the game, and I was pushed with force, thrown to the hard winter ground."

Blaiden had almost managed to open his eyes completely, and as an extra aid, shaded his eyes with his hands.

"I could feel the cold of the ground, but it was nothing compared to the iciness of the creature that leapt upon me. It sat upon my back like a dead weight for a moment, and with that strength, rolled me onto my back."

"You saw what it looked like?" Ania interrupted, the eagerness to find out what she was dealing with flooding her.

He smiled a humourless smile. "Yes, I saw it. She looked like us, yet not like us at all. Her skin was pale, as if no blood resided within her. Her eyes were wide and as black as a jet-stone as they locked upon my own, and her teeth were elongated and sharp, like that of an animal. I could see dark stains on them, even in the dark.

"And she began to bite and claw at my throat. At first I believed she was going to eat the flesh straight from my bones, while I lived to endure the agony, but I was only partially right."

Squinting, Blaiden dropped the hand from above his eyes and began to look around, clearly amazed at what he was looking at. He caught sight of the bizarre plants that Ania had already seen and stared fixedly at them for a moment before looking at his love.

She nodded to show that she, too, had seen them but that he should continue with his story. A finger of panic was coursing down her spine - Ania was sure that Blaiden's story was important, and that his time to tell it was running out.

"There I was, laying there with this beautiful but utterly terrifying creature pinning me down, and I could hear and feel what she was doing. She was drinking my blood, drinking it as you and I would drink water."

Ania gasped in spite of herself, and saw Blaiden nodding at her. "A blood-soul?!"

He continued to nod.

"No. It's not possible." But she didn't really believe that. All she had to do was look into his eyes. And also at the marks on her own body. Had she really believed that it could be anything else?

"What's a blood-soul?"

Both Ania and Blaiden glanced at the girl who had spoken. She was perhaps the youngest of the sixteen, looking as though her fourteenth End of Year had not yet been witnessed, but her face had the marks of age, especially in her light-brown eyes. Looking at them was like looking into the eyes of an Ancient.

"If you had asked me before being in this place, I would have said a myth. But it seems they really are a reality." And, she thought, heard only by herself and Blaiden, not just out reality, but I fear our future.

"They feed on the blood of the living, damned by all the gods for their crimes, and forced to live their eternity alone and in an eternal darkness." As she said it the prophecy that her father had uttered began to resound in her mind but she blocked it out. She would deal with his words later, but for now she had to deal with the situation that she now found herself in, knowing deep down that they were really one and the same thing.

The girl that had spoken looked as though she had been struck and the thirteen others began to whisper amongst themselves.

Blaiden sighed and looked at Ania exclusively, although he realised that he was now talking to the entire group of people. "That's not the worst of it, though, Ania."

The others stopped talking immediately and gave Blaiden their undivided attention.

Feeling as though every ounce of strength was fleeing from her body, Ania looked at him in fear. "What is the worst?" She asked, wishing that he would refuse to answer.

"A man walked upon us, and I first thought that he would also be attacked by the creature who sat astride me. But as I looked, the man reached down and gently took hold of the creature's neck and pulled it away from me."

Ania could only stare at him.

"He spoke to it, telling it not to take too much, that he needed me alive for the tests."

"Tests?" A man from the group said, is mouth only half-moving, due to the damage to the left side of his face.

"I think that's why we've been separated from the others." Blaiden said, his instincts telling him that he was right. "That's why we've been brought here, to this new Garden. We're the ones to be tested upon.

"We're the ones that the blood-souls are to change. To make us like them."

"They smell of death." Ania said.

Blaiden looked at her with despair in his eyes.

She was leaning towards the black roses that grew upon the black rose bush. Everything in the garden was black, even the grass was a dark green that looked black. And everywhere was the smell.

He knew that she was right and also wrong. "Blood. They smell of blood."

Ania looked at him for a second before touching a rose petal with shaking hands, closing her eyes as soon as she made contact, grimacing at the slick oily feel of it.

"They were watered with blood. Watered with the blood of the dying, grown with the life-blood of those who have passed here before us. Everything in this Garden of Death has been nurtured by the fall of the innocent." Looking shocked, her eyes sprung open quickly and she moved away from the roses, turning her gaze to everything around them. "How many have perished here?" She asked no one, once more noting how vast the garden was.

"I don't know, Ania, but I don't think you're quite right."

She looked at him with her pale eyes filled with confusion. "About what?"

Blaiden looked around them to ensure that the small group wasn't in earshot, yet moved closer to Ania anyway. "I don't believe that any of them perished, Ania. I think it would have been a mercy if they had."

He placed his hands gently on her shoulders, then used his left to gently touch her cheek. Blaiden looked deeply into her eyes, hoping that she knew just how much he cared. When he spoke again his words were barely above a whisper, and he voiced Ania's own fears. "I think it is a mercy that we will not receive, Ania. We have been chosen, all sixteen of us, because we have strength of character. Because we have the strength to survive whatever these tests are."

A tear rose in his eye and rolled down his cheek. "You know as I do that we shall soon be separated, my love. That we will be forced to endure our agonies alone."

Crying herself, Ania nodded. "Yes, Blaiden. I know that as

you do. But we shall face it, without losing ourselves, or allowing our hearts to lose each other."

Blaiden moved closer and they held each other, knowing that their time together was drawing to its end.

The Garden of Death was growing darker, the sunlight outside the hundreds of skylights was fading, and a strange atmosphere was beginning to grow among the dark vegetation.

The air of expectancy was almost tangible and both Ania and Blaiden could feel it pushing against them. Nor were they the only ones. The rest of the little group were becoming anxious as the light dimmed, some of them beginning to pace restlessly while others simply sat and looked at the increasing darkness, compelled to search the darkness yet scared of what they might see.

It was getting closer, that time when they would be torn apart, and Blaiden kissed Ania gently, holding her tightly. Their tears mixed together, and that was how they spent their last moments in the light of the day, loving each other and saying goodbye as the world turned, once more, to darkness.

The girl who had spoken to them only minutes before began to whimper and no one consoled her. They were all too scared to offer another comfort, with the exception of the two lovers, who were only able to console each other.

Still alone, her whimper increased to a low wailing, moving to everyone's ears, as other noises began to resound through the garden.

The scratchy, squeaking sounds of heavy iron doors opening brought fear to everyone's hearts, and Blaiden and Ania increased their holds on each other, feeling the other shaking slightly.

In the bottom of the Garden of Death, further than any of the sixteen had cared to venture, the creatures that were to become their doom and their destiny began to edge closer.

They all moved with stealth, yet Ania and Blaiden had no trouble hearing them as they moved towards them. Ania heard the sounds of the black plant life crushed beneath over a dozen pairs of feet, and while she was scared by the oncoming creatures, a part of her began to harden. If this was the way her natural life was to end then she would face it stony-faced. They would not break her.

Every second felt like an hour for those trapped in the Garden, but there was no relief when the pale beings came into view.

Three of the captives rushed to the door and began to hammer a hurried tattoo upon it, begging to be allowed to escape. Two of them (including the young girl, who still whimpered softly) curled themselves into balls and simply lay still upon the ground.

One woman, who had so far made no impression on any, stood silently and began to walk calmly forwards. She made her way to Ania and Blaiden and, without speaking, stood beside them, the same look of obstinate determination forming on her plain features.

Dressed in black, so that they appeared as nothing more than floating heads, they came, the blood-lust beginning to build. Quicker than any of the condemned could register, the captors swooped upon them; sixteen captors for sixteen captives, which was, by no means, a coincidence. The man who had been arranging the tests since time out of mind, whose name no one knew (he couldn't even remember it himself, so long had it been since it had last been used), was always careful to ensure that the number of new subjects always matched the number of his pets.

The screams of thirteen of those imprisoned echoed in the night of the Garden of Death as the creatures descended upon them. Nails, sharp and strong, delved deep into their bodies, teeth, that they had all felt pierce their own skins so long ago, punctured flesh. And underneath the agonised wailings lay another sound. The gulping as blood was drunk, those beings that lived only in darkness taking the sustenance into themselves.

Only Ania, Blaiden, and the woman with dark blonde hair remained untouched, standing close in their stubborn little group. But they were not to be spared. Before them stood three of the beings, smiling viciously and gazing at those who did not scream.

Ania gazed back and, despite her fear, felt herself drawn to them. Their pale skin, while wholly unnatural, was still filled with a kind of cruel beauty. And standing there, Ania knew that both of her companions felt the same. Looking at those beautiful monsters, Ania could see herself in the years to come, could see a dim reflection of herself in the eyes of those who would harm her.

The decision was made, her fate sealed, within her own heart. An ember began to smoulder in her soul, an ember that would turn into an inferno inside of her entire being. Without glancing again at her comrades, without another look at her soul's mate, Ania stepped forward. When the being also stepped forwards towards her, *his powerful hands gently moving the hair from her neck, she embraced his cold body. And when his teeth pierced her already-scarred throat, pain flooding her mind, she did not scream.*

Knowing that her destiny was now before her, embracing it as she embraced him, Ania let herself sink into the pain. She knew that she was finally home; where she was always meant to be.

She lay in the darkness of her cell, staring at the ceiling. The walls around her were built with a type of brick that she had never seen before, thick, grey and constantly cold. The door was also thick and heavy, with a small sliding panel a third of the way down, perfect for eyes to gaze through, although it was mercifully closed. And yet she had still been able to hear the screams of the others.

Ania knew that it had been eight nights and eight days since she had stepped towards her future because the blood-soul had visited her eight times since her introduction to the room she was in.

Tired and cold, Ania moved the cover up to her chin, and curled herself up as tightly as she could, trying to use her own body heat to keep warm. Laying on a thin mattress with only the thin cover over her, Ania wondered how much longer she would be able to endure the pain of the tests without screaming, as she had managed so far.

She could feel the blood trickling from the wound in her neck, but had no more strength, not even to wipe it away. She knew that once the sun rose again, allowing a small amount of light to seep through the crack at the bottom of the door, then the men would return with another test.

Each night was the same. The creature would go to her cell and feed upon her, viciously, ripping at her flesh with his teeth. He would then leave her, feeling close to death, tears of pain and loneliness mingling with whatever blood was left to escape from her wounds. She would lie in a daze, not asleep yet not exactly awake either, until the door opened once more, allowing the sun to enter her dark prison. While she shielded her eyes from the pain of the light, the men would enter her room and restrain her frail and weak body. Each day she had been stabbed with a long thin needle and injected with a thick black liquid. And she knew. Each time, she knew that it was blood from the blood-souls, probably a different one each time.

And then they would leave, shutting the door, shutting her off from the light. But that sliding panel would open to allow a pair of studious eyes to look in on her. It wasn't the man who controlled the tests, she knew that much, but it made no difference, really. The person who watched was only there to observe her reaction to the blood that had been forced into her veins.

Her reaction had also been the same each time, always about an hour after the blood being injected - her body seemed to burn for a minute, an all-consuming fire, and after that the feeling of being stabbed from the inside by a million tiny daggers. Then with a final sense of burning the black blood would be forced back out of her veins, leaving her body by the same way it had entered, dripping slowly to the floor where it turned immediately to dust. And through the walls she was always able to hear the screams of the rest of the test-subjects, suffering as she suffered. Yet her heart was gladdened as she had not heard Blaiden crying out, as she herself had not cried out.

A change had occurred though tonight, and her ears picked up the sound of the heavy door being opened again.

Despite her resolution to face whatever she had to face without showing fear, panic began to bite at her. It was still night, so she knew that only the damned walked the Garden of Death, that the day had not yet been born to frighten these creatures back into hiding.

The cell door opened slowly and the creature walked back inside, his pale skin almost seeming to glow in the darkness, a purpose in his eyes. Ania watched as he walked back towards her, her blood still on his lips, her heart racing fiercely in her chest. This was it. This was the moment she had been expecting since she had first stepped into his arms. This was the moment she was to become a blood-soul, joined with him.

Scared and tense, anxious and anticipating, Ania raised herself weakly, sitting with her back pressed against the cold stone wall, and watched as the blood-soul moved to stand in front of her.

Using his nails he pierced the skin on the fleshy part of his hand, driving the nail deep to maximise the blood flow. He knelt before her and reached his hand out to her, palm to the ceiling, the dark blood flowing to his fingertips.

Ania didn't hesitate, didn't allow time for any doubts,

knowing that ultimately she had no choice; it would be done with or without her consent. She took his hand and raised it to her lips; she began to drink.

The second his blood touched her lips, falling onto her tongue, a fire began to fill her mouth. And as his blood, hot and rich, flowed down her throat, that fire burned stronger, following the trail of darkest red inside of her. It exploded inside her stomach, and Ania pushed him away as the fire started to take over.

It burnt her, pain enveloping her, and she began to writhe on the bed. The pain grew and grew, and she wasn't aware as the creature left the cell, closing the door once more. It increased over and over, filling every part of her, yet still she refused to cry out. And even when she was sure that she was dying, that surely she had *to be, because nothing could live with this pain, still it became more intense and she bit down upon her bottom lip, her own blood mixing with his. And still she would not scream.*

For hours the battle was fought within her frail body, for hours Ania died a million deaths silently, waiting only for the moment when her life would cease to be, sure that the tears she shed would immediately burn up on her skin by the storm of flames that raged within her.

Then it stopped.

She lay there, sweat covering her body, not moving, sure that she had *died after all, that that was the only reason that the pain could have vanished the way it had.* She had to have died. *After all, she could no longer feel anything.*

Yet as she lay there, Ania realised that that wasn't true. She could feel the cold working on her sweat-covered body, could feel herself beginning to shake. And she could feel her heart beating fast in her chest.

Feeling strangely exhilarated, she doubted that she would ever be able to sleep again, for as weak as she felt she could also sense a deep strength working through her, as the blood-soul's blood worked through her. And examining this paradox within her mind, Ania fell asleep.

When the night dawned again, Ania's eyes opened, knowing straight away that her life had changed and everything she had ever believed no longer mattered. She was no longer the same person she had once been.

The second thing she became aware of was that her whole body ached, deep down in the depth of her bones. It felt as though someone was squeezing them.

An image of her parents flickered into her mind. They were standing in the centre of their basement, bare feet on an earthen floor. Candles flickered uneasily in a circle around them as they moved gracefully in sacred dance. Their eyes were closed and their lips moved in silent chants.

Ania knew that her parents had the ability and strength to affect people from a distance, in visions she had seen her parents performing the ritual. But she knew that this had nothing to do with her parents. It was not their magic that worked within her, but the poisoned blood of the creature she had drunk from. It was changing her, altering her body so that she would be forced to feed as the damned did.

Moment by moment the pain began to increase, but it was so gradual that Ania didn't notice to begin with. She simply lay on her bed, staring at the low ceiling above her, wondering what her existence was to be like from now onwards. Was she going to remain trapped in this little cell or was she to be released into a life of darkness?

There was no visit from blood-soul that night; her room remained locked, but she had expected that. His duty was fulfilled, and Ania doubted if her blood, the blood of a fellow blood-soul, would nourish him now.

Ania moved a little on her bed, trying to find a more comfortable position to lie in. After a few moments she began to realise just how *uncomfortable she felt. It didn't matter how she moved Ania could not get comfortable, and as she stood and began to pace around her small cell she noticed that her uncomfortable feeling was passing easily into painful.*

Every bone in her body was being stretched and pulled and squashed. As the blood-fire had swept through her the previous night, this feeling of her body being pulled apart by invisible forces began to build. And now that Ania had finally allowed herself to actually feel *it happening, its strength grew rapidly. As she thought it could get no worse, her body began to burn again, the fire she had felt before returning to consume again.*

Without her knowledge, the night turned back into day, yet still her dual agony continued.

In the world beyond her cell she could faintly hear howls of others as the endured their own nightmares. And as her own pain heightened, she knew that the time when her own screams would join the cacophony was drawing closer.

As the pain peaked, she closed her eyes, squeezing more tears from under the lids, trying to find that last trace of strength within herself to remain silent. But it wasn't only strength that she found in the darkness of her own mind.

She saw a memory, one that, as her parents had rightly predicted, had led her to eternal darkness. It was the memory of her first meeting with Maria, after Maria had lost her son. Almost as if it was happening again, Ania saw herself walking to The Wall, saw and felt Maria throwing her arms around her.

And as she replayed it, seeing every detail again and again, another sensation began to build up behind the pain. It was two emotions combined - the shame at having been fooled, of allowing herself to be taken in by the deception, and hatred of the woman who had brought her here. And this combination of feelings also grew steadily, and Ania focussed upon it. Instead of pushing it away, she allowed the memory to keep replaying in her mind, forcing the humiliation and anger to build. When she finally let go, when she allowed herself to scream, it was more to do with this than the pain. And as she held on to the emotions, grabbing them to stop herself from drowning in the agony, the pain started to became distant. It didn't fade - in fact it continued to grow with alarming rapidity, but she was able to block it out.

Ania lay, looking almost peaceful, upon her thin bed, staring at the ceiling of her cell, still 'watching' her memory play out.

After almost two more hours, she became aware of two things simultaneously. One, that the pain within her had faded dramatically, still there but lowered. And two, she could hear someone at the door of her prison, breathing raspily like an animal.

A chill unlike anything she had ever felt before fell upon her and she felt terrified. At the sound of that noise, the strength that she had built up since she had awaken in the Dark Garden just seemed to flow out of her. Every instinct within her screamed at Ania not to move, not to turn her head towards the door, that looking at the creature (and she had no doubt about it being a creature) that watched her would do nothing to ease her fear. But she had to look, there was nothing else for it. Her neck began to turn, slowly, trying even as it did to delay the moment.

Eyes as dark as the night met Ania's, but no comfort filled her. There was too much in those eyes too many contradictions: madness and quiet sanity; vicious strength and desperate vulnerability. Life and Death.

Ania felt as if she was being attacked by a whirlpool as she stared through the open sliding-panel, and her panic surfaced again as the creature seemed to fade on the other side of the door and materialise inside the locked cell. Ania felt her body wanting to jump, wanting to shudder, but she couldn't move. Every muscle had frozen - she couldn't even feel her heart beating.

The woman, the creature, spread her arms and Ania saw the leathery wings spread out as well, in a compassionate gesture of welcome but that madness still danced in the creature's eyes.

She was unprepared when the thing half-jumped and half-flew towards her, landing squarely upon her chest, forcing the air out of her lungs. Exhilaration and sorrow shone through those dark eyes as talloned-hands wrapped around Ania's throat, cutting off Ania's air.

As the creature lowered her mouth onto Ania's, breathing air into her empty lungs, Ania felt an electric shock run through her body and a momentarily look of shock was forced into the creatures eyes as well, the first solely-human expression Ania had seen there.

Ania was inside its mind, could see a million memories jumbled, could hear a low raspy voice uttering two words over and over: The Hag. Ania could see that the creature itself didn't even know how long it had walked in the darkness. It only knew that this was its purpose for being, maybe it had always been its purpose.

That shock left both of them as Ania's eyes closed, dying yet being reborn.

Power. Strength. Agility. Speed. Those new parts of her became known to her before she had even opened her eyes. And when she did, Ania became aware of so much more.

Her eyes were more adjusted to the darkness of her cell and she knew instinctively that the night ruled once more, that the sun *had departed from the sky. She also understood that her sense of hearing was keener that it had ever been before. Ania could hear the sounds of others; sleeping, and moving, peaceful or scared. She could tell their distances too.*

There was somebody approaching her cell, she could smell his fear as he walked in the darkness and could hear the sound of his blood as it was pumped around his veins.

She smiled. He was bringing her a gift. The door was unlocked swiftly and the bundle thrown uncaringly onto the ground before the door was slammed closed again. Although if she had chosen to escape, she would have had plenty of time - he hadn't been that quick.

Ania laughed darkly at the sound of his rapidly-retreating footsteps.

The hunger that would be with her for an eternity began to fill her soul, and she leapt from the bed onto the floor. As her newly-sharpened teeth punctured the unconscious (but not dead) man's throat, that image of Maria once more swam into her mind.

Before her thirst became too much, before all thought left her in the frenzy of feeding, Ania closed her eyes and shouted within her mind.

Maria, you of betrayal and deceit; of torture and cowardice. The pain I have endured will be nothing in comparison to the agony which will be inflicted upon you. I will take my vengeance, as is my right. Your blood will be poured upon the ground. Your soul will scream. And you will pray for death long before it finds you. I swear this now, to whatever gods now stand with me in this life of eternal darkness.

With her vow now set and taken, she allowed all thought to leave her. She drank a toast to Maria's death with blood.

IV

Fear began to grow as Holly looked towards the eldest of the two who had her trapped in the alleyway. The light of the street lamps caused the knife to shine in the darkness.

She knew that, although the young boy who had led her here also had a weapon (the more traditional wooden stake), it was the boy's father who was the biggest threat - the boy would make no move without his father's say-so. As she looked at him, the fear began to subside slightly, and although she gave no sign, she was smiling on the inside. She would have had to be blind not to notice the way he was looking at her, the way his eyes kept travelling down from her face, taking in her every curve.

An idea occurred to her, but she knew that she might have trouble implementing it with the two of them. If she could take the young boy out of the equation...

Just as she began to speculate, a flash of black moved behind the older man and she knew that her lover had found her.

Although he had no idea of what she was planning, Holly hoped that Michael would catch on. But then, even if he didn't, with two-on-two there was really no reason to worry.

The memory resurfaced in her mind, not her own memory but Ania's. From Ania's point of view, she saw the Dark Garden, could see the men surrounding her. And she could feel herself walking towards the huge man who looked at her with hunger.

This time when she smiled, Holly allowed it to come to the surface. She looked at the man who had trapped her here to hurt her, keeping her eyes fixed totally upon his. She allowed that passion within her to fill her eyes, to make them sparkle, and slowly she began to move towards him, her hips moving seductively.

His eyes had widened, his mouth opened slightly, as he watched her coming towards him.

The older man hadn't heard a thing, his attention was solely on Holly, but Holly smiled wider. Michael had already taken care of the boy.

She had reached him without the man even once turning his knife towards her and she stood before him, looking at him alluringly. Slowly, she stroked his arms with her hands, gently moving her left upwards to caress his face, while the right continued to stroke his left arm.

She began to lean in towards him as if to kiss his lips and as he began to respond Holly acted quickly. Her right hand grabbed his wrist and twisted it, forcing him to drop the knife. As she had seen Ania do, Holly used her strength to spin him around, still holding his wrist and pushing his arm upwards so that it was between his shoulder blades. At the same time her left hand clamped down on his mouth, stopping him from crying out with surprise and pain.

When she spoke her voice was husky and sexy and she whispered into his ear. "That was an incredibly foolish thing that you and your son tried to do."

Still holding him the same way, she began to turn him so that her back was now to the mouth of the alley and he was looking into its depth. She heard him whimper against her palm, and smiled viciously.

"But as you can see, your dear son has already paid for his foolishness." Gently, she kissed his neck, allowing him time to take in the sight of Michael standing with blood on his lips and chin, hovering over the crumpled body of the late Mickey Gibbons.

With one last vicious moment, she laughed genuinely into his ear. "And now you shall pay for yours."

Feeling him whimpering against her hand again, Holly gave up all pretence and bit deeply into her neck, drinking the blood hungrily, not allowing a single drop to go to waste.

Michael, having satisfied his own hunger, and knowing that they were too exposed, wiped his face and walked past the feeding figure. He stood at the entrance to the alley and stood guard, watching for anyone approaching.

No one did, and soon Holly joined him. He looked at her and gently wiped away the few spots of blood that she had neglected to clean and they stood hand in hand, looking at each other, while cheers still rose from the town centre, and the two corpses began to cool behind them.

Ania had at last stilled. Blaiden lay beside her, his arm resting gently upon her waist. As he watched her, he knew that the girl was once again safe, that the danger she had been in was now over. He knew this because of his connection to Ania, and Ania knew because of her connection to Holly.

Her memories had also subsided. She slept silently, peacefully, the fever of her dreams having passed for the time being. Yet still she did not wake up. She had been consumed by her past, it had eaten ravenously at her strength and her will.

As he lay there, his eyes beginning to drop, he knew that it would take Ania a long time before her energy level rose again. It would be a long time before her eyes opened again.

Holly sat on the back step, looking out on the deserted grounds before her. The cloudless sky was filled with stars and she stared at them, allowing their beauty and light to fill her, trying to find reasons, any reasons, not to think.

She was changing. Of course, she had known that: her body had completely accepted her new way of life, she was becoming stronger, faster, more resilient. But she hadn't really considered the fact that *she* was changing, her personality, her soul. How could she have expected not to see new sides to herself? After all she had been through, had she really expected to stay exactly the same?

Michael had retired early, knowing that Holly needed to be alone, and she was grateful. She was grateful to him for so much, but mostly for knowing her well enough to give her space.

She needed to come to terms with who she was, who she was becoming, and it was difficult.

Holly had scared herself, it was that simple. It hadn't hit her completely until they had begun to walk home after disposing of the bodies. She had been killing for over four years, hunting properly for three and had accepted that part of herself, the *necessity* of that part of herself. But it hadn't been until she had found herself in danger that she had realised that she *craved* the killer-side of her nature, longed to experience it more and more. That she had begun to crave the act of killing almost as much as the blood itself.

While she sat outside, the cold December air hardly affecting her, Holly began to think back, marvelling at the difference in herself.

She was no longer the mild-mannered girl, naive to the world, who had first met Michael. She had become physically and mentally stronger, her nature had hardened and sharpened. And she knew that there was nothing that would defeat her; she would go on for eternity, like the stars shining above her, timeless and full of cold beauty. There was nothing that she couldn't do, as long as she embraced the dangerous animal that now resided within every part of her body, mind and soul.

But her depth of feeling had also increased. Her passion and her love had grown. And this was also driving her, hardening her more, strengthening her more; her love and devotion to Michael, to Ania. But for her daughter more than any other.

It was this that worried her. Was it really right for her to upset her daughter's way of life, to introduce her child to this existence of darkness and hunger and death? To drag her from the world of light and force her into the world of darkness?

Holly sat and stared at the dark sky, marvelling at the pinpricks of light within the black expanse. And as she looked up at the sight, she realised that, still, she hadn't reached what was *really* bothering her.

It wasn't the killer side that she feared, but the viciousness that seemed to accompany it. Tonight she could easily have just killed the man, especially after Michael had killed the boy. But instead she had toyed with him, ensuring that his agony was complete before killing him. She had enjoyed it, enjoyed it as he had allowed her to get closer to him. Had enjoyed the sense of his misery as he had looked upon his dead son.

Killing him just hadn't been enough.

Tears of despair and hopelessness fell from her eyes and she looked back at the stars, feeling no comfort from them.

If Ania had been with them Michael was sure that he would have hurt her. Fury towards the woman who had reunited the two lovers raced through his veins. He knew that he wouldn't be able to kill, or possibly even hurt, the ancient vampire, but he sure as hell would have tried if she had been within reach.

But that was the problem: she wasn't within reach. She was gone. As much as he hated to admit it, Michael knew that he couldn't teach Holly everything that she needed to learn. He could be with her, love her, help her to kill and conceal the evidence, but she needed something that he would never be able to give. She needed a teacher.

That vicious streak that had begun to show itself in Holly was, he knew, not her at all but the residues from Ania's past that she was being forced to relive. It was, essentially, *Ania* who had tortured that man, *Ania* who had forced him to gaze upon the dead boy before killing him. It was Ania as she had once been. And it was only Ania who could stop Holly from making the same mistakes.

Frustrated by his own helplessness and useless anger Michael stripped quickly, allowing his clothes to lay where they fell, and slipped between the cool sheets of the bed. He linked his hands underneath his head and looked up at the ceiling.

His voice was low and conspiratorial as he spoke into the empty darkness. "Whatever it is that you have to do, Ania, do it quickly. She needs you."

His eyes dropped slowly shut as, outside, the first snowflakes began to fall.

Ania and Blaiden slept side by side, pale skin touching pale skin. The temperature in their sanctuary hadn't changed despite the drop in temperature outside, yet still they held each other tightly.

Ania's lips opened, still in deepest sleep, and responded to Michael's request in the only way she presently could.

"Make peace with what you are, Holly, in whatever way you must."

Holly was only partially aware that it had begun to snow. Clouds had obscured the stars while she had watched, her tears ebbing before stopping completely. The cold around her had deepened but still she did not move. Too many things ricocheted around in her head, but mostly she remembered how she had felt as she had shown the man his son. Her stomach rolled uncomfortably as she remembered her own enjoyment.

Snowflakes fell onto her blonde hair, on to her shoulders and all around her, falling heavier and faster. A slight wind began to blow, stirring the snow that had already begun to stack up upon the ground.

As if brought by the wind, Holly heard a voice rise in the air and in her head.

Make peace with what you are, Holly, in whatever way you must.

Holly stood quickly. She knew that Ania wasn't near her, yet she still looked around her, peering into the shadows in the hope that she would see Ania's face peering back, but saw nothing.

In an agonised sob, Holly spoke to that consuming nothing. "Show me how! I need you back to show me how!"

In the depth of her dreamless sleep, Ania discovered that not all the magic had left her through the many years, and she sent one more message to Holly.

Holly blinked a couple of times, sure that she wasn't really seeing what was in front of her. The snowflakes began to swirl in a spiral in front of her, none of them reaching the ground. Slowly they began to form a shape in the air, one that Holly recognised.

Ania, formed of the snow, smiled at Holly, her snow-hair blowing back in the wind, her snow-eyes blinking, her snow-chest moving as if with breath. *"I cannot show you how, Holly. That is for you alone. But you* will *find your way."*

Holly watched as that snow-mouth smiled gently again, before the wind dropped and scattered the flakes upon the ground once more.

Knowing that Ania's message was meant to give her comfort, but still feeling none, Holly slowly walked into the house, leaving the cold and the snow outside. She locked the doors and went immediately to bed. As she lay next to her sleeping lover, Holly cried silently. She had never felt more alone.

As the dawn hit the sky with a cold winter light, flooding the snow-covered landscape with its unnoticed warmth, Michael slept soundly. Beside him, Holly moved restlessly, forehead creased in unease as images flickered behind her sleeping eyes.

She was standing where she had once stood all those years ago, in the shelter of the church alcove, waiting for Michael to arrive; she laughed as her puppy gently licked her face, Michael smiling beside her; she stared in shock at the impaled body of her dog, watching as its body twitched with the last remnants of life; she cried in despair as she fled her home, leaving Jesse dead at the bottom of the stairs; she screamed as her contractions overwhelmed her, sweat pouring down her face, pushing out the child she had carried; she ran along the night streets, trying to outrun the feelings of guilt and confusion of leaving her child, trying to ignore the part of her that told her to go back.

Behind her closed eyelids, her pupils dilated and contracted as she alternately remembered sunrises and moonrises, days and nights. Her lives of life and death. Tears seeped from the corners of her eyes, even in her sleep her sense of isolation and loneliness eating at her heart. Yet she did not fight it.

Suddenly her eyes snapped open, spilling more tears that had been suspended in her eyelashes. Holly looked briefly at Michael, grateful that her stirrings had not disturbed him, before turning her gaze to the ceiling above her.

She lay where she was, linking her hands and letting them rest on her chest. Almost as if she were watching them on the ceiling, Holly allowed her mind to go over the images that her dream had presented, forcing it to return over and over, analysing what her feelings told her about what she had remembered. And why.

She glanced once more at her lover as he slept deeply, naked beside her. Her heart cramped with love for him, yet still she felt grateful that his slumber had not been troubled: Ania had been right - Holly had to find her way alone.

Gently, she leant over him, her own uncovered flesh briefly grazing his as she placed a kiss onto his exposed cheek. Then she slowly got out of bed, wrapping her dressing-gown around her, and walked downstairs to the kitchen. Using the powdered milk from one of the cupboards Holly made herself a cup of tea and took it into the living room.

She relaxed onto the sofa, tucking her legs up next to her and held the cup in both hands, absorbing the heat into her now-permanently cold skin.

She had switched on no lights and sat in the dark, staring at nothing, thinking of nothing as she simply sat and drank her tea. When the cup was empty, she placed it on the floor and continued to just sit there. For a moment she wondered about watching something on the television (Ania had an extensive DVD collection, and thinking about the ancient being collecting DVDs always made Holly smile), but she doubted that there was anything that would capture her distracted mind. In fact, she didn't *want* anything to - for, although her conscious mind was controllably blank, she knew that her *un*conscious was working overtime and it was best that nothing divert it from its important task.

And there she sat, not even a hint of tiredness as the sun rose steadily higher in its arc outside, thinking without thinking. She got up twice, once to use the bathroom and once to refill her cup, but did nothing else. She gave her mind the time it needed.

Only seven hours after it had started its ascent the sun began to set, darkness beginning to take over once more.

Movement from upstairs caught her attention and Holly knew that Michael had also sensed that their time was upon them again. Yet still she sat where she was, knowing that his silent footsteps would start to fall on the stairs and would bring him to her.

There were things that they needed to discuss, she knew that, but she didn't know if it was the right time or not - would only know when her eyes met his. Not that she was entirely sure, herself, *what* exactly she would say, but knowing that she would bide by whatever her lower mind had worked out.

His presence was announced by no noises, but she felt him there looking at her, his deep eyes on her and only her, as it had been since the start. With a smile she turned to him and met his gaze firmly. She saw only her own confusion mirrored back to her, and smiled wider. No, now was not the time.

He walked into the room, bare feet on carpet making not a sound and crouched in front of the sofa where Holly sat, casually resting on his haunches. He looked deeply into her eyes.

"Is there something you need to talk to me about, Holly?" He asked her gently.

Still smiling, Holly shook her head, her hair moving slightly across her face. "Not right now, no. It can wait for a while."

Michael reached out, and softly swept the hair from her face, his hand lightly grazing her cheek.

As his cool skin touched her own, Holly felt all of her confusion and conflicting emotions disappear like a wisp of smoke, melting into nothingness and being replaced by something so clear and whole. 'Love' was nowhere close to describing the way she felt for Michael, just as 'thirst' was nowhere close to describing the need she felt for blood. Both words were pale imitations of the real thing, neither meaning anything. As with her blood-craving, what she felt for Michael was like a tidal wave crashing into a poorly-built barrier, in a split second destroying any form of defence. It was passion, unbridled and unable to be tamed, flooding every part of her.

In every part of her, body and soul, she ached for him, and as she looked into the endless depths of his cat-like green eyes Holly knew that he was feeling the same thing.

His hand now rested on her shoulder, slender fingers on the gentle curve of her neck. Tenderly she took his hand and led him back up the stairs.

Outside, the day darkened, the last faint beam of the sun making way for the dark-orange of the street lights and Holly and Michael moved together. In their room, they expressed everything that words could never get close to, feeling the truth of the other's affection.

The night took hold and the temperature plummeted. Inside the home that belonged to neither of them Holly lay in Michael's arms, her head resting on his chest. As she lay there, feeling his fingers stroking her arm, she realised it was the right time to speak.

"I need to go away for a while." She spoke softly, wishing that she wasn't speaking at all. "I need to work something - some *things* - out."

Holly raised herself up onto one elbow and looked at him. "And I need to be alone to do it. I need to find my way." She looked at Michael, anxious as to how he was going to react and was only slightly relieved when he smiled sadly at her.

Michael looked at her, her hazel eyes gazing at him. He wasn't surprised by what she had said, had been expecting it. But that didn't stop it from causing a deep ache in his heart, didn't stop him from wanting to hold onto her until she changed her mind. They had already spent too long apart and he didn't want to spend any more time away from the gaze of those clear brown eyes. But he also knew that this was something that she had to do.

"I know you do." Softly, he kissed her lips, then looked deep into her eyes. "But I'm not going anywhere. I'll be here, Holly, when you find your way back to me."

They kissed one last time, then Holly swiftly dressed and left the room before she could change her mind.

Michael lay in bed until he heard Holly leave the house, alone. Then he slowly began to get dressed, feeling the emptiness of the house pressing against him.

Somehow, Holly forced her feet to keep moving, concentrating wholly on the muffled sound as her trainers hit the pavement. She was vaguely aware of people passing her as she walked through the streets, huddled up in thick coats and scarves against the bitter cold of the night, but she didn't spare so much as a glance at them. It was taking all of her strength and will to continue forwards; her heart was screaming at her to go back, to re-join Michael. Instead, she blocked all thoughts out of her head, especially those of her lover, and pushed herself onwards, counting each step she took.

She was oblivious to everything: She simply walked, allowing her feet to take her further and further away from the place she had considered her home for the past four and a half years. Blind instinct moved her down streets and across roads, yet it was also more than that. Although she was unaware of it on almost every level, Holly was following the same route that Ania had taken when she, too, had left, her feet falling on the same places that her mentor's had.

Gradually, the streets lined with buildings passed on to pavements following roads, buildings sparsely dotted alongside. Although there were now no people walking along - the bitter cold having forced them all to whatever shelter they had been heading to - an intense claustrophobia hit her. Despite the emptiness of the space around her, Holly suddenly felt as though she were surrounded by an immense crowd. She needed to find some real solitude.

Quickly, she turned her back on the road she had been following and began to walk across an open field, feeling that crowded sensation beginning to relax its hold on her as she crossed the barren ground.

For hours she walked north, the clear night sky revealing more stars than she had ever glimpsed before. She moved over field after field, jumping easily and gracefully over hedges that blocked her way, feeling and hearing the crack and crunch of frost that was forming on the mud and grass.

Yet through these hours, she allowed no thoughts to linger in her mind, concentrating solely on the movement of her feet, forcibly pushing away any thoughts or images that tried to sneak their way in.

In the middle of a field that had, until the autumn, been filled with rows of pumpkins but was now only ploughed mud, Holly stopped. There had been no sound, yet Holly turned slowly until she was facing east. As she stood there, wondering what had caused her to stop in the first place, she became aware of the familiar build-up of her hunger. She had not fed so far and the hunger would not wait much longer.

Indecisive, she glanced in the direction she had been following and then in the direction she had turned to. She ran a pale hand through her long blonde hair, moving it from her face.

Shrugging, she began to move east; she had allowed her instincts to guide her this far - she wasn't going to ignore them now.

Gradually, her walk gained speed as the thirst inside of her grew. After only two seconds, her casual stroll had turned into a run.

When she came across the farmhouse standing like an island in an ocean of fields, she began to smile. Pale lights shone out of a few of the windows, spilling soft light on to the ground. Which meant that there were people inside.

The need had deepened in her - she felt famished. As she began to edge closer to the house, the killer began to rise in her, leaping into her eyes and hardening her smile, transforming her features into an animal's, which although was still beautiful would have chilled anyone who saw it.

The animal inside of Holly began to pace restlessly as she grew nearer still to the building, her feet light as she stole in the shadows just out of the light from one of the windows. Just on the other side of the glass she could hear the sound of a television playing and the sound of three people, one of them a child, talking gently together.

Holly could smell them, and her thirst rose once more. It was the smell of blood not yet spilled, of flesh not yet pierced. The memory of that taste was in her throat, and there wasn't a part of her that didn't long for it.

But as she reached a pale hand out to longingly touch the glass, as her ice-cold fingers brushed the equally-cold pane of glass, a strange sensation worked its way through her body.

A tingling started to spread from the tips of her fingers as they touched it and it was soon all through her body. To start with it was intense yet not unpleasant. But the sensation increased and seemed to settle in the centre of her brain. Within only a second it became uncomfortable, and a second later it had turned into agony. It felt as though a million creatures were inside her mind, each of them emitting an ear-piercing shrill shriek while attacking the tissue of her brain with razor-sharp teeth.

Holly's face creased up in pain and she quickly sank to her knees, her hands grabbing her head. In an instant, the pain was gone. As soon as her finger-tips had broken contact with the smooth glass, the pain and tingling were gone. It didn't fade, it didn't dull down to a bearable level - it was just gone.

Stunned, shaking, and completely unnerved, Holly could only sit there, resting on her knees, hands dropping slowly to the ground. When she was finally able to think, a smile filled her face with genuine amusement.

On one of her first nights as a hunter, while Ania was still teaching Holly the basics of her new existence, Ania had explained about a vampire's protection.

They had passed a man on the street, just an average middle-aged man, the type that could be forgotten in a second. But as they had passed him, a strange feeling had passed over Holly. She had moved away from him, like they were both magnets with the same polarity, as if she wouldn't have been able to get close to him even if she had wanted to.

Confused, and slightly worried, Holly had asked her teacher what the hell had happened.

Ania had smiled at Holly. "When a vampire saves a person's life rather than take it, something happens. Some kind of magic passes to that person. They are then protected from other vampires, as no other vampire can then get close to them." Her smile had widened. "Not without feeling slightly strange."

Ania had begun to walk away again, and Holly had followed. "What do you mean, strange? And how will I know if that's what it is?"

Still walking, Ania had turned smiling gently, to look at the vampire that walked beside her. Holly saw the twinkle of amusement in her eyes before she faced forwards again. "You'll know." she said simply.

And sitting on the cold ground underneath the closed window of the secluded farmhouse, Holly understood the reason for that twinkle in Ania's eyes.

Her thirst had been driven out for the time being, by the unusual experience, but she knew that it wouldn't be long before it returned, and she had better find an opportunity before it did. Holly stood and, feeling a sense of compassion for the unknown and protected occupants, she walked away from the house.

She walked quickly away, following a road that was little more than a dirt track, enjoying the complete solitude that the cold night now presented to her. Yet even as she felt at peace something was beginning to gnaw at the base of her spine. Confused at the conflicting emotions she now found herself experiencing, Holly began to walk quicker upon the road.

Not feeling completely in control, feeling as though someone else was directing her actions, she began to run.

After a short time she found herself inside an old and abandoned graveyard. Still with that sense of being led, Holly walked amongst the stone markers, bearing names that had faded over the years. She felt herself moving further into the depths of the cemetery and stood before an old crypt.

Not wishing to but seemingly helpless not to, Holly reached a pale hand out to the door and swung it easily open. Stepping into the tomb, where the air itself seemed dead, she looked around at the small space, wondering why she had come to this place.

Candles that had not been lit in decades stood in cast-iron sconces on the damp walls, and a stone chamber sat in the centre, within which Holly knew would be a coffin, which in turn would hold a corpse. Although given the age of the crypt, she guessed that it would no longer be called a corpse - rather more of a skeleton.

Her gaze dropped to the floor and she saw that the build-up of dust that lay thick all around had recently been disturbed. She focussed on an area that was flecked slightly darker, and leant over for a closer look.

Fingertips brushed through the dust, but as she touched the darker powder that felt more like charcoal a flicker of understanding swept over her.

Holly looked around her again, almost expecting to see her teacher beside her. All the time she had felt as if she were being led, and in a way she had been. She had simply been shadowing Ania's steps, following the path her teacher had taken. Smiling, Holly knew exactly who it had been that had placed the protection on that family.

Almost in a sigh, Holly whispered, "Ania."

Like an echo in her mind, Holly heard Ania's words, words

that had been spoken to her through non-existent lips.

You will find your way.

Holly stood and walked out of the tomb, securely closing the door again. For a moment she simply stood, eyes closed, in the deserted graveyard, breathing in the night, allowing it to fill her.

Slowly, she opened her eyes and looked up at the thousands of stars that shone in the sky. Determination sparked inside of her, and she glance north towards the low wall, knowing instinctively that that was the way that Ania had gone.

With a smile that was harder and stronger than her normal smile, Holly spoke to Ania as if she was standing there. "You're right. I have to find *my* way."

So Holly turned her back on the way that Ania had gone and set off south to find her night's kill, following no path but her own.

Michael sat on the back steps, looking up at the stars. He had fed quickly, then returned to the house. But when he had got back, he'd had to wonder why: there was no one to return to, so why had he hurried? He had lingered in the empty house for only a few minutes before venturing back outside.

His hair was ruffled where he had repeatedly raked his fingers through, and he simply sat on the steps, arms wrapped around his knees, wondering what his two companions were doing, but mostly wondering what Holly was doing.

He just felt so disconnected now that she was gone, so empty. So lost. Loneliness dragged at him and there was nothing that would block it out, not even for a second. And he had no idea how long it would be necessary for him to endure it. For Michael, that was perhaps the worst part. If he had an exact date when his lover would return, then at least he would *know*: it would still be painful to be apart from her, but it would be bearable - all he would have to do would be to count the endless nights before she came back to him. But he had been denied even that much.

As he sat, sitting in the darkness that had been his existence for so long, something else needled away at his thoughts. In all his years, in all of the decades that he had wandered, free, independent and, for the most part, alone, how was it now that he had become so totally reliant on another soul? How was it that, after only a few hours without Holly by his side he now felt weak and vulnerable.

And dead.

Michael looked at the cold light of the stars, beginning to understand something simple yet vital. He had allowed his strength to die, had become so wrapped up in being with Holly that nothing else mattered. And it was no wonder that he had been unable to guide his lover as she'd needed, because he could no longer guide himself.

Anger began to boil under his skin, and he allowed it to fill him up, allowing it to drive away that sense of emptiness. Anger that was directed at no one except himself. He had pretty much given up on everything except Holly, fighting against his own individual nature, forgetting that he was his own person. But, ironically, he knew that this would ultimately lead to losing Holly completely. For as she grew, he would continue to fade.

"No more." Michael whispered to the empty darkness around him. Holly had gone to find out who she was, and Michael was going to spend the time rediscovering who *he* was.

He smiled in a way that had last felt natural to him a few centuries before, the smile of a hunter closing in on its prey. Without another thought, Michael fled into the night.

Blaiden walked through the *Night Cafe*, allowing himself the enjoyment of not being stared at. It was totally empty, not one person sitting at any of the empty tables. He reached the counter and pressed the small buzzer that would bring either Iain or the blonde waitress.

His luck held and, as the door between the cafe and the hallway beyond opened, Blaiden saw the cafe's owner walk through. With a smile, he held the door open for Blaiden and then closed and secured it.

At the second door Iain allowed himself to glance down at the blood-soaked rag that the ancient creature vampire held, but he didn't say a word. Although he hid it better than the rest, he was in complete awe of the two archaic beings with their bleached complexions; in awe, and totally terrified.

Blaiden sensed most of what Iain was feeling, but had no intention of trying to either make the man feel more at ease (as he would normally be inclined to do), or to encourage his nervousness (as he liked to do when he was feeling roguish). Instead, he simply allowed the man to unlock the door and passed through uttering only a subdued 'thank you'.

He walked down the cream-hallway alone and heard the door being locked behind him. In the rose-light, he went to the room that he had been frequenting. Using his free hand, he quickly dipped into his pocket and brought out the key.

Inside, the fire he had ignited still burnt behind the clear fire-guard and the light flickered over the sparsely decorated, but totally comfortable, room.

He walked to the double-bed where Ania lay, her bare shoulders a total contrast to her black hair. He gazed at her face, at the features made delicate by sleep, softened further by the gentle firelight. Her lips, full and dark red, were parted slightly, waiting for what she needed.

Blaiden sat beside the sleeping form and raised the cloth above her face. Positioning it over her lips, he gently squeezed it. He watched as the blood flowed, drop by drop into her mouth, and saw her throat working to drink it down. He continued to feed her that way until the rag he held contained no more blood.

He put the rag into the bathroom sink and washed the remains of the blood from his fingertips. Then he returned to his love's side.

He leant his head against hers and watched the glow of the fire as it danced across the walls, wondering for the millionth time when she would find her way back to him.

V

Gusts of wind propelled the torrents of rain against every available surface. Rivers of rain that had begun that afternoon as small puddles ran unrestrained through flooded streets. The storm had built up throughout the day and had soon caused thousands of pounds worth of damage over the country. Trees were ripped from the ground, tiles were pulled from roofs, and houses were flooded.

Those who had decided to continue with celebrations only half-heartedly watched the clock while also watching the damage that happened to the world outside.

People counted down unenthusiastically, silently wondering, if this was how the new year was starting, what the rest of the year would entail. In a number of homes, the cheers as midnight arrived were accompanied by groans and shrieks as fences outside were demolished, as large branches crashed on top of cars, and a barrage of debris was smashed against, and in some cases through, windows.

In a dense forest, the onslaught of rain turning the ground into a swamp, the air began to vibrate. Animals that had braved the storm now raced for shelter as they sensed the oncoming attack. As clocks chimed and people cheered, an explosion of noise roared through the forest and the darkness was momentarily banished by a blaze of light. Shards of wood flew through the air as a large oak tree was struck by the fork of lightning. Despite the water lashing down flames licked at the now-exposed dry wood which would continue to burn for a number of minutes. Electricity, power, was thick in the air.

Deeper inside that same forest, its windows now shielded by metal mesh, stood the *Night Cafe*. Yet despite the storm that raged outside, the cafe was still open, the soft pink light filtering through the gaps of the metal screens: the doors of that sanctuary only closed when sunlight filled the world.

In one of the few rooms that were occupied, at the precise moment that the oak tree was struck, at the instant that the air of the forest was charged to its peak with power, Ania's eyes flew open, the killer clear in the blue-grey eyes.

Walking through a maze of alleyways, Blaiden fleetingly lost interest in following his prey. He spun around, looking in the direction of the refuge, oblivious now to the rain that still fell over and around him. A smile lit his face and his eyes blazed with happiness. Still smiling, he turned his attention back to his quarry, feeling a new level of excitement as he continued on his hunt.

Michael's prey had a glimmer of hope for survival as the vampire's hands briefly loosened on the collar of his jacket. Miles from the house he now considered home, Michael turned quickly to glance to the east. Smiling a hard smile, he turned back to the man he had caught. Seeing the expression of hunger in the vampire's eyes, the man's glimmer of hope was extinguished like a candle flame.

Sodden clothes clinging to her figure, Holly whipped around, the man she had been holding against the wall almost-gracefully slipping to the ground as she let go.

Her heart hammered an exciting beat in her chest and, elated, she closed her eyes, a bead of blood still glistening upon her lips. She blocked out the musty smell of the garage, blocked out the sound of the rain at it hammered on the roof above her. In her mind, she searched for the truth of what she felt.

Her lips turned up in a smile, exposing the red-stained teeth and that bead of blood rolled over her lip and onto her chin.

Ania was awake!

With renewed vigour coursing through her Holly turned her back to the unconscious man. Almost savagely in her invigorated state, Holly sank beside him and continued to feed.

Never had there been hunger like this! Never in all of her millennia had there *ever* been such a ravenous unquenchable thirst! Quickly, Ania sat up, the cover falling away to reveal the naked flesh beneath. Fluidly, she swept her equally-bare legs out of the bed and stood.

The low flames that still gently blazed in the fireplace sent flickers of orange and yellow over her white flesh as Ania prowled to the far side of the room, her body moving as gracefully as a panther.

With her clothes in hand, Ania's sensual lips curled up into a snarl, her eyes flaring with contempt. She yearned to discard them, to leave the building with the feel of her long hair on her bare back, to feel the cold rain as it fell on her colder skin, to hunt purely as the predator she was.

And a pure predator she was, wholly and unpolluted by any real thoughts. The hunger had consumed all but the animalistic killer that was the core of what she was, and there was no fighting it. In the moments before she had woken, Ania had surrendered to that famished animal.

Just as her hunger had never been as vast neither had her senses ever been as sharp. She could hear each drop of rain as loud as a drumbeat; could smell the blood of the creatures that hid in the forest; could see the smallest speck of dust that hid in the darkest corner of the room.

With a low growl, the creature dropped the clothes onto the floor and turned, still without a stitch of clothing to cover her perfect pale form, towards the door. Hastily, she struck the black button that was positioned beside the door. A key was hung above it, which was rapidly stabbed into the keyhole.

Leaving the key where it was and without closing the door, Ania stepped into the rose-tinted hallway and made her way to the end of the corridor where her acute hearing picked up the sound of keys jingling.

Iain opened the door and jumped backwards in shock. He was accustomed to the speed in which his clientele moved, but he generally had a chance to open the heavy door before any of them had made it halfway to the door. Nor was that his only shock as he recognised Ania.

She regarded him as a lioness would regard potential prey as she moved past him and, trying to swallow the lump that had mystically appeared in his throat, with shaking hands Iain quickly closed and locked the door. Still feeling her eyes on him, he rushed ahead of her to unlock the door between the hallway and the cafe.

With wild hunger dancing in her animal eyes, she walked through the cafe and across the rose-dyed linoleum.

Iain glanced quickly at the deserted cafe, grateful that he had no actual human customers. He had a feeling that if he had, even in the protection of the sanctuary they would have been about as safe as flies caught in a web. He watched as the ancient killer walked naked into the raging storm, disappearing in a flash of pale skin into the dense woods.

Hurriedly, Iain closed the door, not feeling the slightest bit secure: he couldn't shake off the look he had seen in her eyes.

It called to her and she relinquished herself to the night. As the storm seethed around her, she felt an equally powerful storm rage within her. It pounded through every part of her, and she had no choice but to be taken by it.

Lithely, Ania tore through the forest, guided only by blind instinct as she dodged tree roots and the assorted tangle of woodland debris that littered the ground. She felt the exquisite bite of pain as branches ripped into her, the cuts healing almost instantly, and still she ran. A twist of brambles stretched across her path, tearing at her thighs. Not slowing even a small amount, Ania wiped the palm of her hand over a deep gash on her upper thigh before it could heal. Rapture filled her as she licked the dark blood from her hand.

The miniscule taste made her thirst worse and Ania slid to a stop. The time of revelling in her hunger had ended. She closed her eyes and listened to the night. To her left, about fifty yards away, she heard the silent trembling of a young fox that had been startled by her sudden appearance. Her ears pin-pointed the location of the infant vixen and she turned to stare into the darkness, focussing completely now on her prey, ignoring the still-torrential rain as it poured around and upon her. Her eyes narrowed, and her sightline fixed upon the small creature's black eyes. Everything else seemed to fade to nothing, melting into insignificance, while the fox seemed more vivid and intense.

Ania could smell the animal's terror, could almost taste it. Revealing her sharp teeth as her mouth curved into a half-snarl half-smile, all of the muscles in her body tensed up. A low growl escaped from her throat and her muscles tightened a fraction more, the rain flowing over her body, following the contours of her muscles. Then the spring was sprung. She lunged forwards and the fox was caught before it had even registered any movement.

There was nothing tender about Ania as she effortlessly ripped the animal's head from its torso, lifting both pieces above her so that the warm blood cascaded onto her face. Her neck worked frantically as the liquid-salvation went down her throat. But the red waterfall ended too soon, and her thirst was nowhere close to being sated. Callously, she flung the spent animal away from her.

Her eyes narrowed once more, and she gracefully pivoted on

the spot, allowing her senses to do what they were so good at. She found another target and bolted onwards.

While she fed, the forest itself seemed to cower at the simple ferocity of her nature. Animals that had concealed themselves well were sought out easily, found simply by the drumming of their skittish heartbeats as they tried to shroud themselves from the creature that had fallen amongst them.

But soon the animal inside of Ania registered that these simple beings would never satisfy, no matter how many she killed. Allowing her razor-sharp instinct to guide her feet again, she sprinted through the woods.

The man could only stare in disbelief. In that split second before his life was ended, he looked upon the woman who stood in the doorway. Her naked body glistened with rain; her mouth was stained red; and her eyes were wild and intense. No conscious or clear thought passed through his mind in the brief moment between his opening the door to his throat being opened. There was simply no time - his life was over.

Ania was aware of the contradiction of her feelings, and marvelled at them. The energy that coursed through her thanks to the sheer volume of blood she had consumed seemed totally separate to the utter exhaustion she felt. She walked slowly passed trees that, only an hour before, she had flown by. Every rain drop that touched her from the still-gushing skies felt imbued with energy, but also as if it could easily knock her to the ground.

She stopped and looked upwards, standing in the freezing-cold shower of nature, and the water rolled over her upturned face, washing away the small amount of blood that had lingered on her skin.

She heard the crack of a twig behind her, and felt the soft lining of his jacket as Blaiden draped it over her shoulders.

Feeling as if she was living in a dream, where everything felt unreal, she pivoted to face him, *truly* seeing him. She stepped into his embrace, and their lips met, an eternity since the last.

Holly lay looking at the ceiling of the garage, wet clothes hanging up, wrapped in an old blanket she'd found. The board beneath her was hard, but she didn't mind - in a weird way it was almost comfortable. The rafters above her were scattered with cobwebs, and the dust around her was disturbed only by the marks she had made herself. She had already checked the roof for holes or gaps and had found none. Miles away from where she had fed, she lay there, safe from the garage below her and protected from the sun that would be above her, Holly closed her eyes, lonely yet curiously content.

Michael also lay on his back looking upwards, but at a different ceiling than Holly. He rested his head on his arms. As Holly did, he also felt strangely serene. But unlike Holly, something bit at his heart. He tried to put it down to loneliness, a complete contradiction to the peacefulness he felt. If he had ever had the experience of being drunk, or even had experimented with drugs, he would have likened it to that - of knowing in his head that something was amiss, but being so loaded that he couldn't care. Instead he simply lay there, relishing the complexity of his emotions and waited for sleep to take him.

* * *

Claire had been lucky. The brief but violent storm that had ravaged the entire country, destroying homes and killing twelve people, had left her own house with very little damage. There may be things that she had not yet noticed, but all she had seen so far were a couple of smashed plant-pots and a smashed window on the side door of the garage.

Holding the basket full of washing, she peered into the darkness of her garden. Claire balanced the basket on her hip as she unlocked her back door and, continuing to carry it that way, she braved the cold winter night and stepped out. She smiled as she walked towards the garage, keys held in one hand, reflecting on one of the great wonders of her life that no one else seemed to appreciate - the great thing about having big hips, it helped when you needed to carry large items with one hand.

Keeping steady, she leant forwards and unlocked the large garage door, dropping the keys back into her jacket pocket.

Something clattered in the darkness, and she snapped her head around to try and find what had caused the sound. She could see nothing in the night and laughed shakily to herself. She thought herself strong, but put her in the dark and her imagination went wild. It probably didn't help that she had seen far too many horror films.

Her nerves rose a little more as she prepared to swing the garage door up. In her mind she could see something standing there, waiting for her to open it. She could see it there, possibly a zombie, vacant eyes hanging above a hungry mouth.

She shook her head to shake the image away. It went (almost), and she pushed the top of the door. The bottom swung out a little and she hooked the toes of her shoe underneath. Gracefully, she kicked it upwards so that it was high enough for her to reach without having to bend down. With her mind presenting her once more with the image of a horror-film character, she pulled her garage door up a little higher.

Claire reached her hand into the blackness and her fingers searched for the light-switch. Her imagination showed her the vision of a cold hand, nails grimy with dirt, reaching out for hers. Her fingertips found what they searched for and she flipped the switch, hastily retracting her hand.

She ducked under the half opened door as the lights trembled before they decided to stay on. She laughed at her own nervousness, embarrassed yet knowing that the next time she would do exactly the same thing. Quickly, and with that same feeling of acting ridiculously, she glanced around the garage, trying to peer behind the assorted clutter, seeing nothing out of the ordinary.

She walked to the tumble dryer and set the basket down in front of it. She emptied the contents into the dryer and switched it on, jumping as it noisily started its cycle.

Laughing, Claire raised her now-empty hand to her face and rubbed her eyes. "I think I'd better lay off the horror flicks for a while." She whispered to herself.

"I don't know," whispered a voice directly behind her. "I've always enjoyed a good scare."

Claire's hands slowly dropped to her side, and she became suddenly aware of the cold of the night. Her heart thumped loudly; she could feel each bead of sweat on her skin. Knowing that there was, indeed, a hand now reaching out for her, she began to turn.

The woman stood before her, blonde hair hanging past her shoulders, clothes looking damp. In pale skin, her hazel eyes blazed.

Below, dark red lips opened slightly to show the long and very sharp looking teeth.

She had no doubt of what it was, her love of horror films allowing the knowledge to filter through quickly. But now that the imaginary had become reality, was now standing right before her, her fear seemed to melt away. She began to learn that once you face what you fear, the fear transforms to pure reaction.

And as that pale hand got closer, that had been reaching for her all along, she responded by stretching out her own and stepping forwards.

Thirty-five minutes later, Holly stepped out of the shower, wet but clean hair dripping water onto the floor. She quickly dried herself then wrapped the towel around her hair. Naked, Holly walked into the girl's bedroom, using the towel to rub her hair.

She momentarily lost herself in the dark purple of the room, looking at all of the trinkets and ornaments, all purple; everything, even the sheets on the bed, was some shade or tint of purple. As she stood there, she wondered how anyone could actually *sleep* in there - she'd only been in the room for a few minutes and it was already hurting her head.

She looked at the photographs of the now-deceased girl, pictures that were housed inside fluffy purple frames. Smiling, she turned her attention to finding some clothes. Dreading what she would find when she opened the mirrored doors, Holly pulled one of the handles towards her.

It was worse than she had imagined. The colour that had totally engulfed the room had also crept into the wardrobe, infecting the contents. Without holding out any hope, Holly began to look through the clothes that hung from the rails. Even if they had been a colour that she would have wanted to wear, the smallest of the clothes were still two sizes too big.

Sighing, Holly glanced at a couple of piles of clothes folded up neatly at the bottom and crouched down. Halfway through one of them she found a pair of dark blue jeans only one size too big. Her luck held out a little longer and she found a black long-sleeved velvet top, also only one size too big. Searching right at the back, underneath high-heel shoes, she discovered a thin black belt that would at least stop the trousers from sliding off of her hips.

There was absolutely no chance of any of the girl's underwear fitting her, but her own was only slightly damp and would have to do.

She got dressed and looked at her reflection in the mirrored-door. She laughed - she couldn't help it. It wasn't *that* bad, but it was very obvious that the clothes were too big for her.

"Next time I'll have to find someone the same size as me." She said pleasantly to the image in the mirror.

Still smiling, she took her still wet clothes and left the room. In the hallway, she found a navy-blue rucksack and unceremoniously shoved her clothes inside.

With the rucksack perched on one shoulder, Holly stood in the kitchen, looking at the cupboards. It took a few minutes, but eventually she found something suitable and took the can with her.

Outside, the wind had started to pick up again, and it whipped her wet hair around her face, spraying droplets over her face. In the garage, she looked at the dryer that still laboured tirelessly, then walked up to the far end.

Amongst the boxes the girl lay, pale and motionless. Holly crouched beside the body and looked at her. She narrowed her vision and stared at her, taking in every detail. She saw the strands of mousy-brown hair that fell across the soft skin of her face; open yet glazed brown eyes; could see the small scars of acne long gone; could see the creases of laughter lines around her mouth.

Looking at the girl as she was, Holly expected to feel guilty, to feel a crushing blow for the life she had ended. But she didn't. Compassion, even gratitude, but not guilt. Standing up and looking over, Holly gently used the palm of her hand to close those eyes before placing a soft kiss on the skin between them.

"Thank you, my friend." She whispered to the corpse.

She removed the lid from the can and pointed the nozzle at the boxes and squeezed. The lighter fluid arched through the air and Holly swung the can slightly side to side so that all of the boxes were at least slightly damp with the liquid.

Putting the can on the floor, she returned to the house and started searching the kitchen again. In one of the drawers she found a heavy gold lighter and took it outside.

With a final look at who had aided her in her survival, Holly struck the wheel of the lighter. The flame flickered softly as she leant over and touched it to one of the boxes. As the flames caught, Holly closed the lighter and put it in the right-hand pocket of the jeans and simply turned around and walked out of the garage, listening to the growing sounds of crackling and burning as she swung the door down.

They moved together above the covers, the low-burning flames flickering light over their white skins, glistening with sweat. Millennia since their first union, they joined once again, sharing each other more passionately than either had experienced in their eternal lives. They explored each other's bodies and their love felt familiar and brand new simultaneously. Through the night they made up for lost time, euphoria repeatedly reached together.

Ania and Blaiden lay in each other's arms, bare skin to bare skin, as the night moved on silently. They had fed as soon as the sun had hidden its last beam of light, knowing that their night would be spent feeding another desire.

There was also another reason for the hasty and efficient feeding. Leaving their room together, they were greeted by a paler-than-normal Iain. He looked tired, drawn. And, when his eyes darted between the two ancient creatures, unsure.

"I don't want to appear rude," he said, in a voice barely above a whisper and no more than courteous, looking at them in small sips, not allowing his eyes to linger on either of them for very long. "But I need to ask when you will be planning to leave."

Ania stepped forward one step, feeling Blaiden's arm drop from around her waist. Tiredness and a small sense of loneliness seeped through her good feelings as she saw the terror increase in Iain's eyes. But she admired him as he continued to stand his ground and didn't back away.

"Iain, I do apologise sincerely. I did not mean to cause you any distress." She smiled a little, and felt saddened further as it wasn't returned. "I wasn't myself."

Without speaking, Iain handed Ania a copy of the newspaper that he was holding, watching her as she glanced at the front page.

The headline read: VIOLENT STORM CAUSES ANIMAL ATTACKS?

Quickly, Ania scanned the story that was next to a black and white photograph of a forest, where trees were splattered with a dark colour.

She looked up, turning her gaze from the report of the deaths of countless animals plus one man, supposedly killed by animals driven mad by the sheer intensity of the storm.

"We'll stay here tonight and leave when the sun sets tomorrow night." She said briskly, handing the paper back to Iain.

He'd turned to lead them outside, still not speaking. And when they returned after their rapid hunt it was another vampire, new to both of them, who allowed them back inside the refuge.

Now they lay together, Ania's head resting on Blaiden's chest while his fingers gently stroked her naked shoulder, and they both gazed at the embers of the dying fire.

With a reminiscent smile, Blaiden spoke gently, still stroking her shoulder. He smiled wider as he spoke words that Ania had uttered upon their first meeting. "It's your turn to spin a tale."

In his arms, Ania laughed and echoed more of her own words from those many years ago. "Yes, my love. Now it's story hour once more."

Blaiden laughed along with her. "So, who was the girl that was in danger while you slept. And what caused you to be so far from her."

Still smiling, briefly thinking of the vast amount of stories that she could share from her life since they were last together, Ania truly believed that her current one was the most amazing. Her girlish streak seemed to have returned with her lover, and she couldn't wait to see Blaiden's reaction when he heard.

"The girl is Holly, and the danger she was in, as it turns out, was nothing she couldn't handle."

"I'm guessing she had a good teacher." Blaiden interrupted.

"You could say that." She paused and rolled onto her side, resting her head on her hand, raised on her elbow. With a smile, she looked at him, still unable to completely believe that he was lying beside her.

"Well, Holly's one of us-"

"I guessed that." Blaiden said, drowsily.

"A few years ago, she joined with a vampire, Michael. And fell pregnant."

"What..?" Blaiden, who had been on the verge of slipping towards sleep, jerked completely awake.

"The child's blood mixed with her own, and after the child was born, she turned. Quicker and more intensely than I've ever seen anyone turn."

Blaiden lay looking at her, eyes wide. "She turned without being bitten? Without drinking from a vampire?"

Ania nodded. "And the reason that I'm so far from her, is that I'm tracking down her child."

Blaiden sat up, eyes screwing closed briefly as he fought to process it all. When he again looked at Ania his eyes were wild with excitement. "The child survived?"

"Yes."

"The child was born, and it survived?"

"Yes."

"And the mother survived, and is now a vampire?"

"Yes."

Naked, Blaiden got out of bed and, in the darkness of the room, paced alongside it as he struggled to deal with everything she'd said. Ania smiled at his almost-theatrical reaction, yet was unable to prevent herself from lustfully gazing at his body.

"So, a woman who was turned purely by falling pregnant by a vampire, who survived. And a child who was *born* a vampire, who survived." He looked at her. "Have I got that right?"

"Yes."

He ran a hand through his hair and collapsed onto the bed. "Shit."

She burst out laughing at the shocked expression on his face and the quiet way he'd sworn. He turned and looked at her and, after a moment, joined in.

"It's never happened before, has it?" he asked, when they were both finally capable of speaking again.

"The pregnancy, it's rare but not unprecedented. Either surviving... I've never heard of. So, no, I don't think it ever has."

Brow creased, Blaiden looked into the now-dead fireplace. "Do you think the child's still alive?"

Ania shook her head at the question, the one question that she had not allowed herself to ask. "I don't know. I don't believe we can try and guess anything about this."

The twinkle rose in his eyes as he smiled at her. "I don't suppose you want any company for this little quest of yours, do you,

Ania?"

Her heart flew upwards, and she smiled gently. "Only out of curiosity, of course."

"Of course."

Now that they had that issue worked out, Ania allowed her eyes to follow the contours of his body again. And to allow Blaiden to see her looking.

Iain was once more absent as the doors were unlocked and the petrified vampire who accepted their key back barely acknowledged their thanks.

The cloudy skies had done nothing to raise the temperature, and their shoes crunched over frost-ridden grass as they walked together away from the *Night Cafe*. Feeling watched, Ania glanced over her shoulder, looking back through the glass windows. Iain was standing next to the other vampire now and they were both stood behind the counter watching as the couple walked away. Not for one second did Ania believe it was a coincidence, that they just happened to be looking - she knew, down deep in her gut, that Iain just wanted to make sure that they were really leaving.

VI

The twelfth of January was, to most people, a miserable night. Rain had poured from the cloud-entombed skies all day and, although there was no danger of floods, the streets ran thick with water. The pavements reflected the orange lights, the rays bouncing off of the water.

Two creatures stood on a bridge looking out over the water. Blaiden's black jeans and short-sleeved shirt were sodden, his hair plastered to his head. Ania's trousers and long-sleeved top were in a similar state and her long hair hung down her back in a saturated pony-tail. Their arms were wrapped around each other, as they had been each time they had stopped moving.

They had covered the fifty miles in ten days, a great deal slower than they could have travelled, but they were lost in the wonder at being side by side and, wordlessly, they both wanted to revel in it, if only for a short time.

As the night of the twelfth passed into the early hours of the thirteenth, Ania tore her gaze from the river and stared at the place where, four-and-a-half years previously, she had met Holly.

"So, where do we start?" Blaiden leant back casually against the wet railings of the bridge, hands deep in pockets.

She pushed a wet lock of hair out of her eyes. "I don't think I can ask at the hospital, that's for sure."

Blaiden laughed. "No, I don't think that would be advisable." Still smiling, he tilted his head back a little, letting the rain fall onto his upturned face.

"The newspapers would have covered the child being left." Ania said, almost absently, as she looked at him. Lust tore at her as she looked at him, and had to smile - since his return, that feeling never seemed too far away.

"But it may be more than a little difficult for us to trace her that way."

Ania mirrored him, tilting her own head backwards, the cold drops of rain refreshing her. After a few moments, the rain had the desired effect and she was able to focus on the problem at hand and not on the way that Blaiden's clothes were clinging to the curves and lines of his toned body. Well, almost.

Still smiling, she pushed herself gently away from the bridge and walked a couple of steps to the right. Standing exactly where she had stood all those years ago, looking at the place where Holly's first victim had lain. Ania cast her mind backwards, delving deep into her memory. She had followed Holly as she'd run; followed her after Holly had abandoned her daughter; followed her every step after Holly had left the hospital; followed her, knowing that...

"...that the other two would watch the child." She finished aloud.

Without Ania having been aware of it, Blaiden had once more moved to her side. "What, Ania?" He asked quietly.

Eyes blazing with the excitement of inspiration, Ania turned to him. "I followed Holly when she left the hospital. I followed her, and I left the child alone because *there were two other vampires who were watching her*!"

Like a virus Blaiden caught her enthusiasm. "There were *other* vampires as well?!" He saw her nod. "Well, this tale keeps getting more and more interesting." He paused to kiss Ania passionately. "So how do we find them?"

"The old-fashioned way." She replied, her eyes still burning. "We ask around."

* * *

Their routine over the following ten months was essentially the same. They travelled around the area, they fed, and they asked questions of any vampire they came across. And before the night finished they returned to wherever they had chosen to spend their day, and said farewell to the night joined together. They had become used to having to give chase when vampires they had tried to approach turned and fled. Not that either of them blamed the younger vampires - they understood that being approached by two obviously age-old creatures would be slightly unnerving. But trying to flee was just absurd: as all vampires were able to move quicker than humans, both Ania and Blaiden made their fastest movements look like a snails-pace.

On the twenty-second night of November, a cold dense fog filled the gaps between the rows of houses. Two sets of footsteps echoed through the other-wise deserted streets, one rapid and filled with haste and the other unhurried, almost leisurely.

The man who had been in his thirties when he had been turned fifty-seven years previously glanced anxiously over his shoulder, but even his eyesight had trouble piercing through the fog. But he knew that she still followed him.

He'd managed to avoid them for three nights. His knowledge of the area and all its small hidden escape routes was immense. But tonight, after side-stepping them and turning down a small alleyway, she had suddenly been in front of him. Despite the almost alluring spark in her eyes, he'd turned and run, trying to lose himself in the gloom. But her footsteps had followed his.

A voice drifted through the air, soft and haunting, only a whisper.

"Anthony."

His anxiousness stepped up another notch and he quickened his pace a little more.

As much fun as it was, Ania grew tired of scaring him, despite how much he deserved it for giving them the run-around for three nights, so she began to herd him to the street where Blaiden waited, speaking his name lightly into the darkness.

The houses were now long behind them, having given way to shops, and Ania continued to drive him, without his knowledge, right to where she needed him to go.

She heard him stub his toe on a stone, heard him cry out in surprise as he lost his balance and started to fall forwards. She heard the sigh of his silk shirt against his body as he neared the ground. And below those sounds, she heard the silent breeze of another movement.

Blaiden caught Anthony an inch before his face would have come into contact with the cold damp pavement and pulled him to his feet. Still holding him securely, Blaiden leant closer and moved his face next to Anthony's so that he could see the fear in the younger creature's eyes.

"No more running."

Ania had moved directly behind Anthony and gently touched her lips to his ear. "No more running, Anthony; we just want to talk."

Still holding him, they both backed up a little to give him slightly more space. With a smile, Ania spoke once again. "I think it's time you showed us where you live, don't you."

His hand shook as he lifted the cigarette to his mouth and when he exhaled the blue-grey smoke it left his lungs in ragged breaths. The other hand had been holding a glass of whiskey, but after spilling almost two-thirds of its contents over the floor near his feet Anthony had put it down.

The flat he had 'borrowed' from its former owner was sparsely furnished, yet still comfortable and warm. Anthony sat on a blue plush armchair yet looked uncomfortable despite its obvious softness. Ania and Blaiden sat upon the small two-seater sofa, both sitting on the edge, looking intently at the man opposite them.

"There really is no reason for you to be so worried, Anthony." Ania said gently. "We just need your help with something."

"Just a few questions." Blaiden added.

"Questions? What about?" Anthony said after a moments pause.

Ania and Blaiden exchanged a brief glance. It looked like they'd managed to relax him enough so that he could at least take in the situation - his hands weren't shaking quite so much, either.

Ania leant forward slightly, and Anthony's flickering eyes focussed entirely, and warily, on her. "Have you seen me before, Anthony?" she asked.

He nodded, then feared that it may not be quite enough. "Yeah, I've seen you before."

"When? And where?"

He stared into Ania's eyes, trying to figure out her intentions, then sighed, giving up. She was too difficult to read, and also it didn't really matter - if they wanted to hurt him he'd be totally defenceless against them. With this stark realisation reached, Anthony allowed his eyes to close as he searched his memory and tried to work out the time-line of his past.

After a brief pause, while he double-checked his memories, the youngest of the three once again opened his eyes and looked at her. "Five years ago. Either June or July, I can't remember which." He saw her nod slightly, and felt a twinkle of encouragement, that maybe he wasn't in too much trouble after all.

"I saw you outside the hospital, you were waiting outside the hospital grounds. A blonde came running out of the building, you looked at something close to the hospital, then you followed her."

Ania was smiling openly. "You've got a good memory."

Anthony returned the smile, although it still had an edge of caution to it. "I'd wager yours is better."

His sudden demonstration of humour, especially after his continued cautious attitude, shocked both of the ancient vampires into laughter.

"Better than I'd like sometimes." Ania said, her tone serious but still with a smile on her lips.

Anthony relaxed finally into his chair, resting his arms on the armrests and tilting his head slightly so that he could stare at the pale ceiling. Now that she had called on him to remember, the memory seemed completely fresh.

Ania and Blaiden also sat back in their seats after exchanging an uncertain look, and Ania was amazed as to the change in Anthony's whole demeanour in only a few brief moments; it was astonishing what laughter could do.

"I mistook her for one of us, you know." Anthony said conversationally, looking pleasantly at his new acquaintances. "Until I saw the papers a couple of days later, anyway."

"You thought she was one of us?"

He glanced at Ania. "Yeah. Newly turned, but yeah, I thought she was. There was just something about her that seemed to suggest it." He chuckled ironically to himself. "Then the newspapers reported that she'd been found dead-"

Smiling, Ania and Blaiden looked at each other.

"-so I figured she wasn't." He lit another cigarette, and was able to smoke it without his hand shaking.

While Ania stayed sitting back, regarding Anthony with something close to fondness, Blaiden leant forwards slightly and looked at him.

"You keep your ear to the ground, so you know we've been looking for you for a while. Your name keeps being mentioned by every vampire we've asked."

Anthony grinned proudly.

"You gave us the run-around for longer than anyone else managed-"

Anthony's grin widened.

"-but all we wanted were questions answered."

"Yeah, I heard that." he said between puffs. "But I just thought that there was more to it than that."

"What exactly did you hear?" Ania enquired.

Anthony looked at her and raised an eyebrow. "Exactly?"

She nodded, a corner of her mouth raised in a sly smile.

"That two vampires, ancient, possibly even the first, were looking for two other vampires, both young. These vampires were last seen outside the hospital, summer, five years ago."

Choosing to ignore the comments at the beginning of his reply, Ania looked eagerly at him. "You saw me, Anthony, and you saw her. Did you see them?"

Anthony grinned slyly, but not maliciously, at her. "He was average height, mousy-brown hair, blue eyes. Stunning, very bad-boy rebel-type. Looked like he'd been turned a couple of decades, couldn't have been longer."

Ania was nodding, looking at him like a teacher looking at a student. "And the other?"

"Average build, brown eyes. She kept pushing at her nose, like she was trying to push glasses that were falling down. She must have had to wear them before she was turned. She was plain-looking, but there was a sadness about her that made her almost beautiful. Very new, not even a year turned."

"I'm impressed." Blaiden said with a grin.

"So am I." Ania added. "But now the important question, the million pound question, Anthony. Ready?"

He sat there looking at her, at the twinkle in her eyes. There was no trace of nerves in him now, and he thought it was funny how scared he had actually been. "Ready and willing." he said with a wink.

"Have you seen them since?"

He laughed and drew a final drag on his cigarette before putting it out in the small silver ashtray beside him. "No, not seen them, but like you said-" he glanced at Blaiden. "-I keep my ear to the ground."

They had both again moved closer to the edge of their seats and were looking at him in anticipation.

"You know where they are?"

He lit another cigarette and looked at them through smoke,

his eyes twinkling. "Of course."

The next night they stood in the shadows of another house, watching as the lights were turned off in the mid-terrace house opposite. The garden was dishevelled and overgrown; even the 'sold' sign had an air of abandonment and rejection about it: it tilted off slightly to one side, and grass had begun to grow upwards against the post.

Seconds after the last gleam of light ceased to shine through the black curtains and escape through the gaps in the boarded windows, the front door was opened briefly to allow a couple to exit. While the woman locked the door and dropped the keys in to her dark denim jacket pocket, the man stood with his hands in his jeans pocket, looking broodily up at the cloud-filled sky.

Ania and Blaiden watched them, hidden completely from view, as the two of them walked down the road without speaking, walking about a meter apart.

"Affectionate couple." Blaiden whispered with a grin.

Ania also smiled, but her eyes narrowed as she watched them walk further into the night. Whether it was her talents that she had long thought gone or her animalistic instincts, whatever it was, it amounted to the same: She didn't trust them.

"Ready?"

She felt his hand on hers, their fingers twining together, and looked at him. "Yeah."

Hand in hand, the ancient duo followed the younger pair, keeping their distance as they walked through the streets.

Not wanting to give them chance to disappear into the night when they reached the centre of the town Blaiden continued to trail them while Ania hurriedly fed, returning after only a few minutes, wiping the small stain of blood from her lips with the palm of her hand.

A brief kiss passed between them, then it was Blaiden's turn to go out on the prowl. He left, and Ania remained watching while her targets lured a young woman away from her group of friends. Ania faded into the background, blending seamlessly into the shadows, dancing with the darkness, unseen yet still watching as they enacted their little play. They acted it perfectly, and their victim went into death willingly.

They wasted no time in draining the girl and then uncaringly dumped her body in a large bin. Ania watched their callous treatment of the girl's remains with anger beginning to simmer in her heart.

She turned as an arm worked its way back into place around her waist. He squeezed her softly to him and rested his forehead on hers.

"I know, Ania. But we need them, we need to follow them if we're going to find the child."

She nodded, closing his eyes. He was right, she *knew* he was right, yet she still had to bite back on her feelings. She nodded once more, mostly to herself. "Yeah."

Blaiden's voice grew quieter as he watched out of the corner of his eyes when the two young vampires emerged from the gap between the two shops where they had drawn the girl. "Don't look up, not even for a second. Let them pass."

Still with her eyes closed, trusting him, trusting *in* him, she nodded slightly again.

Moments passed and they stayed in their embrace, her hands on his chest and his on her waist. Although she didn't open her eyes - *dare not* open them because the sight of them would cause her to lose control - she sensed when they walked past. However, they were too wrapped up in themselves to notice when they went by the ancient hunters.

Blaiden watched them walking away, and allowed them to lengthen the distance between them. They were still in sight, they could still be followed, but he wanted to make sure that Ania would not suffer a momentary loss of restraint. He could feel how close she was, how hard she was fighting, and he loved her even more for it.

Judging it was now safe, he brushed his lips on the top of her brow and stepped back slightly, his fingers still in place, comfortably on her hips. When she raised her head to look at him he searched her eyes. Although he found no comfort in the fury he saw there, the strength of her self-control that also showed through reassured him enough.

She smiled as he took one of her hands, raising it to his lips and planting a gentle kiss on her skin.

Hand in hand, they walked after the still-oblivious couple, keeping far enough away for Ania to hold the reins of her temper.

Ryan and Jesse ambled almost without purpose, without a word passing between them, and spitefully Ania smiled as she repeatedly remembered what Blaiden had said at the beginning of the night. *Affectionate couple, alright(!)*

They walked a foot apart, Ryan with his hands shoved firmly in his pockets, looking resolutely ahead of him. Jesse's arms hung by her side, but her hands were turned in to her legs so that, even when they had to walk closer together, there was no chance of her fingers even brushing him.

As they followed them into more residential streets, Blaiden voiced her own thoughts.

"They look as if they can't bear to be near to each other."

Ania nodded. "It's as though they need to be together, they're resigned to it, but-"

"-they still intend to be as far apart as they can." Blaiden finished.

Ania was about to add more but noticed that the 'couple' in front of them had stopped walking.

Ania and Blaiden glanced at each other in anticipation. This was it. This was the moment, the place, she had set out for, searched for. Promised her protégé that she would find. Furtively, her gaze darted around, looking for somewhere out of sight.

Directly behind the two estranged-yet-together vampires, who both stared at a house on the opposite side of the street, was a mass of trees in an un-bordered garden. Holding her lover's hand tightly, Ania moved at a lightning speed. She and Blaiden passed by Ryan and Jesse without their knowledge and were instantaneously hidden in the deep impenetrable shadows behind them.

This close, Ania once again had the rising compulsion to move directly behind them both and wrap her fingers around - and in - their necks. Even with her level of control, and Blaiden's hand in hers, she felt the reins beginning to tear, the animal threatening to set upon them.

Another second, maybe two, and those reins would have snapped completely despite all of her efforts. But Ryan and Jesse chose that moment to step forwards and move to the dark house that had been the focus of their attention.

The entire world around them slept; every house sat dark with its occupants dreaming their dreams; no lights illuminated rooms, and not so much as the glow of televisions sending brightness outwards. The world was quiet as two vampires watched as two other vampires watched a dark and, seemingly, asleep house.

Ryan walked a step closer and crouched down. He picked a pebble up, small and light - unlikely to break glass - and gently threw it at a top window.

Not one of the four vampires on the ground below had to wait long to learn if the signal would be heeded. The tiny flutter of the pebble brushing the glass was heard instantly and the girl who had lain awake in her bed swiftly stood and moved to the window.

Ania felt her breath stolen, knocked out of her by pure wonder, and the increase of pressure on her hand making her aware that Blaiden was feeling exactly the same way.

Standing at the window, smiling down at Ryan and Jesse, was a girl so amazingly unique that no vampire would have believed possible, and Ania was compelled to study her.

Her pale skin was darker than those who gazed at her, yet nowhere near what a child's should be. It seemed to glow in the darkness, and Ania knew instinctively that no human would be able to see that glow - it was solely for eyes like hers. She had her father's dark hair and clear green eyes, yet despite the colouring there was no doubt that this was Holly's child - the similarity was too intense.

Ryan and Jesse quickly scaled the side of the building, climbing easily up the wall to the window that the girl opened for them, smiling happily in innocent joy.

"By all that ever was, did you see her, Ania?" Blaiden's voice was almost inaudible even to his own ears. "It's like she's lit up."

Ania smiled. "Yes." she whispered back. "I saw her." She had also seen something else when the girl had smiled - the girl's teeth had not elongated: they were simply teeth of a child. The girl had not tasted blood yet, yet every part of her seemed to scream out 'vampire'.

"Like mother, like daughter." She whispered, to herself more than to her lover.

"What?" He whispered, tearing his eyes from the now empty window.

Ania simply shook her head, smiling at him. She pulled him by the hand, leading him away from the shadows of the trees, walking away from the houses.

He looked at her questioningly.

"We know where she is. For tonight, that is all I need." What she didn't add, but what Blaiden already knew, was that she didn't trust herself to be around those other two - her distrust and suspicion of them was growing moment by moment, and her resolution was weakening.

* * *

For nine nights, Ania and Blaiden had visited the street, always hiding in the same unaltering shadows of the trees opposite the house. A few times they had witnessed Ryan and Jesse also watching the house, but mostly they had the view of the window to themselves. And the window was all they had seen - the child had not appeared in view in those deserted hours of the early dark-filled hours of the morning.

Neither of the ancient vampires could say exactly what they were waiting for, why they continued to spend hours watching a dark window without any sign of movement. That they *were* waiting for something was acknowledged, unspoken, by both of them: the feeling of something approaching was growing clearer to the two of them. But it was just a feeling, a vague weight nestling at the base of spines.

Ania's faint suspicion as to what it could be was pushed aside. She didn't want to be right, didn't want to think that she would have to endure it all over again, or that Blaiden would have to bear the burden once more. So she told herself that she was wrong, *had* to be wrong, not truly believing it, but hoping against hope that she would see no triggers for her memories; that the dam which had only just been rebuilt would stand strong.

Yet, as three o'clock approached, escorting the heavy fog that faded everything, on the morning of the fourth that feeling had disappeared, simply and completely evaporated. In its place was an almost euphoric calm, serenity.

Believing that whatever the feeling had actually meant was no longer an issue, they once again stood looking at the lack of movement in the window. The orange light from the street lamps seemed to soften the fog further. Moisture from the air settled on cars and houses, lighting on the pavements and roads, coating the grass and leaves and branches of the trees. The world sparkled with orange-tinted diamonds in the darkness, yet the fog subdued even this.

Ania held Blaiden's right hand with her left and used her right to sweep through her hair. She smiled at the moisture that collected on her fingers, and knew that her clothes would also be absorbing the water from the air. Her smile widened as she caught sight of Blaiden mirroring her with his own free hand.

He leant close to her, his breath a suggestive sigh on her ear and neck. "I think we're going to have to change our clothes soon. Feels like they're holding half the fog."

With a seductive smile that was invisible in the shade of the trees (yet still glimpsed by Blaiden), Ania turned her head a little so that her cheek was against his and her own lips could speak directly into his ear. "Or take these off and leave it at that." Teasing, she blew softly into his ear, enjoying the pleasant way his breath caught in shocked delight.

Before their playful mood could develop into anything more the sound of a window being opened made them turn.

The girl stood at the open window. Her dark hair rested on her shoulders, covering the pink of the nightdress she wore. Her green eyes peered out into the fog-filled world below, sparkling with the light from the streetlamps. Tears flowed softly down her cheeks and she longingly stared into the night, searching for signs of familiar faces.

Ania felt distant, removed from herself, and faintly she heard Blaiden talking.

"Poor child. She looks so lonely. So sad and so alone."

Barely aware of doing it, Ania let her hand fall from his as she took a single step forwards, her eyes locked on the girl at the window. The orange light moving on the fog seemed to bounce off of her pale face, illuminating each tear as it rolled down her cheeks. It danced over her face, like flames.

Ania felt every part of her fading away as she looked at the girl; the girl who reminded her of another girl, one who had also once stood at a window while flames sent their blazing lights over a tear and blood-streaked face. As she began to fall, the images of the past and present merging into one as her eyes turned up in her head, she had time for one thought to flow through her mind and past her lips.

Blaiden caught her as he had not so long ago and heard her sighed words on an exhaled breath.

"Here we go again."

Holly had to laugh in spite of herself. All of her certainties about following her own path, and yet she still found herself back in the crypt.

Working her way back towards the house that she had run from, feeling stronger and surer than she'd ever felt, wanting to see Michael again, tiredness had swept over her. In the cold clear sky about her, the moons lighting the way as she found herself on familiar ground.

As the crypt had come into view, her tiredness turned into exhaustion, yet she still had to smile. It appeared that her destiny had been to stay a spell in there after all. Moving slowly and deliberately she'd reached the doorway and prised it open.

Now sitting with her back pressed against the damp wall, looking at the dark dust that had once been a part of Ania, Holly felt sleep stealing her away, knowing that it was really Ania's sleep. She allowed herself to slide slowly down the wall, lying upon her side.

She breathed an echo of her mentor, speaking to the darkness around her. "Here we go again."

Michael let his instincts guide him. He'd been making his way home when something made him change direction. Running, he made his way through fields to an ancient cemetery that he'd never seen before and yet was familiar all the same. As soon as he saw it he knew that the crypt was where she was, his lover.

He glanced at the sky before he opened the crypt door. Judging from the lightening colour of the world around him, there was no chance of making it home before the killer-sun rose. Love flooded him as he saw her there sleeping, and he carefully closed the door before moving to her. On the cold floor he lay beside her and gently kissed her lips before wrapping his arm around her.

Smiling at the smile he saw on her face, he closed his eyes. "Looks like we sleep here today, my love."

Anthony, the vampire who had sent them on their way to Ryan and

Jesse, had 'arranged' a flat for Ania and Blaiden, and it was in that flat that Blaiden now lay beside Ania.

Deja vu touched him as he swept a strand of hair from her face before kissing her softly on the lips. "Yes, here we go again." he said, smiling. He allowed himself to drift into sleep, holding her tightly. "Wake up soon, Ania." he added, not knowing that he still spoke. "Don't leave me alone again for too long."

VII

She was hiding behind the door before she was even aware of being awake, hissing as sunlight flooded into half of her cell, pushing herself as far into the wall as she could. Through partially-closed eyes she saw a figure walk in and stand in the centre of the sun-immersed area of the room. Ania focussed all of her will in to becoming accustomed to the light once more, trying to peer through the brilliance that almost burned her eyes.

After an age she was able to see the man who stared at her, although the light still hurt her eyes. But at first she could not define anything about him. It had been eight nights since she had been brought anything to feed upon, and all she could sense of the man in front of her was the sound of the blood as it pulsed through his body, flowing so close to the skin that could easily be pierced. It took all of her strength not to rush into that destructive sunlight and attack him.

As her focus was able to shift away from the red rivers inside of him, she saw the knowing grin on his face: it was obvious that he knew exactly what she was thinking. Ania figured that he wasn't standing in a sun-drenched spot by accident. Still looking at the way he was smiling at her she bared her teeth at him, which only made him smile more.

He wore simple clothes which hung loosely on his frame, quietly disguising the muscle beneath. His slightly-greying hair reached past his ears, and as he looked at the creature in the shadows he brushed one side of it behind his ear. He looked as though he had seen, at most, fifty End Of Years, but there was a strangeness about him and Ania doubted that he was anywhere near as young as that.

The man, who had lived long enough in seclusion - apart from the presence of his guards and his 'pets' - that he no longer remembered his own name, allowed her time to look at him, disregarding the undiluted hatred that shone out at him: it wasn't the first time he'd seen threats aimed at him and, as he planned to continue his tests until death finally claimed him, he knew it wouldn't be the last. His pets just needed to be trained a little.

Lithely, he dropped to the floor and crossed his legs in front of him, still smiling sweetly as she still bared her teeth at him. With his left hand he indicated for her to also sit and then folded his hands on his lap, waiting patiently.

She snarled, deep down in her throat, her lip curled up in contempt, hoping for a reaction, hoping that she would hear his heart speed up slightly in fear, but there was nothing: he remained sitting, completely impassive. Conceding, Ania slowly crouched down, eyes never leaving his, sitting with her haunches resting on ankles, one hand on her knee and the other on fingertips on the floor in between her legs: an animal ready to pounce.

"Do you know how long you've been here, my pet?" The man asked, still watching her serenely, gazing at the silver that threaded her black hair. His voice was coarse and wavery, yet still strong.

He expected no answer and received none, only that unadulterated hostility. Still smiling as if he was engaging in a pleasant conversation with a good friend, he answered his own question.

"The answer is, even I don't know." He chuckled to himself, a pretence of good-natured embarrassment. "I know that only you and two others from the group you came from have survived, but beyond that..." He shrugged. He leant forward, a comrade about to share a tremendous secret.

"But one thing that I do know, child, is that it is a long time since you lived in the sun, a long time since you became a blood-soul."

Ania snarled again, her temper beginning to rise.

"It has been a long time since this cell-" he pointedly looked around at the small space. "-became your home." He met her eyes again, still smiling that infuriatingly sweet smile. "Many End Of Years have passed."

Ania fought to stay still.

"Since you have been blessed, you have been locked in here, feeding only when we bring you food, when I allow you to feed."

Every muscle in Ania's body tensed.

"You are stronger than most I have seen. But even the strong fall weak if caged for long enough." Although he still smiled, a hard glint sparked momentarily in his eyes. "I can keep you caged, or I can allow you a little freedom."

The continued tension in her muscles began to hurt, but Ania held tight and refused even the slightest quiver to work through her.

"I can let you hunt, let you roam, in that garden. In the dark hours you would have ownership of the night. I make the choice whether to free or contain you, but you can decide what you'd prefer."

He widened his grin once more, his friend-forever smile. "Which choice do you favour?"

The growl started low, building from deep in her throat, growing louder. What she had denied she allowed to trickle through, her muscles beginning to tremble and shake with raw energy, shivering with the foretaste of the attack.

The man seemed to misinterpret the shaking of her body, nodding in understanding at her supposed-gratefulness. He either disregarded the vehemence that burned in her eyes, or no longer saw it.

The flow of her anger began to rush quicker, the slow trickle that she allowed herself swelling into a raging river. Her muscles tensed a little more, and she vaulted forwards, leaping towards the man encased in sunlight.

Her skin began to burn the instant the light touched it, pain attacking her as she was attacking him. Yet she didn't scream out - she merely focussed once more on the arteries and veins of blood that were within her reach. Her nails raked across his face and her teeth sank deeply into the flesh of his arm. She was distantly aware, as hot blood touched her tongue and ran down her throat, that others had rushed into the room and fought to separate her from the struggling man. The taste overwhelmed her, but as she was able to ignore the hands on her trying to drag her away, it was only a few moments before the pain of the sun became too much. She surrendered herself back to the shadows, standing against the wall, with the man's blood smeared across her lips and chin, breathing heavily and smiling.

The three men, large and heavy built, stood and stared at her, creating a wall to protect the man behind them who staggered and struggled to regain his feet and composure.

He leant against the sun-warmed wall, his right hand covering the wound on his left arm, looking at his pet through the slight gap between two of his guards. Their eyes met as she stared back at him, seemingly oblivious to the obviously painful condition of her now-burnt skin. His blood seemed unnaturally bright upon her lips, and brighter still as her mouth opened wider to reveal her teeth, the lower half red.

His face creased in anger, his former demeanour nowhere in evidence, his eyes flaming with fear disguised as aggression. "We will talk again soon."

Still trying to stem the bleeding he hurriedly left the room, followed by the three minders, who backed out of the room, not turning their backs on her. As the door was quickly closed and locked, they heard the low animalistic chuckle of the creature inside.

It was worth it! The pain of her injuries, whatever punishment they could come up with, it was worth all of it and more just for the change of expression on his face! Just for that cheeriness to have been obliterated.

Despite how much it hurt Ania couldn't help but laugh as she replayed the moment when his smile had slipped from his face. She collapsed onto the floor, her stomach beginning to hurt from laughing so hard, tears streaming from her eyes.

It took a long time for her chuckling to taper off, and when it did she felt drained. She licked her lips, finding traces of the man's blood and ran her fingers over her chin, gathering all remnants and licking her fingers clean. Only then did she allow herself to begin wondering just how badly she might be hurt.

Slowly, Ania stood and slipped out of her dress. It was a replica of the one she had worn when she had been brought to the Devil's Lair, and had been given to her days after the visit from The Hag. It dropped to the floor and she kicked it gently away with her toes. Naked, she stood there and closed her eyes.

Breathing slowly, Ania allowed her other senses to expand, cataloguing the amount and extent of the harm that she had, unintentionally yet knowingly, committed upon herself.

Although there were a few bad burns upon her feet and legs where her dress had risen in the attack, and a couple of scorched patches on her neck and shoulders, most of the damage was focussed on her face. Timidly she worked her fingertips over the skin of her face, her eyes still closed, feeling the flawless smooth skin that became flaked and raw the further she moved her fingers. Repeatedly she ran her fingers backwards and forwards over the same area of her cheek: smooth then rough, perfect than blemished.

The intense pain had almost-entirely disappeared the

moment that she had been shrouded in shadows again, but she was still aware of the dull throbbing on the surface of her skin.

Now that she knew that she wasn't that badly hurt Ania dressed again and lay on her bed. Ignoring her hunger that had been woken from its uneasy slumber at the first taste of the man's blood, she rested her head on her arms and stared up at the ceiling.

Although she had no idea of it, all perspective of time had been lost and had no meaning, she had spent most of her past nine years in a similar position. Nine years of focussing on the same spot on the pitch-black ceiling in a pitch-black cell, diverting her attention from pain and thirst and loneliness. Nine years of thinking backwards in time, hating and driving all positive thoughts away. Nine years of watching her memories played out on the darkness above her. Nine years.

Her eyes narrowed to slits, her eyes filled with blinding thoughts of revenge.

In the beginning, when the years had first begun to pass one night at a time, Ania had managed to balance her anger at Maria with thoughts of Blaiden. But she found only loneliness and sadness accompanied memories of and wishes for her lover, while her determination to fulfil her oath filled her with boundless strength and willpower, her force building with each and every drop of hostility and loathing. It didn't take long for Ania to realise that if she were to survive her new life and become what she needed to be in order to reap what she was entitled to she would need that strength, and the remote possibility of Blaiden's comfort was pushed aside.

Through practice, Ania paid no attention to the pains of her thirst as she watched the centre of her hatred over and over again.

She replayed the moment that she approached The Wall, cautious enough to wait before decided to more forwards. Over and over, she saw Maria sitting on the stones of The Wall, looking at something far away in her own mind. She saw her looking dishevelled, and lonely. And it was always the humiliation of being drawn in, of dropping her guard because of how lonely Maria had seemed; the previously vicious woman, who had looked abandoned on those stones. Followed by the moment of elation she had felt while being embraced by the girl who had spent so much time attacking her with her words, that pitiful girl who had delighted in *the pain she had caused.*

And then her memory shifted back further to the confrontation of the then-pregnant Maria. The sound of the Maria's uneven footsteps moving over the loose stones behind her, the whispered venom spat out, aimed at the back of her head. Your parents are freaks, Ania, *she had said.* Your parents are freaks, and you're a freak just like them.

Ania smiled cruelly, and whispered into the darkness. "No. Not just *like them. Not anymore. I'm something different now."*

Her smile faltered a little as the thoughts of Maria drifted away like smoke to be replaced by another, newer, memory. The man offering her a choice, but really threatening her with an eternity in her cell. The choice of freedom or captivity.

Her smile was refreshed. "What's one more vow?" she whispered.

Still lying with her head on her right arm she brought her left out and moved the fleshy part of her hand to her mouth. She bit gently down and drank her second blood-toast, swearing revenge also on the man who held her captive.

Careful not to take too much of herself, she placed her hand back beneath her head, the punctures already healing, and watched in an ecstasy of hatred as the set of memories repeated and replayed continually through the hours.

Seven days later, a famished yet calm and collected Ania once again hid in the shadows as light shone into her cell. This time when the man entered her room he was joined by six men. They stationed themselves along the wall directly behind him, all of them in the sun yet not one of them looking comforted by it.

Each of the seven men were looking at her warily, and given her past action Ania could sympathise. Holding her open hands up slightly in what she hoped was a gesture of harmlessness, she slowly and gracefully sank to the floor, sitting with her legs crossed. She put her hands on her lap and looked at the man with a sweet smile.

He felt more unnerved than he already was when she copied the position that he had favoured at their last meeting - it was the second time he had met her and the second time that things had not gone as he'd planned. He was *the one who was supposed to look calm and serene; he* was *the one who was supposed to sit first. And his confidence was hit again as she signalled, just as he had a week before, for him to sit opposite.*

At first he didn't. He merely stood and looked at her with unveiled caution and mistrust. When he was sure that it could be argued as being his own idea, he finally sat, grateful for the presence of the people behind him. Not realising that he was doing it, he folded his hands together, covering the still-healing holes.

Ania's head tilted slightly to one side in amusement as she saw his unconscious action, but she killed the urge to laugh. She could laugh all she wanted later, but for now she had an incentive to maintain the illusion of submission. She waited for him to speak.

His chain of thought had been ripped apart at not seeing the snarling monster that had attacked him but a beautiful and tranquil woman, her pale skin once again smooth and undamaged. He had been prepared for all but his own disturbed concentration. Finally, while she watched him all the time, he was able to gather his thoughts enough to be able to talk. His voice shook, giving away the true level of his unease.

"Have you decided which choice you favour?"

Ania, who could have argued that it was obvious which option she had chosen - mainly because she was not attempting to kill him - only nodded slowly.

Despite the rehearsals he had repeatedly practiced in his head, all of his speeches and equally-obtuse questions were now no longer anywhere to be found.

Without a trace of his former limber movements, the man awkwardly struggled to his feet, ensuring that his gaze came into contact with no one, embarrassed at his newly-acquired telling-signs of old age. Having straightened himself up, he looked at Ania. He opened his mouth to speak, but no words came. He merely nodded before walking out.

Ania watched the other six men leave, then the light was cut off once more. Her smile grew harder when she heard the men walk away without the click of the door being locked.

The old man had granted her limited-freedom! And he did it without realising that by doing so he had just committed suicide.

Blaiden knew that what he was doing was risky, but so was *not* doing it. The body felt heavy over his shoulder as he moved through the night, praying to all he had ever believed in that he would not be seen. He knew that the weight of the unconscious man was all in his head, a symptom of the unease of his actions - over the millennia of his existence he had needed to carry, and dispose of, bigger and weightier victims; and had done so without problems.

In the distance Blaiden could hear the sound of drunken laughter. He froze for a second, head turned in the direction of that far away sound, scanning the orange-bleached darkness with his cat-like green eyes. Sighing, he realised that the man no longer felt quite as heavy and began to sprint towards the flat. Effortlessly, he was able to unlock the door to the flat and, without the slightest struggle, he took the man inside. After securing the door, still only having to use one hand, he walked into the bedroom.

She hadn't improved; it was obvious to him as soon as he crossed the threshold of the room. Ania lay on the bed, the quilt twisted around her as she thrashed and writhed on the mattress. Her normally-sensuous mouth was pulled upwards in a snarl and blood trickled over her chin from the cuts that repeatedly appeared and healed as she again and again raked her lips with her teeth. Her strangled breath wheezed out as she gasped for air, and her opened but unconscious eyes were rolled up to the whites.

Blaiden quickly dropped the man to the floor, who groaned in his senseless state. He took out the handkerchief from his pocket and held it ready. His teeth sank deeply into the man's wrist, who again began to stir, and immediately held the cloth underneath the raised hand, watching as the white material turned briskly to red.

Cursing himself for not being more prepared, Blaiden had to watch as precious blood dripped onto the floor while he removed his jacket. Using it as a tourniquet, he wrapped it tightly around the man's lower arm, just above the wound, pulling it tight. He then rushed to the bed, his hand covered in blood from the red cloth. Employing the same technique as he had before, Blaiden fed the blood to Ania, having to hold her still with his free hand as she continued to move.

When the rag was wrung dry he returned to the man on the floor and removed the make-shift tourniquet. Blaiden remade the wounds and repeated the entire procedure, careful to ensure that the man remained knocked out but alive.

It took over an hour to bleed him totally and feed him to Ania drop by drop. Finally, utterly exhausted and emotionally drained, Blaiden sank to the floor next to the bed. He stared at the corpse that lay on the floor, and then glanced at the curtain-cloaked window. A trembling sigh left him and he ran his fingers through his hair. It would begin to grow light soon and there was no chance of him being able to take the body and dispose of it - the risks were just too great, the gamble too unsure.

It was an effort to turn his head to look at Ania, but he managed it. She lay calm and still, her breathing smoother, no longer jagged.

His head drooped to the bed and sitting in a position that would leave him aching when he awoke Blaiden fell asleep.

Unbeknownst to either vampire, Michael had thought of feeding Holly in the same manner as Blaiden fed Ania. Although, luckily for Michael, Holly didn't need as much blood nor was her rest as uneasy. He was able to simply collect a small amount from his own kill to feed her with.

Back in their own bed, in their own home, Holly lay in deep slumber, Michael laying by her side.

He had carried her home from the vault where they had slept, running most of the distance, all the while working out how he was going to be able to feed and look after her. And he had been fine, fixing his attention on what he needed to do. But with nothing else to shift his attention to, he was left in limbo, and left there alone.

It was glorious and striking and Ania felt her breath stolen. Everything was shrouded in beautiful shadowed-darkness, and all around her was the blood-rich perfume of the plants. It made her own blood rush quicker through her and caused her mouth to cramp with desire as she tasted the scent in the air she breathed. Around her she heard the others, her new kin, as they tracked their way to the other end of the garden, toward the prey that waited there. Yet she hesitated a moment longer before following in their wake, basking in the mere sensation of the huge space before her.

And then she was running, charging forwards, exhilaration building in her as she overtook the others, racing over blood-grown grass and blood-watered trees, flying onwards to the real thing. In a blur of darkened shapes, she passed by all of the plant life, and the pale faces she went by were unclear and without form. The flight filled her and she drowned in the spirit of the night and of the hunt. She could feel herself getting closer to those who were brought to be prey, and her excitement grew.

Their faces became clearer, and an ice-cold smile found its way onto her lips as she recognised one of them.

He cowered behind the trunk of a large tree, his huge body shaking in fear, snivelling and whining. His wiry beard was imbedded with flakes of dried blood and dirt.

There was none, but if there had been, the sight of the pathetic creature would have driven away any sense of doubt or pity from Ania's heart. She felt the growl of repulsion vibrate in her throat, sickened by the weakness she saw in front of her.

The six feet five inch man looked up as he became aware of her presence, still uttering the sounds of his immense cowardice. He recognised her; it filtered into his eyes, and his pleading-noises increased.

From the Dark Garden, he had been brought solely for this reason, and Ania thanked the rulers of coincidence and fate that she was the one to have claimed him. So long ago she had overpowered and defeated him and now she had the opportunity to do it again, only in a more extreme way.

He jumped and squealed as the Garden of Death erupted into screams and the sound of rushing and panicking feet as the other blood-souls reached and sought out their own victims.

Although she loved the extent of the terror that was in his eyes she couldn't stand the way that his whimpering grated through her. Snarling, she flung herself at him.

As she raked his skin with her nails, lapping the blood up like a dog, she glanced at a female blood-soul that rushed past her, chasing a young girl.

Their eyes met, and Ania grinned in pleasant surprise as she recognised her as well. It was the woman with the dark blonde hair, the one who had stood with her and Blaiden when they had met their destinies.

Feeling happier than she had done for an age, Ania turned her attention back to the cowering thing before her. Ending the sham, Ania ripped into the man's neck with her teeth, greedily drinking the hot crimson liquid.

Even though she continued to drink in the same manner, time seemed to slow down as her eyes flickered to her right and she saw another blood-soul feeding.

Blaiden was more devastatingly beautiful than she remembered, his skin glowing with the same unnatural light that she knew radiated out of her.

He also chose that moment to look up and their eyes met and caught. Ania's heart seemed to stop and speed up simultaneously, and her body ached in longing. She kept on drinking but all she wanted to do was run to him, and touch him, and kiss him. And as their eyes stayed locked, she knew that he was feeling the same.

With an effort, she tore her eyes away, concentrating once more on the dying man beside her, a pain in her chest as if she couldn't breathe.

She peered out through the gaps in the leaves and branches of the tree, enveloped in the scent. He was looking for her, searching, and every part of her yearned for him. All she wanted to do was jump out of the tree and run to him. But Maria's face kept floating in front of her, and her anger and hate made her keep still. When her vows were kept, after she had fulfilled her promises, if there was an after, maybe they would be able to get back to where they had been. Where they were meant to be. But until then, she forced herself to watch him walk away.

Below her to the left stood the heavy door that was between her and real freedom; so close. What she was planning was extremely risky, but she refused to be a prisoner any more - and the added incentive of being able to get to Maria was extremely persuasive.

For hours, Ania sat silently, hidden in the mass of leaves, listening to the wanderings of the creatures she was now joined with. She heard them walk amongst the death-plants, moving meaninglessly now that there was no more prey to hunt, no reason to chase; almost body without soul.

As the hours turned, Ania began to grow anxious. She heard the others beginning to tread their paths back to their cells, and she was tempted to jump down and follow suit. Deep unease settled at the base of her spine and she started to grow twitchy as time proceeded onwards. Desperately Ania searched at the leaves and branches, trying to see if there were any dangerous gaps that she had missed, but seeing none did nothing to relax her.

The air around her started to warm and she came close to panicking. She knew that there was time - just - for her to abandon her plan and rush back to the captivity, but safety, of her cell. And knowing that it was a false sanctuary did nothing to free her from the feeling that she should.

Knowing that there was only one thing that could help, she closed her eyes and summoned Maria's face, but at first it wouldn't come. All she could see was darkness lightening to daylight. Panic rose close to the surface again and she doubled her efforts to keep it at bay. This time there was no delay. Maria's face was there, totally clear, even down to the contemptuous sneer. Anger and hatred returned to her like an old friend, and her nerves instantly steadied, fear at the impending sunrise simply disappearing. She waited.

All around her, the world lost its magic as light filtered through from the skylights. Ania nearly laughed as she realised that the nearest skylight was nowhere near her or the door - the nearest shaft of killer-sunlight a minimum of thirty feet away, and no danger to her at all.

Even though she longed for the darkness, all nervousness had left her and excitement hit her strongly when she finally heard the heavy door being unlocked.

The three guards that walked into the day-filled Garden of Death were luckier than the rest of their acquaintances. Even before the door had swung all of the way open, Ania had jumped down and broken the necks of two of them and the third was dead before the door came to a stop.

She stood beside the three corpses, looking down at them, amazed at how easy it had been. Quickly, she moved the three bodies to the base of the tree in which she had hidden, then simply walked out of the door, removing the keys and closing the door.

Ania stood in an alley with a high wall in front of her, and had to stifle laughter. She looked to the left, and the alley ended in a door about three hundred feet away, and the same to the right - and every step of the way was basked in beautiful shadow, the height of the walls around her preventing any light from ever entering the four feet wide passage.

"Whoever you are," she whispered gently. "You really didn't

plan for all eventualities, did you?" Smiling, Ania glanced in both directions, wondering which way to turn.

The hunter inside of her was new and inexperienced, yet she allowed it to take control. She closed her eyes and turned first left and then right, allowing her senses to tune in to the subtle differences that could not be seen. She recalled the scent of blood, summoning it as she had Maria's face. With it clear in her mind, she glanced in both directions again, smiling. Although there was a large chance that her imagination was deceiving her, leading her astray, Ania was sure that the distant smell of blood, of living prey, was slightly stronger to her left.

Shrugging, she decided to trust it. The worst that could happen was that she could be wrong.

Still amused at the absurd ease that she had managed to escape the Garden, she crept as silent as smoke down the left half of the alleyway. Standing at the door she placed a hand on the wood and pressed an ear against it.

Ania had to cover her mouth with her hands to stop the laughter bubbling over her lips as she heard seven different snoring patterns. Listening again, she focussed as hard as she could and was able to decipher the slow and restful heartbeats of seven men. She backed away from the door a little, to make sure that she wouldn't disturb the people inside: the seven men, who were all asleep!

Despite the fact that she was enjoying the lackadaisical attitude of those who had kept her isolated and imprisoned for so long, along with so many others, she knew that she couldn't maintain her strength of concentration while she was laughing at them. And as she had made it so far she wasn't going to make a mess of it now.

Once more she brought to her inner eye the seat of her determined anger, all amusement fleeing in a rush. Her eyes opened and she focussed her contempt on those behind the door. In one easy motion, she swung the door inwards.

There was plenty of clutter and debris for her to choose from as she entered the room. Lying on the thin and simple beds, the seven men hardly stirred as Ania breezed through the room, raising the heavy stone goblet she had picked above each of them in turn. She struck them all in the same spot, just above the nape of the neck, loving the dull thud that accompanied each hit.

Hunger awoke in her as blood flowed from all of them, but she forced it away: it was not time for that.

Putting the goblet down, Ania gathered the first man in her arms and began to walk out of the door. Suddenly, she stopped and retraced her steps back into the room. Dropping him back down on his bed - slightly less gently than she could have done - Ania cursed her own incompetence. Just because they were unconscious now didn't mean that they would stay unconscious, and if they woke up while she was otherwise engaged they could cause her a little inconvenience.

She scrutinized the room once more and found what she needed. Hastily, she grabbed the long coil of thin rope and began to unravel it. Looking at it, she realised that she had no idea how to securely tie someone up so that they couldn't escape.

As potentially destructive as it was, she allowed her mind to wander to Blaiden and, most importantly, the story he had told her about his encounter with his mother's husband. She did her best to limit her thoughts to his description of the way he had tied Kaytan up; and only to that.

Closing her eyes, she pictured it in her mind, working it through in her imagination. When she was as confident as she was going to be, she approached the man she had dropped.

Her hands worked quickly and accurately and he was soon effectively trussed. Feeling that her time was wasting, Ania cut the rope with her sharp and strong fingernails and tied the other six identically, hanging the remaining rope around her neck and one shoulder.

It was taking too long and unease began to creep in again - she had been so fortunate, her luck had been incredible, and she doubted that it would hold for much longer. Holding the man as she would an infant, Ania carried him to the doorway. Using all of the speed that she could muster she rushed to the door of the Garden.

Because of her anxiety it felt like it took an age, yet within just two minutes all of the seven secured and inactive guards were slumped at the base of the tree, sitting and laying next to their three late-comrades.

Although she was sheltered from the direct shafts of light, the brightness of the day was beginning to blind her - after almost nine years of constant darkness, she was struggling to readjust. The warmth of the day was also something she had forgotten, and it was this that was fogging her senses as she stood in the Garden, squinting at her victims, living and dead.

The fog in her mind evaporated once she was standing in the cool shadows of the alleyway again, the door behind her closed and sealing the fragments of light away. Even though the shadows weren't as dark as she would have liked, they were enough for her to think clearly - and for that new huntress streak in her character to step forward and reign.

Ania began to stalk the path, this time moving to the right, to the door that she had not yet opened. As she had at the door now behind her, she gently leant against it and listened.

Fourteen heartbeats thumped and pounded behind the door, not one of them slow enough to mean that its host was asleep. A few of the men spoke quietly to one another, laughing occasionally.

It complicated matters, that much was true, but the animal predator that had been born in Ania celebrated - for her, knocking those unconscious men in their sleep was an act of profanity, not worthy of her. But those fourteen men were awake, so it was now a hunt instead of a low ambush.

Her teeth were bared in a silent snarl that had started as a smile and her hand snaked down to the handle on the door and curled around it.

The man who had built the Devil's Lair when he had been young and fully aware of who he was - along with the full knowledge of his name - sat and only half-listened to the partially-drunk ramblings of the small number of his guards. The other half of him was preoccupied with one of his youngest pets, the one who had surprised him.

He moved the jug of Wheat-Ale to his lips, glancing at the scars on his left arm as it rose before his eyes.

The strength and will she had shown, to move into the sun just to get to him! It worried him a little, wondering what else she could be capable of. But it excited him as well, just that degree of power. And despite the wounds he still carried, he still doubted that she would cause him any real harm. Not him.

He looked at the door to his right, which stood wide open, the day streaming in. He could see the tree in the clearing outside, the chains hanging limply against the trunk. Another branch of light wound its way from the skylight in the ceiling. Yet the sun no longer offered him the guarantee of safety it once had.

The large jug was raised to his mouth once more and he drank deeply, his head swimming pleasurably. The room around him began to spin and tumble a little, and he closed his eyes as nausea rolled through his stomach.

They flew back open when the door banged noisily against the wall.

The intellectual part of Ania had enough time to think about retrieving the heavy stone goblet so that it could resume its new purpose, but she was overruled by the instinctual part of her. Thought was swept away, drowned by the cold sea of her emotion.

The door banged open, but Ania's advantage of surprise was lost as the brightness attacked her. It only lasted a second, that shocked paralysis, but it was enough to save some of them, enough time for them to accept what was standing there.

Her eyes squinted to slits, pupils contracting to almost nothing, and then she was in amongst them.

She had already immobilised one before any of them realised that she had moved into the room, and shouts of fear and confusion filled the air. Two of them froze, incapable of any form of movement, only able to stare at the glowering woman.

It was then that Ania made her mistake, not a dangerous mistake but a mistake all the same - she went forward to those statuesque forms and hit them first before turning her attention to the others. It didn't take long, but five of the guards were quick and smart enough to take advantage of her distraction. They scrambled away, pushing a couple of their 'friends' to the floor as they fled into the sun-filled world outside.

She snarled briefly in their direction before dismissing them from what passed for thoughts in her current persona.

One of the men, who had been chosen for his post specifically for his size and physique, had curled up in the middle of the floor and rocked himself gently.

Her eyes passed him over, that lesson already learnt. Briefly, she looked at the other six guards who scrambled and shoved throughout the room, and she laughed throatily. Not one of them was smart enough to even try and escape through either of the two wide open doors.

She took them out resourcefully and easily, not noticing as she had to move through the two separate darts of sunlight. Then she hit the curved giant that still rocked upon the floor, just in case his mind decided to begin working again.

Ania looked at the destruction she had brought in only a few minutes, running her eyes over the bodies on the floor. Then she turned to face the only other person who stood on the room, sharp teeth exhibited beneath the cold curl of her smile.

He could have run, he had the time and opportunity to make his escape. But he was completely absorbed in her, in what she had been able to do. And he still did not believe that she would hurt him.

Her eyes didn't leave his as she edged forwards, moving lithely over debris and outstretched limbs without even flicking her eyes down once. When she was standing in front of him, head lifted slightly so that her eyes were still on his, her smile widened and she growled softly.

Finally, the man actually saw what was in the depth of her blue-grey eyes, and he began to shake. The jug that he had held throughout the commotion slipped from his grasp, smashing on the floor and splashing a generous amount of the ale on to his trouser legs, the strong smell invading everywhere.

The swift and violent pounding of his heart as the actuality of his plight got through to him was musical in her ears, and her own heart sped up to match his. Her eyes closed momentarily as the euphoria of the pre-strike filled her.

He screamed loudly as she bit into his neck, careful not to hit that wide river that would cause him to lose too much blood: she was not going to let him escape that easily.

While the blood flowed from his neck down her throat, the two elements of Ania's nature switched and conscious thoughts took the place of instincts, so she found it easy to stop at just the right time. She extracted her teeth from inside his throat, a dribble of blood dripping from each of the holes, and let go of him. He fell heavily to the ground. It was only when he was crumpled at her feet that the side of her that was capable of complex thought was able to look around.

Stepping over him, she first closed the door that the five

minders had rushed through, half of the sun disappearing. This time though, when the light hit her she did *feel it*, but chose to ignore it for the time being.

The weight of the rope that was still wrapped around the top half of her body reminded her of what else she still needed to do. She lifted the rope off over her head and looked at the nine men laying around the room.

Not one of the first seven men she had taken to the Garden of Death stirred even a little as she dropped the other nine next to them, and she almost stopped to check if they were all still breathing. The knowledge that it meant nothing important even if they weren't, Ania sat in front of them, trying to think about what she had to do next.

She sat there for a long time, in the shade of the trees, the lack of a reason to move dulling her senses and she seemed to sleep with her eyes open, thinking and seeing nothing. For hours she remained there, a blood-soul sitting dazed in a sun-filled room, the day leaving her in a stupor, sitting alongside those she had brought to the Garden, everything in her mind obscured and veiled. The day passed unseen and unnoticed in the place where it was not an ally.

As it began to fade, as the sun rolled downwards in the sky, awareness started to filter back into Ania's eyes. The embers of thought and intelligence grew brighter and burst into blazing flames. Almost as if a shock had passed through her, Ania bolted to her feet, eyes focussing on the skylights above her.

"Twilight comes." she whispered.

And she realised that it was true. One hour at most before the last of the light disappeared, and at most two before real night took over. So why was she standing still?!

The cooling air and the darkening world allowed her mind to work, and she knew instantaneously what else had to be done. As if she hadn't spent most of the day sitting in a thoughtless trance, Ania's speed was unprecedented.

She rushed into the room where her final attack had taken place, the position of the descending sun leaving the room almost completely darkened. The smell of the Wheat-Ale had impregnated the entire chamber and Ania flung the door to the world outside wide open.

Her eyes closed, pure pleasure filling her as a cool breeze

sighed over her too-warm skin. It refreshed her, awakening her all the way to her soul. When she had absorbed as much as she felt she had time for, she looked around the now-disorganised room, hoping that her memory had not deceived her.

It didn't take long for her memory to be proven right. "There you are."

She walked to the stack of shelves that were laden with large jugs of the potent ale. Out of the eighteen that were there, twelve were empty and six were filled to the brim.

Feeling the ticking of time in her body, Ania grabbed one of the jugs and carried it to the Garden to begin her concluding task.

When she was done, two jugs remained on the shelf and she left them there, not needed.

It took her a little longer to find the last thing that she required. Having searched that room thoroughly and not finding it, she rushed to where the guards had been asleep. The day was fleeing and she felt time pressing on her, which made her concentration a little wavery.

Finally, she found what she needed in a place she had searched meticulously four times. Holding one fist-sized stone in each hand, she held her arms at full length in front of her and scraped them slowly together. Sparks erupted in a shower as the stones touched, safely fading to nothing half-way to the floor.

Arms by her sides so that the stones were sure not to accidentally touch, Ania almost skipped out of the room in joy.

The smell hit her as soon as the door opened in the darkening Garden, despite its immense size, but above it she could smell the sweat and blood of the people she had caught.

She had trailed the ale around the perimeter of the entire Garden, starting behind the door and moving anti-clockwise, coming to a stop on the other side of the doorway. Ania had made sure that not even one drop had spilled onto the threshold, to guarantee that the flames would not block the only way out - at least not until the whole thing burned; she was not going to be responsible for trapping anyone.

While she stood there, contemplating the hastening approach of the finale, she smelt the increasing anxiety of first one, then two, then all sixteen of the bound men, and she turned to face them.

They recoiled as she aimed her icy killer smile at them,

laughing as she saw them glancing in fear at each other and their surroundings. And at the deepening dark.

Moving slowly, she skirted around them, still smiling, so that she was positioned behind the door, at the beginning of her trail of the intoxicating drink. Ania's ears picked up movement in the far end of the Garden and she looked in that direction, her smile strengthening: and she made sure that they saw her looking. She heard all sixteen of their heartbeats speed up excessively as the clamour of the opening cell doors reached even their dull ears, and she could smell adrenaline rushing through every single one of them.

Purposefully menacingly, Ania turned slowly to face all of them as they sat on the ground beneath the large tree.

"Night is here." She said in a low melodious whisper.

They all stared into the depth of the Garden, and a couple of them managed to work their way on to their knees, but their bindings prevented them from getting any further.

Ania sat and watched their futile, yet highly entertaining, attempts at loosening the ropes. She continued to smile at their pleas for release, simply holding the stones and waiting.

Their rushing footsteps made rapid progress through the Garden - they could all sense a change, not just by the weighty aroma of the Wheat-Ale, but by the very mood of the air. They came on the run, charging forwards en masse, taking only a dozen seconds to cover the vast distance.

The group of eighteen blood-souls came to a stop, staring at the sixteen roped men before them and at the open and unguarded door. In awe, and in one coinciding movement, they all turned their attention to Ania, some smiling in wonder and some with mouths agape in amazement.

Serenely, Ania continued to simply sit there, just watching with interest, letting them look but careful not to catch Blaiden's eyes - that would be too much for her to take.

It was only when the captive sixteen resumed their pleading and straining to loosen their bonds that the blood-souls turned from Ania to look once more at their former warders, those who had brought and kept them in confinement (though Blaiden's eyes stayed on her slightly longer before he turned away, smiling).

As a pack the hunters moved towards the group, slowly encircling them. The same expression of hunger, hate and rapture blazed from thirty-six eyes, and identical venomous smiles curled above matching sharp teeth.

As the unified pack moved closer, tightening the circle, the terrified centre occupants recognised the futility of any action and simply sat in utter terror.

Ania felt no compulsion to join her kin - she had brought this to be and her enjoyment came from simply hearing the thundering sound of their hearts pounding in heightening fear as her demon-family allowed the tension to build.

She lost sight of the man who had created this place, her last glimpse of him before the circle closed completely was of him laying stuck on his side after unsuccessfully trying to get up, staring. Staring up at those surrounding him, those he had caused to be and had tried to tame - the man who had created a tornado and tried to bottle it and was soon to be caught in its eye. He looked at his pets encircling him and the others.

She wasn't able to see her people feed, but she was able to hear them.

Once the attack began, as the world inside what was the Garden of Death for the last time erupted in screams and the sound of ripping and tearing, Ania turned her back on them all. She knelt upon the ground, an arm's length away from the root of her closing act, the skirt of her dress tucked safely behind her. With the sounds escalating behind her, building to a crescendo, she stretched her arms out and slowly struck the two stones against one another. The spray of tiny blazing flares arched upwards before settling upon the soaked earth.

Ania was flung backwards as the flames shot high. Startled laughter rushed out of her as she watched the fire run quickly along the trail she had laid out. She dropped the stones apart from each other on to the ground and jumped to her feet, turning to watch the rapid advancement as it fled, lighting the whole area.

Those behind her had paused to also watch the torrent of flames, the reflection dancing in all of their eyes. As creatures of instinct they all understood its purpose and went to finish their final repast within the Devil's Lair, continuing with intense vigour.

Ania stood for a moment, watching them feed as the sound of their devouring was muffled by the crackle of burning plant-life, shimmering yellows and oranges passing over pale skin, smoke *beginning to rise on the air.*

The flames had run their course, and Ania left the Garden for the last time through the doorway which was flanked by fire, an almost-overwhelming and consuming sense of freedom filling her to bursting point as she moved along the alleyway. Her soul swam in joy, her feet light as she reached the penultimate doorway, the frightening notion that this was a dream worming its way into her mind; she was shaking as she crossed the room, half sure that she would awake before she reached that final open door, to awaken in her locked cell.

Yet the door continued to draw closer and a cooling breeze worked its way through to reach her, and she didn't wake up. She arrived at the doorway, the breeze now hitting her square in the face, and she didn't wake up. Her bare foot lifted up and came down upon the ground outside; she was standing half inside and half outside of the building, and she didn't wake up. One more movement and she was out, nothing above her now but the blanketing blackness of the night sky. And she did not wake up.

Before her joy burst from her totally, Ania looked at the distorted tree in the centre of the clearing. Striding over to it, bare feet on summer ground for the first time in years, she knew that she had been wrong.

The chains were cold, she knew that they must be, but to her skin they felt warm. Her fingers walked over the links of each of them in turn, feeling the blood and rust flaking onto her flesh. Easily and without any effort, she ripped each of the three chains from the tree and dropped them to the base.

That had been her closing act.

Behind her, she could hear the growing noise of the Garden of Death burning and the approach of the other blood-souls. She ran into the forest, the gentle wind aiding her momentum in whipping her hair and dress backwards, still able to hear the destruction of the Devil's Lair and the fleeing steps of her kin as they also ran. But as her feet quickened pace, as her blood began to race through her veins, she dismissed it all, even Blaiden. Even Maria.

She ran in the night, with the open star-speckled sky above her, and no walls to confine her.

She had spent all day sleeping in a barn, amongst the scythes and scoops, stacking them and arranging the mass of equipment to make a crude shelter to hide beneath so that the thin streaks of light that would inevitably dart through the gaps in the building would not reach her. She had hidden there in plenty of time before the sun had begun to climb the sky and had slept the day away.

She woke when the light began to fade to darkness and crawled out from underneath the cover of where she had slept. She lengthened and twisted her limbs, stretching all of her muscles taut. It had been cramped and uncomfortable, almost every part of her body ached and throbbed. And it had also been the best night of her life, because although it had not been cosy it had been her choice. Where she had chosen to sleep. And she could have chosen to leave. And it was her freedom of choice that made it perfect.

She could have left the barn before twilight and night interchanged, but she wanted to wait until the darkness was complete. Not only because it would be easier for her to track Maria and fulfil the most important of her vows, but because she wanted to lose herself in the night again. She wanted to experience the rush of intoxication that the dark had infused in her, to run as she had once only walked - with the night as her only consort.

As she waited for the darkness to completely overtake the world, sitting and looking out, opposing thoughts began to fill her, a wordless argument breaking out between the two sides of Ania's soul.

The peace that she had always felt in the depth of the night she found was still there, had escalated in to something even more powerful and awe-inspiring. But for the animal newly born in her, it was not enough, nowhere near enough. The predator wanted Maria, wanted the blood vow finished and completed.

Ania felt the conflicts fighting inside of her, and ran a hand through her tangled hair. But no matter what the calmer part of her felt, she knew that she needed to find Maria, had to put an end to it all so that she could start to make sense of the path she now followed. And she felt sure that if she chose to walk away from this chance then that clamouring and clawing for revenge would never stop, never fade: eternity would be unbearable with that regret beside her.

The last sliver of the day left the world around her, heavy clouds drifting in the sky, and as full night came to force the huntress *in her blood stopped its relentless screams for retribution and began to demand a purer hunt. And on that there was no conflict.*

Ania closed her eyes and rose to her feet, and when she stepped onto the ground outside she opened them again with the killer dancing inside.

The night guided her flight, onwards first over the fields and empty spaces, long grass caressing her bare legs as her dress rose above her knees, and then through small clusters of trees.

The small wooden house sat isolated and lonely, as did the elderly woman inside. She dozed in the chair in front of the roaring fire, a heavy and warm shawl covering her.

She dreamt of her husband, dead for so many years, and although not all of her thoughts of him were kind she still missed him, her life having turned to simple survival.

The light scratching on the surface of the door roused her from her light sleep, and she awkwardly turned to look behind her, a cold finger of dread creeping up her old and twisted spine. As a child she had been told, as had all of her siblings, that when her turn came the Herdsman or the Herdswoman would arrive to escort her onwards. And if he *came he would mark his arrival with a gentle tap and if* she *came she would mark her arrival by tenderly scraping the tips of her nails upon the door.*

As the door slowly opened and she saw those burning eyes stare at her she began to shake in fear, all thoughts of her long-dead husband chased away. In the brief time between the woman she saw as Herdswoman entering the room and reaching her, her hoarse and croaked scream filled the tiny house.

Ania bathed in the small tub that she had moved in front of the still-blazing fireplace. The water from the large barrel had warmed surprisingly quickly on the stove, and it felt so pleasant - smiling, Ania decided not to even try *and remember when she last bathed in warm clean water.*

Guilt tried to leak into her thoughts, but she fought them off. Self-condemnation was both pointless and unrequired. She was now a different creature and her nature had changed. All animals fed on what their natures dictated, and guilt was not a part of that ruling. And she had treated the woman's now-soulless body with respect, gently seating her back in her chair and wrapping the shawl around her once again: there had been nothing callous or unfeeling in those actions.

Out of the water she stood naked in the firelight, letting the heat dry her skin and hair before slipping her dress back on over her head.

Walking from the house she saw a long black hooded cloak hanging on an outcrop of wood by the door. She plucked it from its place and when she had closed the door behind her she whipped it backwards and draped it over her shoulders. The buckle was quickly fastened at the front as she walked back the way she had come, moving through the scattered groves and back into the grass-blanketed sweeping fields.

Mystical beauty filled the world as a break in the clouds exposed the blindingly-bright moons, circles full and perfect. Ania stopped short as the world was tinted with blue light. Her mouth opened slightly as she gaped in wondrous and soul-breaking adoration. For the first time since her crimeless conviction, Ania was standing in the moons' dual glow with nothing in between to dull the rapturous light.

Desire for her pool of years ago came close to devastating her, her heart aching for it stronger than it had ached for Blaiden, and tears sprang from her eyes, distorting the world momentarily. Almost angrily, Ania wiped the moisture away with the palm of one hand, her heart speeding up and her chest beginning to rise and fall quicker. She closed her eyes and struggled to control her pain and sadness, fiercely pushing her emotions until they were once more changed to hatred and anger, the familiarity of it strengthening her again.

Her chin was almost touching her chest, her hands rolled tightly into fists, and that animal inside paced restlessly, chanting with its growling voice inside Ania's heart: Maria! Maria! Maria!

In calculating slowness, her head raised once more towards the moons, eyes opening to fill with that light. Coldly, she looked at the circles in the sky and when the break in the clouds closed and drifted past and the light faded once more, Ania turned away and ran, that growl still echoing inside with every step.

The maid gently and tenderly ran the brush through the girl's silky dark blonde hair, smiling as she watched the young maiden dance her doll up and down upon her lap. It was just such a shame: first the girl's father dying, and then the girl falling silent. Not that any of the household staff or those from the village believed that the 'accident' had been the least bit accidental - Maria had received too many benefits, had gained too much wealth out of her husband's passing, and the time of mourning had been almost non-existent. But it definitely was a pity about Elizabeth.

Even from two stories up, the inebriated laughing and clamouring of Lady Maria and Mistress Katherine was clearly heard, and the maid's mouth curled slightly in distaste; although she knew better, she hoped that the poor girl's ears were as muted as her tongue.

Finished, she lay the brush upon the vanity table, smiling again as the light from the candle flame sparkled in Elizabeth's shiny hair.

A light clatter outside the window made her turn, but the heavy curtains draped across and she could see nothing. Glancing uneasily around the room, she saw nothing out of place; the prettily decorated room, toys concealing all surfaces, was just as it always was - tidy and neat, with an air of immense sadness layered over it.

Trying to dismiss the knots that were forming in her stomach, she gently stroked the girl's shoulder.

Doll still in hand, Elizabeth turned her beautiful - yet achingly broken-hearted - blue eyes to the woman who had raised her, both before and after her father's death. Although she was clearly Maria's child, her features a perfect replica, her face and her soul had not been tainted by cruelty or malice or jealousy. There were no sign of her mother's poisoned perspective of life in those mournful eyes.

The maid, and sole companion to the child who had only seen eight End Of Years, smiled warmly. "All done, my young Mistress Elizabeth." She gently stroked the girl's flawless cheek. "And as beautiful as ever."

Slowly and light as a feather, yet lacking in nothing because of it, the youngster hugged her briefly, before moving away.

Worry seeped through her as she saw Elizabeth staring, eyes wide and terrified, at something over her shoulder. Her arms instinctively went out to her young charge to offer a sense of protection. *Before she could turn to look behind her, the flickering of the candle flame beside her caught her eye. As she moved her head to look at it, she became aware of the fluttering sound as the curtains flapped in a breeze.*

And of breathing drawing closer.

It wasn't clear in her mind (nor would it ever be) how she had managed to find Maria's home so easily, how she had tracked the woman to a part of the village that was unknown to her. But she didn't really care how - all that was important was that she had. She growled softly, almost a purr.

Inside the big house, the sounds of intoxicated foolishness drifted to the street where Ania stood. The entire lower level was filled with light, and a gentle candle-light shone pale through drawn curtains on one of the upper floors.

A gentle gust of wind blew the hood of the cape from her head, freeing her silver-streaked black hair to fly backwards. The scent of blood to be spilled, of vengeance to be taken (although they were the same) rode on that breeze to reach her, not washing over her but aiming straight for her and slamming into her soul.

Her eyes had narrowed, fixing on the faint light above and to her right. Her blue-grey eyes, already searching for a route up to that window, darkened to an almost black-blue.

It would be easy to just walk through the main doors to the house - there were plenty of servants in the building, yet Ania knew that she was quick enough to be able to kill them all without too much added inconvenience. But the memory of the guards escaping from the Lair haunted her. She was not going to risk Maria discovering her and fleeing the same way. There were also lots of dark windows, most likely leading to rooms vacant of life, but that did not feel right either, too craven.

The clouds had increased, the bright moons now completely concealed behind the dense blankets, yet Ania saw every detail of everything around her. Anticipation had brought the world into sharp focus as it sent the blood coursing violently inside of her. But as she began to close the short distance from where she stood to the sturdy wall, she felt all sense of emotion drop away. What minimal thought she had been capable of in her assassin's mind was erased in entirety the moment that her fingertips came into contact with the stonework.

Almost as if she was being lifted, Ania crawled the wall with quick ease, the tips of her fingers and toes found the tiny gaps between the large stones and boosted her upwards. Within seconds, she was perched on the thin window ledge, bare feet half-suspended over a thirty-five feet drop, palms resting flat against the cool glass.

She could smell two separate hosts of blood in the room, one young and one old, their scents strong and clear even through the window, their heart-beats as loud as thunder to Ania's ears.

Snarling slightly, Ania crouched down, now only the tips of her toes remaining on the ledge, the rest of her feet hovering over nothing, her balance not faltering even a little. She raised her arms above her head and her fingertips traced the edge of the large window, hands moving in opposite directions. At the bottom edge, she slid a strong nail in between the glass and the window frame, feeling it snare the catch across, hearing the almost-soundless clatter as the lock slid free.

Continuing to use her strong nails she began to lift the window up, rising to her feet again. She secured the window with the catches on either side to prevent it from crashing down and simply stood for a moment, watching as the breeze made the thick curtains sway. Then light feet stepped inside, Ania unaware of the man who had seen her fleeing away into the night.

Although she had heard the woman talking, the words currently held no meaning for her, indecipherable noises of another species.

As she slipped out from behind the curtains, she looked at the two embracing humans before her. She had already halved the distance between them when the girl saw her.

The young blonde haired girl pulled back from her companion, alarmed blue eyes frozen on Ania's. The woman's arms went out to the girl in her care, and she could hear the maid's heart speeding up. Now standing directly behind the woman, able to see the strands of fine grey hair that had escaped from the tight bun just above the nape of her neck, Ania saw the minute movement as the woman glanced towards the flickering candle flame.

Breathing heavily, Ania bared her teeth slightly, catching the slight widening of the girl's eyes. She also caught the inaudible sound as the girl's lungs quickly expanded with more air than they *were used to.*

She could not allow the child to disclose her presence. Lightning quick, as the girl was still gathering the air to scream, Ania had taken hold of both the maiden's and maid's heads and drove both violently to the hard floor. The heavy and dull thuds and cracks as their skulls impacted resonated briefly in the air, and Ania immediately drew in the scent of two blood-types as they seeped on to the floor.

Moving around the spreading and joining pools of blood, almost black in the poor light, Ania stepped over the still limbs of each of them and walked out of the room as the candle flame flickered for the last time before vanishing entirely.

Sighing, he placed yet another large jug of the ridiculously over-potent blue wine onto the tray, their twelfth of the evening. Wishing for the millionth time since his late-employer had been met by either Herdsman or Herdswoman that he could walk away from the now-cursed, detestable and condemned household, the chief steward straightened his shoulders once more and smoothed the slight creases from the dark green uniform he wore. Although he knew that his decorum would not be noticed, his pride in his profession (not to mention the respect he still held for the memory of his late-Lord) refused to allow his disdain to show. He picked up the tray and walked from the kitchen.

He had served his whole adult life within the surrounding walls, so he knew that something was wrong the moment he stepped into the long shadow-filled hallway. Not inclusive of the loud raucous laughing from the room he was heading to, the house around him was silent, a deserted and empty atmosphere throughout.

Goosebumps broke out over his arms, spreading through his body like a rash and his hands began to shake. The jug shuddered, the wine splashing over the lip of the flask, cascading onto the tray. An icy-coldness pervaded his flesh, settling deep into him, as instinct and his senses made him aware that he was alone. Other than the two drunk and oblivious Ladies of the house, he knew that not one person lived; that somehow all twenty-three maids, scullions and servitors were all dead and gone.

The soft whisper of cloth behind him froze even his tremors.

He stood, statuesque, as the shifting sigh drew nearer, bringing the faint bitter-sweet aroma of blood with it.

To Ania, the aroma of blood was not faint but pungent and compelling. It was spattered over her dress and cloak, and it enveloped her like a cloud, dark red instead of white. It comforted her rather than instigated her hunger once more, although that was partially because it had already been catered for. The compulsion to feed had built too high, too much blood had been spilt for her to control the thirst any longer, and the last two she had killed had more than satisfied.

She stood behind the man who seemed suspended in time except for his speeding heartbeat, who she assumed from his uniform was the main steward, and acted quickly, her movements no more than a blur. Both arms moved forwards, one stretching up around the arm held to his side, snaking across his chest and up to the opposite side of his face, her thumb in front of his ear and her fingers pointing to the back of his neck. The other rose underneath his outstretched arm, ready to catch the tray before it could fall. Without pausing she turned her body slightly to the right, using the momentum of her torso to spin his head the same way.

Before his neck broke, before his head was turned to face behind him, the head servant of the almost-devastated home felt nothing but a brief cold feather touch.

Immediately, his body grew limp and began to sag. Ania took the weight of the tray as his hand began to buckle, lifting slightly so that his falling body would not knock it, and still supporting him by his chin followed him downwards as he gently slid to the ground.

Balancing the tray still slightly above the height of her head, she straightened up and brought it down to waist level.

From a room before her, Ania heard the harsh loud high-pitched giggle and her eyes swept the doorway. Everything in her peripheral vision darkened, faded, while the door seemed to brighten as if it was lit from within, growing clearer so that she could see every minute grain of the wood.

Her teeth felt razor sharp behind her lips, longer and more powerful - hearing Maria and Katherine so close, within reach, reinforced to Ania just what those teeth were for. A cold trickle moved down her spine, like water being poured, and she felt focus and clarity and thought *flow back into her. The wild huntress still bayed for their blood, for their deaths, but it was no longer a wordless animal cry - intelligence and lucidity verbalised those desires. The two sides of Ania's soul fused and merged together, forming a being that was stronger, calm and cruel in equal measure, and more capable of carrying out her vow because of it.*

Left hand continuing to balance the tray of only-slightly spilled wine, Ania used her right to raise the hood of her cloak over her head. Shadows fell onto her face, veiling her features and concealing the venom within her hidden eyes.

Urgency, anxiousness and anticipation had no place in her as her silent footsteps took her closer to the door, leaving her only a wintry stillness. With a hand that was steady, she pushed the door open. The volume from the room seemed to double as the door swung all the way back, lamp and firelight spilling out into the hallway, and Ania stepped from the dark shadows to the soft brightness of the room.

Vast and richly furnished, ornaments and objects of value placed decoratively throughout, the room lost all sense of finery and elegance solely by the presence of the two women within. Expensive dresses were sodden with spilt wine, lavishly sculptured hairstyles were in disarray, and not a trace of propriety was notable on the two figures who lounged on plush seats, raucously braying laughter into the air.

Ania looked at them, still unseen. The years had not been kind to them. Old age had oozed into their skins early, formerly flawless complexions now marked with wrinkles and pitted with scars of recent blemishes. The makeup that had been generously applied only accentuated the unpleasant features that had once been pleasant, defining the lack of beauty instead of concealing it.

"About time!" Maria spat out when she became aware of the added presence in the room. "I thought that the labour of carrying a tray *had become too mu-"* Finally turning towards the doorway, *Maria stopped speaking mid word as she saw the black-clad woman who stood there and not the servant she had expected.*

Katherine also sensed the change and ceased laughing, first looking at Maria and then turning to see what had caused her to quieten so suddenly.

Still in the grip of the inexplicable tranquillity, Ania

gracefully took a couple more steps forward into the room.

"Who are you and what are you doing in my home?! And where is the steward?!" The viciousness that was, and had always been, the norm in Maria's tone was spat outwards as she stood, trying to regain her superiority at the appearance of the uninvited guest.

Katherine followed Maria's lead as she always had, and also stood and stared with hostility.

"Your steward has left his post. As have your maids and all others under your service."

Ania saw the puzzled and unsettled glance that passed between them.

"Yet I could not allow you the indignity of providing for yourself, so I brought your refreshment myself." Ania gracefully walked to a small table to her right and placed the tray onto it, turning back to them while ensuring that the shadows cast by her hood continued to cover her face.

They were still staring at her and Ania saw the flicker of recognition in their eyes caused by the sound of her voice, faint and unsure but there.

Her hands fluttered upwards to the buckle and from the darkness of the hood she watched as they saw, actually saw, *the paleness of her skin and the splatters of red that could be only one thing.*

At the sight of the blood that marked the too-pale skin, the glance that passed between Maria and Katherine had moved from anxiousness and was now filled with fear.

Almost theatrically, Ania turned her back to them as the cloak was undone and she swept it smoothly from her shoulders, laying it elegantly across the back of a nearby chair. With her head lowered, purposefully staring at the floor to continue disguising her face, she turned back to face them.

Long, pale and blood-soaked fingers tucked her hair behind her ears. She could hear their hearts thumping, could smell the sweat on the skin, and breathed it in like air. Her lips curled in pleasure as the nervousness in them rose like their heart rates. Like wine she drank it in, savouring the moment now that it was finally before her. Allowing the cruelty to now filter through into her eyes, she raised her head to look solely at Maria.

Both Maria and Katherine stepped backwards in shock, Maria's stunned gasp and hushed words of negation as she stared at the familiar face, last seen through eyes of insane hate, hovered in the air.

"Maria?" Katherine whispered, her head turned toward her friend yet her eyes still remained on the woman she had led, supposedly, to her death. "Maria? It can't be?"

Ania still smiled as she kept her eyes on Maria's, almost as if Katherine was not there, did not exist, and when she spoke it was directed only to her.

"You've aged, my friend, and not well. The years - long, long years - have marked you unkindly." She pointed at a large red blemish on Maria's chin. "Makeup cannot hide your imperfections, though you try."

Maria continued to stare, while Katherine glanced uneasily between the two.

"As for me," Ania continued, her voice sickly-sweet, as she began to slowly step forward and to the right, angling away from both Maria and Katherine. "I have not aged at all." Lightly, she laughed. "Although I have changed, my years have been frozen for all of that time."

Casually, Ania reached the two lamps that stood on another small table and pinched out both of the flames. Still moving, she slowly circled behind Maria so that the heat from the fireplace brushed her with warmth. Maria now stood in between Ania and the open doorway, but both she and her friend had turned to watch Ania's movements. Circling onwards to the other side of Katherine, Ania made her way to the identical table which held identical lamps.

With those flames extinguished, the dwindling fire emitted the only light in the room, and shadows played everywhere, bouncing over Ania as she remained walking until her circle had completed. Once again in front of the door she stopped and smiled at Maria again.

"And for all of that time, my 'friend', I have thought about only one thing."

Both of the women, whose intoxication had rapidly disappeared into sobriety, picked up on the emphasis of that word, the way she had almost hissed the word 'friend', and they moved closer together after a brief glance.

Ania tilted her head a little so that she would have almost looked friendly if it hadn't been for the danger in the depths of her darkened blue-grey eyes.

"Blood for blood."

The word had not even reached their ears before Ania leapt forwards, speeding forwards.

But not to Maria.

Katherine screamed out as Ania whisked her away from her companion's side. Before Maria could turn to look at the space where her friend had stood, Ania was stood in a shadow-enriched corner with Katherine in front of her. She had pushed Katherine's right arm behind her back forcing it up between the shoulder-blades, holding it securely in place with her own right hand. Ania's left was in front of the girl, her nails gently, threateningly, moving backwards and forwards across the terrified girl's throat.

Maria made a move forward, but Katherine screamed as Ania nonchalantly pushed her arm slightly higher, the nails at her throat prodding softly, indenting but not breaking the skin.

Katherine was breathing rapidly, almost panting, and Ania shushed her, her breath cold on the girl's warm skin. Ania forced away her calmness for the moment - it could not serve her purpose now - and she looked at Maria, while Katherine trembled in her arms, and invited in her cruelty and vengeance to take control.

Slowly, she increased the pressure behind her nails, no longer stroking her former-tormentor's throat but raking it. She felt the soft flesh split and move aside to allow her nails entrance to the softer tissue beneath. Blood trickled from the gashes as she repeatedly scored the skin - back and forth, right to left.

Katherine didn't struggle or squirm; Ania was holding her too tightly for that. But she cried and whimpered, pleading for help.

"Does it hurt, Katherine?" Although she spoke to her captive, her eyes remained on the girl standing opposite. "I know it does. I was once in your place. You took me to that place. And I went through more pain than the two of you could ever conceive." She turned her face so that her mouth was against Katherine's ear and added in a whisper, "But I'll make you try!"

In a flurry of movement, Katherine yelled out in agony as she was spun around to face her attacker. Pain erupted all over her body, waves of stinging overtaking each other, seemingly without cause. Maria stood, unable to move, as her friend screamed, and watched as she was flung onto the floor.

When the night had begun, Katherine's clothes had been in good condition, if a little dishevelled. Now the material that showed too much lay in tatters over and beneath her bleeding body, the cuts and gashes open wide to allow the rushing exit of her life-blood. She lifted her head, staring out through untidy hair, imploring with her blue eyes for Maria to help her, the blood running in thin streams turning her face into a horrific mask of pain.

Ania leapt to Katherine's side, crouching beside her and stroking the girl's blood-soaked hair, looking at Maria once more.

"You once deceived me, Maria." Her voice was guttural, one step above a snarl. "You feign friendship, real friendship; made me believe that you were capable of caring, honestly, for someone else."

Glancing down at Katherine, she grabbed the girl's strawberry-blonde hair. Katherine let loose another shrill yell as her head was yanked upwards.

Again, Ania spoke to Katherine while looking at Maria, speaking in a confidential whisper, only for Katherine's ears. "I'm going to give your friend a choice, dear Katherine. It was she who led you to help delude me; it was she who led you to lead me into that dark place for a misdeed never perpetrated except in her unhinged mind and her bereft soul."

Katherine wept at the contradiction of her position, more out of the gentle and almost-tender words that were being spoken to her than the pain of her injuries. Her tears stung her as they seeped into her many cuts.

"As you lie here," Ania continued. "You have more than honoured the debt caused by the evil of following her request. And I will give Maria the chance to prove her loyalty to you, Mistress Katherine."

Relief ran though her, and she looked at Maria with hope.

Ania raised her voice, speaking now to Maria, still holding Katherine's head up, though more amiably than before.

"Your friend is now at your mercy, Maria. I will allow her her life if you give yours to me."

Maria looked at Katherine, taking two steps back. "No." She said without hesitation.

Ania let go of Katherine, standing up and moving away,

leaning against a wall, and watching. Neither of the two other girls saw the cruel bestial smile on her dark red lips.

Struggling, ignoring the pain that ripped through her body, Katherine pushed herself to her knees, holding her bleeding hands out towards her friend. "Maria? Maria, please?"

There was no confusion, no conflicting, on Maria's face, only a blank refusal. As Katherine reached forwards, scrambling on lacerated knees, holding out her hands for her redemption, Maria simply walked backwards, staying out of her reach. No emotion looked back at Katherine as she pleaded, and she dropped her arms by her side in despair, collapsing backwards. "Please." she whispered in a sob.

Anger swam through Ania, that her 'friend's' begging had not moved Maria in the slightest, that she had made no attempt to even try, and so in mercy she acted quickly. She ended Katherine's life in a rush, breaking her neck in an instant, quickly and efficiently.

Crouched beside the now-fallen body of Katherine, through hair that had moved to almost obscure her eyes, Ania glared at Maria.

Viciously, she forced thought completely away, turning against its reasoning. The last thought that she had before the animal took over once more, was that Maria would receive no such acts of mercy.

Two sounds erupted in that room before more blood started to pour: a low, almost silent growl, and a high pitched scream.

Upstairs, in a room that had given entry to the creature that had massacred the household in such a short time, a small and youthful hand twitched as its owner fought slowly yet steadily towards consciousness, tiny slim fingers trembling in the sticky red puddles that surrounded them.

Maria gasped, struggling for any trickle of air to slide down the now bruised and swollen pipe that had once been her throat. Amongst the debris of broken trinkets, fingers sliced on tiny sharp slivers of ornaments, she pushed herself backwards, leaning against the wall that she had been pinned against, only a strong hand on her neck to hold her a foot above the floor.

There was a low snarl at the far end of the room, and Maria

sobbed. *The coughing fit that followed caused tears to roll down her cheeks and brought the taste of her own blood to the back of her throat.*

It also brought a growling-chuckle from across the room.

Still sobbing, a ripping pain settling in her lungs, Maria wished that she could see where Ania was. Luckily, the pain in her throat and lungs had overtaken the pain she knew was still lurking in the newly-vacant sockets where her eyes had once been; although, she was unable to forget the squelching popping sound that had been made when Ania's nails had impaled and removed them.

Where the growl had resonated from a strong crash exploded as something was smashed. Maria jumped at the unexpected noise, then screamed coarsely as a fingernail was lightly passed across her slashed and bleeding cheek.

Cringing, she tried to push herself further into the wall. Cruel laughter was first directly before her, then it was almost out of the room, and then it was beside her, all before a single second had passed. And knowing that Ania was doing it to scare her did nothing to ease her heart.

"Maria..." A soft whisper tickled her left ear.

"Maria..." Now in her right ear, without a single sound of movement.

"Maria..." Now at her far left.

Her throat was still too swollen to allow speech but she prayed silently that her tormentor would leave.

Elizabeth raised herself to her knees, struggling to understand why her head was hurting so much and why it felt so heavy. It was also beyond her comprehension why the floor beneath her palms felt so tacky. She rested on her hands and knees, eyes closed, to allow her head the time it needed to stop spinning.

Ania looked at Maria, a contemptuous curl on her lips. Speedily, she picked up a shard of a broken vase and slashed it across Maria's chest, slicing both the dress and the flesh beneath, the deep wound spilling blood instantly. And from her new position close to the doorway, she laughed as Maria screamed.

But the predator was growing tired of teasing. It yearned for more pain than had already been administered; for the climax of the suffering.

Angered more by the weak whining from the lips of the coward at her feet, she could hardly contain her strength enough to be able to have her final say.

The rush of air that was a soundless scream blew onto her face as she hauled the blind and bleeding woman to her feet, strong arms forbidding Maria to collapse as her knees buckled.

"You deceived me." She growled softly. "You led me to that dark place. You led me to a lair of blood-souls. That is enough to justify this." She could feel her temper trying to break free, and rushed on. "But worse than that, you denied Katherine."

Maria groaned in despair as Ania's voice continued to deepen and darken. She was blind, but she could still see what was coming well enough.

"She was punished for your malice, and you did not intervene. You were given the chance to save her life by reaping the harvest of your own deeds, but you declined."

Maria could smell the scent of blood on Ania's breath as she was pulled closer.

"But retribution is, however,-" 'yours' *was how Ania meant to finish, but the predatory creature in her was only able to finish with a rumbling growl.*

Covering eyes that were not there, Maria screwed her eyelids closed, desperately trying to prepare herself for what was approaching. But nothing could. Wheezing, unable to send any air to her lungs, Maria felt herself thrown across the room. She felt and heard a brittle snap as she landed on her back, and a brief serene calm before a red river of agony swept over her. She tried to scream but she was choking, suffocating in a room full of air.

There was a light scuffle of shifting debris as Ania pounced and landed beside her, but Maria couldn't turn her head away from the intense power that she felt next to her: she found she couldn't move at all.

Ania knew that Maria would soon be dead, with or without her help. Not only by the blue tint that had begun to infect Maria's lips and skin, but by the smell – the smell of flesh dying.

But it wasn't enough - she couldn't allow her to die naturally.

Softly growling, she attacked. Her nails dug deep, stripping thick lines of flesh from the frozen form. Leaning over her, she sunk her teeth into the woman's shoulder and pulled back, the mass of skin hanging from her mouth. She spat it onto the floor beside her, not wanting to pollute herself by ingesting even the tiniest drop of Maria's tainted being.

It was enough, barely.

Ania managed to tear off half of Maria's skin before the girl died. It was a combination of blood loss, shock, and the inability to breath, but the result was the same: she died, blind and in pain, and without a single thought of her daughter, thinking only of herself as she always had done.

Elizabeth sat with her blood-stained hands covering her face. She was huddled against the base of the bed, knees to her chest and gently rocking herself. Her breath came out harshly between sobs, and her head pounded with each hitching sigh.

She had seen the maid as soon as the pain in her head had eased a little and her vision had cleared. She had frozen in the act of getting, wobbly, to her feet and her legs had collapsed, spilling her back onto the blood-soaked floor and triggering the sickening thud in her head again.

It was too much for her innocent mind to cope with, and escaping the dark room never passed into her thoughts. All she could do was sit and rock herself, hoping that her head would stop hurting.

Ania felt invigorated! She felt light-headed, and complete, and –

"Free." She whispered. She smiled, genuine and pure as that simple word filled her with wonder. She was free! Free of the Lair, free of her vows, free of the contemptuous control of those that lay dead in the room.

She glanced at both of the bodies, first at Maria and then at Katherine. Her lengthy strides took her to Katherine's side. Agilely, she knelt beside her and smoothed the mangled and tangled hair from the girl's ravaged face, death having leaked beauty back into it.

"All debts are cleared, Mistress Katherine." She said, speaking tenderly. "May the Herdsman and the Herdswoman guide and lead you onwards, with compassion, understanding, and love." Lovingly, she softly kissed the cooling skin of Katherine's cheek.

With a slight reservation, she stood and walked to Maria's

side. Fighting off the wave of anger that tried to break through she knelt next to her. The skin on Maria's face had been left unpeeled for this purpose and Ania looked at her, seeing past her own emotions.

As death had injected Katherine with beauty again, Maria simply looked lost, a little girl wandering in nothingness. Looking at her, the last edge of her vengeance melted away, and when she spoke it was sincerely and in perfect honesty.

"All debts are finally cleared, Mistress Maria. May the Herdsman and the Herdswoman guide and lead you onwards, with compassion, understanding, and love." In completion, Ania's lips brushed Maria's cheek.

Quickly she stood, her back straight and her head held high. She looked at the glowing embers in the fireplace; there was only one more thing that she must do.

Blaiden watched as Ania turned restlessly, her brow creased, her eyes flickering rapidly behind closed lids. It wasn't the frantic throes of her almost-insatiable hunger but simply the twinges of a replayed nightmare.

He leant against the wall, tired and worn out, anxious and scared. He could sense that her memories were almost finished claiming her, that she would soon be released from its debilitating grip. But he also knew that whatever the memory was, it was climbing to its zenith; that soon the worst would be replayed.

The smoke filled the hallway, flames rolling like waves across the ceiling in the kitchen, the acrid taste of the smoke scratching at her throat. The reflection of the fire danced in Ania's eyes, her heart seemingly set alight as well.

The night called her stronger, purer now that there were no more vows to be fulfilled. Once it was completed, once the house was nothing more than ash and rubble on scorched ground, she would be able to tread a new path in the night. Her heart flew, ablaze with wild happiness, and she turned to the front door, the flames behind her.

The mutterings that she hadn't heard until she began to open the door hushed into a heavy silence as she stepped out. There were perhaps forty people, all gathered around the steps below the door she now walked through. The flames that were rearing through the hallway behind her rendered her a solid-black silhouette until she had descended all three stairs, the crowd stepping backwards as she advanced.

They all stared at her, eyes moving swiftly over her blood-spattered face and intense eyes, lingering on the teeth that were exposed between her smiling lips.

Ania felt an irresistible surge of power rush into her as she looked back at them. The scent of their fear was as strong to her as the smell of the building burning behind her, yet so much sweeter to her soul. The people from her village, whom she had always feared and been weary of, now looked at her in fear. The semi-circle of the crowd around Ania and the stairs moved backwards as she took another step forwards.

Walking on, straight through the centre of the crowd, Ania smiled wider as they shifted to make a path, a very wide path, for her to walk through. As she passed them, watching as they cringed away and averted their gaze so as not to catch her eye, Ania realised something: not one of them recognised her.

She reached the outer circle of the group and came to a sudden stop. Everybody had moved from her way; all except two. And they recognised her.

Ania's parents stood side by side, preventing her from leaving the path that had been made for her.

It seemed to Ania that the years had been unkind to all but herself. Her mother's back had begun to twist forwards, and the purpose of the sturdy wooden stick in her gnarled hands seemed clear. Lines had etched their way across her forehead and beneath her eyes, and her hair had become faded and listless. Her father had escaped slightly better. He still stood tall, but his head was almost completely bald and the hair that did remain was white and wiry.

But their eyes had not aged. Intelligence, passion, ability and fury shone out at her, burning stronger than the fire in the house behind their former-child. They looked at Ania with hatred, and Ania's power drained from her.

She opened her mouth to speak, to try and explain, but before her pointless words could be spoken, both of her parents raised their right hands and, without uttering a word, pointed at the house.

Ania felt a sliver of cold ice worked into her spine as she turned and looked where they pointed.

Blaiden sat on the bed beside her, talking softly to her, telling her that it was okay, that he was with her. There was no point trying to restrain her – she was thrashing too wildly now for that and he would only end up hurting her more.

He felt helpless, and his heart ached at the sight of the tears spilling rapidly from between her closed eyes. When she began to sob in anguish, Blaiden began to silently cry as well.

Michael held Holly in his arms. She was still, but she had begun talking in her sleep, repeating the same words over and over.

"Oh, no. Please, no. Oh, no. Please, no."

Quietly, Michael hushed her, telling her that it was okay, and that he was with her. He wiped away the tears that slowly spilled from her tightly-closed eyes, wishing he could do more.

"Oh, no. Please, no."

"Oh, no. Please, no."

The words hung in the air as Ania repeated them, staring up at the window she had forced open to first enter the house. A dagger seemed to have been driven into her heart, piercing mercilessly through to her soul. Shame and guilt crashed into her as she saw the flames consuming the building, the tiny figure silhouetted against the fire.

The building was an inferno, the entire bottom floor an almost-solid mass of flames, the heat reaching out towards the edges of the crowd, whose eyes remained steady on the blood-soul before them.

Ania peered deeper into the flames, searching for a possible way to reach the girl she had thought dead. But she knew that, even if she was able to reach her, there was no route to take the child out safely. But all that she had ever been, before the revenge against Maria had pushed aside all else, came into force. It was because of her that the girl was up there, surrounded by an advancing wall of flames, and she had to at least try.

Hurriedly, she turned to go back to the building, but before she had taken that first step she felt her arm grabbed.

Her mother's claw-like hand was wrapped around Ania's arms, the fingers strong despite their condition. Her father stood by her mother, and they stared into her eyes, the last ounce of her strength stolen by the wrath that emanated from them. A terrible rumbling vibrated through the ground and Ania tore her eyes from her parents to look again at the house.

The smoke and flame that billowed out through the open door shifted and jumped along with that rumbling, and in aguish Ania turned her eyes upwards to the girl.

The palms of her hands were pressed against the window pane, which had jumped its catches as the building shook, sliding down closed again. Blood covered her face, and her blonde hair had also been dyed crimson. Tears coursed thickly down her face and her blue eyes were terrified as they looked outwards at those below who did nothing to help.

Ania felt pain twist in her stomach as those blue eyes found her and fixed only on her. In the brief moment that lasted beyond an eternity, before the house collapsed in a mass of flame, smoke and rubble, Ania could see the girl screaming mutely for help. And although not a single sound passed her silent lips, Ania heard the screams inside her mind.

And then she was gone, an earth-shattering roar as the building collapsed in on itself, taking the girl with it, the scream in Ania's head cutting off abruptly.

The crowd erupted into screams, running back towards the village in a bid to escape the billowing flames.

In the night, before the blazing debris, only three people remained.

Tears rushed from her eyes and she wanted to sink to her knees, but her mother's grasp forbade any movement. Instead she turned towards her parents, her eyes downcast in despair and remorse.

When he spoke, her father's voice was filled with the same venom that was in his eyes.

"'It is a darkness from which there can be no salvation.'"

Ania's head shot up to look at him, shocked momentarily out of her tears.

"'It is endless and timeless.'"

Vindictiveness gave her mother's words a childlike edge. "Now leave, blood-soul, and do not return!"

She didn't drop her daughter's arm, but pushed it away as if *the mere touch of Ania's skin would infect her.*

Then without another word, they turned and walked away.

The last sight that Ania would ever have of her parents was of their backs as they denied her as they always had.

Horrified, Ania turned back to the still-burning pile of debris and knelt, watching it burn.

When the flames had faded to embers, she raised the hood of her cloak, shadows falling over her tear-stained face once more, and fled into the night.

VIII

Blaiden woke, knowing instinctively that the sun was still too high in the sky, and felt momentarily disorientated. He stared upwards at the ceiling, allowing the disjointed images from his dreams to fade, and wondering what had forced him to wake. Beside him, in a bed that was not his own, Ania lay still and calm. He sat up and turned so that he could see her completely.

The covers were tangled around her calves and the rest of her naked body was exposed. She lay on her side facing him, her eyes still closed.

As he looked at her, Blaiden realised what was different, what it was that had made him wake up. She was calm and still, she didn't writhe in response to her dreams, didn't mutter in despair. There was no trace of anxiousness anywhere on her hauntingly beautiful face; she was at peace.

Smiling at her serenity, Blaiden allowed himself to drift back into the realm of sleep.

In the same instant, Michael's eyes opened. He was greeted by the wondrous sight of his lover facing him, eyes restful behind closed lids, sleeping clearly without dreams or anxiety.

Smiling, he bridged the gap between them, his arm draping over her waist, and softly kissed the tip of her nose.

Forehead touching hers, Michael closed his eyes again and slept once more, the smile not leaving his lips.

* * *

Despite the memory having reached its conclusion, both Ania and Holly continued to sleep – their emotions and their minds had been ravaged by the onslaught of the dream, and they were both still in need of rest.

Blaiden was able to fulfil Ania's need for blood solely by small droplets rung from a rag once more, her hunger almost non-existent and her sleep was serene and undisturbed.

The nights passed for both Blaiden and Michael in the same way: they hunted and fed, then returned to their slumbering lovers to satiate their slight hunger. Then, they simply waited, hoping that the night would end with closed eyes opening, sleep finished.

But on the eighteenth of December, Blaiden heard a familiar and unwelcome sound – from the depths of her sleep, Ania moaned in despair. Although her body remained still, Ania's head snapped left and right, as if to shake loose whatever her mind was now showing her.

Defeat hit him, and he raked his finger through his hair – he felt frozen, unable to move from his space in the doorway. He could only watch as Ania began to dream again.

Ania once again stood, this time alone, before the house, the flames devouring the building from the ground up. She could feel the heat from the fire and the trembling that emitted from the ground as the house shook at its foundations. The black trousers and black top that she wore confirmed her belief that she was dreaming, and it was not a dream based on memory – but that realisation did not offer one shred of comfort.

Tears stung her eyes as she raised them to gaze again at that window and the girl trapped within, hands pressed against the glass. As their eyes caught and held, Ania sank to her knees, weeping in anguish as that familiar guilt and shame crashed violently into her heart. Those pleading blue eyes, clear and aware of the fate about to befall her, looked longingly out from the blood-stained and ashen face, and that young mute mouth opened repeatedly to scream silently for help that would never be received.

Still crying and still refusing to drop her eyes from Elizabeth's, the trembling beneath her began to intensify, the rumbling that vibrated the air almost like thunder to her ears. Before her the centre of the building began to buckle, the whole structure pitching first one way then the other, a doomed boat caught on a raging sea of fire.

Ania longed to cover her eyes, to put a stop to the torture that her own conscience was forcing her to endure, but she continued to watch, determined to honour the girl's memory even after the years without number.

As she watched, the house lurched forwards once more and the girl's hands were pushed by a sudden force pushing even harder against the glass.

As was the way with most dreams, time slowed. Ania saw the girl's expression turn from complete fear to momentary surprise as she was moved forwards. Ania could hear the time-stretched sound as the frame around the glass broke away from the brickwork, sending both the window and the girl out into the flame-heated night air.

Ania was on her feet and running closer to the collapsing house, time speeding up again as she closed the distance, straining to reach the place where the girl would land before the impact could actually happen.

The girl's body thudded into her outstretched arms, sending both of them crashing to the ground. Sobbing and laughing, Ania clung to the child, holding her safe. Still laughing, she glanced down at Elizabeth, those beautiful and grateful blue eyes staring back.

The sound of burning wood faded, muted, as Ania looked at the child she held, as the girl began to change. Those blue eyes turned to sharp cat-green, the blood-stained blonde hair darkened to deep brown, and the features flickered to slightly different arrangements.

Of Elizabeth there was now no sign: Holly's child now lay in Ania's arms, and Ania felt her stomach tighten.

Although most of her abilities had faded through the many years she had walked the night, on occasion her dreams still held significance. And looking at the girl, Ania realised that her father's prophecy had been wrong on one point: there was *salvation in the darkness.*

And its name was Laura.

Holly awoke with a start, her body trembling. Beside her, Michael snored gently, but the sound was distant.

The image had burnt itself deep into her mind and heart, and she felt a dark strength surging through her.

For the first time since she had run from the hospital, she had seen her daughter, had seen the beautiful child she had grown into. Although guilt and remorse for the missing years swam through her, what she felt most of was pride and love for the girl her daughter had become.

And just as it was the first time she had seen her child, Holly uttered her name for the first time.

"Laura." She whispered, tears leaking from her eyes.

* * *

Blaiden stared in dazed surprise at the empty space in the bed, the space beside him where Ania had lay when he had once again closed his eyes. The starlight from the night outside and the gentle orange glow from the streetlamps now entered the small room. This also confused Blaiden in his post-sleep state – he had drawn the curtains to protect against the day.

Standing naked before the window, Ania stared at the night outside, a tired smile on her pale face.

"The night's call woke me." She turned slowly towards him, her arms rising to wrap around herself in comfort. Her pale face was as beautiful as ever, the soft orange glow touching lightly upon her skin to highlight her features. But her blue-grey eyes shone with weariness; as was always the way with Ania, her eyes alone revealed her true age.

Blaiden gazed upon his lover, searching her eyes deeply as she stood before him. The shock of finding her awake was receding to allow other realisations to rise through his reviving mind. He had expected when she finally awoke for the hunger to have overtaken her as it had previously, for the predatory huntress inside of her to have banished thought and reasoning. He had expected to find either an empty flat or the eyes of a savage killer staring back at him. What Blaiden had *not* anticipated was seeing the vulnerable fragility in those infinite depths. And it unnerved him.

Still smiling sadly, Ania sat upon the edge of the bed, twisting her upper body so that she could look at him. Slowly, she moved into him, her head tilting to one side, eyes falling gently closed. Tenderly, she touched her lips to his, kissing him softly, breathing his soul into her own, and feeling a little of her sadness banished away.

Eyes still closed, she rested her forehead against his. "Thank you." She whispered.

His arms wrapped themselves around her and he pulled her tightly to him.

Without words, their embrace continued, neither wanting to be the one to end the peace they had found. But, although the hunger was nowhere near the level it had been after her past obligatory-

reminiscence, it was still there and with every peace-filled moment it grew slightly louder.

As it reached the point where it could no longer be ignored or dismissed, Ania once again whispered into her lover's ear. "It's time to hunt." Playfully, she nipped at his neck, her tiredness beginning to fade at the thought of feeding.

Still holding her, Blaiden started to laugh, feeling better than he had in weeks. He kissed her neck in response before they simultaneously and, in almost-choreographed movements, rose from the bed.

During her long sleep, Blaiden had ensured that Ania's clothes were cleaned, and as she walked the short distance from the bed to where they were folded Blaiden was watching her, following every tilt and sway of her body. Heat began to fill in the pit of his stomach as he watched her lithe movements. Quickly he moved to where she was and turned her around to face him. Lustfully he kissed her, pushing her backwards against the wall, his entire body in contact with hers, feeling Ania responding to him. His hands moved over her body, wanting to touch every part of her and he moaned in pleasure as she raised one of her legs to wrap around his, urging him to move tighter against her.

And as the night deepened outside they made good use of their time together, both sensing that it would not be long before they were parted again.

Holly had dressed as soon as she had greeted the night, longing to be outside in the darkness – longing to hunt.

When Michael walked into the kitchen he saw the back door open and Holly sitting on the steps, gazing at the world beyond the garden, the cold air pervading the house. She didn't look around as he walked over to her, nor did she look around when he kissed the top of her head. He sat beside her, and allowed himself to take in the peace of the evening. The freezing cold air made no impact on his cold skin as he stared upwards at the stars in the dark sky. He was almost lost himself in the calm beauty of the night that it took him a moment to realise that Holly had finally turned to look at him.

The beauty of the night was, as always, echoed in Holly's face, but the edge that he had glimpsed in her briefly in previous moments was back and much stronger than before. Barriers had been set firmly in her hazel eyes.

When she smiled the barriers dropped a little, but *only* a little - the walls still held strongly. She leant into him a little and kissed him, tenderly (but slightly dutifully). "I need to feed, Michael." She said when she pulled back a little.

Standing up, he put a hand out to help her up. A shot of unhappiness flew into him as a cruel spark jumped momentarily into her eyes. It flickered out just as quickly, but he could not quite convince himself that it had not been there. Just as he was about to drop his hand, to withdraw the gesture, her eyes softened further. She took his hand, and gently pressed her lips to its palm.

"I'm sorry, Michael. Residue of the dream, I guess."

As he helped her to her feet, Michael kissed her, fighting away the question that he really wanted to ask. He just had to trust that whatever the reason behind her lying to him, whatever it was that she was keeping back from him, she would tell him when she was ready.

Walking away from the house, Holly tried to fight away her distraction, but she longed to be away from Michael. The decision that she had made, although painful to her heart, was totally right; but she needed time and solitude to come to terms with her choice - in her soul she already knew that making the choice was easy but living with the reality of it would be anything but.

Michael quickly chose his prey and moved off through the quiet streets, knowingly giving Holly the space that she required.

As he walked away Holly didn't turn to watch him go: her mind was focussed purely on the issues going on in her mind. That and the hunger that was beginning to grow.

Yet she stood for a while in the centre of a lamp lit street, allowing the thirst to rise, to let it push aside thoughts of the path that she had decided to tread.

A woman walked past her, glancing nervously at the pale-skinned dark-clad woman who just stood and stared at nothing. But when that pale-skinned dark-clad woman noticed her, turned her hazel eyes to her, the woman's nervousness shifted up a gear and she hurried on, glancing back over her shoulder despite her feelings that she would be better advised not to.

She skidded to a stop, looking all around her. The woman in dark clothes was nowhere to be seen.

It was cold, but somehow the chill of the night didn't seem enough for the shaking that had begun in the top half of her body. Laughing uneasily, she wrapped her arms around herself and continued on her way, breathing white air from her lungs.

The trainers that she wore barely made a sound on the pavements and all around her was the quiet of empty streets. She passed by closed dark shops, moving past the secured, and often gated, doors and windows without hearing another sound anywhere around.

So the shock she felt and the scream that echoed through the deserted area as she was grabbed was to be expected.

Holly pulled the girl into a narrow gap between two buildings, forcing her along the five feet until they were stopped by a large black wheelie bin. There was no hesitation, no play acted out. Holly was focussed, single-minded, on the blood so close to the surface of the skin, so much of it within reach.

Her left hand simultaneously turned the girl's head to the side and covered her mouth, while her right held her shoulder, forcing the girl's body against the wall. Holly's teeth were buried in the girl's throat and she drank greedily, filling herself with the taste.

The flames that worked through the contents of the bin sent thick acrid smoke billowing out along with the sweet smell of roasting meat as Holly walked out of the once-again empty alley.

She brushed aside a lock of hair from her face as she moved along the streets, passing more dark shops. As she neared a group of buildings that were under renovation, the graffiti spray-painted boarded windows that had yet to be replaced concealing all evidence of the work that had so far been done, in a street close by an argument was breaking out. As a bottle was smashed upon the ground, Holly turned sharply to face the noise, her back towards a supposedly-locked door.

Despite the speed that was now the norm for her, Holly was too shocked to be able to react as the door was flung open and six hands reached out quickly to grab her.

As she was moved backwards more hands held onto her, one rough and dirt-encased hand clamped over her mouth and nose, Holly was able to smell the excitement of the seven men that were around her. Shock turned to anger as the realisation of what they wanted managed to get through to her.

Under the stench of hormones and alcohol the pleasant smell of sawdust and cleaning products lay over the new additions to the interior, but Holly was not in a position to appreciate it.

At the back of the would-be shop amid the scattered remnants of shelving a dust sheet hung in the alcove between two rooms, which billowed back as she was thrown through. Travelling through the air, she heard the drunken laughter of those that had brought her there. Her steadily-building anger was cut short as she landed sharply on her back, her head snapping back onto something metal and very, *very* hard. Blood began to seep out between strands of hair, smearing itself over the head of the sledge-hammer that had inflicted the injury. Eyes closed, Holly breathed in the metallic scent of her own blood, the animal inside beginning to claw its way towards consciousness. Eyes still closed, she let it.

"She out?" A slurred voice broke through the drunken laughter.

"Dunno."

A worn out trainer nudged at her left calf, and that animal inside growled silently. But she kept her eyes closed. Even when hands began to crawl up her trouser-clad legs she kept still. She blocked out the touch of the hands as they moved further up the outside of her legs, blocking out the laughter of the rest as they drew closer. She focussed on the sound of the two men's rapid breathing as they began to lean in to her face. She focussed on that, and of the smell of her own blood.

As one of those hands began to creep in towards the inside of her thigh and what lay there, the growl turned into a howl of rage and Holly's eyes flew open.

The two men who had been looming over her shot backwards, eyes wide in shock. They exchanged a troubled glance as they saw the white-hot murder staring back at them. The others, who had yet to *see* the creature that lay before them, laughed at the two friends' jumpy behaviour.

They laughed louder as the two who had been about to start stripping the girl got quickly to their feet and pushed their way past the rest of the group, the door that they had brought Holly through banging noisily both open and shut as they ran out.

But the laughter in the building didn't last.

The one who now stood closest to Holly was caught before

he'd even noticed that she had moved.

Within a single moment Holly had gotten to her feet and grabbed the man, turning him so that he was facing the others. Standing behind him, slightly to the left so that she could also look at the four men (all who looked as if the effects of the alcohol they had consumed had entirely left their systems), she had pushed his right arm up between his shoulder blades. Her other hand was buried in his greasy curly brown hair, pulling his head back to expose his neck a little more.

When one of the four, the more sober of the group - and the bravest - began to move forward, Holly fixed her attention on him. In a guttural voice, she spoke. "Take one more step and I'll break his arm."

When he twitched as if he was about to move forwards despite her warning she pushed the man's arm further up behind his back, feeling the tendons straining under the pressure.

The man's agonised scream seemed to convince his friend that the warning was real. He put his hands up above his head, palms open, and backed up a couple of steps.

Lowering her voice, but not so low that the others would be unable to hear her, she whispered into her captive's ear, all the while keeping her eyes firmly on the other four.

"You really have tried to fuck with the wrong person." She smiled darkly, the danger in her eyes increasing. "If you have any doubt of that, look at your friends."

His head shifted the tiniest bit as he did as she said.

"Have you ever seen them look so worried, so scared?" The question was rhetorical, and Holly was not disappointed by receiving no answer. "And all because of a *woman*." A sarcastic laugh bubbled momentarily to her lips. "But they don't seem scared *enough*." Holly's heart was racing in anticipation, anger and enjoyment joining together. "Let's change that!"

Roughly she buried her teeth into the man's neck. She let him fall to the floor, blood soaking the floor around his collapsed body. Spitting the lump of flesh and gristle out of her mouth she moved onto the four scrambling would-be attackers.

Thought turned to pure action and she killed them all in a flurry of movement, blood, and brief screams.

Torn and tortured bodies littered the blood-stained floor, the sweet smell of sawdust now hidden beneath the overpowering smell of blood instead of alcohol.

Holly stood still, breathing heavily, eyes closed. She stood tall and strong amid the chaos she had created, looking peaceful despite the rapid movements of her chest. But she wasn't peaceful; she was focussed. Her true nature had reawakened and it demanded full control which she gave it freely. As she stood, still and complete, she breathed in the smell of the blood, filling her soul with it, readying herself. Abruptly her eyes opened, their dark merciless depths still blazing.

She fled into the cold outside, rushing footsteps close to silent upon the pavements as she chased into the night, easily tracking the path of the two who had run. She passed by shops and buildings in a blur, seeing nothing but the invisible trail that her would-be rapists had left her to follow.

The sound of a large group of people chatting and laughing together grew louder as she neared and she slowed to a stop, hiding in the shadows of the overhang of a shop doorway. Penetratively, she scanned the crowd.

It took her only two seconds to separate them from the depths of the group where they were hiding. All she had to do was ignore all of the people who looked relaxed and look only for the nervous glances of people filled with unease.

She smiled slightly as she moved out of the shadows, walking casually towards the group. Her trainers crunched upon shards of broken glass and she stopped to look down. She crouched down briefly to sweep up a particularly long shard and held it in her hand as she straightened, turning it one way and another, admiring the way the light from the street-lamps bounced off of it. It seemed like too much of a coincidence, but her heart maintained it as a fact - this was part of the bottle that had been broken not too long ago, the one that had caused her attention to be moved from the danger she had been about to face.

She curled her hand tighter around it, feeling it cut slightly into her palm, then began to run.

She became a blur of blackness and she dodged easily past those in the group who had not wronged her. The two men who had laid their hands on her both fell to the ground simultaneously, their knees slamming into the cold-pavements. Those directly next to them laughed, suspecting that alcohol must have had something to do with their sudden descent.

Only when their gargling attempts to ask for help reached the others' ears did they stop to look properly, finally seeing the way that both men had hands wrapped around their own throats, straining to curb the gushing of blood between fingertips.

Holly, who had passed through the crowd to the other side without being seen, didn't concern herself with looking backwards. The shocked gasps and dull screams that reached her ears was enough. Passing a bin, she casually threw the blood-enriched blade of glass, licking the residue of blood from her hands.

Michael stood and watched her pass, knowing that she was so caught up in her own mind and thoughts that she didn't even sense him there. Sorrow pulled at his heart as he watched her, wondering what the hell had happened to the woman he loved.

From the house he now occupied, in sight of the house that he had to watch, Blaiden watched Ania walk away, dissolving easily into the deepening shadows, resigning himself to the years would have to pass before they would be reunited.

* * *

Holly knew that she was causing the distance between herself and Michael but knew that, for the time being at least, it was unavoidable. There was only one other person that Holly could discuss her decision with, one person who would understand with perfect clarity the situation and Holly's wishes. And Holly could sense that that person was nearly home.

Michael sat at the kitchen table, staring at the open doorway. Holly was on the other side of that door, looking out to the garden beyond.

The January weather was mild, and the smell of spring was already in the air, bringing with it the shorter nights, which he was beginning to dread. It would mean the three of them (for he was also aware of Ania's drawing closer) closed off for longer periods of time. It should have filled him with joy, the prospect of spending more time with Holly without the hunt, but until she had unburdened herself with whatever it was that had caused the chasm between them there was only the tension.

Ania had felt the house and the people there pulling her closer. For the first time in the week since she had left her lover with his task, Ania felt her heart begin to brighten. It seemed an age (even to *her*) since she had last set eyes upon the woman she had taken in. And with the sadness that had permeated her since leaving Blaiden behind now started to ease its grasp upon her.

Walking familiar steps as she neared her home, she could hear another pounding in her blood, recognising it as the sound of Holly's heartbeat joining with her own. Stepping onto her property she felt close to complete as she saw the blonde haired woman standing near the open back door and looking out over the garden.

Joy overwhelmed her as she crossed the garden towards her friend, an honest smile enveloping her face and filling her with warmth when Holly turned to face her.

The two women embraced, both realising that this reunion symbolised a change between them: they were no longer student and teacher but now simply friends and equals.

As Ania held Holly against her she could feel the strength that reverberated through her companion. It made her feel proud that Holly had managed to find the power within herself, yet simultaneously saddened that she had had to lose so much of the gentleness that was the key to who she was.

"She's beautiful." Ania said when their arms dropped from each other and she could look into Holly's hazel eyes. "You're daughter."

Smiling did soften her eyes slightly but only in sadness. "I know she is. I saw her through your eyes." Holly smiled at the picture of her child that was constantly in her mind.

Ania scanned Holly's eyes and shared what was hidden behind them, feeling what Holly was feeling.

In unison, both turned to look at the open door and the figure that now occupied the space.

"Welcome home, Ania."

Michael smiled genuinely at her, which she returned. But Ania saw the wearied set of his features behind his smile, and noticed the edge of the atmosphere between the lovers.

"Thank you, Michael." She said after her subtle appraisal. "It *is* nice to be home."

He walked slowly to Ania and they hugged briefly before he turned to Holly. His lips met hers softly while he took her hand. "Talk to her, Holly." He whispered. "Let her help you with whatever it is that I cannot."

Holly squeezed his hand once before he walked back into the house, closing the door behind him.

Without either of the female vampires uttering a word, their feet echoed the movements of all those years before as they walked out of the garden and into the fields beyond.

Clouds had covered the stars, cutting off the small sliver of the moon, and the two friends walked as they had before through field after field, relishing the silent company of the other amid the midnight open meadows.

Although her instincts allowed her a glimpse into her friend's private world, Ania longed for Holly to speak, to unburden the thoughts and fears that had caused the distance between her and Michael. But she would not ask, would not try to force Holly to speak; Ania knew that the words would come only when Holly was ready.

After walking for almost thirty minutes Holly stopped suddenly, an unusual smile on her red lips, gazing at the ground serenely.

Ania stopped beside her and simply regarded her with eyebrows raised.

After a few moments Holly turned her eyes to Ania's, an unadulterated sparkle of amusement shining through. "This is where I was, Ania." she said, still smiling. "Do you remember all of those years ago?"

Puzzled, Ania closed her eyes, frowning in concentration, and opened her senses to the place where they stood, letting its memory sink into her. As it did, the creases in her forehead smoothed and she also smiled. "Yes, I remember, Holly."

"Somehow fitting, I suppose. That my feet should lead me to the spot where the fire of the change began to burn through me; where the *pain* of the change started."

Tentatively, Ania closed the distance between them, one hand coming to rest on Holly's shoulder while the other touched her cheek. Ania searched her eyes once more, fighting against the temptation to just *sense* what was wrong - the only way for Holly to cope with whatever it was, was for her to *tell* it. "So what is it that pains you now, my friend?"

Even as she continued to smile tears sprang up to fill her eyes. "She is beautiful, isn't she? My child? My Laura?"

Ania smiled sadly as she saw the gentle tears slowly track down Holly's cheeks. "*Very* beautiful."

Ania started to wipe Holly's tears away but the blonde vampire shook her head and took Ania's hands from her face. "I don't mind these tears, Ania, because they're for her."

Holly sat on the ground and looked up at the cloud covered sky, seeing out of the corner of her eye as Ania sat beside her. "As difficult as it has been to accept the new sides to me, I *am* happy with my existence." Briefly she glanced at her friend. "You know that?"

Ania nodded and watched as Holly lay down, hands under her head, and continued her appraisal of the night sky.

"Even if I could, I wouldn't change back to how I was; the person I used to be was too innocent, too unable to cope. I'm faster, stronger, and more resilient."

Ania mirrored Holly's stance so that she could also stare at the clouds above and simply allowed her friend to speak all of the words that she'd had to contain.

"I love the night; I love the darkness of my life." She turned onto her side to look at Ania, which Ania also copied. "But I've lived in the day, Ania. I've had my time in the light which is why I *can* love the darkness. But Laura hasn't. She hasn't had the years of walking with the heat of the sun on her, of having to shield her eyes when it's too bright."

Still smiling her sad smile Ania simply nodded.

"I can't drag my daughter from the light and push her into darkness. I *can't.*"

"Holly, that is, and always will be, your choice. But are you sure about it? Can you really walk away from her?"

"Ania, the idea of walking away, of not having her by my side, *ever,* makes every part of me ache; it pulls at me, almost as if I can't breathe. But it's *because* it hurts that I know it's right."

"You have no idea of how much I admire you for that-"

Holly felt a little of the burden momentarily roll away, but as Ania continued speaking it slammed straight back.

"-but it may not be as simple as that."

In the open field, with a blanket of clouds covering the stars, Holly felt her anger beginning to rise as Ania spoke of the two vampires that she had seen. There was no relief, not even for a second, as she learnt of Jesse's survival, only a bitter burning in the pit of her stomach. That the woman who had (for all Jesse knew) killed Michael had been visiting his daughter! It was just wrong!

The hatred that was burning in her forced her to her feet, and Ania watched as Holly paced rapidly back and forth, her hands curled tightly into fists. She felt a strange sense of déjà vu looking at the set expression on the youngster's face.

When Holly passed by for the seventeenth time, Ania was on her feet in a flash and had grabbed Holly by the shoulders. That fury in her shone out towards Ania for a moment, but Ania didn't drop her eyes; she had been where Holly was.

"You saw my memories, Holly." Ania kept her voice low and calm. "You saw where these feelings of hatred and bitterness lead."

With Ania's words, Holly caught a glimpse of Maria and Katherine, dead and mutilated, and of Elizabeth screaming silently through a window. And although the anger still thrummed in her head, its beat in time with her heart, Ania's words had the desired effect; the pure hate she had felt dissolved, leaving her feeling empty and tired.

"Don't allow yourself to follow my path: choose your own way."

"He watches her at your request?" Holly was eventually able to ask, still looking deep into her friend's blue-grey eyes, and even felt a flicker of a smile touch her dark lips. "Blaiden?"

Ania's ancient eyes sparkled with youth at the mention of his name. "Yes, he watches - and protects - your child."

"Then, for now, that's enough." Sighing deeply she linked her arm through Ania's and they started back to the house.

Although she knew that she needed to, to find a sense of closure, Holly was in no rush to say goodbye to her daughter for ever, and intended to wait until she was ready.

Michael lay upon the bed, smiling. He'd heard them as they

approached the house, their voices light and laughing. They talked of Ania's lover and the simple joy that touched both of their voices was incredible. Holly's light footsteps moved on the stairs, leading her to the bedroom door. He ached at the sight of her in the doorway, and longed for her as she sat beside him on the bed.

"I'm sorry, Michael." She placed a hand on his face, her thumb caressing him. "I'm so sorry for causing the distance between us, for pushing you away."

He shook his head. "It doesn't matter now. And you could never push me away for good."

Holly smiled at him and let her thumb move over his cheek to softly graze his lips. Looking into his green eyes, she searched for an answer. "Do you love me, Michael?"

His hand gently stroked her soft blonde hair. "With everything I have, and for eternity."

"Then love me."

After such a long time, the distance between them finally closed as he pulled her to him, hands moving over every inch of her, freeing her pale skin of its confines.

IX

Holly stood in the doorway looking out over the garden, the uneasiness she felt almost making her tremble. The world before her was too bright, the rich reds and oranges that were painted over the normal-dark scenery hurt her head, causing her temples to pound. She was tired, had been as soon as the pale light had filtered into her blissfully-shadowed surroundings over thirteen hours ago. She had spent the day sitting out of the sunbeams but watching as they trekked steadily from east to west in front of her.

The pain in her head would go, she knew, when night came back but until then she bore it. For the last two months she had spent every other day watching the daylight, raving silently at her own cowardice. Since her daughter's twelfth birthday, Holly had persistently criticized her hesitation at travelling to say goodbye to her child. In the six and a half years since Ania's return Holly had found herself using every excuse she could find to postpone the moment that she would have to commit herself to leaving her child.

With the palms of her hands she rubbed her eyes sending black spots across her vision. She then used the index fingers of each hand to rub her temples in small circular motions.

Michael's hands on her shoulders made her jump - her senses, instincts, dulled by the burning brilliance of the day. Despite the headache that resounded on her entire mind, Holly couldn't help but laugh.

Standing in his boxer-shorts, his hair ruffled from sleep, his hand rose to try and screen the yawn that overtook him. When he was able to, he smiled sheepishly back at Holly. "The same?"

She was aware of the apprehensive way in which he glanced outside, and admitted defeat. She stepped wholly into the kitchen and closed the door. After the brightness, Holly was momentarily blinded while she waited for her eyes to readjust.

"Yep." She said as they both sat at the table. "Still the same."

He sighed deeply. "How long is it going to go on for, Holly?"

The short-lived burst of temper she felt at his question gave way to simple irritations at her own annoyance. She knew how difficult she had been to live with - especially since the anniversary of Laura's birth. Unable to come up with a reply, Holly simply sat and looked at him.

He reached across the table and took her hands in his. "You know that you've gone back to where you were six years ago? Trying not to deal with what you've decided about Laura..." A sad shadow flittered across his eyes. "...pushing me away."

She squeezed his hands. "I know, Michael. I'm just...struggling." Holly took one of her hands from his grasp and brushed her hair away from her face. "I just need to wait until I'm ready - *really* ready - to say goodbye; especially when I've never even said hello."

"Holly, I know how hard it is - you know I do." He reached across to once again take her hand. "But you need to do this. If you're ever going to, you need to let her go."

"I know, and I will. As soon as I'm ready."

When Ania walked down the stairs an hour later she found Holly and Michael still seated opposite each other at the kitchen table, hands still linked.

As Holly had again grown distant with the consuming thoughts of Laura, Ania's spasmodic bouts of self-isolation stemmed from the ache she that she felt for Blaiden. And it was only when around Holly, where they could rest in the pain of the other, that it eased.

The three vampires set out into the twilight to feed, each of them preoccupied with their own doubts, insecurities and pain.

Within the drunken Friday night crowds there was a very brief exchange before the three of them moved their separate ways, turning their divided attentions back to the mutual need.

Walking away from the others, Holly noticed a young girl walking alone. To anybody else she would have appeared normal, everyday; just a little above plain with her soft features and mousy brown hair. But Holly saw the paleness of her skin, the depth of hunger that hung far back in her eyes.

Moving away from each other at angles, Holly knew that the new-vampire hadn't noticed her in any real way, and she started to dismiss the girl from her thoughts. But as a somehow familiar freezing-figure of blackness rushed past her, turning the august air momentarily cold, Holly stopped, her eyes closed, a memory of a woman's voice playing in her mind. *"This area is ours, and we don't tolerate new-borns on our patch."*

In a moment her preoccupation, the doubts that had been a

constant in her life, was wiped out of her mind as she herself became a blur of darkness following those that followed the new-vampire.

They were surrounding the girl as Holly reached the small clump of trees close to the fields where she walked often. They had grown in size in the eleven years since their attempt on her. The twelve men and women grew closer to the terrified-looking brunette, encircling her.

It was the look of helplessness in the girl's eyes that caught Holly in place; at least until she heard the laughter of the other twelve. Rage that she had bottled up since hearing of Jesse and Ryan's interference in her daughter's life, no matter how mild it was, exploded out at those in front of her. She rushed forwards and had thrown three of them to the ground before they had been aware of another vampire being present. Leaving them bleeding upon the ground without another thought, Holly grabbed for another two.

Instead of having them in her grasp Holly found her arms caught in strong hands while another vampire approached her. In her peripheral vision she could see the other six still surrounding the now-shocked young brunette, each of them looking at her with caution.

As the male approached her, another on each side of her holding her tight, he began flicking his chin with his thumb nail, purposefully drawing her attention to its length and sharpness.

Unseen by any, Ania held onto Michael's arm, pulling him back so that he was once again by her side. Furiously, he shot her a glance as she prevented him from going to his lover's aid.

"She does not need your help, Michael." Her silver voice was quiet and secretive.

He looked back at Holly, watching as the man approached, and prayed that Ania was correct.

Holly had no intention of letting him get any nearer to her - his intentions were clear. Gathering herself up she put into practice everything that Ania had shown and taught her, both in reality and through her dreams. A roar pushed through her snarling lips and she twisted easily out of the grip of the two that held her.

Even she was unaware of how she was doing what she was doing - her mind was blank and only the red-rage-fuelled pain she inflicted mattered.

After a short time, barely even five seconds, Holly stood beside the terrified brunette, breathing hard, her clothes and hair drenched in the blood of those that lay still and motionless on the ground.

She reached a hand out to help the girl gain her feet but was not at all surprised when she scrambled away from her. Her eyes never left Holly's, not even when she slipped in a blood-sodden patch of earth.

As Holly watched the girl flee a sad thought crossed her mind: that child did not have what it took to survive her new life.

Hearing the ground squelching under foot as she began to walk away, Holly spoke to the broken body of the woman who had once spoken to her. "Do that again and I'll kill you."

She wasn't shocked to see Ania and Michael standing beside a tree, Ania looking proud at her reactions and Michael looking uncertain as she approached.

"I need a shower." She said simply, loving the sound of Ania's soft laughter.

Michael still looked at her warily, more at the wild-strength that he still saw in her eyes than at the display of fearlessness that he had just witnessed. But he smiled as she spoke again.

"*Now* I'm ready."

As they went back to the house so that Holly could bathe before they continued on their disrupted hunt, Holly kept her reason for her readiness to herself: that she just couldn't stand the thought of that look of terror on her own child's face.

* * *

Four nights later the orange glows of the streetlamps illuminated three figures as they strolled along the streets, each of them carrying rucksacks. One woman walked in the lead, her long dark hair stirred only by her movements. Behind her walked a couple, hand-in-hand, their bodies brushing against each other. Ahead of them another man turned as the silent steps moved closer. The woman in the lead quickened her steps and the man before her also began to close the gap between them.

Almost laughing with happiness, Ania wrapped her arms

around Blaiden's neck and felt his arms wind around her waist, his hands coming to rest on her hips. She pulled him to her and they kissed.

Behind them, far enough away so that they weren't intruding, both Michael and Holly were smiling. But while Michael's smile was totally genuine Holly's was forced, strained. She was happy that Ania and Blaiden were together but it was not why they were there. She could feel how close she was, how close *Laura* was, and she was impatient. Now that she had finally got to this place, she needed to see her child.

They indulged their passion for a few minutes then Ania and Blaiden turned and walked to the younger couple where introductions were made. Michael and Blaiden shook hands and Holly hugged him softly. While in his arms she spoke gently into his ear. "Thank you for watching my child."

With his hands on her shoulders Blaiden stepped back a little to smile at her. "A pleasure, Holly." He took her hand and raised it to his lips, kissing it softly.

Holly smiled wider, but all three of the other vampires were able to see just how tense and keyed up she was.

Blaiden glanced at Ania, who simply nodded. Still holding Holly's hand, Blaiden turned and started to guide her further along the road with Ania and Michael walking behind them. Despite the situation, Michael struggled to fight back the small bite of jealousy at the sight of someone else holding his lover's hand.

As he passed a house on the other side of the road Blaiden glanced briefly at its dark windows, and Holly felt her stomach roll and her heart jump. She looked first at the house and then backwards at Ania. Meeting her friend's eyes Holly's suspicion was confirmed: that was where her daughter was.

Disappointment gripped at her as Blaiden continued along the road instead of stopping as she'd hoped he would. Longingly, she glanced back at where her daughter lived and only looked at where she was going when Blaiden turned to walk to a house. Although she still longed to catch a glimpse of her child, it wasn't as bad as she had feared - she was still in sight of the house.

Blaiden unlocked the door to the home that he occupied and the four walked in.

Holly was barely aware of the guided tour as Blaiden showed

them around, including the bedroom that he had prepared for the younger couple. The one thing that she did notice was that it faced the street, allowing a diagonal view of the only house that she cared about seeing.

"I was in this one," Blaiden was saying to Michael as Holly wandered over to look out of the window. "But I thought that the two of you would prefer it."

The conversation between the three older vampires continued behind her but Holly no longer heard it. She wrapped her arms around herself and looked longingly at the place that she knew her daughter was, the aching in her heart stealing her breath.

"Holly."

Ania's hands on her shoulders brought her back. She wiped tears from her face and dragged her gaze away from the window. Michael and Blaiden were no longer in the room, had left without Holly realising, and she could hear them talking gently downstairs.

Risking another glance, just one more, she turned back to the window and stopped. Slowly, Ania's hand dropping from her shoulder, Holly moved back to her former position.

The light was on in the window she'd been watching, and Holly began to smile and cry together. Holding the curtain to one side, her dark hair draping over her shoulders, one side pushed behind an ear. She was looking out into the street, searching for something.

As Ania joined Holly again at the window, she was just in time to see the beautiful twelve year old girl step back and allow the curtain to fall closed again, blocking out the night and cutting off their line of sight.

A conflict of emotions swept through her in a torrent, pushing past every defence she had tried to set up in her heart. Love for her daughter; despair at the decision that she'd made; longing for the years missed; anger aimed at herself, at the woman beside her, at the man who had fathered her child, at the man who had watched her while Ania was gone; uncertainty of what the future held for Laura.

Groaning, her hands went to her temple as if the thoughts in her mind were trying to escape and she was trying to hold them in. Ania's arm once more around her was too much and she pushed her friend violently away, running out of the house and through the streets.

If she had waited just three minutes longer Holly would have come face to face with her daughter as she left the house to meet Ryan and Jesse.

It was too much! It was just too much for her to be able to cope with! The sight of gorgeous daughter, almost a teenager, so close and yet she might have been a million miles away: she still couldn't be next to her.

Wandering around streets that were totally unfamiliar to her, noticing nothing about where she was walking, Holly found herself in a playground.

Sadly she smiled as she looked at the swings and made her way over to them. Sitting down, she started to swing herself gently backwards and forwards, enjoying the reminiscent feelings that seeped through the pain and confusion; it had been her favourite thing as a child. She allowed the rhythm to become the focus of her attention, letting it - *encouraging* it - to drive out other thoughts.

They were nearly in sight before Holly realised that anybody was approaching. Quickly she leapt from the seat, leaving it swinging, and rushed away, hiding within the large climbing frame. Out of view, she felt anger boiling up at the sight of her daughter walking into the park with Jesse at her side. It subsided as she watched Laura take the seat that she had just vacated only to return as Jesse sat beside her. With difficulty, Holly forced herself to stay still.

"You're mother and I were good friends."

Jesse's voice reached her and Holly watched as her hands twisted in her lap.

"What happened?" Laura's voice this time, young, sweet and innocent.

Holly listened as the tale of how Laura came to be was recounted. With each word that came out of Jesse's mouth Holly could feel the compulsion to just sweep her daughter into her arms and away from everything growing - but knowing that it wasn't an option, Holly transferred her anger into herself, digging fingernails into the palms of her hands. As soon as she could get Jesse alone then she could transfer the anger to where it deserved to be.

They had fallen silent; Laura was crying and staring at a photograph that she had taken from her pocket. Holly's pain was refreshed when Laura spoke in a small crushed voice.

"Why have you done this, Jesse? Why can't you just leave me to be a normal kid? Why can't you just let me be normal?"

As Jesse turned to Laura Holly was able to see that she was also crying - but she didn't feel the slightest bit of sympathy.

"You're all I've got of her. If we let you be, in time, you'll die. If I let that happen to you, I'd lose whatever was of Holly. I won't let that happen." She took hold of Laura's shoulders. "You have to be with me always."

Holly relished the sting of pain as her nails split the flesh of her hands. *You manipulative bitch!* She thought as she imagined all that she would like to do to Jesse. *I'll make you pay for trying that with my child!* She knew that her anger was coming off of her like waves, and hoped that Jesse sensed some of it.

Pride like nothing she'd ever experienced before swallowed the rage as Laura moved away from Jesse, telling her clearly that she needed time to think and that she didn't want them to visit her for a couple of weeks.

Jesse sat alone on the swings watching Laura walk away, not even suspecting that someone else was also watching the girl go, just waiting for the second that she was out of sight.

Her teeth felt sharp, her nails felt deadly, and she smiled as the blood in her temples pounded intensely. Her muscles started to tense deliciously tight as she readied herself to spring. The second that she let go, propelling herself forwards, her arm was dragged back, her shoulder jarring in its socket.

Ania ignored the fury in her friend's eyes and continued to hold her tight. "You will achieve nothing by reacting now. The choice has been offered, Holly. Laura has to make the choice."

Resignedly, Holly allowed herself to be led back to the house, skirting around the edges of the park so as not to be seen, not daring to look back at the still-sitting form, knowing that her resolve would shatter in an instant if she did.

She hated Jesse with more passion than she had ever believed possible.

But, for having left things far too late, she hated herself more.

* * *

Thirty-eight days later, as decorations started being sold for the upcoming Halloween celebrations, Holly and Ania watched as Laura and Jesse walked out of the house. Ryan walked out a moment later, locking the door behind him. When they started to walk down the path towards the outskirts of town Holly and Ania followed; Ania's hand fixed tightly onto Holly's arm as a rein in case she tried to rush ahead.

Although it wasn't a problem for her Holly knew how cold it was and longed to go to Laura and wrap her up in her cloak to keep her warm. Instead, she just watched as she walked in obvious awe of the night, her t-shirt and jeans the only barrier between her and the cold.

They followed as the three walked the streets. After a short time they found what they had been searching for.

Holly watched as Laura guided the man, a drunk, into an alleyway. She watched as Ryan bit the man's neck and her breath caught as Laura approached him: She knew that she was not alone in it, knew that Ania, plus the two who had set this in motion, was also waiting, watching.

Holly flashed back to her first kill, to the man she had fed from when she had run from the hospital. She could remember how the taste had flooded through her, blocking out everything else, consuming her. As she watched Laura she knew that it was something that they now had in common.

Fading deep into the shadows, black cloaks with raised hoods making them indistinguishable from its depths, Holly and Ania waited for them to pass.

"She can't go back now, Holly." Ania whispered, watching the spark of anger growing in her hazel eyes. "Do you still wish to say goodbye?"

"She made her choice alone." Holly whispered back, smiling viciously, loving the strength that her anger was giving her. "And the only ones I'll be saying goodbye to are Jesse and Ryan."

Ania mirrored the ferocious grin before they started walking again.

At the corner of the road where Laura had lived with her adopted parents Blaiden and Michael stood casually, both with hands in pockets, looking along the street. As Holly and Ania joined them, Laura was just stepping through the door leaving Ryan and Jesse standing uncomfortably outside.

Ania began to tell them what they'd seen while Holly simply stood with her arms crossed beneath her cloak, the hood still throwing shadows onto her face, gazing with hatred at the two who waited for Laura. She didn't say a word, or acknowledge any of the others: she simply waited.

Her arms fell to her side as Laura walked back out of the house only a few moments later. Fury unlike anything she'd believed possible, intense, focussed and centred, ravaged all that had ever been in her life; all thoughts that raged in her heart were full of venom for the two that walked either side of her child, that had manipulated the innocent girl into making a choice she should never have been offered. As they moved in the opposite direction, showing Holly only their backs, she pelted towards them.

Both Michael and Blaiden turned, surprised but ready to follow, but Ania's strong hands held them both in place.

Neither liked the feral glint in her eyes and smile. "This is for her alone. Let her do what she needs to do."

Everything that she had ever denied, each pang of hatred and anger that she had kept inside, now pounded through her veins as she moved with speed, the length of her cloak flowing behind her, her head lowered to stop the hood from revealing her face.

Holly could see the way that all three looked uneasy, more tensed up. Smiling dangerously she moved behind them in between the adults, her arms raised and ready. She struck both of them in between the shoulder blades and at an angle so that they fell in opposite directions, leaving a gap which she easily moved through. Before either of them had landed, Holly had enveloped Laura within her cloak, holding her away from Ryan and Jesse.

Holly hated the way that Laura was struggling in her arms, fighting to get free. She had her arm across Laura's chest and put her mouth next to Laura's ear.

"Stop struggling, Laura; you're safe. I'm your mum."

Holly was surprised at how quickly Laura became still and relaxed, allowing her to simply rest in her arms.

Her arm remained around Laura, now in protection instead of restraint and she used her free hand to lower the hood of her cloak, letting the street-lights throw some illumination onto her pale skin.

She allowed the anger to filter back through to her eyes as she looked on the two vampires who remained on the ground, seeing the shock in both of their eyes.

"You will never touch my daughter again."

When Jesse and Ryan turned to look at each other Holly turned with her daughter and began to walk away.

Walking along, they both kept turning to look at each other, both trying to accept the reality - that finally they were next to each other. They reached the corner where Ania, Blaiden and Michael stood.

Laura felt uneasy as she saw the two paler creatures in front of her, but when Michael stepped forwards, smiling, everything else faded away. His green eyes, so much like hers, shone with joy. She stepped forwards and felt his arms go around her.

Ania and Blaiden stayed out of the way as those before them - the *family* before them - hugged, searching each other's features; absorbing the truth of each other's presence.

Placing a gentle hand on Holly's arm, Ania smiled at the youngster's happiness. "We need to collect our things from that house, Holly."

"I need to get my things, too....Mum." Laura, like Holly and Michael, grinned widely as she used that word. "They're at Ryan and Jesse's."

Ania looked at Holly with meaning. "We'll get the things from the house, you and Michael and-" she smiled briefly at the child "Laura collect her things, and we'll meet where we discussed."

Puzzled, Blaiden and Michael exchanged a quick glance before the group split up into two. Ania and Blaiden watched them walk away before turning back, holding hands, to gather their belongings. Walking past Laura's adopted parents' house as they walked past, nonchalantly entering the house that had never been theirs.

Michael easily forced the door open, doing nothing more than leaning against it until the lock broke and the door swung open, almost spilling him into the hallway. In unison, Laura and Holly giggled quietly, their laughter startlingly similar. With her arm still around her daughter, as it had been for the whole walk, they stepped into the hallway, pushing the door closed behind them.

Holly found the light switch almost straight away but cared nothing for the blue walls or the dozens of different sized pictures portraying sunrises over every conceivable landscape.

Laura went upstairs to collect her small rucksack of things, and Holly and Michael stood at the bottom of the stairs grinning at each other at the wonder of the situation. They turned together to look to the top of the stairs as Laura began to walk down with her bag over one shoulder. Her feet reached the second step down when the front door opened again.

Ryan and Jesse walked in and Holly and Michael stood side by side, blocking any route to the stairs and to Laura.

"You can't do this, Holly!"

Jesse stepped forwards, nervous at the way her once-gentle friend now held herself with such strength and will. "I don't know how you can be here, but you can't do this! You can't take her away from me!"

Leaving Michael to stand guard at the base of the stairs Holly also stepped forwards, eyes blazing once again. "She is *my* child, Jesse! I *can* do this! I will do what is best for her!"

Almost dripping with spite, Jesse's voice rose. "So where have you been?! *I've* been here; *I've* guided her! *I've-*"

In a rush Holly was millimetres from her. "*You've* been there for her?! You manipulated her; you forced her to choose! You've ripped her life from her!"

Ryan had moved next to the two shouting women, but with one glance from the glaring blonde he moved quickly away again.

She looked back at Jesse, loving the uncertainty and fear that she saw there. "And now that she has been *made* to choose," she continued, her voice low but deadly. "*I* am here to guide her."

Shaking her head Jesse looked at Laura, then back at Holly. "You're not taking her from me." She said weakly.

Holly's hand found Jesse's throat and pushed her back against the wall, hissing. "You don't have a choice!"

Ryan had moved again to intervene but Michael was there before he could get close. Mirroring Holly, Michael forced Ryan away and against the other wall.

Laura stood at the top of the stairs, frozen, as she watched.

Holly glanced over at Michael and they shared a brutal smile. Looking back at Jesse, she increased the pressure on her neck. "You will stay away from us; you will stay away from Laura." She let go and stepped slowly away, hearing Jesse cough while she rubbed her bruised neck. Michael followed her example and they motioned for Laura to come downstairs.

Halfway down now, Laura stopped. "No!"

Jesse's hands were wrapped in Holly's hair, pulling her backwards. Michael turned to rip the brunette away but pain thudded into his back and he was sent crashing into the wall. Ryan began to land blows on Michael's head and upper body, while behind them Holly struggled to turn to face her attacker.

"No!" She screamed again and started down the stairs to help the parents she had only just found.

Ania dropped in front of her. "No, Laura."

She could hear the fight continuing and tried to dart quickly past, but she had no chance against Ania. "I need to help!"

"No." Ania said simply.

Laura was blocked as Ania stood in front and Blaiden appeared behind, but although she couldn't see what was happening she was still able to hear.

Michael swept Ryan's feet out from under him and when he fell face first to the floor Michael dropped his knee onto Ryan's spine, pinning him. He looked over to see how his lover was managing and had to smile.

Holly's hair was in complete disarray, as was Jesse's; but Holly had far less cuts and bruises - he could only see one large gash across Holly's cheek. Jesse on the other hand was sporting numerous cuts across her face and her lip was already swollen, one of her eyes already closed. Holly had Jesse on the floor, face first as Ryan was. She was stood over her, foot planted squarely on her back, Jesse's arm raised above her back and pulled tight.

"Ania?" Holly didn't turn, continued to stare at the whimpering form below her.

"Yes, Holly."

"We're leaving now. Can you take Laura outside?"

Ania held her hand out to Laura who, after a second's hesitation, accepted and allowed herself to be escorted down the stairs. She saw the positions of the people in the hallway and hurriedly closed her eyes - it was not something she wanted to see.

Holly looked at Ania as they passed by towards the door and

smiled.

Jesse felt the pain in her arm lessen just the slightest bit and took advantage of Holly's obvious distraction. Using her legs she managed to flip herself over, ignoring the pain in her arm as it was pulled from Holly's grasp. She kicked out at Holly, pushing her to the side.

Holly was unable to stop herself from falling forwards into Ania, who bore the force with hardly any reaction. When Jesse tried to sweep Holly's legs out Holly was able to move out of the way, causing Jesse's kick to go wider than she'd intended.

Laura's instincts were nowhere near their peak so she had no way of avoiding the kick that sent her flying into the wall. She cried out as she connected, pain in her lip as she bit down.

Holly was by her side instantly, checking the damage. When she was sure that it was nothing serious she gently kissed her daughter's forehead. She focussed on Laura's face, fighting to stay calm, as she spoke. "Ania, take my daughter outside."

Ania whisked Laura outside with Blaiden following. Holly waited until the door closed before turning to Jesse.

Shocked that she had harmed Laura, Jesse simply sat where she was. Both Ryan and Michael looked uneasily between the two women, whose friendship had once been thought unbreakable.

Holly continued to fight to hold herself together. "I swear to you, Jesse, if you come anywhere near my child again I will kill you."

Holly spared no more energy or anger on them. She walked out of the house with Michael one step behind, the cold entering the house to add more pain to Jesse's injuries.

Stunned, Ryan and Jesse looked resignedly across the hallway at each other. They were on their own, alone; there was no one else now for either of them.

When Jesse began to cry Ryan put his hands in his pockets and stared at the floor.

* * *

The approaching sun had started to add bleached colour to the world outside as Laura lay asleep in the bed, her dark hair hanging over her face. Holly reached over and tucked it behind the exposed ear, smiling as Laura smiled in her sleep at the touch. At the doorway as she left Holly stopped with her hand on the door and looked back. She had never felt so much love, such unconditional love, as she looked at the sleeping form. Still smiling, she pulled the door almost closed.

It felt so strange to her, being back in the house she had left nearly thirteen years previously. After she had been led away from attacking Jesse in the park, Holly and Ania had planned ahead for every possible outcome, deciding that Holly's old house would be perfect to spend the day before travelling back to Ania's home. And, looking around, Holly was grateful for the wonderful job that Ania had done cleaning it up. There was still a dark stain of blood spilled at the foot of the stairs where Jesse had lain; a pool of dark red underneath a now-removed picture hook where her puppy had been impaled; but there was no other evidence of the past.

She walked into her bedroom and saw Michael laying there. Deja vu gave her goosebumps as she thought back to the other times they had shared the room, and the bed within it.

Smiling as he smiled at her, Holly closed the door.

"So, what now?"

Ania had been close to sleeping when Blaiden spoke, bringing her back. She felt exhausted, but it was a good kind of exhausted - it seemed that all of the pain of the past had been healed.

They sat on the sofa, Ania's head on Blaiden's chest, his arm around her shoulder, their free hands clasped together, his thumb softly moving over hers. She sighed contentedly. "Holly's asked me to help Laura, prepare her as much as I can for The Hag. And then to guide her afterwards."

"So you'll be her Grace-Guide."

Ania smiled at the long-forgotten term from her childhood. "I guess I will, yes."

He pulled her tighter to him, his head now rested against hers, both his arms around her while hers encircled him. "Here?"

"No. Tonight we'll begin to travel back to my home. Travelling separately though: let Holly and Michael and Laura have the time they need alone."

"You'll be back to travelling alone?"

Ania's heart plummeted. Hesitantly, she answered. "I guess

so."

"Don't suppose you want any company, do you, Ania?"

Ania moved away a little so that she could look at the mischievous grin on his lips. Playfully she pushed him. "Tease!"

He laughed and drew her back into him. "So? Do you?"

With a failed attempt at acting indifferent, she couldn't help smiling as she rested her head back against him. "I guess you could tag along..."

For no apparent reason Ania's heart hammered in her chest as she slowly climbed the stairs. She had no idea what had caused her to wake, but what she felt left her feeling uneasy. Her whole body tingled as if an electrical current was passing through her. At the top of the stairs she closed her eyes, allowing her instinct to guide her to where she needed to go.

Her eyes opened again and she walked towards Laura's room. Slowly pushing the door open, she saw Laura sitting up in her bed, her dark hair over her shoulders, and all innocence gone from her eyes. Looking at those depths as Laura looked back was like looking into her own - they seemed ancient.

Smiling, Laura turned to look back into the room, opposite where she sat. Her heart pounding louder, Ania stepped into the room.

She felt scared; she couldn't help it. The memory of the first time that she had been in The Hag's presence was too clear in her mind.

The Hag was smiling at Laura as Laura was smiling at her. Their features were totally different but the expressions mirrored each other perfectly, as did the shared knowledge in their eyes; it was the look of people who had found a long-lost friend.

Ania watched, speechless, as The Hag slowly hobbled on ancient legs to Laura's side; and more surprising was the lack of fear in Laura as The Hag reached the side of the bed. Ania couldn't move, could barely take it in. All she could do was watch as The Hag gently wrapped her leathery wings around Laura, as Laura responded by embracing the being's neck without alarm. The Hag kissed Laura softly on the forehead before stepping backwards. Still smiling, she regarded Ania, who noted the total and whole sanity in those deep eyes, before her form faded to smoke and disappeared.

Ania stood where she was, focussed on the spot where The Hag had stood, the startled expression on her face melting into bewilderment. Eventually, she looked at Laura and slowly walked to the bed. Sitting on the edge she looked at the child who looked back, the smile not leaving her face.

Ania remembered thinking that Holly's child was probably the first born-vampire. After seeing the exchange between Laura and The Hag, the way that they had seen each other without confusion, she knew that she had been wrong: There had always been another.

There were no marks on Laura's neck, no signs of the attack that all vampires went through at the time of their turning. Ania smiled in wonder and amazement at the vampire who had never been turned, nor subjected to the pain or fire.

"You weren't killed and brought back." Not a question.

"No."

"You really are a rarity."

Laura nodded and began to giggle, the ageless wisdom in her eyes being replaced by a child's delight. Being quiet so as not to wake anyone, what had just happened a secret between them, Ania joined in.

* * *

Dusk filled the world with blues and purples as Holly locked the door to the house for the last time. She looked between the two groups who stood three feet apart, those that had already said their temporary goodbyes.

She walked to the couple and hugged Blaiden, kissing him gently on the cheek. Walking into Ania's embrace she felt tears - happy tears - slide from her eyes. "Thank you, Ania."

Ania squeezed her tight before they moved apart. "We'll see you soon."

Still smiling and still crying, Holly moved to her child and lover.

Ania winked at the youngest of the trio, unseen by her other three companions, before they turned away, smiling wider as Laura giggled quietly.

Ania and Blaiden watched them walk away, a vampire family of three, leaving to start their existence together. Holding hands and both smiling happily, Ania and Blaiden followed them along the same path, moving from the shadows into eternal darkness.

They followed, but always at a distance.

The End

Printed in Poland
by Amazon Fulfillment
Poland Sp. z o.o., Wrocław

58859719R00179